"EARL EMERSON IS A WRITER'S WRITER. In THE PORTLAND LAUGHER, Emerson demonstrates one more time that he is a master of witty dialogue; clever, complex plotting; and lucid, meaty prose in the best tradition of American crime fiction. THE PORTLAND LAUGHER is his best yet, a masterful demonstration of how to write a compelling, wonderfully intricate mystery and make it look easy."
—AARON ELKINS

"Emerson is at the top of his game. . . . How many can claim authorship of not one, but two of the most highly respected ongoing series in the mystery genre? . . . Those who are up to speed have been waiting three years for THE PORTLAND LAUGHER and they will not be disappointed."
—*Mostly Murder*

"Earl Emerson's fine new private-eye novel is a tale of blindness, madness, murder and love."
—*The Oregonian*

"Earl Emerson manages to be both very funny and very serious. This is the big, exciting breakout book his fans have been expecting!"
—LIA MATERA

*Please turn the page
for more rave reviews. . . .*

"[HIS] BEST YET."
—*The Seattle Times*

"Earl Emerson and Thomas Black only get better and better! Emerson's plotting is original, suspenseful—so well done that the richness of his writing seems almost a bonus. . . . I crawled into the middle of THE PORTLAND LAUGHER at bedtime, and emerged at dawn, in awe, once again, at what a truly superior writer Earl Emerson is! Emerson's ear for language, his eye for visual detail, and his genius at creating suspense in a roller-coaster plot makes THE PORTLAND LAUGHER sing all the way through. Chilled my veins and made me laugh out loud and fooled me when I got too smug."
—ANN RULE

"A superbly worked-out plot, a narrator with a likable voice and Emerson's clean, witty prose."
—*Publishers Weekly*

"Earl Emerson is the best in the business. Outrageously funny, gritty, compelling—his books have it all."
—EILEEN DREYER

THE PORTLAND LAUGHER

Earl Emerson

BALLANTINE BOOKS • NEW YORK

A Ballantine Book
Published by The Ballantine Publishing Group
Copyright © 1994 by Earl Emerson, Inc.

www.randomhouse.com/BB/

Library of Congress Catalog Card Number: 94-4786

ISBN 0-345-39782-7

Printed in Canada

First Hardcover Edition: October 1994
First Mass Market Edition October 1995

10   9   8

TO MY MOTHER AND FATHER,
JUNE AND RALPH

"These are the flustered old ladies—of both sexes (or no sex) and almost all ages—who like their murders scented with magnolia blossoms and do not care to be reminded that murder is an act of infinite cruelty, even if the perpetrators sometimes look like playboys or college professors or nice motherly women with softly greying hair."

—*Raymond Chandler*

1

MY LACK OF VISITORS CONTINUES TO BAFFLE ME.

While other patients have been receiving guests and colored balloons packed with helium, while children rustle around outside my room, while the rest of the world talks about last night's TV offerings, I have been abandoned to my own devices.

This abandonment may be caused by two things. One is that I am in a state not unlike a coma, wherein I can hear and think but cannot speak or move. Another is that I have become something of a monster.

I am incarcerated in a lifeless body. I languish in a stupor.

What I have learned is that when you are in a coma, nobody rushes to you with explanations. From where I lie, it is all guesswork.

The absence of one specific visitor causes particular anguish. As I view it, there are three circumstances that might keep her away: one, she has been in some way incapacitated; two, she is unaware of my condition and/or location; three, she knows where I am but has been made aware of what I have become and thus cannot gather the brass to face me.

Images skip around inside my skull, images that sane men's brains do not house. Time is spooned out. Objects lurk at the outskirts of memory and retreat before I can grasp them. The possibility that I have killed torments me. Only slightly less terrifying is the prospect that I have been killed and simply have not yet completed the act of dying. Ordinarily, I am a man of serenity and reason, of some calm, but these panicky safaris haunt my days.

I remember who I am but can recall only snatches from the past weeks. One of these snatches prickles the hair on my arms and breathes a film of sweat onto my limbs. I am certain I have done something monstrous but cannot recall what.

The phone rings, and several times it rings at the precise moment a nurse or an orderly walks into the room. What I sometimes hear on the other end mystifies the nurses and orderlies, but it does not mystify me.

Some of the calls run so long that the nurse summons a coworker and passes the receiver—and in that instant the sound gets a little louder and I catch a sample. Something deep inside me turns over and starts to shrink.

Lost and flickering mirages of the past bombard my afternoons. Images of an elderly black man holding a kitchen knife. Of a dead horse and next to it a pit containing two exhausted and blistered young men with shovels. Of a little girl hiding in a closet, eyes as big and blue and bright as an electrical arc. Of a face popping out from the bushes at the end of my driveway as I climb into my truck. Of two men shooting pistols at a plastic bottle in the darkening woods. I am badgered by senseless images, each more unreasoning and inexplicable than the last. My brain has blurred into a one-man freak show.

And then he is here, my visitor. I can hear him and I can smell him, but I can smell him before I can hear him. He has been in a tavern somewhere nearby because he could not possibly have driven in this condition.

His name is Elmer Slezak, but he prefers a nickname he picked up on the rodeo circuit years ago, long before he became a cop and then quit that to become what some people have called Tacoma's sleaziest private investigator. The nickname he prefers is Snake. He believes it confers

a certain Runyonesque rank. Snake is mostly hoot and hol-
ler, the spit-filled pennywhistle of Northwest private eyes.

He drags a chair across the waxed floor, and I hear the
whistling in his nostrils as he sits nearby. During the first
ten minutes he does not utter a word.

Knowing I am in a hospital and that my sole visitor is
a man named Snake, I conclude that I have committed
some hideous breach of social or moral etiquette.

2 AFTER SOME TIME PASSES, ELMER "SNAKE"
Slezak clears his throat and speaks. His voice
is low and rumbles with phlegm.

"Shit, oh dear, Thomas, I made some mistakes in my
time, but letting this happen to you makes me out a pea
brain."

The plastic seat back on Slezak's chair squeaks as he
rummages around in his pockets. I think I know what he
is rummaging for and confirm it when the odor of cigarette
smoke suffuses the room. Snake knows smoking is not allowed, but rules mean nothing to him.

"Damn it all to hell, Thomas," he whispers. "I thought
you were ready to dance barefoot through the firecrackers
with old Lucifer. Damn it all to hell. Now they tell me
you're probably going to end up some sort of BB stacker
in a bearing factory."

More tobacco smoke. Snake knows how tobacco smoke

annoys me, but he puffs away as if I am beyond annoyances.

"And where the hell is all the firepower?" he says. "They's no guard on the door nor nothin'. I told them to put a guard on the door. I spent twelve hours in a vest yesterday out in the corridor—but I can't march around out there forever. And you know Philip ain't going to help. And where the hell is that plucky little lawyer filly you been pretendin' not to chase all these years?

"Thomas, my friend, now maybe you believe me when I tell you some people shouldn't be allowed to make footprints on the planet. You find them. You whack 'em. Boy, they sure did hit you hard. They sure did. I never seen you hurt like this. Not ever."

Another few minutes pass, during which somebody from the hospital staff enters the room and berates Snake for smoking, to which he replies that I had been the one smoking and he has merely been holding the cigarette as a favor.

After the staff person leaves, Snake fires up another one and says, "I been lookin' all over, Thomas. I ain't slept in two days but I ain't seen nothin'. In one sense, you were right. You start something like this, you better be ready to finish it, or it'll finish you. You were right about that. But I ain't seen nothin' since they scraped you up and brought you in here."

After some minutes, Snake realizes he has finally found his perfect audience and commences to wearing out topic after topic. It occurs to me that there must be windbags all over the world just waiting for friends to lapse into comas.

It is going on forty-five minutes, maybe an hour of Snake telling stories and various tall tales, when the phone rings. Elmer Slezak lets it go ten or twelve times, rushing through to the conclusion of a story he calls the Great Dee-troit Pimp War, before he climbs out of the chair, tramps across the room and snatches up the receiver.

"Snake here," he blurts. I can hear the laughter for a moment, but then he is pressing the receiver to his ear so tightly I can hear nothing but the loud sucking as he makes love to his cigarette. The phone call, coupled with Snake's stoic acknowledgment of it, causes beads of sweat to crawl down my armpits like insects crawling down a corpse. Suddenly I am dying of thirst.

After twenty seconds Snake speaks into the phone. "Listen, pea brain. Didn't your mother ever tell you not to get into a pissing contest with a skunk?"

Leaving the phone off the hook so we can both listen to the laughing, he sits down. After about thirty seconds the phone makes the racket they make when the connection has been cut off. Later, when a nurse comes to the door and tells him visiting hours are over, Snake says he will be out "in a jiff." The nurse racks the phone, and as soon as she leaves it rings. It seems to ring forever.

Snake does not move until it stops.

Then he walks around the bed and slips an object under my pillow. As he leans over me, his breath is foul enough to kill nestling songbirds, reeking of tobacco and booze and dentures, for Snake has lost most of his teeth in fights. Snake has been on a binge. I heard a woman once describe him as a man waiting for the right time to kill himself, and, though this was never my impression of him, you could see how it might fit.

"Shit, oh dear. This'll tide you over, buddy. And remember, there's no point to it if you don't outlive the bastards."

The object he slips under my pillow is small and compact and hard. I am thinking it is a flask of whiskey. One of Snake's running gags is to make me promise if he ever ends up in a nursing home with "brain damage" that I will supply him with beverage. What he presents is simple insurance that I will do the same for him someday.

After he leaves, I am lulled by the chitchat of two women down the hall who obviously did not grow up with English, by the hum of a mechanical floor polisher, the jangle of keys, by a man in a distant room speaking with the hardy conceit of authority, and then by a close whiff of perfume as a gentle hand picks up my wrist and feels for my pulse.

The count, which bangs in the back of my skull as she whispers the numbers, is slow and rhythmic from many squandered hours goofing off while the rest of the world works: playing pickup basketball in the neighborhood or peddling a racing bicycle through the Arboretum and down along Lake Washington.

"Mr. Black," her accented voice says lowly. "Mr. Black. So slow. You were an athlete, weren't you?" Yes I was, sweetheart, yes I was, but what is it exactly that you mean by the word *were*?

3   THE EPISODE HAD BEGUN WEEKS EARLIER ON THE third Monday in September.

The weather pattern had chalked high clouds across Seattle's horizon and ricocheted enough spotty sunshine into the boxy cityscape to keep shopkeepers in shirtsleeves, women in summer skirts, and gardeners in dirty knees.

Doodling and daydreaming and waiting for my appointment was all I was doing when Kathy exploded into the room, slammed the door, and seated herself directly atop my writing pad. She had a habit of sometimes acting like a pushy cat and of earning the same easy forgiveness.

I tugged my mechanical pencil out from under her thigh and peered up into her violet eyes. A long, thick plait of black hair dropped over her right shoulder. She wore a black skirt and white silk blouse. Black pumps, which she kicked onto the floor.

"Thomas. I don't think you need to talk to that Galli woman. It looks like they're going to reduce the charges to misdemeanors. Trespassing. Malicious mischief. I've convinced Jody he's doing well at that. And I got him in to see a good psychologist next Thursday." She began fussing with a pen, a definite signal she had something else on her mind.

I leased a cubbyhole of an office in a wheel of law offices along with Kathy Birchfield, two other female attorneys, and two paralegals. Generally, Richard, one of the paralegals, and I were the only males in sight who hadn't recently been in neck braces or handcuffs, for the lawyers saw mostly personal injury cases and criminal defendants—the angry and the sullen.

"You're looking good, Sister."

"Likewise, I'm sure. Sorry I didn't see you this weekend, but I was up in Anacortes at Mother's."

"How is good old Mom?"

Kathy smiled a smile that, had I been fifteen, would have injected enough adrenaline into my system to kill me, then spoke in the long-suffering tone she seemed to reserve only for me. "Yeeees, we were discussing you and Philip, what to do about the two of you."

"Mom has always been rather partial to gumshoes. I noticed that. A woman with keen insight."

"Mother does think you're cute, but, to be honest, her advice was to go with the cold cash. Philip's inheritance and all. Philip's charmed her."

"Surprise, surprise."

Kathy sighed. "You've always been a trial. From the minute they seated us in alphabetical order in that history class at the U of Dub, I knew I was in trouble, Thomas."

"You were in trouble long before the University of Washington, Sister."

"Not until I met you, I wasn't."

"If you hadn't followed me around the campus like a lost kitten I might not have noticed who you were."

"Very funny. I've never followed you anywhere. Besides, *you* were the one who would have flunked that class without *my* notes." Kathy was motionless for a moment, gazing out the window at the street below, and for that moment the only sound in the room was her clicking pen. "I've been doing a lot of thinking."

"I figured you had been."

"Yeah, well, this proposal you came up with for us to get together has got me confused. I know it's been two weeks, and I feel awful about it, but I honestly don't know what to do. We've known each other all these years and we've always been friends, and I rent the basement apartment in your house, and now that I'm engaged to Philip, you all of a sudden want us to be lovers."

"You didn't think it sounded like such a bad idea two weeks ago."

She gave me a chiding look. "I went to Mother's to get away from you two and to try to get some distance on it. It would break Philip's heart if I broke up with him now."

"It would break my heart if you didn't."

"I don't mean to look at this from only one angle, but he's so proud. Philip is."

"You'd be doing him a favor," I said, touching her hip. "Pride is one of the seven deadly sins. You might cure him."

Laying her hand over mine, she said, "You and I have always been so godawful platonic with each other, and then you come up with this."

"Can't say why we didn't think of it sooner."

She gave me a bewildered look. "But I have this little voice somewhere deep inside asking questions."

"Let's hear some of them."

"Well, for one thing, we've been friends for so long it's hard to comprehend where we turned the corner and flipped it into something else. If we even did."

"We're still friends."

"But we had so many chances to be lovers, and we passed them all up. I don't know. I thought there was something . . . I thought we didn't have the chemistry. I thought you thought we didn't have the chemistry."

"We always had the chemistry. What we didn't have was the nerve."

"What do you mean by that?"

"You should know."

"Well, I don't."

"Listen, Kathy. People have best friends and they have lovers. Lovers come and go, but best friends are forever. If we wanted to stay friends forever, we both figured keeping sex out of it was probably the best way. I *thought* we both figured that. There is a certain intrinsic distrust of romantic love in the notion that you can either be friends or lovers, and we shared it. Both of us. Didn't we? Now I've decided we were wrong. And I think you've decided the same thing. At least, I hope you have. I love you, Kathy—"

"You do?"

"More than I ever wanted to admit. Yes, I do. And I'm pretty sure you love me. If you don't, I wish you would tell me so I can start getting used to it."

"The trouble is, I had myself convinced I loved Philip."

"Sure. Or you wouldn't have agreed to marry him."

"But what would you do if I didn't love you?"

"Go live in the Himalayas. Do about forty years of heavy thinking. Learn to levitate. I'd come back and be on Jay Leno. I'd levitate dogs and old ladies."

"You can't kid about this."

"Okay. I'm sorry. But you know me. I can kid about anything."

"I've noticed."

"I'm just so wounded that you haven't dumped the F person yet."

She thought about that and then stroked my cheek. I stood and grasped her shoulders and looked directly into her eyes. They were a deep blue-black in some lights, violet in others, the kind of eyes one of her law professors who had designs on her had hypothesized could raise the dead. "Listen, Thomas. Serious. You really have thrown a monkey wrench into my life, and you can make sport of Philip all you want, but I'm in a confused time here. Also, I should warn you that your incessant jokes about him do not help your cause."

"I know they don't. And I've made a vow. No more jokes at Philip's expense. No more jokes about shaving off his body hair once a week and selling it to a mattress factory."

"For reasons that I could never quite figure out at the time, from the moment Philip came into my life you took an immediate and total dislike to him."

"What I am is a fairly perceptive judge of character."

"Yes, you are, Thomas, but I'm sorry to tell you that you're wrong about Philip."

"The F person isn't all that thrilled with me either."

"I've been trying to analyze why we're such good friends, you and me, and what would happen if we tried to push it further. There's something about passion that tends to erode friendship, don't you think?"

"A number of married couples I know would disagree with you."

Her jaws clenched and the evocative sound of nylon on nylon filled the room as she crossed her legs and leaned on her stiffened arms, knuckles white on the edge of my desk. I was well aware that her having discussed this with me but not with Philip signaled a strong bias in my favor.

I leaned forward and felt the soft down on her upper lip as I kissed her. I did it the way I thought she wanted it done and waited as she turned her head to see if anyone in the office had observed through the glass door. "Expecting visitors? Oh, no. Not whatshisname?"

"We're having lunch."

"Lunch? What are you doing for dinner?"

"Sorry. He's taking me to hear *Carmina Burana* at the Opera House tonight."

"Take him to Mitchelli's. They were once listed as Seattle's best place to dump a lunch date. I think you can get out the window in back. In case he doesn't get the idea, I'll have a load of wet cement poured into his BMW while you're inside. How do you want to pay for that, ma'am? Cash or credit card?"

"You know I love you, Thomas. I'm just not sure it's *that* kind of love. And I'm not sure how I feel about Philip anymore. I'm so totally confused. I feel like I need six months on a deserted island to think this over, only I know I'd go crazy in a week."

"Can I come? I've never seen you crazy."

"I didn't think it was possible to be this confused." She gave me a probing look, then a quick kiss. "Philip still thinks we're engaged. I feel like such a traitor talking about all this with you, but how can I tell him?" Her face and hands were hot, but her kiss was as cool as that of an ex-lover. This time she didn't check the anteroom afterward. She gave me a reckless smile, put her palms on the edge of the desk, and kicked her legs out from the desk one at a time, like a schoolgirl waiting for the bus.

"I think you're swell, Thomas. You know that. My biggest problem with Philip, aside from the fact that I might be in love with you, is that I'm afraid I'll lose your friendship if I marry him. And my biggest problem with you is he really might be the one. He worships me, you know. And I kind of like being worshiped."

"I think you kind of like having two guys pursuing you."

"Maybe. Just a little. If nothing else comes of this, I want us to be friends the rest of our lives. You and me."

"And if nothing came of it with you and him? Would you still be friends with him?"

"Somehow, I don't think so."

"Doesn't that tell you something?"

"I want you to promise we will be friends. Forever."

"Pen pals. Remember. I'll be in the Himalayas."

"That is not a promise."

"Until one of us dies or starts washing the socks of a cretin we will be friends."

She laughed. "Philip's going to do his own laundry. In fact, he's got all the household chores divided up. He likes to plan things. And he's very progressive."

"Compulsive, I'd say. Anal compulsive. So. You admit he's a cretin?"

She laughed again, and in doing so, exposed the basic snag in our circumstance, which was that she laughed at all my Philip Bacon jokes, even in the rare instances when Philip was in the room, even when it threw him into a tizzy, so that she was making a show of choking our rivalry with words but actually was fanning it with laughter. In fact, I wondered if, subconsciously, she hadn't wanted to engineer this prickly little triangle from the start. Perhaps her amusement was the reason he hated me so.

"Philip is such a wonderful human being, Thomas, and he respects you even if you don't respect him. He's going through some hard personal times right now."

"Sure he is. He's about to get dumped."

"No, it's something to do with his family."

"What? They finally discovered inbreeding produces mutants?"

She stared out the window. "He loves me so much."

"Does he love you enough to try to steal you away from your fiancé?"

"He didn't have to. I didn't have a fiancé. What is this? A proposal?"

"I thought you knew that."

"Thomas, Thomas, Thomas. What am I going to do?"

Spotting something three floors below in the street, Kathy slid off my desk with the smooth, deadly motion of a black mamba, slipped her shoes back on, gazed out the window a moment, then peered back up at me. She said, "I guess one of the traits I liked about you was that you've never been intimidated by me."

"Do you want me to be?"

"No. But other men are."

"That's because you're gorgeous."

"Thanks."

"And it scares them shitless."

"It never scared you."

"Not shitless." I grinned.

"I have to go now. Just one more item, Thomas. Elmer Slezak's out there talking to Beulah. I pray to God you're not doing business with him again. You know how I hate liars."

I glanced toward the foyer but saw only a young man and an older woman seating themselves under the George Wesley Bellows portrait in the anteroom. My noon appointment, Mrs. Lake and guest.

"Snake? Those are mostly tall tales. One other thought. He's not six feet tall."

"Of course not. Elmer is a shrimp."

"No. Your lunch date. Dreamboat out there in the street. Ask him how tall he is."

"What brought this up?"

"You said you don't like liars. Maybe because I actually am over six feet, I can see this clearer, but a man's five-eleven, five-ten, sometimes even five-eight, he says he's six feet. He's not six feet."

"Why would you care?"

"I don't like liars either."

Kathy gave me a funny look when she left the office.

4

KATHY WOULD SOON EMERGE FROM THE BUILD-
ing, step across First Avenue and onto the
cobblestones of the tiny park where she would greet a man
with one brown eye and one blue, a gentleman whose
proper calling in life, as far as I was concerned, was to sell
used cars with bad brakes to Gypsies with bad eyes. The
problem was that I seemed to be the only one on earth
who viewed him this way.

Despite the fact that he taught in an elementary school
and bought gas that made his engine ping, Philip Bacon
was reputed to be independently wealthy. The only indications of affluence I had seen, and I had looked carefully,
were a Rolex wristwatch with a cracked crystal, an irritating penchant for quoting to me from various conservative
newspapers, and a certain remote smugness as he tooled
around in his dented BMW.

One hand in his khaki trousers pocket, he wore a cotton
shirt with a sweater draped so carefully over his shoulders
that it might have been glued on. Like a tourist from We-
natchee, he was handing out coins to indigents in the park,
most of whom were already headed for the grocery up the
street to buy wine.

Snake cracked open the door behind me. "How's it
hangin', big fella?"

"Fine." I continued to watch the street below.

14

"Thomas, maybe the lady out here mentioned it already, but I recommended you."

"Haven't seen her yet. Who's that with her?"

"I don't know. She ain't got a son." Slezak was a bandy-legged private investigator with shaggy, gray-brown hair and a grizzled beard that resembled something left over from a five-day drunk, a beard he caressed whenever it occurred to him. Snake was five and a half feet tall and weighed a hundred and twenty-two pounds if you slipped a brick into his pocket.

"When I spoke to her on the phone, she said she tried to hire you but you begged off. Your aunt Missy finally croak and leave you that avocado farm?"

"Thomas, my boy, rule number one: never do business with someone you've been porking."

I glanced into the anteroom. "Mrs. Lake?"

"As horny as a three-peckered billy goat standing in a two-dollar wagon."

Downstairs, Kathy crossed the street, strode over to her fiancé with what I could only call a carefree gait, and kissed him with the very lips that had been pressed to mine minutes ago. I couldn't decide if the kiss was as heartfelt as the one I'd received. Nor did I have a clue as to what was going on in her head when in the space of five minutes she could kiss two men, each of whom professed to love her. She and Philip walked arm in arm up First Avenue beyond Doc Maynard's and the Old Timer's Cafe, then disappeared.

Standing beside me at the window, Snake said, "Just got back from Dago after that case we had together. Went on down to Mexico chasin' hot nooky and homely señoritas and chewed too much of the ice in my tequila and got sick. Before I got outta there I coulda stood flat-footed and pooped over a fence. New window?"

I dropped into my rolling executive chair, skidded it backward a few feet, and clasped my hands behind my head. "Client broke the old one. Hired me to follow his wife."

Snake fell back onto the sofa, throwing his arms out along the wall, crossing his legs so that a silver-toed cowboy boot was propped on one scrawny knee. Talk of cases where anything had been broken, windows or otherwise, was Snake's forte. He grinned wide enough to flash a gold tooth in the back of his mouth. "You weren't bangin' the bride, were you?"

"He thought she was having an affair, and she was. Not with me and you know it. I didn't want to take the case in the first place, but I was having a blah week, so I thought: why not? I found out he was beating her, so I knew I couldn't tell him she was sleeping with another guy without her getting busted up. I held it back from him. He got suspicious and threw a chair through the window."

Snake glanced at the prospective clients thumbing through magazines on the floral-patterned sofa in the anteroom, the young man riffling a *Velo News*, the woman a *Scientific American*. "Never lie to a client, Thomas. That's the first rule."

"I thought the first rule was never pork a client."

"You'll find them two edicts go hand in hand. Once you pork 'em, you have to lie to 'em. You should have told your client his wife was playing footsie."

"I was afraid he would kill her. Kill both of them."

"He could sue, ya know. I been thinkin' a lot on ethicals lately. So will you after you get into this screwball case. Look, it may not look this way, but essentially *I* am hiring you. I'll send your cut after you bill hours at the end of the month. Just have Mrs. Lake mail the checks to me."

"This is a joke, right?"

"I ever joke about money?"

"You're dealing a weak hand here, Elmer. I've got a client out there I don't even know who she is, a woman whose case I don't think I want anyway, and you say I'm to have her send you the fee? You still owe me two hundred bucks you borrowed in San Diego when you lost that push-up contest with those sailors."

Elmer lowered his voice almost to a whisper, stood, and

said, "I was cheated out of that two hundred, and if you want to cheat me out of this, then so be it. Just watch yourself. After horsing around in her boudoir, I couldn't walk a straight line for an hour, couldn't spit for a day, and still can't look myself in the eye. And you'll want the case. There's no way you could pass up this babe. Just remember. Rule number one in the detecting business."

"Yeah? What is it now?"

"Everything is not as it seems." He left by the door that led directly to the hallway.

Mrs. Lake was somewhere between forty-five and fifty-five years of age. She wore nearly opaque sunglasses. Her copper-colored hair was pulled back and knotted at the nape of her neck. Her cheeks were painfully tight and, like a new penny, she was shiny all over.

As I got up to invite them in, the office Muzak began a slow instrumental version of "The Great Pretender," and, without any preamble, the young man in the anteroom launched into song, dropping to one knee beside Mrs. Lake like a suitor in a hokey act. I would have asked them in just then, but I was attracted to his talent the way we're all attracted to talent and wanted him to finish.

She wore a black-and-white-checked gingham skirt with a wide black belt, a floppy white T-shirt, high heels, and no nylons on her tan legs. Before she came in, she hung up a man's scuffed bomber jacket in the other room. She carried a small purse, which she used to store the black sunglasses, after carefully folding them into an expensive hand-tooled case.

There was a primness to her movements that betrayed everything Elmer Slezak had said about her. She was a little too classy for the likes of Elmer Slezak. Elmer daydreamed to excess and sometimes fogged reality with desire. It wasn't that he thought he was lying. What he thought was, that by a certain twinkle in his eye or a growl in his voice, I would know he was exaggerating and take his words for what they obviously were. Sometimes I did and sometimes I didn't.

We shook hands, Mrs. Lake and I, and then she sat in the blue chair. She had looked at me as if I reminded her of somebody else, someone she might have known long ago. It was a memory she had to pull back from a good distance off, and it seemed to sadden her.

She said, "This is my friend, Jerome. Jerome Johnson. He's involved in this as well. Jerome is my house guest for a few weeks. I think of him as a surrogate son." She gazed at him affectionately.

Johnson wore jeans, penny loafers, a starched white shirt, and a tie. His curly hair, which might have been red when he was younger, wafted straight up off his head. His complexion was smooth as milk. He wore John Lennon glasses and probably did not shave more often than once a week. He looked eighteen, twenty tops, not the kind of guy you would notice anywhere; more the kind who would sell you cuff links at Nordstrom's before he faded into the wallpaper. His handshake was cool and tentative where hers had been warm and supremely confident.

"We believe you know a Mr. Bacon," said Mrs. Lake.

"Who?"

"Philip Bacon?" The young man sat down in the red chair.

"I know him."

"Are you close friends? This might not work if you're close friends. Mr. Slezak indicated you might not be."

"We're not what most people would term *close*."

"I'm assuming we can speak in confidence."

"Absolutely."

"The reason I ask all this is because we want you to follow him."

"Bacon?"

"Somebody has to find out what he's up to."

My sentiments precisely, but I hardly expected a woman to come into my office and pay me for it.

5

"HE'S HOUNDING BILLY," VOLUNTEERED
Jerome, butting his glasses up onto his nose
with the knuckle of his thumb. "I'm Billy's foster brother.
Billy calls himself Billy Battle now, but his legal name is
William Blodgett."

"You see, Mr. Black," said Roxanne Lake, eyeballing
me. "We need to find out what Philip is up to. We know
he's following Billy, we just don't know why. The way we
figure it, Philip is either going to hurt Billy, or, more
likely, Billy is going to hurt Philip. Whichever the case,
we want you to find out and put the kibosh on it."

Philip was a lot of things—a snob, pedant, sycophant, a
prude, an overly educated and largely ignorant commenta-
tor on society—but I doubted he was a thug or that these
people had any real cause for worry. I doubted they were
revealing their real motives either, but I didn't care. Somewhere along the way their real motives would surface.
They always did. "Why don't you explain what you think
is going on?"

"It gets a little complex," she said. "Billy and Philip and
myself and Jerome here, we come from the same neighborhood, Madrona, and Billy committed some crimes that
probably affected everyone who lived there." Filled with
middle- to upper-income homes, Madrona was a section of
central Seattle on a sloping hillside overlooking Lake

19

Washington and facing the Cascade Mountains and the sunrise. "I would have thought you would have heard of Billy Battle. The trial made the papers, what, seven years ago? Although it was Blodgett then."

"Billy just recently was released from Monroe Reformatory," said Jerome. "Before that he was up at Echo Glen out past Issaquah, where they keep young offenders."

"Philip lived in your neighborhood?"

"With his folks," said Roxanne Lake. "I moved to Madrona with my third husband and lived there until the divorce. You want to hear about that, give me about two days. Jerome and Billy lived down the alley from us with Billy's mother. Billy's been in trouble since he was little. Starting fires. Stealing from the grocery. When he was about eight, he tied old man Clark's dog to the bumper of a UPS truck. As he got older, he got more devious. From Echo Glen he went straight to Monroe."

"What indications do you have that Philip is following Billy?"

"Jerome saw him. The problem is, Billy's apt to do something particularly nasty when he finds out, which means he'll end up back in prison. Either that or Philip's going to kill him. You realize, we do not want either of those to occur."

"I find it hard to believe Philip means to kill anybody, although I can almost believe he might be following somebody."

"We're a little dubious ourselves. Don't you see? That's why we need somebody to find out what's going on."

"What was Billy sent up for?"

The woman and the young man exchanged looks. She responded. "Assault."

"It didn't have anything to do with Philip?"

"Nothing except Philip was one of the people who stepped in and stopped it. Later, he was also a witness against Billy at the trial."

Dark and unwavering, her penetrating eyes were

freighted with that same belated ghost of recognition I had glimpsed, or thought I had glimpsed, when we shook hands. She thought she knew something about me, a perception I believed might have come from Slezak, who would have given her some background. When she crossed her legs, the skirt, without objection from her, crept higher. Her body looked twenty years younger than it had a right to, and she didn't care who knew it.

She fished a gold-plated cigarette case from her purse, glanced around the office for an ashtray, tightened her thin upper lip when she saw that there were none, and tossed the lighter back into her purse.

From what I knew of him, I believed Philip might harbor enough Tom Mix six-gun values to get siphoned into something like following an ex-con around because he thought it was a heroic pursuit, or because he had hatched some scatterbrained ploy to serve society in an as yet unnamed manner. It occurred to me that Philip tailing an ex-con was like a naked boy following a bucket of hot coals down a slide. Yet, to me, the possibility of Philip doing anything blatantly illegal was beyond the pale. Philip Bacon did not have the sand to correct a schoolgirl making the wrong change on a box of cookies, much less to harass or confront or certainly to kill a grown man. In addition, for all of his vexing traits, one had to admit there was a fundamental decency and rectitude about the man.

"Mrs. Lake—"

"Call me Roxanne."

"Roxanne, why don't we simply talk to Philip and ask him what he's up to? I'd be happy to do that without mentioning your name."

"We've thought of that already. We're afraid it might exacerbate the situation. If you speak to him and scare him off, he may go out and get somebody else to do whatever it is he's planning."

"You're sure he's following Billy?"

"Jerome saw him last week when we had Billy over to the house to sort through some clothing. He's grown out of everything he ever owned before he went to the joint—all that weight lifting."

"Did Billy see him?"

"Billy spends all his time these days looking at girls," said Jerome. "I thought it was better not to tell him he was being tailed." Johnson shifted uneasily in his seat. "We've been writing back and forth all these years. It wasn't easy because some of what Billy wrote me was pretty scary, but his mom, our mom, Millicent, thinks I'm a good influence, so I tried to stay in touch. I'm his foster brother. Billy used to have these—I don't know what you would call them—fits maybe. He'd get angry and go non compos mentis for a minute or two. Then he'd be all right. You just had to stay out of his way for that one or two minutes. He'd go at whoever he was fighting with both mitts in the air, roaring like a gorilla. One afternoon I saw him buffalo half the football team. It never seemed to last. One, two minutes, tops."

"Don't be silly, darling," said Mrs. Lake. "Billy's always been crazier than a tick in turpentine. My grandma used to say that about her first husband after he was killed by a moose in Saskatchewan."

"Yeah, well. You have to understand Billy. He was only fifteen the last time we knew him. The joint calmed him down a whole lot." Jerome's voice was waterlogged with hope. Having a foster brother in jail had to be an unacceptable burden for such an ingenuous young man, a particle of family history best left unmentioned in most social matrices.

"It calmed him down enough for him to attack some kid up at Echo Glen," said the woman. "Then a month later he calmed down enough to knock out a woman counselor and tie her to a chair. That's what got him into Monroe, darling. Calming down. Maybe he will straighten out. Maybe he won't. I'm reserving judgment."

"And you don't know anything more about Philip's connection to Billy?"

"I hardly knew the man at all," said Mrs. Lake. "All I

know is that the night Billy was arrested, Phil and a couple of other neighborhood men, including my ex, Jon, grabbed Billy and held him for the cops. Then they testified at his trial. All except Jon, who was too chicken. He thought Billy'd come back and get him if he testified."

"You think Philip is afraid Billy is coming after him for testifying?"

"Could be."

"I'm at a loss as to what to tell you. Philip is pretty good friends with someone in the office here, and it probably wouldn't be kosher for me to take your case. I could talk to him for you, but you've ruled that out."

Roxanne Lake crossed her legs the other direction and looked at Jerome. "Why don't we tell him some of what went on in the old neighborhood."

Touching his nose, Jerome tried to compose himself. His face was beginning to flush. "Roxy, I don't think all that stuff in the old neighborhood was about Billy."

"Philip does. We know he thinks it was about Billy. Maybe if we tell Mr. Black here, maybe he'll realize why we have so much reason to be worried."

Jerome glanced at me and touched his nose again, then his glasses and the back of his neck. Finally, he sat on his hands. "Look. Maybe I'm not one to talk, but I don't think he did half of what people think."

"Why wouldn't you be one to talk?" I asked.

"Well, I stole a car with him once. But I didn't know we were stealing it."

"You stole a car?" Roxanne Lake asked.

Johnson gave me a sheepish look, turned to Roxanne. "We killed a horse too."

"You did what?" Mrs. Lake asked.

"I don't like talking about it, but when you're young, you can get into all kinds of situations. We were in Oregon, and Billy told me he'd been hired to take this horse to Seattle to give riding lessons. Billy didn't even know how to ride. Neither of us had a driver's license. We were down there in his uncle's car, which I later found out he stole. No trailer. So we cut this fence and roped a horse with some clothesline, then walked the horse way the hell up the road.

"That was when he told me his idea was to kidnap a horse and tell the owner we had it here in Seattle and ask them to wire money to ship it back. Say we found it running in a field or something. Billy always had this plan for the two of us to hire a call girl, and he was always trying to get money for it. Before I could stop him, Billy whacked the horse with a hammer. He was talking nuts, saying we could kill horses everywhere, bury them, then ask for shipping money. He said all we needed was a clothesline and a hammer."

"What happened?" I asked. Jerome sounded almost shocked to be recalling these events. It was clear that he harbored a certain fondness for Billy and also a certain fear. It was also clear that it bothered him to exhume events from a troublesome youth that wasn't all that distant.

"After four hours in the middle of the night with these little army spades trying to dig a hole, Billy gave up on the whole thing. You shovel long enough, you decide burying dead horses isn't what you want to do with your life."

"You never told me any of this," said Roxanne Lake.

"It's not exactly something you want on your résumé."

6 "LISTEN, MR. BLACK," SAID ROXANNE LAKE. "Jerome is older now. Mature. He's got his degree. The only setback on the horizon is this thing about Philip and Billy. If Philip is really your friend, you'd be doing him a favor. Bailing him out, so to speak."

She had been talking and caressing Jerome's shoulder at the same time, the way a mother touched a grown child. Appearing chagrined, Johnson paled, peered past his knees, swallowed and rubbed the knuckles of one hand. It was a soft hand that had not been inaugurated by physical labor. In the manner of people encountering a painful subject, Johnson slowly faded out of our conversation, as if he had fallen asleep with his eyes open.

"Let me start from the front," said Mrs. Lake. "This all happened over a series of years. Maybe three, four years. There were the animal mutilations. I was there the day Mrs. Wald found her tabby hanging in the cherry tree. There would be a couple of incidents, and then it would be quiet for months."

"You're saying Billy did this?"

"Jerome doesn't think so, but everyone else does. He set fires. I don't think there was a house in the area that hadn't been burglarized. Somebody broke into mine, and, even though we could tell they must have been in there for

25

hours, they took only a few old love letters I had stored in an armoire."

"They caught a burglar," said Jerome. "And it wasn't Billy."

"That's debatable," Mrs. Lake said, wetting a fingertip and touching it to a tiny piece of lint on her bare knee.

"Can't you just go see what Phil Bacon's doing?" said Jerome. "I never saw Billy set any fires. And I don't know about breaking into houses. He might have once. I know he stole cars and he killed that horse—and I guess you could say he wasn't a very pleasant person to be around sometimes. But I think there was a copycat in our neighborhood who knew the blame for everything bad would land on Billy."

"You have to understand something," said Mrs. Lake. "Jerome is extremely loyal. When Millicent, Billy's mother, took him in, he didn't have anything or anybody. He'd lost his folks, his home, every toy or book or scrap of clothing he ever owned. His parents' house burned down in the middle of the night, and he went to Millicent's in a pair of pajama bottoms. I think he was eight years old."

"Ten."

Roxanne Lake gave him a glance that was a mixture of the maternal and the patronizing. There had been something vulnerable about Jerome from the beginning, and I began to see it was his eggshell yesteryears.

"Let me ask you something, Roxanne. What's Elmer Slezak's part in this?"

Lake kicked her top leg up as if a doctor were testing her reflexes, then did it again, watching her foot bounce. "I simply ran into him somewhere and he happened to mention he was a detective. I asked him about this. He said his stew had too many nails in it and recommended you."

She was a slim woman with bony features, sharp shoulders, thin arms, and broad hips that looked broader while she was sitting. I had the feeling she was both drab and unremarkable without makeup. If I had to guess, I would have said she had been gawky as a girl, awkward as a teenager, faltering as a young woman, and that she had achieved some grace only in middle age. I had the feeling she had no children of her own, that Jerome was some sort of mothering project, that perhaps she took on such projects from time to time. She dressed rich, she talked rich, but she had not been born rich, because she had never been to an orthodontist.

"Mr. Slezak reminds me of a little banty rooster. Don't you think?" The phrase gave me pause. "Mr. Black, you should be made aware that there were two deaths in the neighborhood. One of them was a girl who disappeared. Billy's girlfriend. She broke up with him, and then about three weeks later disappeared under the most unusual circumstances. At least, we assume she's dead."

They were silent for a few moments, each of them reliving the past.

"Look," I said. "I hate to take a case that my gut instinct tells me is a waste of time, and I'm not sure the information will be worth what it will cost, but if you want me to, I'll find out what is going on between Philip Bacon and Billy Battle."

"Money's not a problem," said Mrs. Lake. "We're extremely concerned, and we'd feel so much easier if you looked into it." When she got a checkbook out and scrawled a check, I noticed she did not bother to put the figure in the accounts section of her checkbook. "Or should I write it to Mr. Slezak?"

"To me will be fine."

After obtaining some routine information from them, I stood, signaling the end of our interview. Johnson had been thoughtful and introspective throughout. "Phil's a pretty reasonable-type person," he said. "Don't you think so?"

"I do think so."

Johnson took out his wallet and retrieved a small photo

of himself standing next to a fence beside another boy. They must have been fourteen or fifteen.

"That's Billy," he said, rather glumly.

"He's bigger," said Mrs. Lake. "Billy is a whole lot bigger now. And those piggy little eyes he has in the picture? They're even piggier."

"Can I hold on to this for a while?"

"Sure. I don't even know why I carry it around."

Johnson hung back while Mrs. Lake went into the anteroom to get her coat. His eyes behind the wire-rimmed glasses were the gray of the ocean in a rain, a suitable match for his stormy auburn hair, slightly anemic skin, and the vague and probably perpetual look of bewilderment on his face.

"One more question, Jerome. Where is Billy living?"

"With Millicent, his mom. Our mom. Or sometimes he'll stay on a couch somewhere. He kind of likes fast, low-down girls. Mr. Black? All kids get into scrapes. I mean, everybody I know did. Billy just never got a chance to grow out of that phase. I guess you could say they locked him away before he could grow up."

"According to Mrs. Lake, you're understating the case by a considerable margin."

"Yeah, well, he's not *her* brother."

"I guess not."

Jerome's ostensible motive, to protect his brother, was clear enough. Roxanne Lake's motive, to help out Jerome, though not as believable, was equally clear. Shield Jerome's life from any more chaos. The motive that was off kilter in all this foofaraw was my own. Who but an idiot would sign up to follow his best friend's fiancé?

7

LIKE A PIG ON ROLLER SKATES I CAREENED around the room in my wheeled executive chair. The centrifugal force whipped tears of laughter across my face. The chair nearly tipped over backward, but even then the utter disgrace of my conduct was not sufficient to rein in my elation.

In the midst of my cheap glee, I slammed my feet to the floor and skidded to a standstill. What I had yet to face were some of the inherent bugaboos in this situation over which I had no command. For one, if Kathy ever learned I was tailing Philip, she was apt to hand back every Christmas mug I had ever given her, though I had a feeling she would keep the cutting board.

Even before I'd asked Kathy to jilt her fiancé and become my lover, conversation had been strained whenever the three of us were in a room together. The night I made my big play, she kissed me almost greedily, then wept and stood at the kitchen window staring out at the dark, saying it just might be that I was a day late and a dollar short.

Yet two weeks had passed and she still hadn't given me an answer. More important, she had delayed any further talk of a wedding with him. Two weeks.

Philip Bacon wouldn't have bothered me so much if he had been a regular guy you could throw a Frisbee with, tell dirty jokes to, a guy who as a kid might have jacked

29

off a dog or used a BB gun on the neighbor's attic window, a guy who might fudge on his taxes; but he wore black socks with Birkenstocks, cooled his mismatched eyes almost to marbles if he heard even a whiff of profanity, and had more than once lectured in tones close to browbeating on the advisability of no-load mutual funds. I had never heard Philip involved in a lengthy conversation with anyone in which he did not drop, at some point, the fact that he subscribed to the *Wall Street Journal*. These traits and others seemed to endear him to everyone but me.

After phoning Bridget Simes to see if she was free, I removed a bag from the oak cabinet and filled a thermos with water from the kitchenette next door. Already cached in the bag were several changes of clothing, provisions, three Thomas Guide map books, and a thousand dollars stashed in the lining of a Charles Willeford memoir titled *I Was Looking for a Street*.

As I packed I recalled a dinner at the 5 Spot a week earlier. It had been Kathy's stab at reconciling the two of us.

The 5 Spot was at the top of Queen Anne Hill and had a tile floor and a café atmosphere that made it noisy enough that you knew you were having a good time. Kathy had arranged the seating so that Philip and I were staring at each other across the table, a total of three brown eyes and one blue. Also at the table were Allison, a lawyer from our office, Beulah Hancock, our receptionist, and her current beau.

Kathy knew I didn't much care for Philip, but what might have escaped her notice during their tawdry summer romance was that Philip Bacon despised me with all the pell-mell gusto his naked little soul could muster.

Though he was careful not to let it show, you rarely ran across a man so consumed with venom.

Conversation at the table had veered, for some unaccountable reason, to talk of serial killers. The topic was one Philip had evidently given some thought to.

"But if you knew a person like Ted Bundy," said Philip,

"and you knew he was killing people, and he was getting away with it, what would you do?" He winked at Kathy the way a normal person might wink at a kid or a bad pun. Philip winked at everyone except me, probably because I had a habit of muttering the color of the eye he had winked and then asking if I had been right.

"Blue," I said, quietly.

"When somebody is committing a crime," Kathy said, kicking me under the table, "you take your information to the authorities."

"And if the authorities won't listen or cannot do anything?" Philip asked.

"You're talking about being a vigilante, aren't you?" I asked. "Vigilantes kill people."

"Maybe."

"And what if you kill the wrong person?"

"Mistakes? Sure, Tommy. People make them."

"Even when the state executes somebody and he gets eight weeks of trial and ten years of appeals they make mistakes. How would you like something like that riding around digging its naked little spurs into your conscience?"

"I'm talking about a situation where there can be no mistake."

"No such thing."

"Sure there is. Don't be naive."

"We have a system," I said. "Sure, there's grit in the gears, but it's a system, and it's preferable to anarchy. We're talking order and disorder."

"I thought we were talking law and crime," said Philip.

"What you're talking about is justice at the expense of order. In the end, attitudes like the one you're espousing create more chaos than the problems they are trying to solve."

I had a feeling he knew I had killed once. It had been in the line of duty on the Seattle police force, an event that had drained the sap out of me for many long months and even now churned to the surface more often than I cared to admit. Kathy would have warned him not to mention it.

"But aren't there some people, Tommy," Philip persisted, "who are just plain evil? You told me yourself when you were a cop sometimes you would find a body in a Dumpster and you'd know the man was bad and you'd know Homicide wasn't going to fall all over themselves trying to solve it."

You almost had to like a guy who called you Tommy to your face even though you had told him not to and even though he'd never heard anybody else call you Tommy. You almost had to like a guy who winked at every woman, child, cab driver, and mirror he passed.

"Are we talking vigilantism or judicial death sentences?" I said.

"You realize as well as Kathy here ... that there are times you know somebody has done something but you also know they are not going to get sent up for it. The whole system with all the plea bargaining. We all know justice and the law are two different things."

"So we *are* talking vigilantism?"

"What if you know somebody who is pure evil. Somebody who kills for fun. What if one of them is, say, your brother? You know he is planning to kill again. Don't you have a moral obligation to starch him?"

"To what?"

"You know. Kill him?"

"Saying things is right next to doing things, and the more times you say you would do something, the easier it ultimately becomes to do it. I'll never say I would kill someone."

Eyes wet with excitement, Philip said, "Some people go rock climbing or fly fishing. Others torture and kill. If you can get one of those psychos in your sights, you may be saving a lot of lives."

"Are you telling us you'd kill your own brother?"

"Under certain circumstances, wouldn't you?"

Philip was leaning across the table, his chile verde long

forgotten. I had never seen him so worked up, nor had he ever evinced so much interest in me. Despite the fact that he kept calling me Tommy, I felt genuine warmth and interest emanating from him, an observation I did my best to overlook.

"You're too naive, Tommy. You know what the experts think? That there are between a hundred and two hundred serial killers on the loose in America."

"Nominating yourself judge, jury, and hangman is a dangerous piece of business, Philip."

"The experts say—"

"Screw the experts."

"Why are you so opposed? Because of getting caught?"

"Because you're assigning yourself this same demented power these killers thrive on. A power that twists and corrupts everything it touches."

Philip's reply was glib and rehearsed. He said that in cases where there was doubt, one held back. Being accurate would be its own protection.

I said, "You're talking about anarchy of a sort people cannot even guess at."

"Worse than having killers running around snatching people off the streets?"

"Not worse. The same. Exactly the same."

"How do you figure?"

"Don't you get it? You've just described precisely what you're advocating. Killers running around snatching people off the streets. Except, under your scenario, we would be the killers."

"Your problem, Tommy, is you don't know how tough you are. You could do this."

It was the most patronizing tone he'd used all evening, and for a split second I had one of those myopic impulses you get sometimes, mostly for no reason other than you've got the wrong chemicals zooming through your brain, to reach across the table and slug him, see how tough he was with a fist in his face. It was embarrassing that he could irk me to that degree. What I did instead was pick up the

mason jar my ice water was served in and drink until the
nerves in my front teeth were screaming.

No doubt about it. He had been thinking about Billy
Battle.

8

ON THE WAY OUT OF THE OFFICE I STOPPED AT
the receptionist's island. "Just one question."

"Certainly, Thomas."

Our receptionist, Beulah, was what females, blessed
with empathy and tact, called a "big woman," and what
males without thinking twice called a "fat lady." Once in
a great while Beulah herself joked about her size, the most
recent a remark about her laundry coming back from the
cleaners with a note saying they did not do boat covers.
She was intelligent, cute, underemployed, and had amas-
sed a social life more active than mine but not any more
than Kathy's.

"How exactly did Philip and Kathy meet?"

"Why, I think it was last winter sometime. Skiing,
wasn't it?"

"Don't play dumb, Beulah." As I stared at her, her
Technicolor-blue eyes seemed to sink into her round
cheeks. When the phone buzzed, she snapped it up. I
waited.

"I know you know I know," she said after she had finished with the call. "What I mean is, I know you think you

know I know, but even if I did know, that doesn't mean I would let you in on it."

"Why such a secret?"

She shrugged and dimpled her cheeks. "He swept her off her feet. Isn't that enough? Haven't you watched him charm every woman in the office? It's nice to finally see a man who knows what a woman wants."

"He got caught with a gang of transvestite hookers in the restroom at Hombres and hired Kathy to defend him?" Beulah's high, breaking laugh ushered me clean out of the building.

Our offices were on First Avenue in Pioneer Square, in the Mutual Life Building, a stone structure directly across the street from a small park that was mostly a cobblestone plaza, maple trees, a few benches, and a totem pole. It was a haven for the homeless, for those who had fallen off their medication, and for the recently released.

As towns went, Seattle was a relative babe, a city where a few old red bricks and a hitching post were considered ancient history. Pioneer Square itself was a renovated area of town, with old-fashioned street lamps, cobblestones, and brick alleys. Many of the buildings had been restored to their original specifications. The waterfront was two blocks to the west, and from our office you could sometimes hear ferries sounding off in Elliott Bay.

You could smell the tide, catch the scream of the gulls, and listen to the nostalgic clang of the little green waterfront trolley on Alaskan Way.

Before it burned to the ground in 1889, the original core of the city had been platted out from this area. Afterward, Seattle was rebuilt atop the ruins so as to place it higher, as a protection against the tides, and also to obviate picking up the old city. Many of the sidewalk gratings with their heavy colored-glass portholes looked directly down into dusty shop fronts that hadn't seen a customer in a hundred years.

Bridget met me at the cookie store catty-cornered from

our building, whipping her black Ford Taurus through traffic and parking on Yesler in a truck-loading zone.

Tall, wan, freckled, Bridget Simes operated her private investigation business out of a small apartment on Queen Anne Hill. A competitive runner, her claim to fame was a second place in the girl's state cross-country championships during her senior year of high school.

She had one of those milky complexions redheads get when they hit their late twenties or early thirties. Clad in Reebok running shoes, jeans, a silk blouse, and a neatly pressed blazer, she wore sunglasses perched in auburn hair that she had pinned up into a pile.

"Thanks," she said, accepting a huge chocolate chip cookie in a sack without looking inside. It was a routine we had. "Who are we following?"

"In a minute he's going to drop Kathy off across the street."

"Your Kathy?"

I nodded and stepped into a notch of the building in front of the cookie shop, trying to keep as little of myself exposed to the street as possible. Two long-haired Indians in army jackets sat on a bench across the street talking dialectics and theosophy and passing a brown paper sack back and forth. A moment later Kathy and Philip came into view behind them.

"This man we're following a client of Kathy's?" Bridget asked.

"Not exactly." I gave her his name and the license number of his BMW. "A silver two-door with a little ding on the driver's side where somebody might have kicked it after he parked in their flower bed. You follow on foot, then give me a call when you find out where he's parked." Kathy was stepping on tiptoe to buss Philip's cheek while he put his arms around her waist and held her.

"If he's not a client," said Bridget, "is he a boyfriend?"

"Sort of."

"Looks like more than sort of."

"She's getting ready to dump him."

"I see."

Philip said something to Kathy, then pivoted and walked up Yesler. "I'm off," Bridget said. "Just one thing."

"Yeah?"

"This is an authentic gig? Because I like Kathy."

"It's authentic."

Jaywalking across Yesler while Philip veered east up the hill on Jefferson, Bridget shadowed him from the south side of the street. From First Avenue most of the streets to the east ran uphill. Parts of downtown Seattle were so steep that in the winter the Engineering Department block-aded them before it snowed. Eighty years ago a hill not far away had been sluiced back into the bay with hydraulics.

I headed for my pickup in the lot behind our building. "For a white guy, you've got a great caboose," Kathy said, patting my rear pocket.

"For a woman who was just seen kissing another man, you're awfully fresh."

"I kiss all the men. You know that."

"You're supposed to be upstairs working." She had am-bushed me at the corner of the Mutual Life Building, out-side the toy store. Behind her in the doorway a barrage of kites fluttered in the September breeze over the heads of a bunch of four- and five-year-olds and their guardians, who had crossed the street on the same light with Kathy.

"Thomas, Thomas, Thomas. I saw you conspiring with Ms. Simes. Got a job? Was it that woman with the boy? Looked like Lady Godiva in clothes. You're not going to get caught alone with her, are you? Did you see the way she was looking at you?"

"She wasn't looking at me. And I gotta go."

"I'm glad something turned up."

I grinned. "Not as glad as I am, Sister."

Halfway down the block, in front of Trattoria Mitchelli, I noticed she was still watching, so I squinted, made my right hand into a pistol and pointed it at her. She gave a halfhearted wave. The two Indians on the bench across the street in the park hadn't taken their bloodshot eyes off her,

grinning and swigging from their brown sack. My Lord,
she was pretty with that braid of dark hair trailing down
her back.

Five minutes later I waited in my pickup truck while
Philip Bacon jimmied his BMW out of a parking space
near Eighth and Columbia under the elevated Interstate 5.
Bridget was trotting back down to her illegally parked
Taurus.

When he finally got into the street, he ran a stop sign,
then accelerated up the hill, tires chirping. By the time I
crested the hill, he was almost out of sight. Sticking to side
streets, he continued to roll through every intersection,
stop sign or not, looking left and right for cops and plung-
ing ahead of slow pokes. He was one of those drivers who
compulsively zipped in and out of traffic, even when there
was no need. I could almost smell the smoke coming off
my new clutch.

He made his way to East Madison and drove to Madison Park alongside Lake Washington, where he sat for a
haircut in a small salon. Altogether he had run two yellow
lights and one red. He had rolled through six stop signs.

After the haircut, Bridget did the footwork, wearing a
baseball cap. Philip was the sort of man who liked you to
know he had two or three women lounging on the backseat
of his life, and I wondered if he wasn't on the way to visit
another girlfriend now. After he met Kathy, it became
common knowledge that he had allowed himself weeks to
disentangle himself from several ongoing social contracts.
It wouldn't have been so bad if he hadn't made such a pro-
duction out of announcing that he had finally off-loaded
Vickie, or Debbie, or Buffie. I had the feeling he thought
Kathy spelled her name with an *ie*.

At two-thirty we trailed him to East Alder, to a three-
story subsidized income building painted slate-gray. On the
east side small, narrow balconies overlooked a rockery, a
macadam parking area, and the street. The west side
fronted a busy arterial.

Seattle University was a few blocks away, as were most

of the hospitals in town. The neighborhood was a muddle of apartments and old houses broken up into individual units. Several outpatient apartment houses were located in the area, and in our first hour seven hairless people walked past in surgeon's masks.

9

AFTER A WHILE BRIDGET SIMES GOT OUT AND carried a paper sack that could have been groceries past Philip's parked car.

When she had climbed back into her Taurus, she phoned me. "He's just sitting in there reading a book."

"A Scrooge McDuck comic?"

"Actually, it was something by Marcel Proust."

"Come on. Nobody reads Proust."

"He does."

Three hours later, at five-thirty, Philip Bacon still had not left his car, a fact I could ascertain through the interstices in the junipers and azaleas in the rockery. I had gotten out of the truck twice to stretch my legs and to admire the distant, snow-covered glaciers of Mount Rainier in the late afternoon sunshine. At one point I found myself in a long philosophical discussion with an elderly man in a snap-brim hat and a neatly pressed Hawaiian shirt about whether he should drive to San Diego and live there, or rent an apartment in the same building Philip was watching. We got to talking about women, and he gave me some not-very-useful advice.

It was dark before Philip moved.

A chunky man with a bad haircut and clothes stiff with newness emerged from the southeast exit of the apartment building. He wore a fake leather jacket, jeans that were loose in the waist and tight in the thighs, and a pair of ragtag leather shoes that had been in fashion eight or ten years ago and were sinking into the pavement on either outside edge.

He jumped into a broken-down '73 Chevrolet, a faded green two-door, and drove around the corner on Alder Street. Billy Battle?

Bacon followed the Chevy, and Bridget followed Bacon. Her Taurus was the SHO model, and although outwardly it looked like a family sedan, it was the same model the Washington State Patrol used for some of their unmarked cars. Almost as ruthless a driver as Philip, Bridget could jitterbug through traffic and match him illegal turn for illegal turn. After dark she could present him with four different sets of running lights on the front of her car, a gimmick she installed to keep surveillance subjects from recognizing her in their rearview mirrors at night. I had a similar setup on my truck.

I worked my way down the hill to Fourteenth, then headed north behind them.

It was just after nine-thirty and dark. The three of us had been sitting in our vehicles for hours. Traffic was light. School had started for the fall quarter, so there were a number of students from Seattle University walking the streets, collars winged against the night.

They traveled east on Jefferson, past Providence Hospital, to where Jefferson dead-ends at Garfield High School. The Chevy parked behind Ezell's, and the driver went inside for an order of fried chicken. Then he cruised north on Twenty-third Avenue to Union Street, Pike Street, up Broadway through the Capitol Hill area, and back toward the Central District. Thirty-five minutes elapsed before Bridget reported anything else on the phone.

"The Chevy bought some drugs at the corner of Twenty-sixth and Cherry."

"Probably wanted a chaser for the chicken. Where's the BMW?"

"Pulled over at the curb half a block back. I kept going and parked two blocks in front. I've got my field glasses on him. Get this. A black dude sells him the crack, then walks back and talks to your friend in the BMW. Tries to sell him some too."

"He buy any?"

"Naw. Just drove away behind the Chevy."

At Jackson and Twentieth, the Chevy was flagged down by a bold-eyed black woman in shorts, sneakers, and a T-shirt, who opened the passenger door, spoke for a few seconds, then climbed inside. "Christ," said Bridget on the phone. "I gotta keep moving. The driver of the beamer's been looking at me."

The Chevy parked in front of Gai's Bakery. Windows rolled tightly so as not to lose any of the fumes, he smoked a glass pipe while the hooker disappeared from view below the level of the car windows. Later the Chevy did a U-turn in the street and drove the hooker to a ramshackle apartment house on Twenty-second Avenue just off Jefferson behind Ezell's. The driver went inside with her.

Philip parked in front of the building. I parked around the corner and Bridget stayed down the street.

It was almost midnight when the man in the Chevy emerged from the apartment building and drove away. Bridget followed closely while I trailed along six or eight blocks behind. The Chevy took James toward town and then headed south on Interstate 5.

A few minutes later Bridget phoned. "It's getting real late here. I wasn't prepared for an overnighter."

"I'll break you loose as soon as I catch up." Driving well over the limit, I caught the trio on the freeway on the long uphill out of Southcenter, signaled to Bridget, and watched her drop away.

I-5 was mostly straight and mostly flat. Beyond Olympia, the state capital, they began to pick up speed, going eighty-five and ninety. If they went much faster, either the little Chevy would blow up or my truck would.

In Longview, Philip sped off at an exit, presumably to refuel. Faced with my first option, I stayed with the Chevy. Twenty-two minutes later the BMW came over the crest of a small hill from behind, doing a hundred, maybe a hundred and ten. I started laughing because I had spotted the first State Trooper of the trip. Just as Philip caught us, the blue bubble-gum rack on the trooper's car shimmered in my rearview mirror as he tagged Philip. He would catch up soon enough.

Knowing Bridget was a night owl and would still be up, I telephoned and asked her to get me the owner of the green Chevrolet. A couple of minutes later she called back and said it was registered to a woman named Millicent Blodgett. Her address was on East Alder Street, the same address where we had been parked all afternoon. She was Jerome Johnson's foster mother. The driver of the Chevy had to be Jerome's foster brother, Billy Blodgett, a.k.a. Billy Battle.

Bridget said, "I was just cooking a TV dinner, watching an old movie, trying to cool off. Tamara was really pissed, I got in so late."

"It's your job. She should understand."

"Well, she doesn't."

10 ON FRIDAY AND SATURDAY NIGHTS EVery roughneck teenager in the county who can get his hands on a hot rod cruises downtown Portland, Oregon, a leftover small-town peccadillo that doesn't always endear the place to business travelers. Fortunately, it was Monday and late enough that the hotrodders were gone.

It was drizzling.

A mist that had started somewhere around Longview had grown more substantial as we crossed the Columbia River. It was almost three in the morning. Philip had caught the Chevy again. I was hanging back.

Oddly, with a three-hour drive under his belt, the Chevy took the Burnside Bridge into the ghostly streets of Portland, cruising up and down the deserted avenues under empty office buildings and sleepy hotels. The car followed First Avenue south as far as Clay Street, crossed west a few blocks and doubled back on Yamhill, where the driver tried to chat up a pair of teenaged girls on the sidewalk who marched away on stiff, coltish legs.

Billy Battle seemed to be performing according to expectations. A drug buy. A hooker. Attempting to pick up girls at three in the morning. If he was on parole, my guess was he was not allowed to leave the state without permission, but he blithely ignored that canon. And there was something else. Although nobody had exactly called Billy Battle a sociopathic killer, one thing most sociopathic killers had in common was that they were scavengers of the urban landscape, driving hundreds and thousands of miles a year.

After a scant twelve minutes in downtown Portland, the Chevy headed west on Burnside and took Lovejoy up into the hills. For the first time that night the man in the Chevy seemed to be hunting a specific address.

When I passed them by accident, the Chevy was parked in the dark driveway of a house. The BMW was half a block farther along, also in a driveway. Both drivers remained in their vehicles. Parking on a gravel strip just beyond the two cars, I could see neither one but was near enough that if either motor started up, I would hear it.

After stretching my legs, I hiked down the road that cut through a wooded hillside. The drizzle was cool and slick on my sleepy face. After five minutes in the dark my hair was soaked.

It was 3:40 A.M.

When a pair of headlights swung up the road from the direction of the BMW, I dove into a laurel hedge and felt a shower of fat droplets on my back. Now I was getting cold. Beyond the laurel hedge I was able to achieve a partial view of the Chevy.

After a few minutes a twig snapped twenty-five meters away. Philip was making his way toward the Chevy from the other direction, creeping under some oak trees and through a cluster of tall rhododendrons, making more noise than a renegade Boy Scout troop looking for a knothole in the girls' shower house.

I could only wonder if he was planning to confront the man in the Chevy. Assault him? Murder him? It would be simpler to shoot myself in the foot right now than to go to court to testify against Kathy's fiancé.

But nobody did any shooting. For five minutes Philip lingered in the brush, then crawled back to his own vehicle to get out of the rain. The man in the Chevy might have noticed us except he had his radio so loud that even with his windows rolled up, you could hear every word of every song. He was smoking crack.

I watched the Chevy for another twenty-five minutes. He smoked his pipe and then turned on the interior light. A brown beer bottle sat on his dashboard. After a while he got out, gazed in my direction—I was a little less than ten meters away—and peed against a large rock. I didn't move. Silhou etted against the dim light from his car interior, all I could see of him was a pair of massive shoulders, a head shaved down to stubble, and the steam coming up off the ground between his legs.

When he climbed back inside the Chevy, I heard the clink of empty bottles on the floor of his car. He pulled out a revolver and inspected the cylinder. I hoped he wasn't going to pop any off into the woods. Wouldn't that be the ticket? If Philip made noise in the shrubbery and I took a bullet in the kisser?

Just after five, a Portland cop stopped in front of my truck, flashed his spotlight up through my windshield, and got out, his right hand on the butt of his holstered pistol. I took out my wallet and put both hands on the top of the steering wheel where he could see them. He was younger than me and right-handed, holding his flashlight in his left hand the way the manuals had taught him. He was alone and it was five in the morning and he was a tad nervous.

"Got a driver's license?" he asked, standing alongside and slightly behind my open window. I kept my hands where he could see them, opened my wallet, and handed him my driver's license and investigator's license, along with a ten-year-old snapshot of me in uniform.

"What department?" he asked.

"Seattle. I'm retired. You get a call on me?"

"Actually, I got a call on a green Chevy playing loud music."

"Just up the road. Also a gentleman in a BMW."

"They with you?"

"I'm with them. But they don't know it."

"From Seattle?"

"All three of us."

"What's going on?"

"I'm following the beamer. He's following the Chevy. I haven't figured it out yet."

"You know I'm going to have to ask you to leave."

"You could do me a favor. Ask the Chevy to leave first. The beamer will follow and I'll go with them. By the way, the young man in the Chevy's been doing drugs and he's got a gun."

The cop looked at me and then at the surrounding properties. "Things happened in this neighborhood. They've always been a little spooked up here."

Two minutes later the Chevy rolled down the hill, followed by Philip's BMW. In the early morning light I caught a glimpse of Philip Bacon, and he didn't look a bit tired. In the mirror my own face looked like a shoe that had gone under a lawn mower.

The man in the Chevrolet found a small market open near the Mark Spencer Hotel and bought a six-pack of beer before heading back toward Seattle. In Castle Rock he stopped for gas. The longer we drove, the more erratic the Chevy became, running two tires on the traffic turtles for miles at a time as he threaded through rush-hour traffic. You could see him in there drinking beer.

Once in Seattle, the Chevy went back to the apartment house where we had started. Philip drove home. Home turned out to be a two-story affair in Magnolia, on the bluff overlooking Puget Sound, a palace that made my own house look like a converted paper shack.

When I pulled into my own driveway, Kathy was locking the door to the basement apartment she rented from me, leaving for work. "Look what the cat dragged in."

I grinned like an imbecile. "How was last night's opera?"

11

"THE OPERA?"

After swigging down a glass of water from the kitchen faucet, I got a box of Cheerios out of the cupboard, then a bowl and a spoon. I had to do everything one step at a time in order not to drop things. The worst part was that I knew the real undertow of exhaustion wouldn't suck at me until that evening, or maybe even tomorrow.

"I thought whatshisname was going to take you to the opera last night."

"I'd almost rather you called Philip the F person than whatshisname."

"How about whatshisletter?" I laughed. "So how was the opera?"

"It was the strangest thing. He never even showed up. I called his house, but all I got was his machine. I hung around until almost nine, then watched some TV. He never called. You think he's all right?"

I poured milk over the bowl of Cheerios, dumped a spoonful of sugar onto it, carried it to the kitchen table, sat and scooped up a mouthful. "I'm sure dreamboat is home sawing the z's right now. If he's not at school teaching."

"No, he's taking the first couple of weeks off. He's got this family problem. Something. I don't know what it is.

And he's never stood me up before. Besides, he's not my dreamboat. You're my dreamboat. *He*'s my fiancé."

"A body would think your dreamboat would be your fiancé."

"Except he didn't ask me."

"That was my mistake."

"I can't believe you're doing this to me."

"I just hope whatshisname's excuse for last night is good."

She mulled it over for a few moments. "By the way, do you by any chance know anything about a bumper sticker somebody pasted onto Philip's BMW last week?"

"Huh?"

"Somebody put a sticker on his rear bumper that said, 'You are driving behind a Road Hog.' " I laughed so abruptly it blew soggy Cheerios onto the tabletop. "Now, Thomas, that's really infantile. I mean, some of this stuff might be funny, but don't you think you're getting infantile?" After about fifteen seconds of me spooning up Cheerios and her giving me dour looks, she smiled and said, "Thomas, Thomas. What am I going to do with you? And where were you all night? You worried me."

"I thought Philip worried you."

"You both did."

"I was out, uh, following a serial killer, actually. Two guys. A serial killer and a peckerhead."

Touching my shoulder from behind, she leaned down and gave me a kiss on the lips just as I took a bite of cereal, strode to the back door and said, "I've been thinking about the old days. We used to set each other up with dates. You and I. Why did we do that?"

"Dates, Sister. Not marriages."

"Yeah, well . . ." She smiled distractedly and left. After she was gone, a starling landed on the kitchen window ledge, stared through the glass, then dropped his opinion of me onto the wooden shelf.

I phoned Bridget, gave her Philip's address, and asked

her to drive over and wait. "I'll call if anything happens," she said. "Just get back?"

"A few minutes ago."

"Then he should be sleeping. He must be beat."

"He looked pretty fresh the last time I saw him."

After a soapy shower I slid between cool sheets, took a deep breath, and was out. Sleep was effortless for the first two hours, until the phone rang. The caller laughed into the mouthpiece. Nothing else. Just laughter. The only person I knew who hated me enough to harass me on the phone was Philip.

After tossing and twisting myself up in the sheets for another twenty minutes, I got up and thumbed listlessly through the previous evening's newspaper. The president was down in the polls. Two motorists had gotten into an altercation at a stop sign. One followed the other to a mini-mart, where a shoving match ensued. Angered, the second man pulled a 9mm semiautomatic out of his car and put three bullets into the back of the other as he ran for cover. Next to that was an article about a five-year-old shooting his three-year-old sister by accident. At ten the phone rang again. "He's on the move," Bridget said. "You're going to love this."

"What?"

"He just bought a gun."

"Philip?"

"I'm pretty sure that's what he did. He went downtown to Warshal's. When he came out, he had a box under his arm and he looked like a kid with a Christmas puppy. Right now we're just getting off I-5, heading into North-gate Mall."

"He getting wise to you?"

"Are you kidding? I could tail him from the backseat of his car and he wouldn't get wise. He's got total tunnel vision."

"Look, Bridget, I'm going down to Warshal's. You can get me on the cellular. And do me a favor? Stay out of his backseat." For some reason Bridget thought that was hilarious. •

I bought gas at the Texaco down the street, filling up the primary tank and both reserve tanks, then took I-5 downtown. The jaunt took less than ten minutes.

Warshal's Sporting Goods was on the corner of First and Madison, not far from our offices. I parked in our lot off Western and hopped a bus the few blocks up First to Madison. It was closing in on noon and the sidewalks were full of people. The sky was blue except for some wispy white clouds on the western skyline over the Olympic Mountains. A crisp breeze blew in from the west over Elliott Bay.

Except for two strapping college women swinging tennis racquets and an elderly man with a hearing aid who was fiddling with a rack of fly rods, the store was curiously empty. I went directly to the gun counter.

"Help you?" He was a thin young man with an intellectual look about him, a hawkish face, and greasy black hair that hung limply across his brow. He wore cords and a turtle-green shirt buttoned to the neck.

I hunched on the counter, holding the side of my head with one hand. "I had a friend come in here and buy a gun this morning."

"A tall guy? Curly hair? Real friendly?"

"Not too tall."

"The trouble is, sir, we're really supposed to keep all sales of handguns confidential, if you know what I mean."

I lowered my voice and salted it with conspiracy. I was tempted to tell him Philip was my brother and that I wanted to buy ammo for his birthday, but this deserved better. "Suppose I tell you that I'm an investigator. Suppose I tell you I've been working for a woman whose husband has threatened to kill her and ship her five kids off to Arabia because she wants to leave him. Suppose I tell you this husband already spent six years in Joliet when he was a kid for murdering his mother. Supposing I tell you his wife thinks he might be trying to buy a gun. That he's told

her in front of witnesses if she packs a suitcase, he'll un-
pack it and put her in it. Remember, this is confidential. In
fact, I'm not even telling you. You didn't even hear it." He
nodded. "Suppose I tell you that you might very well be
saving the lives of a woman and five kids by telling me
whether he bought a gun."

The clerk, whose name tag read MOE, spoke in a sibilant
whisper, "My uncle shot his wife."

"No shit?"

"He thought he killed her, so he sat down in the kitchen
and shot himself in the mouth. After she recovered, she
married a dentist from Walla Walla. I always wondered if
that was Freudian, you know, since her first husband blew
all his teeth across the stove."

"Life is a bitch."

"Yeah. How'd this man kill his mother?"

"You don't want the details. After I heard them, I
couldn't sleep for a month."

"Oh, blessed Lord."

"Yeah."

"I'm a writer, you know. Poetic novels. And then there
was my uncle. The details wouldn't probably bother me."

"Yeah they would."

"Some of my friends think the novel I've just finished
might be good enough for a National Book Award. Listen,
it's autobiographical, about my brother and me. I was
twelve and he was eighteen and he went over to Eastern
Washington visiting some buddies and never came back.
They were drinking beer and potting birds and they lost
track of him. He disappeared from this picnic, and two
days later the police found him in a well. He was a good
swimmer, so we know he must have been down there calling for help for a good long time before he drowned.

"Afterward, my father left us, and my mother would
come home from a date and wake me up and crawl into
my bed and tell me the details. All her sexual wing-dings.
I was only twelve and didn't know how sick it was. She'd
be reeking of alcohol and something else I didn't recog-

nize at the time. It was sex. It really fucked me up. I mean, a thing like that can really—"

"Fuck you up. Sure."

"The book? Each chapter is a four-hundred-line sentence. Twelve chapters. It's called *Weeping Until the Well Is Full.* I'd be glad to let you read it."

"That's very generous."

"My ex-English teacher has it now. But I can get it to you if you give me your address. Only thing is, you'll have to wait until the guy who works in the parking garage up the street gets through with it."

"About this customer who was in here this morning? His name was Bacon, wasn't it?"

Moe thought about it and then thumbed through some cards. "A gun and three boxes of ammunition. Bacon, that was his name. Philip. A little younger than you. Real good-looking."

"Some people might think so."

"I gave him a box of the Magnums and two boxes of plain .44s."

"He bought a .44 Magnum?"

"A Model 29. Dirty Harry's gun. That's what he asked for, and we just happened to have one in stock. It was a beaut. Ever see one up close?"

"There's a week's waiting time, right?"

"The cooling-off period. You wouldn't guess how many sales we lose." Moe grinned and I noticed two upper teeth were askew.

"Did he say anything?"

"Said he was going camping where there were a lot of varmints. You hit a marmot or a rabbit with that sidearm, all you'll get is a little cloud of fur drifting off past the sunset. Say, you wouldn't reconsider telling me how that woman died, would you? You kinda got my curiosity running."

"I didn't even tell you about it. You don't even know me."

12 CLAD IN JEANS, RUNNING SHOES, AND A long-sleeved shirt with a sport coat over it, I walked through the cool downtown canyons, buttoning my coat against the wind. After checking in at the office in the Mutual Life Building, returning a couple of phone calls, and riffling through my mail, I went downstairs to number 84 on Yesler Way, sat at Mitchelli's counter and realized, after I had ordered a Dutch baby with maple syrup, that it was time for lunch, not breakfast.

I was scanning the morning *Post-Intelligencer* and thinking about the bind I had gotten myself into when the cellular phone rang. I hated carrying it around with me.

"This man was with Kathy yesterday, right?" It was Bridget.

"What are you trying to say?"

"He went into Nordstrom's and bought something in the Individualist department. Had it gift-wrapped. Oops. He's headed for the car. Here we go again." The present had to be for Kathy, but to what purpose? When was her birthday? I couldn't remember, but I knew it was sometime in the autumn.

It took almost two hours of dithering to find a present for Kathy, for I wasn't the canniest shopper, but I finally found a knowledgeable young female clerk in a drugstore on Third Avenue to help.

"We're on the run," said Bridget, when I dialed her cellular phone. "On I-90 heading east. He drives like a one-eyed man running from a stick fight. We're past Mercer Island. I keep thinking I'm going to get a ticket keeping up with him. I have no idea where they're headed."

"Who's they?"

"Bacon went back to the apartment on First Hill and picked up some man. They're both in the BMW now."

"Is it the guy from the Chevy last night?"

"No. It's some old fart. I didn't get a good look. He took a small suitcase from his car. Could be they're taking a trip. Or it's drugs. Thomas, you know I don't like drug cases."

"Philip doesn't need drugs. He's doped on himself."

I hopped onto Fourth Avenue South and took the new ramp near the Kingdome to I-90. The primary east-west route traversing Washington State, Interstate 90 was an important roadway because Washington was bisected north to south by the Cascade Mountain range, a bifurcation that affected not only weather and industry, but politics. In the winter, the pass reports became an essential commodity to truckers, skiers, and other travelers.

Step by step, Bridget gave me instructions. I found myself in North Bend, the last small town before heading up over Snoqualmie Pass and into Eastern Washington. Tacking up a Bavarian motif on most of the shop fronts, North Bend had tried its damnedest to be quaint, but only about half the merchants had cooperated.

At the Chevrolet dealer, I turned left and followed a two-lane road through a residential section, farther and farther out into the country, past flat grassy fields with grazing horses.

The road was dominated by a sheer rock mountain face, and I found myself passing a blueberry farm and a pasture with twenty head of Holstein cows grazing, crossing over two small bridges, and then heading up a steep dead end. The sign said the pavement ended in a quarter mile, after which the traveler could expect twenty-four miles of gravel.

It had rained a few days earlier, so the road wasn't dusty. It climbed through a clear cut. The mountains were to my right and very close.

The road was hemmed in by fifteen-year-old Douglas fir trees planted, according to the signs, by the Weyerhauser Company. I pulled on a sloppy hat, sunglasses, and a fake beard just prior to passing the parked BMW, noticing that neither Philip nor his companion bothered to turn around. Both had pistols in their hands. Philip was arranging a large piece of cardboard against a gravel bank.

A quarter mile farther on, Bridget was standing beside her Taurus in front of a gated logging road in a small turnaround used by wayward logging trucks and mushroom hunters.

"God, you scared me," she said, laughing and striding to my window. "That beard makes you look like a cracker."

We walked across the wide road on the damp dirt and loose rock and into a thicket of second-growth Douglas fir. In a small hollow ten or twelve feet from the edge of the woods, we knelt, then lay on our stomachs on a bed of dry pine needles. Below us was the lip of a large open gravel pit, the walls forty and fifty feet higher than the flat base. The pit had not been used commercially for years.

We hid behind a rotting log. Philip had drawn a silhouette on the large piece of cardboard and placed it against the hillside. His back to us, the second man instructed Philip on the use of a handgun. I borrowed Bridget's field glasses and focused.

The second man had silver-heeled boots and a tight way of holding his shoulders, bunched up, as if he were a little boy about to get a spanking. I whispered, "He picked up the other joker at the apartment house?"

"I'm sure he was staking the place out."

It was Snake. He hadn't been able to take Roxanne Lake as a client because he already had a client: Philip Bacon. Approached by Mrs. Lake to rescue Billy Battle from

Philip, Snake had snookered me into taking the job. Had he taken it, he would have been following himself. Snake was a master at working both sides against the middle.

Squatting in various Old West gunfighting positions with his Colt Python, Snake gave Philip fifteen minutes of exposition while Philip listened with rapt politeness. At one point Snake threw himself onto his chest, clicked off three blank shots, rolled onto his back, sent a pretend bullet our way, then got up and ran to a rock fifty yards distant, dodging and zigzagging the whole trip. We heard him say, "Don't be afraid to make a fool of yourself, youngster. I seen two different cops get shot because they were afraid to look silly. You look silly, it's ten seconds. You get shot, it's forever."

When Philip fired his first shot, he used the Magnums instead of the less powerful .44s. We watched as Philip's gun hand went up so high the revolver blade sight struck him in the forehead. He stepped back a pace and transferred the heavy revolver to his other hand. His forehead was bleeding.

Before he was striking the cardboard with any regularity, Philip used up a box of .44s. When he switched back to the Magnums, he had trouble hitting even the cardboard.

He left the revolver loaded when they were finished. I knew it was unwise for a person at that skill level to carry a loaded revolver, but Snake was never going to say that. Snake was a gun lover. He had told me many times that more than one indecisive client had hired him after they saw the butt of a gun in his shoulder holster.

What he wouldn't admit but what we both knew was that carrying a gun was more worthwhile in the misfortune it prevented than in the actual use of the thing. People knew you were carrying a gun, they tended to be a little chary and a lot more civilized.

When they finished, Bridget followed the pair to the highway and back into Seattle, where Philip let Snake out on First Hill outside the apartment house. A little later, on the phone, she told me that Philip went straight home from there.

13 I PARKED IN THE DRIVEWAY BESIDE Kathy's Datsun 280Z, reminding myself to wire up her dangling muffler. The university students I had seen on the streets were walking with that energized stride you saw in the first few weeks of school when everything was possible and anything was probable. If only I could siphon off some of their hope. I went inside, scrubbed my face, then ducked around under the back stairs and knocked on Kathy's door.

She was barefoot, clad in a pair of ratty jeans she wore only around the house. She had on a brilliant violet blouse that enhanced her eyes. "Nice blouse."

"Thank you. Come in, Thomas." I had it in my hands, the package, passed it over formally, then perched on the edge of the couch in the small studio apartment she had rented for the last couple of years. "Another present? This makes two in one day. Three, if you count flowers from Philip."

"I hope he didn't get his shoes wet in the cemetery."

"Very funny." I knew I had done the right thing because she was beaming, had turned the unveiling into a performance, sitting in her rocker, the box in her lap. "Let's see. It's not Christmas. It's not my birthday. It's not ... Oh,

Thomas. You didn't? This isn't that sculpture from Kreskies? I hope you didn't do anything that extravagant. I just love that piece."

I grinned uncomfortably. I was exhausted from ten hours of driving during the past twenty-four hours and from the snowballing premonition that her fiancé might be a danger to her.

Like a striptease artist shucking clothes, Kathy opened the package slowly, folding ribbon and wrappings the way her mother had taught her. She rotated the box slowly. Her smile was beatific. "Whatever it is, it fits into a Mixmaster box."

"Sure does," I said.

It took only moments to get the box open, and although her rally was both swift and inventive, it didn't fool anybody in the room.

"Thank you, Thomas. Thank you so much. Thank you. It's just what I needed. A Mixmaster. It'll fit right here on the counter. Thank you."

Four thank-yous. If there was anything I had learned over the years, it was that the more thank-yous Kathy handed out, the more disenchanted she was with the gift. Three was a catastrophe. At least she had not said *sincerely*. *Sincerely* crept into Kathy's lexicon only when she was already laying plans to exchange a present.

After locating "the perfect spot" for it on her counter, she heeled around and said, "Thank you, Thomas. I really mean it."

Eager to cut my losses, I said, "The blouse does something for your skin color. Brings out your eyes too. Very nice."

"I'm glad you think so." For an instant before she looked away, I thought I saw something in her face.

"Why? Where did you get it?"

"Oh, well, uh, I guess Philip gave it to me."

"You guess he did, huh?"

"A messenger delivered it. Tonight's our six-month anniversary, and he wanted me to wear it."

I had bought her a present commemorating their six-month anniversary! To cap it off, I had given her something you poured food into that needed to be cleaned afterward. Had I turned overnight or was I always a geek? And how on earth did you compete with a smoothie who could pick out a violet blouse that perfectly matched a woman's eyes without even having the woman or his mother there to help?

"There's his car outside right now. Would you be a dear and go yak with Philip until I'm ready?"

Ever hopeful that the two men in her life would become fishing buddies, Kathy stood on tiptoe and gave me a kiss on the cheek. She had some twisted vision that the three of us would share our final years on a sunny porch somewhere, she knitting, Philip and I hunched over a rousing game of checkers, an Irish setter named Brandy at our feet. "Tomorrow night? If you're not working? We'll do something?"

"Yeah."

"And thank you for the present. Sincerely."

A beaten man, I went out and hunkered on the front porch while Philip jockeyed his BMW at the base of our driveway. The drive had a slope to it, and it was upon this gradual slope that Philip was rolling up, then backing out into the street, repositioning his car by a couple of inches each time, edging it to the precise center of the drive, yet in the end blocking the sidewalk so that two university students hiking past were forced to step into the street. If he hadn't spotted me on the porch, he might have jockeyed the BMW all night. Philip had once confessed to lining up the pin-striped shirts in his closet according to width and color of stripe.

He loped up to the porch and extended a hand. I shook reluctantly. "Trying to break in a new clutch?"

"What?"

"Nothing. Kathy said she'd be out in a minute."

"Oh, good. Mind if I sit awhile?" He took a seat on the

steps before I could say no. "Oh, the clutch. Say, I was just trying to get it centered. The car."

"Nice job. Sit anywhere you like. Sure. Right there is fine. Sincerely."

He gave me a funny look. Philip was wearing a tweed sport coat over a gray shirt and gray slacks. His shoes were bright with the original shine. Here was a guy who would wear his feet through the soles and onto the pavement before marring the original polish.

"Beautiful day," he said. "I love September, don't you?"

"Hate it. Bump your head, did you?"

He thought about the question, then touched the Band-Aid on his brow. "Knocked it getting out of the car. Stupid thing to do, really."

"Beulah tells me you were up all night with a neighbor?"

"Hollis Bierney. Had a stroke. His wife, Ethel, really needed somebody to be with her at the hospital." Another lie. Maybe he was addicted to lying.

"You're a fine friend, Philip."

"I try to be."

Up close, you had to admit there was something almost graceful about Philip Bacon, an absentminded imprint of poise and finesse. He was always impeccably groomed, but from the look of his heavy beard growth, he surely was forced to shave twice a day. I made a lot of jokes about him, yet if it hadn't been for my own association with Kathy, I probably would have thought them a reasonable match. There were other times, with his helmet of hair and the length of his arms, that from a distance I thought he looked like a skinned-out baboon.

"The Bierneys, huh? Up in Magnolia? You know, I think my neighbor over here, Horace, I think he knows them. Hollis and Ethel? I wonder if he knows Hollis had a stroke? I better go over and see."

"I don't think it's probably the same people," said Philip, yawning.

"Sure it is. How do you spell Bierney?"

"Wow. I'd have to think about that one."

For a minute we sat, elbows on knees, and watched a boy across the street run a skateboard down the sidewalk, watched him discover a slab of sidewalk that had been pushed up into a ramp by chestnut tree roots. He went back to try it again.

"You ever use a gun, Phil?"

"Huh?" I could see him getting nervous.

Kathy's arrival ransomed him. She had pulled her hair back into a loose ponytail, gathered at the nape of her neck with a large clasp. "My two guys, huh? You're not squabbling?"

We gave her identical blank looks. Philip escorted her to his car and backed it out carefully into the street. When he looked back at me, there was a large knot in his jaw.

I jogged around the house to my truck and followed them—not the smartest move ever. I got to N.E. Fiftieth Street, four lanes of confusion and disgruntled drivers, without spotting the BMW. On a gamble, I headed west toward the freeway several blocks away. I took the freeway south toward downtown. His turn signal caught my attention as he snaked through traffic toward the Roanoke exit. He didn't often use a signal, so I was lucky. After the exit they took Tenth Avenue up the hill, parked and walked to a Thai restaurant called Angel's. I grabbed a burger up the street at Dick's while my truck engine cooled off.

They ate a leisurely dinner, then strolled Broadway and drifted into the new multilevel mall behind the facade of shop fronts. Twenty minutes later they drove to Pine Street and parked, while I found a spot on Pike a block away. The Egyptian was the flagship for the Seattle Film Festival, and I had probably spent more hours in that converted Masonic temple than in any other movie house in my life.

After they had been inside ten minutes, I bought a ticket.

In retrospect, I'm not sure what I was hoping to accomplish. That Philip was a liar was a certainty. That he was working a scam on Kathy and everybody else he knew was a certainty. And now, after trailing him for two days and two nights, I was beginning to believe he and Snake were probably planning something for Billy Battle that they didn't want anybody else on earth to know about. That would account for the lies.

Once inside the Egyptian, you walked around a semicircular hallway to get to the two auditorium entrances, opposites, one east, and one west. I took the east juncture, thinking I would stand well back from the curtained doorway and perhaps spot them.

I was near a French poster for *East of Eden* when a familiar voice came from behind. "Are we lost?"

Blood pulsing in my face, I turned and said, "Funny seeing you here."

"I just had this feeling, Thomas. So I go to the ladies' room, and when I come out, voilà."

"Imagine that. Kathy's ESP kicks in, and here I are."

"With egg on your face."

"Voilà."

"Thomas, I can't even believe you did this. What makes you think it's okay to follow me?"

I waited until a pair of short-haired women in army jackets and boots stumbled past, wishing I had had more than two hours sleep and knowing if I tried to grin my way out of this I would look like a week-old corpse. Philip didn't seem affected at all by our jaunts across the countryside, but they had derailed me. I was making one wrong move after another. I took a deep breath.

"Kathy, I'm not following you."

"Of course you're not. You're following me and Philip. I don't think I've ever been this angry with you. Ooooooh! This is just ... so asinine."

"Listen. The truth now. I'm following Philip for a case. He's been lying to you."

Kathy's smile was smug but still irritatingly beautiful. "Lying? Yes, I know. He's not six feet tall. I asked him and he admitted he was *almost* six feet. Satisfied?"

"This isn't personal. The client who came in the other

day? The one you said looked like Lady Godiva in clothes?"

"Does she appreciate juvenile antics?"

"Kathy, this is business. I swear it is. Wait and talk to me about this before you say anything to him. Will you?"

"I'll think about it."

Walking stiffly, she went around the circular wall into the darkened auditorium where the trailers were already running. Without even pretending to be interested in anything other than my imbroglio, two young women stood next to a *Spartacus* poster written in Italian. College students maybe, in jeans and T-shirts with unbuttoned shirts over to keep warm. When I made a face at them, they giggled, turned, and walked into the auditorium, the cute one with the pixie haircut turning around twice to watch me. Their shoulders bobbed with their giggling.

THE BMW ROLLING BACK AND FORTH IN the driveway was what woke me. Up and down. Up and down.

Just before he drove off, Kathy used her key on my front door. It had to be a strange feeling to drop your woman off and watch her put a key into another man's door.

In the darkness, she slipped into the living room and sat

on a straight-backed wooden chair against the wall at the far end of the room, next to the cold fireplace.

"So?" she said.

Pulling myself into a sitting position, I closed my robe and knuckled sleep out of my eyes, switched on a lamp at the end of the couch and watched the lamplight glitter off her violet eyes and blouse. She was angrier than she had been at the Egyptian, probably because she had had time to think about it.

"It's not what you might think."

"Good, because I *think* you're deranged. I *think* you should get fitted for a sweater with no armholes. Maybe get a ride in the little rubber truck you're always talking about so they can put you in the little rubber room you're always talking about. Where were you last night?"

I had to think before answering. She had just spent five hours with the biggest liar in the state, and here she was challenging everything *I* said.

"A woman came into the office the other day. I guess it was yesterday. She told me she thought Philip was following someone of her acquaintance. He was. I followed the two of them to Portland last night. He was there all night. So was I."

"You expect me to believe this?"

"The man Philip is following is not exactly an altar boy, and my client thinks there's going to be trouble. One way or another."

"So you're not following someone? Philip is actually the one who is following someone?"

"He's following this guy. I'm following him."

"Everything you're doing, Philip is doing too. Right?"

"More or less."

"Do you realize what you looked like creeping around the lobby of the Egyptian?"

"A drunken pickpocket working the Republican convention?"

She got up and edged toward the front door. She was angry enough that bullets would have bounced off her.

"Sit down, Kathy."

"How many weeks have you been following us? Just since our engagement? Or before?"

"This has nothing to do with your engagement. My client thinks—"

"Are you sleeping with her? Your client? Is that it? And you don't want me to know? Guys tend to get jealous when they're feeling guilty."

"Feeling guilty? I'm not the one with two guys on the string."

She was silent for a good minute. I was glad to have aroused some jealousy finally, though I didn't necessarily want her to know that. "Okay. I'm sorry I'm taking so long. If I wasn't a woman, I could have given you an answer the night you asked me, but I am and I couldn't and I didn't."

"I think he just drove by again. Check out the window. Was that him?"

She let the comment simmer, but I could see her trying to suppress a smile. "I trusted you."

"Would you let me finish, for Chrissake?"

Kathy sat back down, pulled her knees together and pushed out her lower lip. Her voice was so soft I could hardly hear it. "Go ahead."

"It's real easy to be a bumblebee on a billboard. Let me pull you back and give you a little perspective. My client feels Philip might want to hurt a young man named Billy Battle. Or vice versa. I followed him Monday night. Just to see what it was about. He tailed somebody who was probably Battle. To Portland."

"You had no right to take on a case that had you tailing Philip."

"Maybe not, but he's been telling everybody he spent Monday night with a sick neighbor."

"Philip told me he was at the hospital."

"I know he did. He's lying. You don't seem concerned about it."

"Can I call this client and verify all this?"

"No, you cannot."

She thought about that for fifteen seconds. "Don't you think it was terribly convenient that some woman you've never met waltzes into your office and asks you to follow a man you've been mocking for six months?"

"It was a bit convenient. But then again, maybe I hallucinated the whole thing so I'd have an excuse to snoop on you and that cross-eyed baboon."

"I don't even believe you said that. You would do anything to make him look bad. Admit it. You lied to me just tonight. At the Egyptian. You said you weren't following us."

I lay down on the davenport, reaching above my head to switch off the lamp. "Well, I obviously was, wasn't I?"

"Is Snake involved in this?"

"What makes you ask that?"

"He is, isn't he?" Kathy pushed across the dark room and stood over me, fists on her hips, smelling strongly of perfume and vaguely of garlic chicken and buttered popcorn. "Tell me what Snake has to do with this."

"And why, pray, is old Elmer so important to you all of a sudden?"

"It's just . . ." She stood in the dark breathing heavily. "It just happens that Philip mentioned him this evening."

"Did he now? That's a little curious, wouldn't you agree?"

"He wanted to know if I would trust Snake with my life."

"What was your answer?"

"With my life, sure. With my purse or my extra bus tickets, no. Tell me what Snake has to do with this."

"I'll know in a day or two. But I thought you hated liars."

"Maybe Philip lied to me, but you did too."

I smiled in the dark. "Just a little."

"One of you has trouble being even in the same room with the other. One of you makes sick jokes at the other's expense."

"One of *us* laughs at those jokes."

She gave me a look. "Do you know Philip has never said a negative word about you?"

"Never even acknowledged my existence, has he?" She was silent. "Indifference is its own form of arrogance."

After a long silence Kathy said, "I don't *always* laugh. Sometimes I laugh. Thomas, you say you love me, but I don't know what to think. I really don't. You're the third man in a rubber raft, and you're wearing hobnailed boots."

"Two choices," I said. "You could hug me or you could throw me overboard."

Kathy walked slowly to the front door and cracked it open. The nighttime breeze carried an early autumn chill to it. We hadn't had our first frost yet, but it couldn't be far off. I watched a gust ruffle her blouse. I watched her eyes glimmer with a slice of light captured from the street lamp.

"I thought if I followed you guys tonight, he might do something to help me understand this case. I just thought—"

She laughed so hard I couldn't finish. Throughout our friendship Kathy had never laughed at me—with me, but never *at* me. What made it particularly unbearable was that I could see hairline fractures throughout our history now, fractures in the relationship that I had widened with lies and deceit this very night. What I had done in the past two days had damaged not only our future, but the essential foundation of our liaison. I had broken a trust, had jack-hammered fissures into the only friendship I had ever really cared about.

"Kathy?"

Leaving the door ajar half an inch, she pressed her body and face up against the chink and spoke through the small opening, her voice corrupted from the mean-spirited laughter. "What is it, big guy?"

"At least let me know if you're going to tell him. I owe that to my client."

"Maybe you do, but *I* don't owe your client a thing."

After the door closed, I could hear the laughing as she walked down the front steps and around the side of the house. I could hear it reverberating between my house and Horace's. At least, I could hear it in my head. It was so loud in my head I couldn't tell when it had actually stopped outside. Moments later I could hear it coming up through the heat registers. Or I thought I could. It was with a small pang of guilt that I realized there was nothing quite like being mocked. I, who had been mocking Philip for months, was now on the receiving end. I knew he would never forgive me, and I began to wonder if I was going to be able to forgive her.

When the phone rang, it seemed as if only a minute or two had elapsed. I groped for the receiver, squinting through the darkness at the clock radio. I had been asleep three hours.

It took me a moment to get my bearings. It was the man who had been calling since Monday. The same berserk cackling. First this clown, then Kathy, and now this clown. I told him what I thought of his mother and then I racked the phone. I was dreaming that I was back in school when it rang again. It was a quarter to four. A throaty woman's voice said, "How ever is the world treating you?"

"Hello?"

"Don't you know who I am?"

"Ummm, not really. I guess not."

"If you can't guess who this is, maybe I shouldn't tell you." I began running through a catalogue of women: old girlfriends, relatives, screwballs, former clients, relatives of former clients.

"I'm sorry. I'm drawing a blank."

"Our little investigation. How is it going?"

"Mrs. Lake?" If not completely stinko, she had been drinking enough to take the edge off her reason. "This is awfully late."

"Just got in, darling. I crawled into my big empty bed and was lying here feeling warm all over and a little cuddly, and suddenly I found myself thinking about my detective. How is our investigation going?"

"You were right. Bacon is following Billy Battle. I'm going to look into it further tomorrow."

"You're not married, are you? Because I take a very sophisticated attitude toward things like that."

"Pardon me?"

"I think most people are so constipated, morally, don't you? That's what my first husband used to call it. Moral constipation. I want you to know that anything is cool with me."

"Tell you what, Roxanne."

"Yes."

"When I learn more, I'll give you a report." I hung up knowing this was a call neither one of us would ever acknowledge in the light of day.

15 BACON LIVED ACROSS THE ROAD FROM A string of windswept madronas on a narrow strip of land at the top of the bluff on Magnolia Boulevard West. Across the road were parking stalls for dog walkers, camera hobbyists, and backseat lovers.

Looking almost as if you could walk across the tops of them, maples and other deciduous trees and shrubs from the green belt below the bluff were hacked off each year by the city to keep the wealthy from being defrauded of their view.

The neighborhood resembled San Diego more than Seattle. From any of the houses on Magnolia Boulevard West, you could see the Sound, West Seattle to the south. Sailboats and shipping lanes. Across the water the low lump of green that was Bainbridge Island. Above Bainbridge, the snowy Olympics fairly steamed in the morning sunshine.

It was seven-fifteen in the morning, but you couldn't take chances with a man who functioned without sleep. I had placed Kathy in a bad position, had given her the choice of betraying her fiancé or her best friend. The only way I could think of to extricate her was to spill my guts to Philip, which made me feel a little like the kid who had broken out all the school windows and then immediately turned himself in.

When he answered the back door, he wore only black socks and a pair of boxer undershorts. One of his socks was inside out and not quite all the way on his foot, the toe flopping like the end of a loose condom. Philip gave me a look of bewilderment mixed with extreme pique. "Kathy didn't come?" he asked.

"Phil, baby."

His face was devoid of expression. "So. What? What do you want, Tommy?"

"Listen, pinhead. Don't call me Tommy."

"What do you want?"

"Ten minutes." My intent was to act like a cranky father demanding the return of his daughter's brassiere, but it was a difficult mood to nail down.

"You going to hit me?"

"No, I'm not going to hit you."

"It was just . . . you look angry. I guess . . . Come in."

I had been pumping his doorbell for most of ten minutes, had roused him from a dead sleep, as evidenced by his puffy face, ragged growth of beard, and hair flattened on one side. I had been awake since six, had driven over without breakfast, combing my hair with my fingers, shaving in a rush. I wore a tie and a jacket, pressed jeans, and suede bucks. It was the first time I could remember being dressed better than Philip. In fact, it was the first time I could recall having more clothes on than Philip.

When he left me in the vestibule to walk through the kitchen and up a staircase, I could see that he was built like a marathon runner, no fat and very little lean.

Alone for a minute, I scanned the immaculate kitchen and walked into the foyer near the front door, an area that contained a statue and a couple of prints on the walls. In the next room stood a cabinet filled with cut crystal. Good grief, a single guy who already had his crystal. No wonder Kathy said yes.

The dining room table was littered with newspaper clippings, file folders, and a berry-colored cardboard box labeled BLODGETT—TRANSCRIPT OF PROCEEDINGS. The cover was off the box, and it was filled with hanging file folders, each section labeled and dated. The dates began five years earlier and spanned a period of two and a half months. The heading on the first page read: IN THE SUPERIOR COURT OF THE STATE OF WASHINGTON IN AND FOR THE COUNTY OF KING. STATE OF WASHINGTON, PLAINTIFF, VS WILLIAM DEAN BLODGETT, DEFENDANT.

A newspaper clipping on the table read: OMINOUS CLUES IN MADRONA GIRL'S DISAPPEARANCE. In the bookcase I noted the most recent *Shooter's Bible*. This teacher was doing his homework.

When I heard a noise on the stairs, I hurried into the living room and pretended to inspect family photos lined up on a hutch.

Philip wore jeans now, but still no shirt. "If you want, I can give you a tour," he said.

"You're getting a little sarcastic in your old age."

"At seven in the morning, somebody calls me a pinhead, I tend to get a little sarcastic."

"When we met, I told you not to call me Tommy. Twice. And I know Kathy must have warned you."

"Kathy *might* have warned me. I don't remember *you* saying anything." Philip had a habit of forgetting things I had said or done, of forgetting I had been in the room during a conversation, of forgetting I was on the planet. "This is about Kathy, isn't it? I've had this sensibility the last few days there was something going on between you and Kathy. You realize I've asked her to marry me? I hope you realize that. If you don't know, you should probably be apprised of that fact."

"It's not about Kathy."

"No?"

"Can we sit down?"

He gave me a noncommittal look as he gestured toward a living room teeming with white furniture that appeared never to have been used. I sat in one of two overstuffed white leather chairs opposite a matching sofa and crossed my ankle over my knee.

Bacon sank into the center of the leather couch, then stood abruptly, joints popping. "Get you something? Tea, perhaps. I have coffee if you prefer. Fresh ground? Decaf? A latte? Juice? I can squeeze some oranges. Just take a minute."

"Sit down and tell me why you were following Billy Battle."

Philip sat heavily. "Don't believe I know the man."

"Drives a green Chevy."

"Have you had someone tailing me?"

"You want to explain, or do you want me to tell Kathy you lied to her about Monday night?" I had already told her, but he didn't know that.

Philip mulled over the proposition. "Stoop to anything, wouldn't you?"

"Anything but lying to my friends. I try not to lie to my friends."

Bacon grew silent. Crossing his legs and wriggling his toes when they came into his view, he folded his arms across his hairy chest and breathed heavily for a few moments. I noticed he had changed into a clean pair of black socks. He might have been getting ready to launch himself at me, but that wouldn't be his style. If Philip thought he needed to fight, there would be invitations to a gym to lace up the gloves. There would be rules, plenty of rules along with a referee, and afterward both parties would shake bruised paws and repair to the club to buy each other drinks and to toast sportsmanship.

He said, "You ever meet a teenager who gave you a look that made you want to punch him in the face? Just one look, as if he knew some dirty secret about you, except he didn't know a darn thing? A look of contempt that you thought about all the rest of that day and into the night?"

"Teenagers seem to be pretty good at that sort of thing."

"Not the kind of look I'm talking about. You only get this look from little perverts."

"Let's hear the rest."

"I don't want Kathy to know any of this."

"She's a criminal defense attorney, for God's sake. She's heard her share."

"I don't mind telling *you*," Philip said, running a palm across his sleep-ruffled hair. "But not her. Once you hear the details, you'll be behind me one hundred percent. Deal?"

"I'll think about it."

"It started in Madrona. My folks moved there just before I began at the U. Living with them was cheaper, and that was before my grandfather passed away and left me the money.

"I had been living at home maybe three weeks when one of the neighbors came over with a sack and asked us if we knew where our cat, Calico, was. Somebody had killed him and stuffed him in our neighbor's mailbox. Mom had gotten Calico just after I was born and he was like part of the family. We buried him in the backyard, reported it to the police, and sat around talking about it the rest of the evening, the way anybody would. When we got our mail later that night, Jim's cat was in *our* mailbox."

"Let's cut to the chase."

"This is the chase. It started with pets, then the second summer I was there, we had a fire burned down a house and the family inside. There had been little fires around the neighborhood. Then this house. Except for a ten-year-old boy who barely escaped, the whole family died. It was pretty awful.

"They say it was a misplaced bag of fireplace ashes, but who knows. Then that same summer, a little boy drowned in a wading pool in his backyard. His babysitter could hear him playing out there through the back door, kept checking on him every few minutes. At one point the babysitter heard voices, two children, an older child and the little one, and then the phone rang and the babysitter didn't check on him for a while. Seven or eight minutes later, the little boy was facedown in the water. The medics tried to revive him.

"It wasn't until years later the babysitter was able to admit that the other voice in the backyard that day belonged to a boy who lived a couple of houses over."

"Let me guess. Billy Battle."

"That's what he calls himself these days. It's been Billy Blue. Billy Lime. Billy Blood. Billy Silverheels. He was ten years old, almost eleven, and he had been known to spend a lot of time with the smaller children on the block the way some kids do who have trouble getting along with their peer group. It wasn't until years later people began to suspect. You see, that was back in the days when it was inconceivable for a boy of that age to be capable of murder. Billy's brother died in a wading pool accident himself, when Billy was three."

"I heard Billy had a foster brother."

"You know about this?"

"Not much."

"The Johnson kid. He was nice enough. Not like Billy at all. It was his house that burned down. Afterward, Billy's mother took him in. But don't you get it? Billy had a fascination with drowning. So did his mother. For years

and years her dead child was all you would hear from her.
It must have been drummed into Billy. Pitiful as it sounds,
it got her shunned by most of the neighbors. Most people
could only take so much."

"I thought we were going to cut to the chase."

"I'd say the kicker was the missing girl and the finger
they found."

16

"YOU WOULDN'T BELIEVE THE THINGS
that happened. Somebody used to prop
sixteen-penny nails under your car tire so when you started
off, the nail was driven into your tire. There would be pe-
riodic vandalism with spray paint. Profanity would be
written in animal blood on the sidewalk. A couple of
young women in the area received so many obscene phone
calls their families moved away."

"You're tracing this handcrafted reign of terror to
Billy?"

"Who else?"

"What's your evidence?"

"Oh, you couldn't prove anything. When you asked
Billy a question, he said, 'Huh?' or told you some whop-
per about some other kid. With Billy, it was always some
other kid. And when he did lie, he was very convincing, as
sociopaths often are. The day we lost our cat, one of the
other children saw Billy playing with him. My father went

over and got into a shouting match with his mother, but you couldn't talk to her. When we confronted Billy he said he thought some gang members killed the cat as a part of an initiation. We didn't have any gangs down there."

"Tell me about the missing girl."

"One Friday night she left home to buy some pretzels and a pair of stockings, and she simply never returned. She was fifteen. At first, the police didn't take it seriously because she had run away previously.

"Two days into this, after the neighbors got together and organized a search, they found some things in a vacant house maybe three blocks away. One item they found was a strange pattern of nails pounded into the hardwood floor. If you looked, you could see it was in the configuration of a body with the arms out to the sides. There was cloth on a couple of the nail heads. As if somebody had been nailed to the floor by their clothing. The police came in and looked the place over, but they never reached any conclusions. This kid is a monster, Black."

"What makes you think Billy had anything to do with her?"

"She broke up with Billy just a week or two before it happened. Think about it. Then he helped with the search. He was the one who discovered the vacant house had been broken into. Listen, a police dog found a finger in the overgrown lawn outside the house. They still weren't willing to admit Susie had been killed. They didn't know the girl's blood type, but about six months later the FBI lab got some results of an analysis on the fingernail paint, and it matched a bottle she had in her bedroom. Blodgett was always the prime suspect." Bacon spoke with a triumphant, though plainly profitless satisfaction. "The *only* suspect."

"Blodgett?"

"Blodgett. Battle. Same difference. Billy calls himself Battle these days."

"So let's come clean on why you're following him now."

"When Billy was fifteen or sixteen, he attacked his foster brother with a knife. Real bad. Me and an older gentleman named Walter Clark went to court and testified against him. Billy got out two weeks ago and he's been by Walter's house twice that I know of. He calls Walter and laughs. He never says anything, just laughs."

"He calls your friend Walter on the phone and laughs?"

"He's a creep. This boy has killed and he's gotten away with it. He'll do it again too. Unless somebody takes it upon themselves to stop him."

I lowered my voice until I sounded droll enough that he knew I had run out of patience. "Have you talked to any of these people? The babysitter who claims she heard Billy's voice outside when the child drowned? The father of the missing girl? Eyewitnesses come up with some screwy ideas, especially if there's someone convenient to take the blame."

"Black, the missing girl was his girlfriend and had been trying to break up with him." Philip trained his mismatched eyes on me. "So we're talking two known deaths here. The little boy he drowned and the girlfriend. He killed our cat and who knows how many other neighborhood pets. We caught him assaulting the Johnson boy. We caught him doing that. He was trying to pull the boy's pants off so he could emasculate him, darn it."

I had to wonder why Lake and Johnson had neglected to tell me about this. "What does Billy say?"

"I haven't spoken to him. Why should I? It would have been three dead if we hadn't caught Billy the night he went after the Johnson boy. There must be plenty of other atrocities we don't know about. It took me a long time to figure out why Billy kills, but I can see now. He is an impotent little mouse, with absolutely no juice whatsoever in the real world. No money. No job. No friends. No prospects. And he knows it. When something goes sour in his life, he wants to feel dominant somehow, somewhere—anywhere. So he starts killing pets. Pets don't mean diddly to him, and it makes him feel better; shows him how important he is; how much he can affect somebody's life. After a while, killing pets isn't a strong enough painkiller. I've researched this. Believe me."

If the Johnson kid had been attacked so brutally, it seemed odd that he cared enough to come with Roxanne Lake when she hired me to protect Billy. But then, I hadn't trusted the motivations of either of them. "You're planning to hurt Battle, aren't you?"

"That would be illegal. But I think if I follow him, I might catch him doing something criminal. I saw him trying to pick up some teenaged girls."

"A major felony."

"Get as sarcastic as you like. Maybe you've already discovered. Sarcasm doesn't bother me."

I got up and walked to the living room window. He was right. I shouldn't have cracked wise. Walter Clark was receiving phone calls that sounded identical to the ones I had been getting. On the other hand, Philip claimed he wasn't out to hurt Billy, yet he'd bought a gun and he had lied about it. He had lied to Kathy and the whole office about where he was Monday. What else was he lying about?

A man across the street in a windbreaker walked two well-mannered dogs on leashes while he spoke on a cellular phone. When he passed the scenic view across the street on the bluff, seven smartly dressed Japanese tourists in a rented Toyota stopped him and asked him if he would snap their picture in front of the Sound and the Olympics. He made signs that the phone call was too important to interrupt.

"If he doesn't do anything but laugh, how do you know these phone calls are from Billy?"

"I was there when Walter got one of them. I'm sure I recognized the voice."

"When did you hook up with Snake?"

The question flummoxed him as badly as a dog trying to catch two balls at once. He grew very still on the sofa, stopped breathing and stared at me, mouth agape. "I don't recall anybody named Snake."

"You tell one lie, how do I know you're not lying about all of it?"

"Listen, I didn't have to let you in here. I'm telling you things because I care for Kathy."

"Where were you Monday night?"

Philip Bacon scratched his chin, then fussed with his pant leg while I came back from the window and sat down across from him. "Monday?"

"Yeah, you know. After Sunday. Just before Tuesday. Every seven days or so, if we're lucky, we have another one."

Philip stared at the red Oriental rug between us as if I had not spoken. "You're right. I followed Billy to Portland. Slezak was in your office one day. He gave me his card, and when this came up, I phoned him. He's an intelligent man, although he doesn't want people to know it. Did you realize he once placed second in the world championships at bull riding?"

"So you two are going to grab Billy, put some sixteen-penny nails through his trouser cuffs and ask questions?"

"I have a list of questions." Philip got up and walked to the dining room table, riffled through his papers and came back with a sheet torn from a steno pad. For the first time that morning, though not for the first time since I had known him, he sounded like a teacher lecturing a class. "Who drowned the Torgesen boy? Who killed our cat? What happened to Susie Alberg? Who makes the laughing phone calls? Who stole Mrs. Pitney's private letters?"

"Mrs. Pitney?"

"She lived across the alley from Walter. Jon, her husband, helped save the Johnson boy. But then he wouldn't testify at the trial."

"So you know what happens now, don't you?"

Bacon looked puzzled. "Not exactly."

"Battle turns up missing, and I tell the cops what you just told me. They build a case on you and you spend a good long time in the company of concrete walls and tattooed men."

"I thought this was in confidence. What I told you."

"Confidence and conspiracy are two different animals."

"What if I don't do anything and my friend Walter Clark is injured?"

"Let's work a deal. You promise to lay off Battle for a few days while I look into this. We'll come back and talk more when I have some information."

Bacon stared at his black socks and shook his head. "You don't get it. No matter what happens, Billy Battle or William Blodgett or whatever he is calling himself these days is going to kill again. It might be me. It might be my friend Walter. Some stranger. He's going to kill, I'm telling you. Somebody has to do something about it."

"Have you spoken to the authorities?"

"I called his parole officer yesterday. She didn't believe me when I told her he'd gone to Oregon yesterday. And even if she had believed me, she was going to slap his wrist and tell him not to do it again. The cops brush me off. They need a crime, they say."

"Delay things for a week. Just a week." As I leaned back in the plush chair and studied the house, I couldn't help remembering that Kathy had said everything was paid for. I wondered if it really was. "Let me do some poking around."

"You won't tell Kathy about this?"

"If you stay away from Battle, I'll keep it between us."

"Deal."

"Before I go, do you have anything that might help me get a handle on the scenario, besides anecdotal evidence? Newspaper clippings? Names? Phone numbers? Anything like that?"

The color began rising in his neck. Philip shrugged and said, "Not really," then glanced beyond me to the dining room table littered with materials that he didn't know I had seen, including a transcript of one of William Blodgett's trials.

I thought about calling him a liar again, but what was the object? From his point of view, he had paid for the transcript and probably knew, or suspected, that I had a client, though he couldn't know who the client was. Why give all his hard-won materials away for nothing? In addition, Philip was fond of pretending I did not exist. What better method of establishing my insignificance than to repeatedly lie to my face?

"Just tell me one thing," he said as he escorted me to the back door.

"What's that?"

"You two were lovers, weren't you? You and Kathy. I mean, the way she dotes on you."

I looked at him, walked through the backyard to my truck and got in. He was still standing in the doorway when I backed out into the alley.

17

AFTER PARKING UNDER A WINDSWEPT MAdrona down the hill and out of sight of Philip's house, I picked up the cellular phone and tried to reach Snake. Nobody answered at the first three numbers, so I called one of his ex-girlfriends, a large-boned electrician Snake sojourned with from time to time. A gruff man who definitely was not Snake picked up her phone. I asked him if he wanted to buy some aluminum siding and he told me to get lost.

Eventually I broke down and left a message on the tape machine in his Tacoma office.

The trial transcript on Bacon's dining room table had been provided by the court reporter who had sat on the case. His name and number had been across the bottom of each page. When I dialed the number and asked for Mervin M. Yates, a chirpy-sounding woman said, "In what connection?"

"He was the reporter in a trial I'm interested in. I need a transcript." She asked for the name, then told me to wait while she fired up their computer. Children young enough to duck school on a weekday squealed in the background.

"William Dean Blodgett," she declared happily. "August twenty-first, five years ago. It runs a hundred and seventy-three pages." She gave me a quote per page that was steep enough that I did the math before going any further.

Mervin Yates and his wife Trudy lived about five miles away in Ballard, on a street named Greenbrier near Carkeek Park.

Trudy Yates was a plump, pleasant-faced woman in her late twenties who met me at the front door of a small house on a street lined with small houses. As were all the yards in the neighborhood, their grass was California-brown from the summer's water shortage. She wore a tightly belted bathrobe, battered leather moccasins, and a smile that had a shine to it.

She sat me on a sofa that had a stack of freshly laundered baby diapers balanced on the other end, then bustled from the room, calling over her shoulder. "Almost finished. I had a couple of calls, so I didn't get going right away."

The carpeted floor shuddered under her heel-heavy footfalls. The tea table in front of me was littered with colorful plastic toys and safety pins with Disney characters etched into the yellow plastic heads.

A bloodcurdling scream pierced the quiet morning. When I leaned forward the sofa sagged. In the next room three moon-eyed tykes were welded to a TV.

Trudy Yates thumped into the room carrying a transcript. More yowling from the TV in the other room as the scene dragged on. Yates sighed and said, "What can you do? At least they're watching it where they can come to me if something's bothering them. Otherwise they end up seeing it over at the neighbors. You know?"

I shrugged. Sometimes I thought we were participating in something much like the fall of the Roman Empire.

I took the Aurora Bridge, where everybody seemed to be going twenty over the limit, back toward town, parked on Western behind our building and went into Mitchelli's, sat at a table next to the window under a wall full of playbills and ordered a blueberry Dutch baby. The trial transcript was from the Superior Court in King County in which William Blodgett had been tried as an adult, even though he had not turned twenty-one. It was for crimes committed while he was incarcerated at Echo Glen. It was his second trial in two years.

Blodgett had been arraigned on three counts of assault and one of attempted rape. The proceedings had been complicated by the fact that Blodgett had several times confessed to the assaults in the presence of police officers and social workers from Echo Glen, yet each of the confessions differed in significant aspects. This was typical, I knew, of the small-time criminal mind. A different story for each interviewer.

A woman social worker at Echo Glen had been assaulted. "I saw him coming at me and he had a funny look in his eyes. Just as I realized he wasn't going to stop, I saw stars." She explained that she woke up some minutes later gagged and tied to a chair with her own nylons. Billy's plan, she had assured the court, was to sexually assault her with the help of his friends.

A fight broke out among the youths before any assault could take place. The clash attracted the attention of other personnel at Echo Glen.

If Billy's ship was leaky, he scuttled it when he got on the stand and said, "She deserved what she got. She's been teasing me for a year. I lost control and bopped her and then I went to turn myself in, but after I left the cottage I saw them sneaking in. I went back. It ain't fair. I was defending her. I smacked her but then I protected her. If the law ain't fair, how do you expect any of us to take it serious?" This too was typical of the small-time criminal mind, blaming the crime on the victim and then blaming the system for not understanding.

When asked why, if he were going to turn himself in, Billy had tied her to the chair, he claimed the others had done that. Nobody involved believed him at the time and I didn't believe him, reading about it now.

During the sentencing phase of the trial the word *incorrigible* was bandied about. Because of the nature of his crime, it was recommended that Billy be sent to the Special Offenders Center at Monroe Penitentiary, a unit specializing in the housing and treatment of sex offenders. Even before the assault, the staff at Echo Glen had diagnosed Billy as a sexual deviant.

What worried me was the brief psychological profile that was read into the record before sentencing: "Although this subject has not been institutionalized for any great length of time, he seems to have formed a criminal personality of the type seen primarily in long-term inmates of adult correctional facilities. Despite his youth, this subject is not likely to reform. Billy not only fails to admit his crimes, but refuses whatsoever to show any remorse or concern for his victims."

He was sentenced to seven years and sent to Monroe. By my accounting, he had been twenty-two when released two weeks ago.

I spent half an hour upstairs in the office slitting open envelopes from yesterday's mail, typing a brief report into the computer, and returning phone calls.

When I phoned Mrs. Lake, she said, "Thomas," with mock gaiety, as if we had been the best of friends and hadn't seen each other in months. "We were just thinking about you. What have you learned?"

"Two developments, Roxanne. First: Yeah, Bacon was following our boy. Second: I've had a chat with Philip and

I believe I've convinced him to let me do a little digging into this before he does anything else. Don't worry. He has no idea who hired me. In fact, I think he thinks I'm doing this on my own, out of spite."

"What are you going to do?"

"Find out what Battle's up to, same as Philip was doing. Maybe I can stop it that way."

"That sounds like a sensible plan. How is Phil these days? Does he, uh, still have those dreamy eyes?"

"Maybe they were dreamy. They're a little shifty now."

"Does he have someone he's seeing?"

"Yeah, but it won't last much longer. There's something I've been meaning to ask you, Roxanne. Were you there the night Billy attacked Jerome?"

"Why, yes I was." It had been a stab in the dark, but she was one surprise after another.

"Can you tell me what happened?"

"They got into some sort of dispute and Billy knocked Jerome down. Billy was always very physical. Then he got a butcher knife and backed Jerome up against a fence in the alley. It was a very nasty business. I saw Jerome when the medics were working on him. I didn't know you could lose that much blood and survive."

"I had heard something about emasculation."

"Apparently when they found them he had been about to do something real bad with the knife. It would have fit if you'd known Billy."

Half an hour later I phoned Snake in his office in Tacoma. "Ya'allo," Snake said.

"Wake you up, old boy?"

"Thomas. Sonofabitch. In fact you did. I was out all night chasing fan dancers."

"There are no more fan dancers."

"I must have been imagining it then. What can I do you out of?"

"Not Mrs. Lake's retainer, that's for sure."

"You sound a little pissed, Thomas."

"Wake up and listen to the birdies, Snake. I thought you had a code. Ethicals and all."

"Thomas, I been laid up for two days with hemorrhoids, so go easy on me."

"I saw you up in the hills Tuesday."

"You would have had to be awful good to spot me."

"Actually, a retired nun who works for me spotted you."

"Listen, I got a luncheon date with a three-hundred-pound lady comic who wants me to check out a beautician she thinks she's in love with. Portfolio. Diseases. All that. 'Bout every three months I check out another dame for her and they turn out to be bogus."

"I've spoken to Philip. What are you two up to?"

"Thomas, if you just play this whole thing real soft and easy and don't get too eager to booger things up, it will work out."

"Why the artillery?"

"Guns are my hobby. You know that."

"Yeah, well, up until a few days ago Phil's hobby was feeding peanut butter to dogs. Now I think he's going to kill somebody."

"That may be in the realm of possibility."

"I thought it was."

ON THE SIDEWALK IN FRONT OF THE apartment house on Alder, I passed a pair of young women cloaked in scarves and surgeons' masks. The front door of the apartment house was locked. I buzzed 104, got no reply, then thumbed six buzzers in the top row. When people started answering, I said, "I'm here." Two of them buzzed me in. It was just after eleven.

The second floor was at street level, so she was one floor down. I took the stairs, which smelled strongly of urine and burnt food and curiously of a rain-soaked street in the spring.

After I knocked on the door, I heard banging inside. At the end of the dark corridor a tiny boy rode a tricycle around in circles. I winked. He was still experimenting with a wink himself when the door to 104 opened very slowly.

She was a spindly woman with a thinning gray face and wispy hair through which her scalp shone in several spots. She sat curled up low in a wheelchair looking at me like a pet begging to come in from the rain. Her bony legs were canted inward at unusual angles, as if they were only counterweights. She left one scrawny hand on the knob.

"Is Billy Battle staying here?"

"My son, William Blodgett, though that's not precisely what he likes to be called these days anymore, you see. He's not in trouble again? Would you be with the police?"

"Years ago, ma'am. I'm a private investigator. My name is Thomas Black. And you must be Millicent Blodgett?"

She blushed, though her skin couldn't hold the color long. "You know of me?"

"Just that you are Billy's mother. Jerome's foster mother."

Her British accent had faded like weathered newsprint. "Would you come in and wait? He's not been around this morning, that I know of. Though I got up only a few minutes ago. I stay up late and then sleep in. An old woman doesn't have much to do but watch the TV, feed her children, and keep awake with trashy novels."

"Yeah. Sure."

Greedy for company, she gave me a weak smile, then

pulled the door open laboriously, working the wheelchair
with one hand. Her arms were all bone and dangling skin.
I doubted she weighed more than eighty-five pounds. I
helped her maneuver out of the way and then shut the door
for her as she trundled methodically along in front of me.
You could tell from the look of the place and from the way
she moved that she rarely left this burrow.

The bathroom to the right of the front door had been
outfitted with stainless-steel railings for the handicapped.
Clothing and towels were strewn on the floor. Dirty dishes
and empty food packages cluttered the small kitchen area
to the left.

It was a one-room apartment. The main room served as
a dining area, living room, and bedroom. A sleeping bag
and rucksack were rolled into one corner. A large double
bed, tidily made, was pushed against the painted concrete
block that made up the far wall. The bed had a small
pouch in the center of the mattress where she slept.

"My son's been out catching up on things. I can't blame
him for that."

"Just released from prison, right?"

She gave me a birdlike look of surprise. "You know
about Billy?"

"Not everything. His name came up peripherally in a
case I'm working."

"You really are a detective." She had skin that might
have been cured in a sanitarium, and bullet cracks around
her mouth from too many years of sucking tobacco smoke.
Her graying hair was as limp as overcooked greens. "My
son was paroled from Monroe reformatory eleven days
ago. He's a fine child. We know he'll stay out of trouble
this time, if he can only find a job. Nobody goes out of
their way for ex-cons."

"No, I imagine they don't."

Along the far wall I counted ten parakeets in six bird
cages, newspapers mapped out along the floor underneath
to catch the detritus. There were specks of guano on a table along with a flea or two specking the color of Mrs.

Blodgett's pale pink shirt, next to the coffee stains. The television was running and in poor condition, picture blurred, colors untrue. She must have killed the sound before answering the door. I noticed she didn't have a cable box, just the public channels, a sure sign of poverty these days. It was pitiful when you could judge people by the quality of their television set.

On the table next to the window was an ashtray filled with butts, an opened package of Virginia Slims, and an elaborate antique brass cigarette holder on which a burning cigarette was perched.

"Both the boys had such a rumble-tumble life. But especially Billy. His father used to slap him around. When his older brother, Shem, was alive, everything was copacetic, but after the accident, why, my husband grew attached to liquor more than he was attached to us. Billy's brother drowned, don't you know. It was my fault. I didn't watch him the way I should have done. It's not easy for a mother to know she killed her son. William Senior was an old pirate and he got even worse. He did something to Billy when Billy was little that Billy is just now getting over. You see, Billy played with matches. That's what I had to contend with. A dead son, and the other one setting fires everywhere you looked."

"I don't expect you killed your son, Mrs. Blodgett."

"I did, though. I did. Did."

"It's natural to feel guilt, but mothers don't kill their children."

"This one did."

We sat on that for a few seconds. "Are you expecting Billy back this morning?"

"I couldn't say."

"What did your husband do to him?"

A faraway look moved into her gray eyes. "I think he used to light matches and hold them under Billy's hand. Can you believe a father would do such as that?"

"Unfortunately, I can. Billy doesn't have a real good reputation in your old neighborhood, does he?"

"Billy? Once you've mailed somebody a dead animal, you pretty much lose your good name."

"Does he ever make strange phone calls?"

"What did you have in mind?"

"Calls where he laughs but doesn't speak?"

Millicent Blodgett gave me a wary look and changed the subject. "The administrators of Echo Glen were out to frame Billy. That's how he got into Monroe."

"Mrs. Blodgett. I read the trial transcript about an hour ago. They had half a dozen witnesses. He admitted to most of it."

"Listen to me, Mr. Black. Billy was in Echo Glen under sentence from a juvenile court. That meant they couldn't hold him longer than his eighteenth birthday. That's what they wanted. To hold him longer. No person ever lands in the calaboose in a vacuum. With Billy, they taunted him by using that woman." Millicent Blodgett's voice dropped an octave and got so soft I could barely hear it. Making excuses for deadbeats was hard work.

"This was the woman he eventually attacked up at Echo Glen?"

"He didn't mean to hurt her." The old woman tried to double up her fist, and then made an incomplete stab at the air. "What did she think was going to happen treating a seventeen-year-old boy like that? Boys have hormones. She laughed in his face. Nobody ever mentioned that at any trial. If she hadn't laughed in his face, he never would have hit her.

"Then some of the rough element in camp showed up. Billy was defending her from them! Do you know, all three of those other boys were out within six months? My son spent the next five years up at Monroe."

"Now that he's out, he's friendly again with Jerome?"

"They've always been friends." Except the night Billy tried to emasculate Jerome with a kitchen knife, I thought.

"Has Billy been in contact with anybody from the old neighborhood?"

"Dear God, I hope not. Who knows what damage they'll do to him?"

"Jerome was hurt badly in their fight, was he not?"

"Yes, and Billy was heartsick over it. Did you know, he was in Echo Glen a month before he would even speak?

"Jerome was over on Monday. Spent hours. Cleaned up the kiddies' cages. You know, he's loaned Billy almost a thousand dollars since he got back. Everything he had."

She was a lonely woman who magnified small triumphs into social coups. My visit. Her sons. I wondered if she magnified tragedies into personal failures as well. She had been quick to assign herself the blame for her other son's drowning.

"Why does he go under the name of Battle, Mrs. Blodgett?"

"He hated his father that much. Billy wants to see his father's name buried with him. He swears he'll never have children of his own or go under the name Blodgett again."

"Must have been some father."

"Worse than you can ever know."

"I understand you took in Jerome?"

"After his house burned to the ground. He was only a boy. Billy was. That's why I never told anybody my suspicions."

"And what were your suspicions?"

"Billy had a fascination for fire. I told you that. He set a lot of fires."

"You think he might have burned down Jerome's house?"

"Frankly, I'd appreciate it if you kept this under your hat. Neither of the boys knows of my suspicions, and I'd rather not encourage any more bad blood between them. The state was going to put Jerome in a home, but I never regretted taking him in. I never had one lick of trouble with Jerome."

Millicent Blodgett rolled over to a bird cage, opened the door and put a finger inside. The two parakeets eyed her finger but did not budge. "My boys will both make me proud before I'm in the grave."

"I hope so."

On a small bureau next to the television I spotted a black and white photo of a young woman in a print dress standing in front of an old house, a boy under either arm, the wind whipping her shoulder-length hair.

Billy and Jerome. And Millicent.

It was an idyllic picture of a handsome, strong-minded woman and her two children, and at first I thought it must be Millicent's prettier sister. Trying to keep the shock out of my voice, I said, "Is this you?"

"With the boys. We were happy for a time."

While the boys looked only ten or twelve years younger in the photo, she looked gorgeous, thirty years younger and infinitely happier, although by then she had accumulated one dead child and a missing husband. The last twelve years had turned her into a wreck.

"Is he in contact with anybody from the old neighborhood? Billy?"

"Why would he be?"

"Do you know Walter Clark?"

"The colored? Why, I haven't thought about him in years."

"He testified against Billy, didn't he?"

"You're so set on trial transcripts. Why don't you go get that one?"

"They tape-record juvenile proceedings. And seal them."

"That old man was too old to know what he saw. And the other fellow was even worse. They couldn't see it was just a couple of boys who got out of hand."

"The other fellow? Philip Bacon?"

"That's right. The college boy. He was the one had the affair with that woman down the alley."

"What?"

"I think her husband's name was Jack or Jon or something of that sort."

"Not the Pitneys?"

"That was it. Yes. Roxanne. Roxanne Pitney. Why, I haven't thought about her in years. Her husband didn't seem to give a hoot. Always off at the horse track or someplace."

"Are you sure about this, Mrs. Blodgett? Roxanne Pitney had an affair with Philip Bacon?"

"Everybody knew of it. It must have lasted, oh, a year, year and a half. Why, I think my boys were arguing over her when they fought too. She lived right next to where they had the fight. In the alley."

"What makes you think they were arguing about her?"

The old woman edged forward in her wheelchair, so as to touch me. "That's what Billy told me. They were arguing over the *chick*. They were practically in her backyard. I don't know. Maybe she was fooling around with one of my boys. I wouldn't put it past her. Later, Billy switched his story around and told me they were arguing over the car. Billy's like that. He tries to protect himself by changing his story. I never knew what to make of it. My two boys. One of them going to jail in a police car and the other one to the hospital in an ambulance."

We talked about the birds for a while. Then we talked about Mrs. Blodgett's favorite daytime television programs. Half an hour after my arrival, the hinges on the front door squeaked.

A stocky, bull-necked man stepped into the apartment. His head was shaved. His beard was almost the same dark color as the stubble on his head. He resembled a cartoonist's rendition of an ex-con. He had a look about him, a born-mean look, as if he might have resembled an ex-con in high school, maybe even in grade school.

19

WHEN HE SAW ME, BILLY BATTLE HESI-
tated in the doorway, glowered in my
direction, stepped to his right into the bathroom, and, without shutting either of the doors he'd gone through, peed
into the commode. The splashing resonated throughout the
apartment. When he was through, the old woman's wheez-
ing and the birds' chirping seemed louder than ever. He
washed his hands.

"You can leave," he said in a soft voice I could barely
hear. He wore new jeans, baggy, a T-shirt, and an old pair
of brogans sanded down at the edges by a bow-legged gait.

"You don't even want to know who I am?"

"No. I don't guess I do."

"My name is Black. I'm a private investigator. I came to
talk."

"I'm impressed. Now you can get out." His voice continued to be so soft it was almost inaudible. His arms
floated off to the sides the way weight lifters' arms often
did. The muscle girdle in his neck, shoulders, and arms
was as thick as tree roots and shadowed with bulges. He
was shorter than me but outweighed my one-eighty by
forty pounds or more.

He walked into the kitchen, opened the refrigerator, and
shuffled into the main room clasping a can of diet soda,
which he opened and gulped from. He inserted the alumi-

num tab inside the can and sipped again. "People choke on those things," I said.

"You're not gone?"

"Billy, this man's come to talk to you. He's been waiting a good while." Millicent Blodgett's voice was somewhat shaky, a woman who did not assert herself often. I smiled at her courage. "He's been very polite to your old mom. Now, don't you think you might give him some time?"

Battle straddled a plastic-backed kitchen chair with a torn yellow cover, the only chair in the apartment aside from the one Millicent was sitting in. He had left the front door open, an obvious message. Reaching out to one of the bird cages, he thrummed the bars with an index finger that looked as if it had been broken more than once.

"I read the trial transcript. You've been in a lot of trouble."

"Who are you?" His voice didn't fit his stubbled head and bull neck. Or his reputation. A cat killer shouldn't talk so softly.

"I told you I'm a private investigator."

"So what does a private pig want with a culturally deprived DNA renegade like me?"

"I'm working on something that brought up a few issues from the past. I've been poking around in some things that happened in Madrona a few years back."

"I served my time. I just want to be left alone. Can you buy that, man?"

"You haven't been back to Madrona recently?"

"I wouldn't go back to that place on a dare. If a dog bit the mailman, they'd blame it on me."

"Yeah? What about Portland? Would you go there?"

He gave me a hooded look and said, "You got a hard-on for Portland, do ya?"

"Been down there recently?"

"Billy hasn't left Seattle," said Mrs. Blodgett, who was so nervous about our conversation that our words seemed to vibrate her like a tuning fork.

"Look," said Battle. "Don't hassle me, okay? Right now all I'm trying to do is get along. I'm not causing no trouble for nobody."

"Billy studied every minute he was gone," said his mother. "A couple more credits and he'll have his bachelor's degree."

Roxanne Lake had been right. He had piggy eyes. Little gray piggy eyes that looked as if they might not be getting enough rest. I could see his thoughts back there too. At least one of them. He wanted to kill me.

"Mind if I ask just a couple of questions, Billy? Are you holding a grudge against anybody from the old neighborhood?"

"Me? I got probably six, seven letters from different people when I was in the joint. None of them signed. Said when I got out they was gonna waste me. If you're looking for a grudge, you go back and talk to them people sent those letters."

"Do you have any of them?"

"I did, but there was a fire in my cell."

"You never told me about that," Millicent said.

He ignored her.

"What's your degree going to be in?"

"Forestry management. I figured there wouldn't be no people out in the woods. People is what seems to get me in trouble."

"You're not in contact with anybody from your old neighborhood? How about a man named Walter Clark?"

"He still around, is he?"

With some people, you could tell when they were lying. Or at least you thought you could tell. With Billy, I didn't have a clue.

There didn't seem to be any more to say. On my way out, Millicent thanked me profoundly for the visit. Billy countered by saying, "Ma, don't let that prick in again."

In the hallway the little boy pointed a chrome-plated cap gun at my face. I raised my hands, and, in a Buster Keaton deadpan, he said, "Think about your future."

"Yes sir. I sure will." He grinned and so did I.

Outside the main entrance to the apartment house, I crossed the street and leaned against a parked car, surprising the occupant. He rolled down his window. I said, "In the old neighborhood, I guess they used to call you college boy?"

Nervous as a cat in a roller rink, Philip Bacon peered up at me with his mismatched eyes. Being discovered this early wasn't something he had planned on. He swallowed. "I guess they did. I'd forgotten about that."

"Did I scare you?"

"I don't scare too easily."

"Yeah, sure. Don't forget to clean your britches when you get home."

"You've been talking to Billy Battle, haven't you?"

"What are you doing here?"

"I had some errands and was passing by. I saw him. It was accidental."

"You agreed to stay away."

"I saw him from the street and thought I'd hang around a few minutes."

"In case he tried to kill one of your friends out here in front of his mother's apartment building?"

"It wasn't like I planned it."

"More along the lines of sleepwalking, eh?"

"You know what I mean. I'm not lying, Tommy. Thomas. Thooommmmas. What did you find out?"

"Listen. When you make a deal with someone, don't always expect the other guy to be a patsy."

He fired up the motor and swerved out of his parking spot, then ran the stop sign at the corner.

Snake's souped-up Mustang was parked on Tenth, but even walking around the block and through the shrubbery to Boren, I couldn't find the ex-rodeo rider. I trotted around the block again, in the other direction in case he was playing games. Then I staked out his car and waited two hours, watching the clouds in the southeast sky gang up on Mount Rainier. I had the feeling he had parked there and taken a cab just to fool with me. Snake loved to fool with me.

Late that afternoon Kathy came into my office and stood with her back against the door, arms folded.

"I spoke to Philip."

Putting my feet up on the corner of the desk, I said, "Figured you did."

"No way this is a case, Thomas."

"Say again?"

"Philip said nothing is going on."

"When did you talk to him?"

"About an hour ago. He told me not to say anything to you about it, but how can I honor that when you're following us around? He also said he hasn't been to Portland in over a year."

"That sonofabitch is lying through his teeth."

She crossed her ankles and leaned her weight against the glass door until the glass bowed slightly. "That's what Philip says about you."

"That I'm a sonofabitch?"

"That you're lying through your teeth."

"He says that? Through my teeth?"

"Not in so many words. But that's what he means."

"So who are you going to believe?"

"Why would he lie to me?"

"Why indeed? At least we're both over six feet tall. We both have that going for us."

"Aren't you ever going to grow up? You know what the trouble with you is? You're the Peter Pan of private eyes."

"The Peter Pan of private eyes. I kind of like that, Wendy."

"You're hopeless." Kathy turned and walked out of the office. For the rest of the day she avoided me.

That evening there was a message on my machine from Slezak. "He's stalking the old man. Phoning him. Trying to make his life unlivable. So we do the same to him. Stalk the stalker. Give the little fucker a taste of his own medicine. It's just for sport, Thomas. What do you think about that, old boy? We ain't hurtin' nothing. Just for sport."

Snake wasn't in when I returned his call. Not at any of the numbers.

EVEN THOUGH MY MIND IS RACING A mile a minute, my days pass as if I have been embalmed.

I am lying on my back. I feel nothing.

At infrequent intervals I recall bits and snatches of my history but these are not nearly enough to alleviate the panic that embraces me.

I have not moved.

I cannot get my eyes open.

Nor can I speak.

The panic revolves around two things. One is what I have done. The other is what might have been done to me. To date, no one has explained my condition. For all I know, this state I am in is irreversible.

I may be a new breed of idiot.

If I am to remain in this state forever, I will find some way to end it. If I can get him the message, Snake will oblige me, probably with a drink or two under his belt and a pillow squashed flat over my head. No. Snake will lug me to the window and heave me out. Yes, if I ask him to, I am pretty sure he will kill me.

In college I once read an article about a man who had awakened out of a nine-year coma thinking only a few days had elapsed. If I were to hazard a guess, I would say only a few days had elapsed. There is something more than painful about the paucity of foot traffic in my room, for, unlike the new kid in the orphanage, the business extends beyond abandonment. No matter how much comfort I extract from nurses humming over their chart inspections or from the chirp of their rubber-soled shoes on waxed floors, I expect the keening silence to be broken up by visitors.

Yet, no visitor hovers over my bed.

No one peers into my deadened face for signals of cognition.

No anxious relatives inquire about recovery.

No process servers flirt with nurses over my dormant carcass.

Except for the occasional ringing phone, which the staff has learned to ignore, my room remains as quiet as a reunion of deaf mutes.

At one point a nurse airs the bedding, does some business with the equipment that is keeping me alive, and covers me up again. Miraculously, she falls short of finding the article Slezak stuffed under my pillow, and for some reason I derive comfort from her lapse. It is not much, but I have a secret and I'm amazed how much this secret pleases and entertains me, for even the lost and the bewildered can feel the cheap comfort that radiates off a secret. Even half-wits like me need secrets.

At my side I manage to get a couple of fingers to flitter momentarily. A tendon in my arm tightens and the muscle contracts. I still cannot open my eyes, but I believe that in a day or two I may be able to move. In another room in the distance, I hear a child's squeaky voice, and along with the voice comes a longing. To have a kid in my room. To have anybody in my room.

Hours or days or minutes later, someone knocks.

It may be my doctor. It may be the door to somebody else's room.

My sole visitor to date is Elmer Slezak, but this knock is too gentle and tentative to be Slezak. The door swings open—I can tell because the hallway sounds become magnified—and hard-heeled footsteps approach. Slowly. I have a sense that I am in some danger, but what do I know? I cannot open my eyes. After a bit, I smell perfume. The only thing I am certain of is the perfume.

The visitor stands beside my bed and clears her throat. My guess is that I look like I have been run over by a herd of dirty cats. After a while she takes up my limp hand and clasps it. My hand is cold. Hers is hot.

She kisses my fingers gently.

She rubs the back of my hand across herself. Across her face and then across her bosom.

If you have to be in a coma, this is the way to proceed. Without letting go of my hand, she eases her weight onto the edge of my bed, and I feel a sharp, stabbing pain in my ribs, the first pain I have felt since regaining a state of consciousness cogent enough for thought. It is clear from the pain of the jostling that I am injured severely. My ribs are stove in. Something in my neck aches. For the first time a brace on my neck becomes noticeable.

"Thomas," she whispers. "Thomas, I'm so sorry. I should have been here sooner." She fondles my limp hand and then says, in that flippant, semiteasing tone she uses only on me, "I suppose you can't hear a word of this . . ."

As I listen I marvel at the sweetness of her voice. At the thrill it gives me. "When somebody gets into this kind of fix, Thomas, you wish you had treated them better. I'm no exception. I'm just so sorry." She kisses my hand and holds it to her face. I feel something wet slide down onto my wrist. A tear. Another.

"They tell me your brain scans look normal. So what's wrong with you? Nobody seems to know. It scares me. I just wish . . . I wish I had never met Philip. I wish none of this had happened."

She gets quiet for a while.

More weeping. Her voice grows weaker. "Thomas? Get better. I need to know you're alive and well. I need to know that so I can walk away from you."

As she sits on the edge of the bed, her gentle breathing is broken up only by an occasional crying hiccup. I can feel her intense body heat.

"Thomas? I'm afraid we're going to bump into each other some day and we'll each be with someone else but we'll look at each other and know we're in love still. And we'll know there's nothing either one of us can do about it. It will kill me. I couldn't bear it. And I love you so much. You're my favorite person in the whole world."

Kathy sits with me, and after a very long while, out of the blue she begins a joke. She is doing her best to pretend that I am alive and well. "Three guys," she says. "You'll like this one. Three guys are bird hunting and they're from three different states. The first guy takes a bottle of moonshine and throws it in the air and blows it to pieces with his shotgun. 'Why'd you do that?' the others ask. 'I'm from Kentucky and we already have way too many of those where I come from.' The second hunter takes a bottle of wine, throws it in the air and blows it to pieces. 'Why'd you do that?' the others ask. 'I'm from California and we already have way too many of those where I come from.' Whereupon the third guy picks up his shotgun, points it at the California hunter and pulls the trigger. 'Why'd you do that?' asks the guy from Kentucky. 'I'm from Washington State and we already have too many of those where I come from.'"

Kathy collects awful California jokes which she tells to no one but me and which are quite popular in the Seattle area. Also awful lawyer jokes, as do a lot of lawyers. She says nothing further for some time. Then she says, "Oh, Christ!" She is crying again.

I am right to wonder why she has not visited until now. It isn't only that my sense of time has been skewed. She has avoided me for reasons I am not privy to.

As I mull over these points, I manage to wiggle four fingers on my right hand. It is the hand on the far side of my body, and she does not notice. I can move. My God, I can move!

She kisses my cheek, my brow, my lips, and then I realize she is standing, walking across the room, those hard-heeled footsteps, and I strain and grimace to get my eyes open. I can move! Don't leave yet!

My eyes open. I cannot believe my good fortune.

My eyes open and my fingers twitch and I struggle to look around the room.

It takes some time before I can focus. The light is blinding. My face is full of tears. I blink. I am in a hospital room. A TV set is perched high on the wall opposite, the screen dormant, as I have been. The wallpaper is printed in pink patterns. It is the sort of pleasant room women are trundled into after giving birth. It is the sort of room that should have balloons and flowers and newborns. Instead it contains a bewildered man. A window is situated to my left. I can see a darkening, cloud-filled sky.

It is only with a monumental effort that I manage to roll my head so that I can look at the door. If Snake is standing guard, I cannot see him. If the police are around, I cannot see them either. All I know is that Kathy is no longer with me.

I cannot say why precisely, but when I hear someone from the hospital staff at the door, I shut my eyes. There is succor as well as novelty in my new ability to withhold secrets. Until now the secrets have all been on the other side.

Although there is every possibility that I can speak now, I am not going to experiment; not in front of others. Revealing my new powers seems a risk. Playing possum is, I feel, the best course of action. Of course, it occurs to me also that I am like this because I have gone crazy.

It is not until late into the night, lying with my eyes open, staring at the ceiling, that I manage to get up the reserves to move my arm, the one without the needles and tape and the two-way drip. I move slowly and carefully with the patience of an invalid. I twist and reach for the lump under my pillow, rolling slightly to one side, reaching high. The pain is nearly unbearable. After many minutes I am rewarded. It takes me a while to guess what it is, and when I do, I wonder why Snake has wedged it under my pillow.

Somewhere in the distance in the hospital I hear the faintest hint of music, or I think I do. Roy Orbison is singing, "Crying," his later version when his voice is weaker, the notes not as pure.

21

AT TEN O'CLOCK ON THURSDAY, BATTLE emerged from his mother's apartment, drove the green Chevy to the Thriftway on East Cherry and sauntered inside. He wore the same jeans and T-shirt and broken-down shoes he had dirtied yesterday.

Nibbling a piece of fried chicken from a sack, he came out of the grocery store and sat in his mother's car. He had been inside nineteen minutes. He rolled down his window and swapped quips with a brassy black woman as she walked into the store. He catapulted chicken bones out his window. He drained two beers.

Tires screeching, he pulled out onto Cherry Street and headed west. As he drove, he launched a crumpled sack of garbage across the seat and out the passenger window, where it bounced on the macadam like a stray tennis ball.

He hooked a left on Twenty-third Avenue, drove south past Garfield High School, his head on a swivel as he passed clumps of teenage girls. He turned west again and went over the hill through the Yesler Terrace projects, down the hill on the overpass that crossed Interstate 5 and past the Smith Tower downtown.

Eventually he navigated the one-way streets and no-left-turn signs to an area near the Kingdome that had a kind of a truck-route, empty-warehouse, no-man's-land cast to it, the type of place where you're afraid to leave your car parked on the street. He found a spot beside a brick wall that had a faded ad for Gillette razors.

He parked the car cockeyed, as if it were an abandoned auto, then hiked in the direction of Pioneer Square. On the way, he downed another beer, which he pulled from his jacket pocket, then flipped the empty bottle onto the street where the glass splashed against a phone pole. He had not locked his mother's car, a mistake in this part of town. I did not know how many beers it took to make a twenty-two-year-old man his size drunk, but I had a feeling if I followed him I would find out.

Double-parking a block or two behind him, I rolled forward only when Battle threatened to get out of sight. He did not turn around. In fact, he hardly glanced at his surroundings. What he seemed interested in were street signs and anything in a skirt, both of which were becoming more abundant as we neared Pioneer Square.

As I paced him, I picked up my cellular phone and pushed a button. "Bridget?"

"Thomas. Where are you?"

"Downtown."

"I wish I was getting mileage. Philip's been to the laundry. Then the supermarket, where he bought three bottles of wine, a magazine about lady body builders, Tinactin, a package of fat-free sweet rolls, a basket of fruit, a small box of toothpicks, and some wart remover. He's an easy tail and I can use the extra money, but I wish I knew why we were on this. I have this unsettling hunch it actually does have something to do with Kathy."

"Tinactin is for crotch rot. And wart remover? My God, he's got genital warts."

"He seems like a nice enough guy."

"How could he be, with genital warts? Besides, if he had to live his life over again, he'd still be in love with himself."

Battle made his way through the winos in the small park across from the Mutual Life Building and stood under the shedding maples in front of my building with his hands in his pockets. At a bench in front of Doc Maynard's, he told two sleepy-looking men in tattered clothing to move. They got up and left without discussion. Battle didn't have the look of somebody you wanted to argue with.

He sat and directed his piggy little eyes at our building, looking away only to track the occasional female pedestrian.

I parked behind our offices in the lot across Western Avenue. When I circled the huge block and came up behind Battle on First Avenue from the north, he was still on the bench. I stopped a hundred feet away, placed my back up against a building, and slid down until I could feel the coolness of the sidewalk through my trousers.

Despite the relatively warm September day, I wore a pea coat with the collar turned up to hide my face, tacky mirrored sunglasses, and a baseball cap pulled tightly askew. I hadn't shaved and was confident Battle would not recognize me. When I moved, it was with hunched shoulders and a hitch in my gait. I carried a limp bedroll wrapped in twine.

At two minutes after eleven o'clock he walked across the street against the light, flipped the bone at a driver who tooted his horn, and proceeded to the front of the building, where he climbed the marble steps, cupped his hands against the glass door, and peered into the foyer of our building. Seconds later he came pounding down the steps

in a fast, bow-legged shamble. I expected someone to exit
the building, someone he didn't want to bump into, but nobody showed.

He rounded the corner, passed the toy shop, the Japanese restaurant, Mitchelli's, and went across Western directly to the lot where I parked my truck. He seemed to
know what he was looking for and approximately where to
look.

After some fooling around, he found the small sign that
said RESERVED FOR T. BLACK and walked behind my vehicle.
I had asked Kathy not to let the lot owner print my name
on the sign, but Kathy thought I was being paranoid.

I walked up Western a hundred feet, but by the time I
turned around to see what Battle was up to, he had his din-
gus out and was pissing on the driver's door, the front tire,
then the headlight, crab-walking in a struggle to water as
much of the vehicle as possible.

Afterward, he stood on the sidewalk, yawned, knuckled
his nostrils, scratched himself, buttoned his trousers, then
walked back around the block, kicked two more homeless
men off the bench in front of Doc Maynard's, and crossed
one knee over the other, looking as relaxed as a father at
his daughter's choir practice. After making certain he was
settled in again, I went back to my truck and discovered he
had dragged a church key or maybe a sharpened screwdriver across the paint on the driver's side, carving out a
three-fanged snake. Could it be he knew I was following
him, that he was toying with me? Was Battle that sharp?
I had thought not, but now I began to wonder.

While waiting on the other side of the park, I fell into
a conversation with a man who told me he had lost his job
eighteen months earlier, his house shortly thereafter, and
then his three cars, boat, power tools, and wife, in that order. He told me he was sleeping in parks and shelters,
where he had been robbed twice, once of seventeen dollars
and once of ninety-three cents, so he was carrying a knife
in a sheath inside his coat. It was with a certain despairing
braggadocio that he showed it to me. Gamy and broke, he

was not lacking in optimism or the ability to tell a joke on himself. I told him I was a private investigator. "Oh, yeah?" he said. "How long *you* been out of work?"

Some time later when Philip Bacon showed up on foot, I scanned the sidewalks and found Bridget forty yards behind him on the other side of the street, wearing a shawl and hat and looking seventy. He disappeared into our building and she waited catty-corner from the building, leaning on a cart she had been dragging.

I took out my cellular phone and called her. She stood in the doorway of a shop to answer. "How did a poor old woman like you ever afford a cellular phone?"

"Who is this?"

"What do you have in the cart? Old underwear?"

"Thomas?" She looked up at the building, didn't see me, then glanced around the street.

She never did find me, although she looked directly at me several times. I dialed the office. "Beulah? This is the big guy. Don't use my name. Is he there?"

Beulah paused while she thought it over. "I suppose you're referring to a certain someone's fiancé? A gentleman you once called Old Blue Eye?"

"You know I wouldn't stoop to anything that juvenile."

"Hah! They're in Kathy's office. Talking. Would you like me to turn on the intercom so we can listen?"

"That's it? Talking?"

"Thomas, Thomas, Thomas. Where are you, anyway? Is there something I should know?"

"Yeah, you should know how they met."

"You're not going to give up, are you?"

"Forget I called, Beulah. And do me a favor? Don't tell anybody."

"I'll think about it."

Ten minutes later, with Philip still upstairs, Billy Battle hopped a bus. Battle went to the back where the rowdies and delinquents sat and squared himself up with the aisle. All the commuters who got on after us, including three gang members, made a point of avoiding Battle. He looked that scary with his shaved head, heavy brows, beefy shoulders, and killer stare.

He rode up First Avenue and got off at Pike Street, where he stood in a crowd on the corner waiting for the light. Sidling through the throngs in a slouch, I followed him across the street and into the Pike Place Market. I stopped at a stall and bought a Red Delicious, knowing that a man biting into an apple has almost no face.

A cobblestone alley named Pike Place ran the length of the market. On the other side were merchants and shops. From the backs of some of the stalls to the west, windows looked out over the bay. The Pike Place Market included bookstores, fish stalls, leather-craft booths, people hawking flowers, vegetables, honey in the comb, belt buckles, earrings—you name it. The main thoroughfare between the produce tables was packed wall-to-wall with moving bodies. Virtually every film company that came to town found an excuse to shoot here.

It took me a while to figure out exactly what Billy Battle was doing in the crowd, but after the third or fourth woman glanced around with a cross look on her face, I figured it out. He was twenty-two years old, had spent seven years in the pen, and now he used up his noon hour goosing women. For an ex-con who claimed he didn't want to go back inside, Billy Battle seemed bent on trampling every little rule he could find. I wanted to grab him and break his thumbs, but it was more important that I didn't expose myself.

When he reached the north end of the Market, I saw his shaved head making its way to the street in a swift hustle. Behind him there was some loud talk, but he didn't turn around, walking with the arrogant strut of a man who had won more than his share of fights.

Battle sat on a wall in the small park at the north end of the market next to an Indian who had seen better days. He said something to the Indian, and the Indian, who was drunk, shot his cuff and glanced at what appeared to be a very expensive wristwatch. To our backs three or four freighters were anchored near shore. A ferry steamed across the Sound toward town from Bremerton.

Within minutes Roxanne Lake walked up the sidewalk on Western and went into the Seattle Club, a workout and fitness center. She wore white stretch pants that were tight enough to reveal the dimples under her knees. On top she wore a loose-fitting black sweater. She carried a flight bag with a taped racket handle protruding from one end. Squash or racquetball.

Battle went in after her but came right back out. I had a feeling they hadn't spoken, that she hadn't seen him. For the next two hours, when he wasn't watching women, Battle watched the entrance to the Seattle Club. Though he said nothing, he had eyes rude enough to get him into a fistfight. After a while I began to wonder if that wasn't his intention.

When she finally emerged from the health club, Roxanne Lake was laughing with another woman, a redhead, younger, built heavier, but looking as fit as Lake. They went a couple of doors down to Cafe Sport and took a table inside.

This was the first time I could remember tailing somebody who was in turn tailing a client. Billy Battle had staked out my office, bullied homeless men, vandalized my truck, goosed women, and now was spying on his foster brother's patron.

After forty minutes sipping lattes and munching salads, Roxanne and her friend paid their bill, then stood outside talking for another twelve minutes, during which I walked past them twice, garnering vague looks of disgust from Lake and the thousand-yard stare from the redhead. It was funny how unappealing you could make yourself by crippling your posture, forgetting to shave, twisting your mouth, and donning a few tasteless items. My pea coat was the same one I used when working underneath my truck.

With Billy trailing half a block behind, the two women walked to what I had always considered the back door to

the Westlake Center, a small multistory mall with open
balconies that had been built in front of the elevated mon-
orail terminal.

They were singing harmony, Jerome Johnson and four
others, a quintet, on the first level of the mall, using the
natural acoustics of the structure as much as they could be
used. It was clear that these young men owned the place.
Everybody within earshot was mesmerized.

All five wore white shirts, black bow ties, well-worn
jeans, and black shoes polished to a sheen. I figured there
were two hundred people watching from the balconies, including numerous store clerks, as well as a dedicated core
group of about fifty on the main floor in a ragged semicir-
cle. The crowd was dressed more formally than the quintet, businesspeople out for a quick lunch and some
shopping, the occasional housewife or retiree.

Battle went up the stairs at the west end and watched
from one level up. I got there in time to see him elbow
three pumpkin-butt women aside and stand nonchalantly
on the rail, gazing down at his foster brother and cohorts.
The women gave him scathing looks and stood off talking
about him. You could tell they were debating whether or
not to contact security.

The group was good. Damn good.

They sang vintage rock 'n' roll love songs in ways that
brought tears to the eyes of many of those watching. "So
Much in Love." "Just a Dream." "Come Softly to Me,"
originally done by the Fleetwoods from Olympia, which
started off with that great *dum dummm, dum do dumm,*
harmony. Even the janitors carrying their trash sacks
around had stopped to watch. You could see a hundred
smiles in the crowd. Each number featured another of the
singers, each taking a turn at lead, and each lead would
stand forth from the group and use the same corny hand
gestures I had seen Jerome Johnson use that first day in
my office when he'd dropped to one knee and sung a few
bars to Roxanne Lake. He was the featured singer when

they did "A Teenager in Love," and they did it at least as well as Dion and the Belmonts had.

When he sang, he stepped forward into the crowd and addressed his words directly to a pretty young blonde with cherry-red lips and a long red coat. He worked hard at being both romantic and chivalrous, qualities women did not see much anymore.

These weren't the five best-looking young men in town, the wittiest, or the richest, but right now they had every woman in the place eating out of their hands.

Fifteen minutes later when they finished, one member stepped forward and addressed the crowd, began passing out business cards. They called themselves Remember When.

Mrs. Lake began talking to Johnson, laughing loudly and flirting with the other members of the group. A few minutes later they all left together, walked through the mall, took a corridor that headed east, and wandered into Clippers, the restaurant in the Mayflower Park Hotel around the corner. Battle followed, but I didn't. There were too many people in that tight corridor who knew me.

When I went outside, I spotted them from the street-side windows as I walked down Olive Way between Fourth and Fifth.

A few minutes later Battle walked almost six blocks before he found a small grocery. He came out with a paper sack, fiddled with something inside, then tipped the sack up to his lips. A quart of beer. He had the first bottle about finished before he got back to Clippers, broke it on the sidewalk and opened a second, nursing this one.

He walked back to First Avenue and took that toward Pioneer Square and my building. On the way, he stopped at three porn shops. I followed him into one. I was curious to see what materials attracted him. I watched him buy five or six magazines and a video. They all involved sado-masochism.

He spent the next hour outside our building. When he headed in the direction of his car, I jogged around the block to pick up my truck. Now that the afternoon light was different, the scratches that bastard had put on my paint looked worse.

Ignoring the parking ticket under his windshield, he sat in the car under the shadow of the Kingdome for twenty minutes. I had the feeling he was thumbing through the pornography.

It was almost six. I had eaten the Red Delicious long ago and was snacking on some cold pizza. I phoned Bridget. "Did you see him?" she said. "He spent almost two hours up in your office."

"Phil did?"

"After your office, he was like a fly homing in on some dead meat. Right past that building on First Hill we were watching Monday night. But he didn't stop. He spent half an hour in the Magnolia public library near his house. He spent the rest of the day driving from one automobile tire store to another, taking price quotes with a small notebook in his hand. He's in a Goodyear store right now."

"Do me a favor. If he heads over to my place for a date with Kathy, get lost, okay?"

Battle was moving now. He went across town and dropped down into his old neighborhood, Madrona. He parked his mother's car on a side street on a downhill and waited. I could only assume he was waiting for dark.

22 BECAUSE IT WAS SEPTEMBER, AND because we had the added conspiracy of a heavy cloud cover, it got dark early that evening. The tang in the air announced there would be rain before dawn.

In his mother's car, Billy Battle's head was propped above the lip of the front seat like a pot in a window. I was parked higher on the hill a block and a half away, so that he could not see me unless he made a concerted effort.

I phoned Bridget and told her to break off surveillance of Philip for the evening, "Unless he's about to go into a cathouse."

"You're funny, Thomas." Twenty minutes later she drove up the hill from the lake, past Billy Battle, past my truck. On the phone she said, "I don't think he's doing drugs. He's just sitting there staring. Want me to hang around?"

"Go on home. Your dinner's probably waiting."

"Are you kidding? It was my turn to cook. Tamara's going to want to eat at Canlis or someplace."

After the streets grew dark, Battle fired up the Chevy and coasted down the hill. He coasted until the neighborhood leveled out, then cruised the blocks. When a man is twenty-two, the neighborhood he grew up in seven years earlier can take on awesome dimensions, particularly if he has not visited in the interval.

He slowed and stared up at several houses, and after he rounded the corner, I jotted the addresses in my notebook.

When I rounded the corner myself, I found I had lost him. I put the truck in reverse and backtracked to the opening of an alley.

Lights doused, the Chevy was midway down the long narrow alley, parked behind the same houses he had been inspecting from the front minutes earlier. I stepped out of my truck, stooped, and sighted through his car windows, using a distant streetlight as a guideline. There was no silhouette inside.

He had parked and waited patiently until the sun set, and now he was loose.

I was going to look like a moron if he did something ugly here.

I moved the truck out of sight, leaped out, and walked up the alley.

The windows of the Chevy were fogged from the inside, a cold dew beading up on the metal roof. I was tempted to remove the distributor cap to discourage a quick flight, but that not only would have tipped my hand, there was also the possibility he would return and catch me at it. I had no idea where he had gone; how far away he was. For all I knew, he was behind a garage watering the lilies.

I scouted the alley, peering over fences and into windows at families sitting down to dinner, at a baby in a high chair, at a father tossing a toddler high over his head. In another house an elderly woman leaned against her kitchen counter watching a ten-inch black and white television.

It was not until I had gotten almost to the end of the alley that I heard noises in a yard at the corner. I detoured into the dark opening of a garage and listened.

A muffled radio sounded from one of the nearby houses.

When he walked past my hiding spot, Battle was as quiet as a cloud. I glimpsed a wild look in his eyes and, even though it was growing chilly, a sheen of sweat on his brow. He broke into an unhurried jog. A dog howled, rattled his chain, and scratched at a fence. I tried to estimate how long Battle had been out of sight. Five minutes? Six? Losing him in his old neighborhood was a sorry move. Was five minutes enough time to break into a house and kill someone?

When Battle's headlights brightened the alley, I stepped back into the recesses of the garage, bumping up against a tiny little black Morris Minor that obviously hadn't run in years. Battle's Chevy passed me at speed.

I bolted into the alleyway and ran for my truck. I headed downhill toward the lake, veering dangerously around a slower car. I couldn't shake the thought that I might have witnessed a murder. Finally, blood pounding in my ears, I glimpsed his taillights.

Battle wended his way down to the water, drove north on Lakeside, up the hill and through the University of Washington Arboretum. As I followed, I dialed 911 on my cellular phone and reported a prowler at the Madrona address. I wanted to tell the 911 operator we might be dealing with a psychopath, but I didn't know how to convey the urgency I felt without being taken for a nut case. I would have stayed in Madrona myself to make sure things were all right, but I had a feeling about Battle. If he was on some sort of rampage, it was more important to stay with him. Stop him.

Battle emerged from the Arboretum and took the floating bridge across Lake Washington, two lanes in each direction with no shoulder, one of the longest floating bridges in the world. We found ourselves jammed up behind a stalled vehicle. The lights reflecting off the lake gave a serene glow to the water. A sailboat with only running lights motored parallel to the bridge on the lee side on what was probably his last run of the summer. We could see four people on deck. They had binoculars and were looking at us. On the other side of the bridge, to the south, the waves were all chop and froth. In Seattle a south wind usually meant clouds and rain.

Battle took the first exit on the other side of the bridge and hung a right, proceeding into Medina and then Bellevue. Twice he executed sloppy U-turns without warning, circling back past me. Either he was lost or he had spotted me, and I was reasonably certain he had not spotted me.

For almost an hour he snaked through Bellevue, twice wandering into residential culs-de-sac and making angry turns. At a service station he filled his mother's tank and asked for directions. I watched him pay for the gasoline with a handful of crumpled one-dollar bills he dug out of his jeans with two fingers.

His destination turned out to be Hunt's Point.

Located on a spur of land to the north of the northern-most floating bridge on Lake Washington, Hunt's Point was La-la Land, known to be the richest neighborhood in the state, where a modest house in the little municipality might sell for one and a half million. Many of the estates had boat moorages and not a few had tie-ups for seaplanes.

The only person I knew on Hunt's Point was Roxanne Lake.

Battle proceeded north past the hamlet's city hall and along Hunt's Point Road. I followed. He drove all the way to the end of the spit, where he turned around and headed back toward me. I pulled into a long dark drive where my headlights swept across a monstrous cedar that must have been three hundred years old, then flipped my lights off and took my foot off the brake. He had already passed me too many times.

He pulled into a driveway on the side fronting Fairweather Bay. The houses there faced west.

I came back and found a side out two driveways beyond the one the Chevy had used. I placed a sign in the window: CAR TROUBLE: BACK IN TWENTY MINUTES. Then I jogged back down the road.

It was ten-thirty and quite dark.

I crept behind the Chevy and shined a pocket flash through the driver's window. The front seat was littered with broken cookies, torn-open condom packages, pornographic magazines, and empty beer bottles.

The numbers carved into a wooden plaque hanging from the tree over the drive matched the numbers on the check Roxanne Lake had written me.

If he had been on a legitimate social call, the reasonable thing to do when lost would have been to phone ahead and procure directions, but he was not reasonable. Nor was this a social call.

The woods between Hunt's Point Road and the house were so dark Battle could have been thirty feet away pointing a gun at my head and I wouldn't have known.

It was a large house with a lot of lights. It had been remodeled extensively, and the first thing one saw after a garage the size of an airplane hangar was a circular drive under a canopy of cedars.

When I scooted on my stomach under a twelve-foot rhododendron, the damp earth chilled me through the knees of my jeans and the palms of my hands.

Billy Battle, who had been at a side door of the garage, quietly stalked between there and the north face of the house, stood on tiptoe and peered into one darkened window that had a slit of light showing from somewhere deep inside the mansion. Checking the windows one by one, he began a counterclockwise circuit of the structure. Then he disappeared somewhere in the darkness alongside the house.

The lawn was as smooth as the felt on a pool table, and my shoes sank into it like it was a sponge. I had the feeling my footprints would still be visible in the morning.

Fortunately there were no dogs. It took a few minutes to take up a position in the shrubbery in the woods on the north side of the pool house. Behind me, the distant porch lights of a neighboring house tweezered through the bushes.

The pool house looked as if it had been built onto Roxanne Lake's main house sometime within the last ten years. The lights were bright, and the water reflected off

the walls and ceiling in brilliant parallelograms and trape-
zoids. It was misty inside, but not so misty I couldn't see
Jerome Johnson walk past the long row of floor-to-ceiling
windows in a baggy pair of cobalt-blue swimming trunks.

Even using the field glasses I had brought, it took a
minute to find Billy Battle in a thicket near the doorway.
His back was toward me and he was peeping through the
window on tiptoe. He was young enough to be doing this
as some sort of prank, but somehow I didn't think so.

Not after Madrona.

Raucous music from the pool house bombarded the yard
and waterfront. Inside I could see Jerome clearly, and from
time to time, the top of a head that I took to be Roxanne
Lake's.

Already adrenaline was thudding through my system. If
he so much as shook a fist at them, I would cross the lawn
and strike him like a falling house.

The only other person in sight was an elderly servant in
an apron who dispensed beverages and afterward ad-
journed to the front of the pool house in a doorway, for I
could see light spilling onto the lawn from around the corner, along with her cigarette smoke. If Battle circled the
building, he would bump into her.

Jerome bounced on the diving board, performing can-
nonballs and other inexpert dives, sounding off in a Tarzan
yodel at the apex of each dive. Mrs. Lake remained out of
sight much of the time, and when she did come into view,
she wore a floor-length silk robe. Her hair was mussed and
damp.

Jerome had stumbled onto a sweet setup. Here was a kid
just out of college, scrounging around for a career, yet he
had a benefactor who could offer him midnight swims,
million-dollar beachfronts, servants, and even private in-
vestigators when the need arose. Even from my vantage
across the lawn, the music was loud, something with a
heavy beat and lyrics that I was incapable of deciphering.

After a while the splashing subsided. Battle remained in
the shrubbery, abandoning his post only once, to turn

around, unbutton his fly, and squirt a heavy stream onto
the lawn. He was the peeingest guy I'd ever met.

I quietly moved to a higher vantage point, where I could
clearly see a forty-by-eighteen-foot pool. At the shallow
end was a closed-off sauna. Two chaises longues with
mussed towels on them sat outside the sauna's door. A
video camera on a tripod sat in the corner, directed at the
ceiling at a cockeyed angle, an open bag of accessories on
the pool deck below it.

The elderly woman in the apron stood back in the doorway that led to the main house, arms folded, a burning cigarette wedged between her stubby fingers.

Two heads were visible above the level of a cedar hot
tub at the far end of the pool. Mrs. Lake and Jerome. Billy
watched them. I watched Billy. After drinks were served
twice more, each event triggered by a small hand bell Mrs.
Lake jingled, the servant was dismissed for the night.

Shoulders slumped, head lowered, the old lady tramped
up the hallway fumbling in her apron pocket for another
fag. I had the feeling she lived somewhere on the premises
and that she did not approve of her boss.

After she left, the two of them wallowed lackadaisically
in the hot tub for a good long while, then Jerome climbed
out, walked around the pool near Billy's spot outside the
window, and stepped into a pair of sandals. His wet skin
was pale, and he had that narrow, rippling stomach muscu-
lature many young men seem to have naturally. His arms
and shoulders were small and lacked definition. He would
be an easy man to beat up, but then, Billy knew that already.

As he circled the pool slothfully, I noticed his chest, one
arm, and his lower back when he turned, all of which bore
scars that showed he had taken some nasty knife cuts. I
couldn't quite get a handle on their relationship, Mrs. Lake
and Jerome, but he had a hangdog look about him as he
walked down the long shadowed corridor into the main
house.

After he left, Roxanne made a long, lingering phone call

from the hot tub, her head tilted back on the rim next to her half-empty wine goblet. Billy remained motionless at the window.

When she finally hung up the phone and clicked off the music, she climbed out of the tub, toweled her hair, and walked around the pool toward Billy. She stared mindlessly at the windows at ankle level, directly at him.

I knew she hadn't seen him yet because she didn't jump. Nor did she scream.

The whole thing made me extraordinarily nervous. As she got closer, Billy refused to lose his nerve, refused to duck into a squat. She stood directly opposite him, though higher, squeakily wiping a spot on the window with her fingers and pushing her face up against it, cupping her hands against the glass. She was looking out at the lake.

My sense had been that Roxanne and Jerome sustained an almost mother-son relationship, but this notion was betrayed somewhat now. She was not wearing a bathing suit. Was not wearing a stitch.

There was something remotely bizarre and not a little bit sad about this woman in this luxurious house standing alone in the middle of the night gazing out at the lake with an ex-convict and a private eye outside gawking.

Hands cupped to the glass, Roxanne Lake stared out at the lake for much longer than I could have guessed possible. When she eventually turned around, she circled the pool and flipped the lights off so that she was shadowed in the opening to the hallway.

Then she reached up and touched the back of her wrist to her face, did the same thing with the other wrist on the other side of her face. Twice more she made the movement. It wasn't until her shoulders began bobbing that I realized she was crying.

It was a kind of forlorn, passionless weeping, the empty sobbing of someone who fooled around with melancholy every night. Billy saw it too, because it was then that he turned and jogged away in the darkness toward his mother's car.

It wasn't until that moment that I felt the proper rude contempt for our transgression of her privacy, Billy's and mine. The thing that made it worse was that as he had jogged away, Billy had been chuckling to himself. I could never tell her about this. I was certain the nudity meant little or nothing to a woman like Lake, but for her to know we had seen her crying would surely bankrupt her pride.

23

I FOLLOWED BATTLE BACK TO HIS mother's apartment house and watched him park her car and go inside. I was tired and he was finished for the night, so I went home. When I got there, Philip's perfectly centered BMW was blocking my driveway.

Ordinarily I would have honked until he came outside, then given him a sickly smile and one of those beauty-queen waves I had perfected since meeting him, but I was dog-tired, and he was inside fooling around with my woman, and besides all that, I couldn't abide the thought of looking him in the eye. Either eye.

On the way into the house I kicked his driver's door in the same dent some other trailblazing patriot had made weeks earlier. And again.

The answer machine had a message from Bridget. Another from a permanently confused but very good-natured cousin on my father's side.

Saturday morning I awoke with some apprehension and checked to see if Philip's car was still in the driveway. It was not.

I drove to Madrona and located the house Battle had scouted in the dark twelve hours earlier. I had a weak hunch this was the house Billy had grown up in, that perhaps he had left something buried in the yard when he went off to jail, something besides dead hopes and half-forgotten troubles.

Dwarfed by the vegetable garden beside it, the shanty was a throwback to another era, the kind of place you see alongside a highway in the desert. It might have been a garage once, or a playhouse slapped up by the chauffeur for a rich kid.

Though tidy and neat, it was the shabbiest residence in sight, a one-story shack facing east but not precisely lined up with the street. The roof was crooked, and I doubted it covered more than three small rooms. The yard extended to the lot south of the house and supported a rectangle of mulched earth that was littered with ripening pumpkins, tall, brown cornstalks, beans, lettuce gone to seed, and a row of staked tomato plants. The vegetable garden was ringed with huge, fat dahlias on stakes, chrysanthemums, and scores of zinnia plants in orange, purple, red, and yellow.

I wasn't prepared for the old man's height or age or the dignity with which he carried himself. He greeted me with a sugary smile and a wrestler's handshake that must have been killers fifty years ago. He was three or four inches taller than my six-one, and his black skin was as wrinkled as an elephant hide. If he realized he was in danger, he didn't give a clue when he opened the door. Despite his age, he had only a mild stoop. What was special about him was that I could see in his face that he was immediately prepared to like everything about me. We introduced ourselves. He was Walter Clark. He had testified against Billy Blodgett.

In the center of the room on her knees sat a towhead of

about three with an oversized coloring crayon in one hand and a bag of Skittles in the other. She had an assortment of coloring books in front of her, along with a tiny, purple container of fruit juice of the type that comes with a straw stuck to the side of the rectangular carton.

Clark tossed a look over his shoulder and came back smiling. "Nicole. Meet Mr. Black. Mr. Black, this is my excellent and wonderful friend, Nicole. Nicole and I commune together from time to time when her mother has errands. Lives just down the block."

"May I come in for a minute?"

"Didn't I invite you? Come on in. Come *on* in." He stressed the *on*, like a carnival barker urging yokels under the tarpaulin for a look at the camels and the big-bellied dancing damsels.

Clark eased himself down into a rocker that must have been as old as he was, motioning for me to sit on a sofa that looked as if it had fallen off a truck onto the freeway. I sat near the end, but still it sank, and something in the innards nipped the underside of my thigh. Nicole eyed me carefully and continued to color, from time to time taking a tiny and purposefully delicate sip of juice.

"Now, what can I do for you, Mr. Black?"

"I think you know a guy named Billy Battle?"

"Ummmm, yeah. Under that name and maybe a couple of others. I been in the doghouse with Billy for a spell now. Long enough for the nut to grow into the tree."

"Did you know he was here last night?"

"He been to town awhile."

"No. Here. At your house. Around in the back."

If he was frightened, if he was even concerned, he gave no hint. It was the sort of information a man didn't want to hear from a stranger, and when he thought about it, his eyes clouded up. "Much as you hate to admit it to yourself, Mr. Black, there's some people born with trouble in their heart. Last night the police come knockin' 'long about Arsenio time. Asked me about prowlers. I should have guessed the likes of Battle was behind it. You with the police?" He pronounced it *pole*-eece.

"I'm a private investigator. Working on something that involves Battle."

Walter Clark placed an elbow on either arm of his rocker and thought about it. He took a good long while, the way only people who have learned to live can take a good long while. The longer I sat with him, the older I guessed he was. At the door it had been his late seventies, but now I had him pegged in his nineties.

Buttoned to the neck, his plaid shirt was worn so thin the light shone through the elbows when he lifted his arm. The pants had come from a business suit that had been stitched back around World War II, when he would have been in his forties. If his brown wing tips hadn't been buffed that morning, they had yesterday. He didn't have much, but he took care of it.

"I knew he was out of the boogerhouse. I always felt sorry for that kid. Billy's dad used to beat hell out of him, and the old lady too. It was just a shame."

"Is that how his mother ended up in a wheelchair?"

"Naw. That was a different event entirely. Near as anybody could calculate, she just up and lost her desire to walk to the paymaster. Decided she wasn't going to walk no more. Ain't that a somethin'."

"Yes, it is."

"I'm about the oldest one down here on the hill. There was Mrs. Stanton on the next block—her two sons were prisoners of war over there in Korea." He pronounced *Korea* as if it were a disease. "I got a picture of them in the other room from *Life* magazine. We had a lot of famous personalities come outta this neighborhood, but you can probably guess the Blodgett kid takes the prize."

"I can kind of guess he might. Mr. Clark, do you mind if I go out back and take a peek around? I'm curious as to what Battle was doing here last night."

"Go right on ahead. You find out, you tell me." He stood up, which was enough of a project for him that I felt guilt over precipitating it. He took Nicole's hand and walked her through the room in front of me, into a kitchen with incredibly ancient wallpaper, past a large, tan standup gas heater. I watched to see how steady he was, but he didn't need assistance. The floors were covered in torn linoleum with a pattern of twigs and lilies that had probably been on somebody else's floor before coming here.

In his bedroom I glimpsed a pair of battered slippers, a four-poster bed, and a tiny, portable black and white television on a dresser. There was nothing else except two quarters lined side by side on the dresser. It might as well have been a motel room for a migrant worker.

When I strode across the bare boards of the screened back porch, they seemed to whisper secrets. A hand-crank meat grinder sat on a sagging plank shelf next to an assortment of clay planting pots. Gardening tools stood in a cardboard box in a corner. They had undoubtedly been hosed off and dried before being brought inside. Everything on the porch smelled spare and slightly ancient, like old dirt in a garage that had housed buggies the last time it had seen sunlight.

Except for the garden, it was a simple yard.

I found no footprints, booby traps, broken windows, or pried-open doors—no evidence of a visitor last night or any other night. Along the backside of Walter Clark's property ran an unpainted wooden picket fence. A bird feeder constructed from an old coffee can hung from a plum tree. A grungy neighborhood cat crouched under the feeder, waiting for some hapless sparrow.

Clark called to the cat, then stooped and petted it as it brushed up against his leg. "See the kitty?" said Nicole, squatting to touch the animal warily with her index finger stuck straight out. "See the kitty?"

With the cat on her heels, Nicole staggered across the uneven lawn and began ripping zinnias out of the garden's border. I noticed how the old man positioned himself so that he could watch her and still let the weak sunshine stroke his face. Clark eyed me with deep-set, nearly black eyes scummed with gray deposits I took to be cataracts. "Now maybe she's out of earshot, you can tell me what this is about, sir."

"I was hoping you could tell me. Battle was in your backyard last night. I know, because I watched from that garage."

Clark swung his head slowly and said, "Pitney's place. He keeps saying he's going to restore that old car, but any fool can see it'll rust before he gets to it."

"Jon Pitney?"

"Yep. Where you was hiding was just about the spot that started all this ruckus. That's where we caught Billy trying to whittle down his little brother. I heard yellin'. Time I got them in my sights, the skinny one was covered in blood. Head to toe. I never seen the likes. Cut this way and that. He had this peculiar look on his face, as if to say, this can't be happening." After seeing Jerome's scars in the pool house, it was hard to believe he and Billy were still friendly. But then, maybe he regarded Billy the way circus people regarded lions and tigers, as something to be friendly with, but careful around.

"We all just circled him and told him to get realistic. He tried to hand the knife to one of us, but nobody would take it, it was so bloody. And then we grabbed him. He fought, then set on the ground his ownself and started bawling. It was a strange sight."

"And you testified against him?"

"Me and my friend Philip. They asked Jon over there, but he said he was too scared Billy'd come back and get him." And now he's back, I thought. Clark must have been thinking the same thing because he said, "I do what's right and trust the rest to the Lord. It's always worked for me. I got faith it always will."

"You and Philip have been friends for a long time?"

"My heavens, yes. Philip wrote some sort of prize-winning school paper on me and my pap and grandpap. Came over and interviewed me and everything. My word. We been friends a long, long time."

"You remember what the boys were fighting about?"

"Now, don't you leave here thinking they were fighting. When I was a young man, I saw a similar transaction down in New Orleans between a big jack pimp and some nasty little shrimper was messing with one of his women. That wasn't no fight neither. No. The little one was cutting the big one to pieces. It ain't a fight when one man's dying and the other isn't even bleeding. No sir."

"But you don't know what it was about?"

"Couldn't tell you."

We stood in the sun for a while watching the little girl wad up zinnias in her dimpled fists. The cat was sitting on his haunches staring at the street, arrogantly facing away from us the way cats do. "Her mother is single. Never was married. Going to school and working both. Now she's going to have another one. People these days are fuckin' out of both legs of their drawers, Mr. Black. Ain't it something? With all them diseases."

"It's something, all right. How'd you get tomatoes like that?" Walter Clark ran his hand patiently over his high hairline and grinned. When he finished telling me his gardening secrets, I said, "Don't let him get close if he shows up, Billy."

"He already been here twice and done nothin'."

"Last night and when else?"

"He showed up a week ago Tuesday, I think it was. Wanted me to recant my testimony from the trial. Recant. I told him I said what I saw and I saw what I said and I wasn't going to recant for him or St. Peter or nobody else. He done his time. What was the good?"

"That's an interesting question. What did he say?"

"Said he was trying to clear up his name."

"Did you tell Philip Bacon you'd had a visit from Battle?"

"Sure. We stay in touch, and I spoke to him that very week. The kid must have come straight from the joint. It was like he still had a cold chill on him. Said if I thought he was the one at fault, I hadn't been looking carefully enough. But I know what I saw, and I also know Billy's always been one to blame anybody and everybody for his own transgressions. Never owns up to anything even when there are eyewitnesses right there."

"Did he threaten you?"

"Being here was a threat."

"I guess it was."

Clark and I watched a man across the alley carrying a bundle of leaky newspapers to his garbage cans, holding the bundle away from himself distastefully. It was Saturday morning, and the tousled hair and bare feet and puffy rings under his eyes were sure signs that he had just gotten up. "That's Jon over t'there now."

"Pitney?"

"Yep."

"Mr. Clark. Do you have any protection?"

The old man gave me a quizzical look. "If you want to know about protection, I don't keep no conundrums around the place. Not that I wouldn't mind another go 'round. I been too old for regular lovemakin' maybe five years now. Not that I don't have my lady friends, but they're too old too. Every once in a while I'll find one willing to try, but all we do is end up rasslin' and laughin'." He gave a good-natured little hoot thinking about it. "It's pitiful to get old, Mr. Black, but it sure beats the alternative."

I grinned back at him, and for a moment we were just two kids in the back of the gym class making dirty jokes. "I meant a gun. Do you have something to defend yourself with in case Billy Battle comes back?"

"Had a gun once. Thought it was a good idea to keep it around the place. Then I read that a child was more likely to die from a firearm in the home than a burglar was. It made sense to me. All you got to do is follow the papers to see who's dying. I like children around, so I took it downtown and pawned it. Let some other fool have it."

"Remember, if Battle comes back—"

"I ain't worried, Mr. Black. 'Sides, who'd miss this old carcass?"

"She would." I nodded at Nicole trotting toward us across the bumpy turf. "And so would her mother."

"No, sir. I'm just an old man. Ain't nobody going to miss an old man."

"Don't count on it."

I crossed the alley, walked along a narrow sidewalk next to the garage with the Morris Minor inside, and knocked on Jon Pitney's kitchen door. It opened at my touch.

24

PITNEY'S HEAD WAS HUGE IN PRO-portion to his body, and though he was fifteen or twenty years older than me, he reminded me of a little boy, complete with big hair, a cowlick in back, and a look of recklessness in his eyes that was close to charming. The tail was out on his shirt, and the zipper on his trousers was broken at half-mast.

"Mr. Pitney? I'm interested in a guy named Billy Battle. Formerly Billy Blodgett. I think he used to live up the alley, here."

Pitney gave me a startled look and broke into a sweat. After a moment he invited me into his kitchen. I had never seen a guy break into a sweat so quickly.

Dried dog food littered the kitchen floor and snapped like breaking pencils under the soles of my shoes. Tiptoeing gingerly to a chair, Pitney sat, crossed one leg over his knee and flicked dog food from the arch of his bare foot. The speck rebounded off a wall and rocketed into another room. Except for the dog food and his own disheveled state, the home was immaculate. Yet, it was a far cry from Roxanne's present lifestyle. I wondered what had changed for her.

Pitney gave me a jaundiced, half-bashful look and spoke in a carefree slang that I sensed was more affectation than anything. "For a minute I thought you were after *me*. Last time somebody who looked like you was after me it was for some poker losses. You're not after me, are you?"

I stepped carefully across the dog food and handed him a business card. "Thomas Black. I'm interested in what happened out in your alley seven years ago."

"Yeah, I noticed you over there talking to Walt. He's quite a specimen. He tell you he used to play ball with Satchel Paige? He was a gardener and estate handyman down here for the Riplinger family for years and years. His dad had the job before him. They came out here somewhere around the turn of the century. Had eight people living there, and that was before they added on a room. His grandfolks was slaves. He has some stories to tell, that one."

"What can you tell me about Blodgett?"

The sweating began in earnest. "They wanted me to testify in court, but I figured they had enough people who'd seen what was going on. You know?"

"At that time you were married?"

"It was not the first time around for either of us, and we figured we were going to do it right, but I gambled a little too much and she got to screwing around. I lost a couple of jobs, and she went back to work and got pissed at me. I guess Roxanne did more than her share to keep us together, when you think about it. After me, she married some rich old coot."

"Did you know the Blodgett kid or his foster brother?"

"A little. We had them paint our house that same summer. It was Roxanne's project, but I was the one who had to stick around and oversee it. Then she blames me for not finding work all summer."

"You knew Bacon too? Phil Bacon?"

"Sure. Roxanne was screwing him."

"I'd heard a rumor, but I didn't really believe it."

"Oh, you can believe it."

"You seem to take it pretty casually."

"What else was there to do? Besides, it's water under the bridge now. He lived up the alley here with his folks. They've since moved somewhere out of state, I think. Roxy used to trot down there and borrow eggs and sugar and stuff from Rosemary, then stand around gossiping all evening. How do you know about all this?"

"I'm talking to everyone from the neighborhood, trying to get a clear picture. They were *sleeping* together?"

"Yep. Why? Is the kid coming back? I heard he was out of the jug."

"He is. He's in town."

"I knew that little shit would be back. That's why I didn't testify."

"So, Philip . . . I really don't have a clear picture of him with your wife. I hope you don't mind my asking."

"Nothing to it. It lasted . . . I don't know. A year. A year and a half, maybe. I didn't blame her. She was screwing other guys the whole time I was dating her. You gotta realize, Roxy never had a real boyfriend until she was almost twenty-four and out of college. She was not a particularly attractive woman and, to tell you the truth, she was afraid of men when I met her, even though she had already been married twice. Believe it or not, she married a guy who was gay but didn't really know it until he got married. Lasted three weeks. They never even did it. It wasn't until she met me that she started getting her confidence around guys, and then I guess she went overboard. But hell, I indulged her. Hope is different. Goes to church twice a week. Tries to get me into Gamblers Anonymous.

I guess maybe I am a project for Hope. But that's good. Should keep her busy until she gets old and dies."

"But Philip and—"

"Roxanne was just the kind of woman who needed a lot of male attention. People get recognition in different ways. Me, I gamble the family Christmas bundle on a Huskies basketball game. She once tried to screw the paperboy, back when there were paperboys. I never did find out what came of that. The boy's father, a preacher of all things, came over here and was pretty irate. As long as Roxanne stayed with me, I didn't much care."

It was an odd attitude, but not any odder than his tone of voice, which was as flat and unaffected as a puddle of water under a parked car. Pitney was either a singular actor or genuinely had not been disturbed by his wife's affairs and their subsequent divorce. There were people who kept so much turbulence in their lives that a divorce was a mere ripple. I wondered if Pitney was one of those people or whether something else was going on.

"You say it lasted a year or a year and a half?"

"Actually, except for the paperboy and Philip, I think she was faithful during our marriage. Well, maybe she wasn't, but those were the first I really knew about. The kid used to hang around out back, waiting for her to come out and use the car."

"The kid?"

"Phil. I'd go out there to empty the garbage and there he'd be standing in the dark. Once in a while I'd tell him she wasn't home and save him some time waiting in the cold. He always got real embarrassed. What Phil was never going to realize was that Roxanne especially liked it when it was wrong, and screwing one of her friend's sons while her own husband was at work was about as wrong as she could make it.

"Hell, Philip was still bugging her after she remarried. Some rich old fucker from down in Oregon somewhere. Lived off investments. This guy used to rent a jet to fly to Vegas for a show, then fly home again that same night.

New Mercedes every year. Gave the old one away to a friend. I was in line to get the next one, but he was murdered. Yeah. That's the kind of luck I've had my whole life. Real shitty."

"Sounds like his was a little worse."

"Couple of men broke into his house in Portland. Broke in and killed him. At first I thought Philip might have had something to do with it. He has this affair with my wife. She gets rid of him. He hangs around. She and I split, and she marries this rich old geezer. Phil continues to hang around. Then six weeks later the rich hubby is murdered. I thought about sending the cops an anonymous letter, but they caught these other guys."

I glanced around the house. The furniture was old but clean. The paintings were inexpensive prints. The kitchen table needed replacing. If Roxanne had gone directly from this domicile to the one at Hunt's Point, she had stepped up the social ladder a good many rungs in one huge leap. It must have been a shock.

"So Roxanne inherited the old man's money?"

"I mighta got back with her after that, but by that time I was hooked up with Hope. She came up to the house one day with her married sister trying to sell religion. I invited them in, and the rest, as they say, is history."

A moment later Hope came through the back door carrying two paper sacks of groceries. Before Pitney could introduce us, she commented angrily about the floor. She was a pear-shaped woman with kindly brown eyes, limp hair, and a shaky hand with the makeup brush.

"One last thing," I said, after his wife went back out for more groceries. "After you were divorced, did you ever talk about Philip with your ex-wife?"

Pitney jerked on his broken zipper as if he could fix what hadn't been fixable before. "I guess we did. I guess we talked a little bit about everything. Going off like that and snagging some rich old guy . . . she had decided to do something for herself, was all. Hook the brass ring while she still could. You see, Roxy loves me. Even now. But don't ever let Hope know that. It would crush her."

"She tell you anything about Philip Bacon?"

"Only that he was still stuck on her. Poor boob."

25 AFTER CALLING OUT FOR SEVERAL minutes that she was coming, Millicent Blodgett opened the door, then reversed her wheelchair directly down the little passage into her parlor. Although I knew she wasn't, she seemed thinner than on my last visit, her bony breastbone protruding through the vee of her robe.

"Get some new stuff?" I asked, gesturing at a VCR and a new color television. The old TV was on the floor in the corner next to her bed.

"You understand, Mr. Black, Billy has made it perfectly clear that he doesn't want me speaking to you."

I winked before I could stop myself, realizing it was something Philip would have done. "Want me to leave?"

"You're here, you might as well sit down and have some tea. You have time?"

"I've got some time. Did Billy come home last night?" It was almost not fair because, not knowing how to refuse, she would have answered any question I asked.

"Last night, Billy and a friend I had never seen before carried all this in. They set up the telly, drank some beers, ordered a pepperoni pizza, then made a few phone calls and were gone."

"Who was the friend?"

"Some colored boy I didn't like the looks of. Would you care to sit through a movie with me?" Towering above Millicent Blodgett, I couldn't help but smile at the naughty look she gave me. She had parakeets, a son recently out of the slammer, a stolen TV, a private detective in her parlor on a Saturday morning, and little else. There was tea in the kitchen and a bottle of gin peeking out from under her bed. Stolen videos. Cigarettes. Fleas.

We cooked popcorn on her stove. I heated up water for the Twinings tea. She sipped a soda and then filled a plastic cup with hot water and spiked it with gin from under her bed. She lit up a cigarette, fitted it into her brass cigarette holder, and waved it around grandiosely. We watched horror flicks, which was all she had—slasher films, actually. Billy had stolen over thirty slice-and-dice movies. Lots of screaming. Madmen running amok with knives and hatchets and shotguns. Mrs. Blodgett might have been watching a first run of *Lawrence of Arabia*, she was so enthralled.

While we watched, Millicent told me about her first marriage in England, to an American serviceman who died in a freak air accident. She claimed she had never completely become herself again after the romance, a statement I readily accepted.

After a while, now clearly in her cups, she said, "He had one of those phones that you carry around with you. I had never actually seen one before."

"Who did?"

"Billy."

"Did he make a call where he laughed?"

"I think you call it a modular. His friend lent it to him."

The gin and tea worked its way through her system midway through the first flick. When she rolled into the bathroom and shut the door, I got a chance to go through Battle's belongings. Along with books on most of the notorious serial killers of our era, he owned a well-thumbed copy of every book ever written about Ted Bundy. It was common for killers to collect this sort of thing, but on the other hand, enough of the general populace read these tomes that most bookstores now had true crime sections.

Aside from the books and a knapsack that looked as if he'd strong-armed it from a third-world student, Billy had pitifully few possessions. Some neatly folded clothing. There were no journals. No weapons. No drugs. No photos. And no money.

When she emerged from the bathroom, Millicent Blodgett smoked until the apartment detector went off, then after I opened the sliding window on her small patio, smoked some more. I was no expert, but from the paper thin sound of her lungs, she would soon have her own oxygen tank.

It was early afternoon when I emerged from the apartment building into the blinding afternoon sunlight, feeling like a kid who'd been at the movies all day. I went straight home, peeled and gulped a couple of bananas, made toast with marmalade, changed clothes, wheeled my new Eddy Merckx out of the spare bedroom, peddled over to Seventeenth and coasted down through the University of Washington campus.

Tired and hungry, it was dark by the time I got home, having ridden sixty miles through Renton and around Mercer Island and then back to Seattle over the floating bridge. It was the first real exercise I'd had in a week, and as I wheeled my bike back into the spare bedroom, it occurred to me that when Kathy moved in with me she would need most of that space for her clothes. My weights, the racing bike, the spare wheels, the truing jig, would probably end up in the garage, where Kathy figured they belonged anyway.

Monday and Tuesday I got sidetracked testifying in court. Earlier in the year, I had worked on a personal injury case in which a young woman and her sister had been rear-ended by a hit-and-run driver. It had taken me three weeks to find the driver, and then he turned out to be a gang member and drug dealer. In the course of my investigation I had uncovered some information that needed to be turned over to the Seattle police, and now I was paying for it with two days in court. I was slated to be in court Wednesday as well, but was unexpectedly released by the deputy prosecuting attorney Tuesday afternoon.

At loose ends, I went back to the office, opened mail, and wrote my quarterly check for my Errors and Omissions Insurance. Outside my window the weather was holding, a sort of junior league Indian summer, sunny but not too sunny, warm but not balmy. The word was we were in for a hellacious winter.

The new information concerning Philip and Roxanne Lake's affair seven years ago was interesting, but not necessarily pertinent. I kept running it over and over in my mind, realizing that it was one of those little cancers of fixation that crop up in cases from time to time and that threaten to consume everything.

The fact that her fat-cat fourth husband had been murdered in Portland was interesting, but not necessarily pertinent.

The fact that Billy Battle had driven to Portland and had spent the night sitting in his mother's car in a residential neighborhood was interesting, but not necessarily pertinent.

What *was* pertinent was that Billy was missing.

I had been speaking to his mother daily, and she was worried. I had been in contact with Walter Clark too, but he'd had no visitors.

I had seen Philip once or twice, and each time he had badgered me about my progress with Battle. I had phoned Lake's place once a day, reaching Jerome on the second day and a servant on the first and third days. Battle had not been around.

Elmer Slezak neglected to return any of my calls.

On Tuesday afternoon I phoned every number I had for Snake, without success, then spoke for half an hour on the phone to a gentleman Kathy was representing in what we called the Dog Rocket Case, a case where a man was being sued by a woman who had taken her dog along on their date. On the way to the boat show in the Kingdome, he had been forced by traffic to slam on his brakes, a move that sent the dog, who had not been using a seat belt, through the windshield. Over the course of three days I learned that this woman had lost two other dogs in various car accidents and was presently living on the settlements from same.

A woman came into the office who had me investigate the scar on her boyfriend's calf after he claimed to be working for the CIA. Supposedly he had been tortured in East Africa on a case, thus the scar. I told her what I discovered, that he had been fired from a string of sales jobs and had a wife and two kids, along with another girlfriend.

"Will you kill him for me?" asked my client, a heavyset woman with gorgeous auburn hair. I looked at her and she burst into tears. "I'm just kidding. Bad joke. Gosh, I hope he lives a happy life. Of course, it's going to be without me. Gosh. I hope a runaway steamroller doesn't gun him down. I'd hate to go to his funeral with his wife and his kids and his other girlfriend and see him all jammed up in a pizza box." She began to laugh hysterically, and, at that point, mixing tears with laughter the way it sometimes rains when the sun is out, she got up and left.

I was tilting back in my chair under my World Association of Detectives certificate on the wall when the phone rang. "Thomas. I've been meaning to have you over for dinner or something."

"Mrs. Lake?"

"I told you to call me Roxanne, silly. I got your messages, but I was out of town for a few days. What all have you turned up?"

Leaving out Friday night's episode outside her pool house, it didn't take long to give her a rundown. "Can we get together?" I said. "I need to check my expenses with you. And I have a couple of questions."

"I'm at Casa-U-Betcha on First with a friend."

"Ten minutes?"

"Wonderful."

26

CASA-U-BETCHA WAS A TRENDY Mexican restaurant where on Friday and Saturday nights the noise of the wall-to-wall singles in the bar made eating a rather irregular experience, but where, if you dropped in during the week, you could get a terrific Caribbean jerked chicken without a lot of excess excitement.

Roxanne Lake and a friend were holding down a small sidewalk table in front of the restaurant, Roxanne wearing slacks, a blue jacket, large earrings that clanked when she turned her head, and a bone necklace that, judging from the way it dented her blouse, weighed at least a pound.

In his early fifties, her colleague had wispy white hair cut in tufts, which denoted either a very bad haircut or a very fashionable one, a black blazer, beige slacks, and a turtleneck sweater. He wore pince-nez glasses on the bridge of his stubby nose. His belly was as round as a small barrel, and his fingers looked too fat and short to play a piano or type, although he probably did both.

As I approached, they were playing a game where male pedestrians and the occasional male driver on First Avenue were rated according to perceived prestige, rank in the cosmos, and, most importantly, sexual prowess: all guess-work, of course, and self-parody, although I might have been mistaken about the self-parody. Regarding a lone male parallel parking a sports coupe across the street, Roxanne said, "He'd make an appalling lover. He's far too pretty to think about anybody but himself. Look at how he's decked himself out. Probably spent more time coordinating his outfit than you or I."

He said, "But give me a bungalow on the beach and two days with *that* one."

The game came to a halt when her male companion decided to acknowledge my presence, though Roxanne clearly would have made me listen to their inanities far longer. I wondered that Roxanne's universe had so easily broken me down to the social status of a servant. Not that I gave a damn.

Her companion was well known in the city both by sight and reputation, Charles Tibbeford, a painter who did portraits of children and picture books for New York publishers. His coffee-table books were perennial best-sellers in Seattle.

We shook hands and, on his insistence, exchanged cards, mine going into his billfold and his into my jacket pocket with some gum wrappers. I pulled a chair up to the table, and when the waiter appeared, I ordered a Sprite while the two of them giggled like a couple of sixth-grade girls who'd found a dirty book. We waited for the order in silence, and after some moments Roxanne sized up the situation. "You can talk in front of Charlie. Charles and I are very close."

"I must be going," Charles said gently.

"Don't be silly," Roxanne said.

"I would rather keep this discussion private," I said.

"Charlie *is* private, for God's sake. I told you."

"Some things have entered into this."

"Now you've intrigued Charlie, and he simply has to stay."

"No. I must go," he said, but she leaned against him, weighted his forearm down.

"Okay. Sure. Seven years ago Philip was your lover. You hire me to follow your ex-lover, because, you say, he is possibly going to injure the foster brother of a young man you have as a house guest? There are a lot of alternate scenarios for why you might have hired me, Roxanne, and a lot of people besides a paranoid detective would jump to conclusions."

She turned pink, blinking, the smile on her lips slipping and then turning into a faltering grimace. It was only then that I noticed her makeup had been applied in a slipshod manner. Her cheeks were too low.

"If you want me to tail somebody, you should be candid from the beginning."

"I was candid. Philip was not my lover."

"Your ex-husband swears he was."

"He was *one* of my lovers."

"There's a difference?"

"You have a gold coin, or you have a bag of coins."

"Anyway, some honest background would have helped a lot. And saved you money, besides."

"And Jerome. He's a guest in my house for a few days. Nothing more. Now. About this other. Would you like me to list my lovers? Is that it?"

"Oooooo," said Charles. "I really must be going. This is all very delicious, but it is not something for my tender ears. You can fill me in later, precious." Tibbeford stood, gave me a plump hand, and said, "If she's really going to list all her lovers, you'll need someone who takes shorthand. It's been agreeable, Thomas. I hope we bump into each other soon."

"Sure."

He leaned down, kissed Roxanne on the cheek, and whispered, "I approve. I definitely approve." When Tibbeford walked away, he looked like the back end of a dizzy pig in trousers.

Being turned into an object in their game while I was

still within earshot annoyed me in a big way, but the comment had not been Mrs. Lake's, and the look she directed across First Avenue gave little enough hint of sanction.

"Mr. Black, I didn't realize one of the prerequisites for hiring a private detective was providing a list of former lovers."

"Why would it be unless you're asking me to follow a former lover?"

"I don't think it's that simple. You've been getting into things I didn't ask you to get into. And why were you talking to Jon?"

"A thing like this leads where it leads, Mrs. Lake. I spoke to Jon because he was one of the people who interrupted the assault that put Billy behind bars. Because he lives across the alley from the house of a man Billy visited Friday night."

"Clark?"

"That's right."

"How is the old man?"

"I imagine about the same as the last time you saw him."

"He was a dear. I still can't get over this thing about my lovers." She lit a cigarette and sucked until her mouth was a hundred radiating lines. "Would you like me to start with my best friend's father in eleventh grade? I was sixteen, almost seventeen, and I had about one lousy date a year. If that. Samantha's dad got stinko one night when I was sleeping over, and I managed to end up in bed with him, where I promptly, a little too promptly I found out later, lost my virginity. He cried afterward. Isn't that rich? I had had a crush on him for ages, and I couldn't have been more tickled with myself. This is how stupid I was. I thought we were going to run off together and get married."

"I didn't mean to embarrass you, Mrs. Lake."

"Don't be silly. I wasn't embarrassed. Want more? It probably would have helped if I had computerized things so we could do this in chronological order, or in reverse chronological order. Or alphabetical. Or would you prefer a list of the lovers I've had while married? Jon sometimes wanted the details before he would sleep with me. Am I shocking you, Thomas?"

"Forget it."

"Just wondering."

What I wanted to say was that I thought she had thumbed through too many bad novels and eaten yogurt in front of too many old French movies. "I'm not interested in your life story, Mrs. Lake. Just in your relationship to a man you've asked me to follow. I wouldn't be the first detective tailing some sap for reasons that were bogus."

She sipped her margarita and eyeballed me over it. She was annoyed, but at the same time she liked me a whole lot better for having had the nerve to put her on the spot. "You believe I've hired you under false pretenses, Thomas? Is that what you believe?"

"I'm asking, is all."

She watched a car rumble by and didn't speak until we could both smell a gritty whiff of exhaust. "I'm still trying to figure out how to give you this list of my lovers."

"Forget it. I only need to know about Philip."

"Your job is to keep Philip from hurting Billy or vice versa. That was the arrangement. I didn't hire you to come back to me with tidbits like this about Philip."

"You don't get it," I said. "What we have here are a number of complications you might have warned me about but didn't. One, you and Philip had some sort of affair. Two, he didn't get over it and made a practice of hanging around your house. Hanging around the alley in back, the alley where Billy was arrested. Three, Billy was not jailed for assaulting a stranger, the way I was led to believe. He tried to kill his foster brother. It seems an odd thing not to have mentioned at our first meeting. Four, when I told you the other night I had followed Philip and Battle to Portland, you didn't mention you had lived in Portland. Nor did you mention that your fourth husband was murdered there."

Roxanne Lake sat back and surveyed me while the emotions ranged across her face. I was sure she imagined she had an excellent poker face, and I was even more certain she would have been stunned to know that every little thought danced across her features the way it might on a sassy little girl.

"Listen, I was still a fairly young woman when I decided to do what most of you men have been doing from birth, to divorce love from sex. Granted, it's harder for a woman. After all, we have these hormones raging around inside telling us to have babies and keep house and wash dishes and all that crap. I guess I got hurt enough times when I was younger that I gave up on the big L word. And since I got wise, life has been a whole hell of a lot simpler, believe you me."

It was sad testimony made more miserable by what I had witnessed Friday at the pool house.

"Okay. Your points one by one. Yeah, Phil and I had a fling. Yeah, Phil didn't take it all that well when I wanted to move on to greener pastures. I suppose I should have made a clean break of it, but he would hang around and plead and I would relent and it would continue. And sure, Billy stabbed Jerome. It was in all the papers. I wasn't going to harp on it with Jerome in the room. Jerome seems regular enough, Thomas, but he went through years of counseling. He majored in psychology in college the way a lot of people who are messed-up major in psychology. I'm sure you realize, psychiatrists are the most screwed up people on earth. Every major nut case I went to high school with is a psychiatrist now. Either that, or he killed himself in medical school."

"Go on."

"My last husband, Randall Lake, was murdered. It too is a matter of public record, and it has absolutely nothing to do with this."

"I think there's a possibility that it does."

"I very much doubt that."

"In Portland. Up in the hills north of Burnside. You

lived on Monte Vista in a Spanish-style house with a tile roof. Big yard."

"My, my. You *have* been digging. This is going to make a great cocktail party anecdote. I'm paying a detective to tell me about myself."

"Battle spent most of the night Monday before last in Portland parked outside a house on Monte Vista." I gave her the address. She nodded. It was her old house. "Philip followed him and stayed out of sight. Why would Billy go there?"

"Look. Can't you just hire some gorillas to bust him up? If he was in the hospital, none of this would be happening."

"Battle?"

"Philip. Philip is the problem. If we can get Philip into line, the rest of this should resolve itself. Nothing really serious. Break his arms, both of them." She thought about it. "Maybe his thumbs too."

"I hope you're being facetious, Mrs. Lake."

"Isn't he going to marry your girlfriend? I would think you would be delighted to see him in plaster."

"Let's get this straight, Roxanne. Philip is not the problem. Philip is following Billy because he thinks Billy is on the verge of doing something ugly. I'm beginning to think so too. One of the things Billy is doing is chasing around in your past. Why would he do that?"

"This is a decidedly sore subject. I divorced Jon and married Randall in the space of about a month. Six weeks later Randall was dead."

"Did Billy ever come on to you?"

"Why do you ask a question like that?"

"Because . . . kids get funny ideas sometimes. They hear stories about somebody, the way he might have heard stories about you. Kids hear stories and they begin thinking about somebody in a totally new light. You have to remember, if you took the hormones out of any teenager on earth and injected them into an adult, they would probably be committed to an insane asylum within hours."

"You're probably right about that. I don't think he ever came on to me. No. You know, Thomas . . . I'm not sure . . ."

"What?"

"Nothing."

For the first time that afternoon, I could not read her face.

27

"I MET RANDALL LAKE WHILE I WAS still married to Jon at a party somebody from work gave. He was the wealthiest man I had ever met, and, even though he was twenty years older—well, thirty years older—he was still young at heart. He took me to Disneyland on our honeymoon. And then Hawaii because he had always wanted to ride a boogie board, and then to Bangkok. He was the kind of guy who would tell a dirty joke in an elevator just to make all the blue hairs tighten up, and then he would turn around and work in a soup kitchen every Thanksgiving and Christmas.

"Six weeks after we were married, two burglars broke into our home in Portland and butchered him. They probably thought nobody was home. Like a lot of wealthy people, Randall liked to pinch pennies, and part of that was keeping most of the lights off most of the time. If I had been there, instead of up here fooling around with Philip, I probably would have been killed too."

"You were fooling around with Philip the night your husband was murdered?"

She sighed and her face sagged. "Philip was with me. The cops found out, but it never got in the papers. The cops didn't think much of me, and I guess for a while I took it pretty hard myself. The Portland police became suspicious because Philip and I had an argument and he left my place in time to have driven down and killed Randall."

"What sort of argument?"

"At first it was yelling, but then it got physical. I slapped him and scratched him and kicked him, even. He mostly curled up on the floor and took it. Finally, he shoved me into some furniture and ran out crying."

"Philip?"

"Oh, he used to cry all the time. Anyway, when they found the actual killers a couple of days later, it put Philip out of contention. I never even went to the funeral. Randall's relatives thought I was cold, but I really could not make myself go. I won't say we had a raging romance, Randall and I, but we were well suited to each other, and if that night had not happened, we'd be together still."

"Who killed him?"

"Runaways. One was seventeen and the other sixteen. Street kids. They'd been on the loose for about a year. Homosexual hustling. Burglary. Shoplifting. Car prowls. Rolling winos. Their names were Harold Turner Weissman and Kenneth Toby Senters."

"Why would Billy Battle be interested in a seven-year-old murder that had nothing to do with him?"

"I have no idea. You know about his former girlfriend, don't you?"

"That she came up missing?"

"Everyone in the neighborhood assumed that he killed her. That was maybe six months before he tried to kill Jerome."

"I'm concerned about Billy's interest in Monte Vista in Portland. Billy has also been prowling the old neighborhood. He's talked to at least one of the people who witnessed against him. What I've been trying to tell you is that I need to know about some of these other things. Philip knows about them. Billy knows about them. Remember, I'm not a reporter for the *National Inquirer.* I'm working for you."

"What do you want to know?"

"Has Philip been in contact with you?"

"Not for two or three years. Yes, he was twenty-four and I'm pretty sure I was his first love. What can I say?" The pride in accomplishment came out in a small, simpering smile. "He spent most of that year I was divorcing Jon trying to convince me to move in with him and marry him. I said, 'Hey, this is silly. I'm so much older than you.' We broke up, I don't know, three, four different times. After one of them, our house was broken into. Jon thought Philip did it.

"The only things missing were some underthings of mine and some old love letters I had stored away. But it fit the pattern. Almost everyone in the area had been hit. Billy was doing it. I'm sure of it."

"Was anything like that stolen from the other houses? Underwear and love letters?"

"Not that I ever heard about. Lord only knows why Billy took those things."

I had been thinking all along that Billy might have had an obsession with her, but I didn't say anything. "But your husband thought it was Philip?"

"The scorned lover and all that. Then when I married Randall, Philip really went crazy. He called me up one night and said he was so blue he was thinking about killing himself."

"Is that how you got back together?"

"Basically. I drove up from Portland to talk some sense into him. The night Randall was murdered, that was the last time I saw Philip. I said some things about his manhood I probably shouldn't have. He called me a tramp. That's when we fought."

"Mrs. Lake, the costs on this are starting to mount."

"I told you before. Cost means nothing to me." I presented her with a bill, which prompted her to take out her checkbook and dash off a check. She sipped from her drink and watched while I fingered the check. I noticed for the first time that the tip of her nose was perfectly blunt, so that if she slept on her back, somebody could have balanced pennies on it. "I have to see my broker and then I'm going to play racquetball at the club. Do you play?"

"No. Sorry," I said, lying because it was easier. I was more convinced than ever Roxanne was holding back, but as long as she was paying the bills and giving the orders, I would let her string me along. Sooner or later I would find out her secrets anyway. "Did you ever sleep with Billy?"

"I told you he never came on to me."

"The questions aren't the same."

She was quiet for a moment. "Dear heavens, no. Everybody knew he was a psychopath. I like my kicks, but not like that."

"What about Jerome?"

"What are you asking me?"

"Have you slept with Jerome? I know this is very personal, but if you have, it might explain some of the things Billy is doing. I think he might have a crush on you."

"This is too personal."

"Then forget I ever asked. I apologize."

"No. No. You deserve an answer. Besides, I'm the one who told you I have nothing to hide. My love life is something I've always kept in the open. No. Don't be ridiculous. Jerome has grave problems. He doesn't need some ex-slut like me sucking his blood. Jerome is like a son to me. I have not been sleeping with Jerome.

"I've only just learned some of Jerome's early life. It's actually fairly fascinating. Jerome's mother was married to a man named Johnson back in Philadelphia, then she married Twerligger and moved out here with him. His mother had two girls with Twerligger, Jerome's younger sisters.

Then, when Jerome was ten, his father put some hot ashes next to a wall and the house burned down. Everyone in the family died except Jerome. I guess one of his sisters survived twenty-four hours. He was a ward of the state for about a week when Mrs. Blodgett took him in. She had lost a son in a tragedy a few years earlier, and I think she had an empty spot she thought Jerome could fill. He turned into a pretty normal kid."

"Did Jerome ever tell you what the stabbing was all about?"

"Jerome has a real hard time talking about that time, and I don't push him on it. You know, Thomas, you've got me thinking. Ten days ago when Jerome told me he'd seen Philip watching the house, the first thought that came to me was that Philip was back and was as obsessed as ever. But then, when I spoke to Elmer Slezak about it, he told me Philip was engaged."

"He thinks he's engaged."

"Is she nice?"

"Nice enough she deserves better."

"Philip did some strange things seven years ago. When I heard Philip had followed Jerome and Billy to Bellevue Square, I was sure it wasn't about me. Now, you've got me wondering."

"Let me keep working on it. We'll find out. What about these guys who killed your husband?"

"Weissman and Senters. Their fingerprints were found inside the house. They had bearer bonds traceable to Randall. Credit cards. Some of his clothing. And they had a small tape recorder Randall had only recently purchased. And of course, they both claim they're innocent."

28

IT WAS TUESDAY NIGHT AND MITchelli's was jammed. An insurance company from up the street was throwing some sort of bash, so the atmosphere was raucous. The lawyers from our office were there, as well as boyfriends, husbands, and two male companions Beulah had invited.

Kathy was sitting alone in a booth near the door under an Italian movie poster. When I sat down across from her, we accidentally bumped our knees under the table, and she immediately pulled back. Her dark hair was hanging loose and her violet eyes glittered with the coldness of museum stones.

"I'm sorry. I'm here with Philip. I believe he's in the other room conferring with your buddy, Elmer Slezak. I wish you would quit introducing Snake to my friends."

"I didn't introduce them."

"I could have sworn Philip said you introduced them."

"He probably did say that."

"But you just said you didn't."

"That's right. I didn't."

"Anyway, I don't want Snake in the office. Ever again."

"Don't high-hat me, Kathy. It's my office too. I'm working a case for a client. Despite what he's telling you, some of it overlaps Philip's past. More of it overlaps his present." Kathy clucked her tongue and stared off behind me at the revelers from the insurance company. "You are very testy tonight," I said.

"I'm still waiting for you to tell me you're no longer investigating Philip." I shrugged. There was nothing else to do.

When I walked past the telephone and into the men's room, I felt as if I were walking out of one life and into another. There was no mistaking Kathy's realignment of allegiances.

I met Philip in the tight passageway between the restaurant and the pizza parlor. He pretended he had not seen me and tried to squeeze past. "Hey, hombre," I said, blocking his route. Even after he stopped and looked me in the face, it took a moment or two before he allowed recognition to set. "Are you being good?"

"Busy. I've been busy." He winked. "What have you found out about Billy?"

"Phil, I want to talk to you, but right now I need to see Snake."

"Kathy said you asked her to stop seeing me. She said you're trying to break up our marriage plans. I don't screw around in your life. Why screw around in mine?"

"I didn't ask her to stop seeing you. I asked her to start seeing me." For the briefest of moments his shoulders tightened, as did a cord in his neck. His left hand doubled up into a fist and it looked as if he were going to throw a punch.

"You know what I think? I think you're scum. That was a miserable thing to do, trying to break up our marriage plans."

"Have you told her you were implicated in a Portland murder seven years ago?"

Philip reverted into a cardboard cutout of himself, stiff and flat and motionless. Though it lasted only four or five seconds, it seemed like minutes, and when it ended he sputtered, "If anything happens to my friend Walter Clark because of your shenanigans, I'll see that you pay. You understand?"

"Kathy hates a liar. When she discovers all this bullshit you've been spreading around, she's going to hit the roof."

"There's no reason for profanity. Besides, Kathy's already hit the roof, old boy. All she talks about anymore is how you've changed. In fact, the other day she called you a rat."

"Thank you for sharing that with me."

"You have to understand, at this point all I can do is commiserate with the old girl."

He laughed as he strode away. At the end of the corridor he turned and said, "By the way, we thought early December would be about right for the wedding. Think you can make it?" He winked again. The brown one.

29

SNAKE WAS HUNCHED OVER A STEIN of beer at the bar. He wore his silver-toed, silver-heeled cowboy boots, a Stetson, well-worn jeans that made his spindly legs look like blue pencils, and a tweed sport coat with elbow patches over a fringed cowboy shirt. I knew he had a gun in his hat and a knife in his boot, but in addition to that, his favorite revolver, a long-barrelled Ruger Blackhawk, was generating a bulge under his jacket even the bartender could pick out. I scooted onto a stool beside him and ordered a 7 UP.

"You look a little down in the mouth," Snake said. "Life going sour on you?"

"You could say that."

"Let's drink to it being a temporary situation."

"Sure. Yeah. Thanks."

"Hey. You see that gal at the end of the bar standing next to Grandma? You think there's something strange about her? Some of those transvestites can really do a number with the makeup pencil."

"I've left messages all over the state for you, Snake."

"You think she's a man? Does that sound like a man's laugh?"

"Tell me where Billy is."

Slurping foam from the top of his beer, Snake eyed me over the thick rim of the glass and said, "What's the matter, you lose track of the little maniac?"

"You already take him out and shoot him, did you?"

"You actually lost him?"

"Friday was the last time I saw him. I was in court yesterday and today. I know you know where he is."

"Don't rip your shorts over it. We'll find him."

"Tell me the truth. Are you and Philip setting up a hit?"

"You wired?"

"Don't get paranoid, Snake. You know we're friends. I wouldn't wear a wire on you."

"We're on the side of law and order, here, Thomas. You and me both. And Phil. Don't get yourself confused about that."

"You talk Lake into hiring me to find out why Philip is following Billy, without telling her that you and Philip are following Billy. Then I talk Philip into letting me follow Billy, which you're getting paid for, by myself, while you sit on the sidelines earning your fee from Philip and trying to wrangle part of my fee to boot. So here I am, doing your job twice over and you tell me not to get confused."

"I did you a favor. I heard you refer to Phil as the Mutant from Magnolia and I figured you wouldn't mind following him around. Admit it. You were having a good time."

"Some favor. Kathy barely speaks to me now."

"Don't blame me if you can't keep your babes in line. For years I been telling you all she ever needed was a good poke."

"Just be careful. You're talking about my best friend in the world, here."

"Sure. Lake say anything about me?"

"She said you remind her of a little banty rooster."

"Did she now?"

"When she said that, I realized she must have seen the tattoo on your belly. Must have been to bed with you."

"Never made it even close to a bed. Did it on her kitchen floor. She wanted to be on top, but I told her when you get to be my age, you need gravity feed. She actually said that? Little banty rooster?"

"Let's get back to Battle. Friday I followed him until midnight and then let him go, thinking he would stay home. But he didn't spend the night there. Or the next night either. Since then I've checked the jails, hospitals, and the neighborhoods where he hangs out. Checked the impound lots for his mother's car. I can't find him, but I don't think he's left town. He's got too much unfinished business."

Snake polished off his beer and observed the woman at the end of the bar who was wearing, among other things, a beret and a pair of three-dimensional reindeer earrings large enough to ornament a Christmas tree.

"You think she's a guy? Damn, she looks flighty as all get-out. I like flighty women even more than I like depressed women. Depressed women are hard to get next to but they expect nothing once you get there. In fact, they would rather be disappointed, that way you don't upset their edition of the world. Flighty women, on the other hand, are not afraid to get involved on a whim. Flighty women are disappointed when nothing much comes of an episode, but they're so flighty they usually come up with their own rationalizations for it. This gal I was going with last year told me she was sure I walked out on her because

I had a terminal illness and didn't want her to know. Pancreatitis, she figured. With flighty women, you don't even have to make up your own excuses."

"If she's a man, that'll be the third one you've accidentally picked up since I've known you, Snake."

"She's ugly enough to be a man. Doesn't she have a great laugh, though? I'd almost go with a man to be around that laugh."

"I know you know where Billy is."

Snake was a secret keeper. It was the reason he had been attracted to police work first and private investigations second. He liked secrets, discovering them, keeping them, spilling them, but most of all, knowing them. When you knew secrets, you *knew*. And *knowing* was a state of mind preferable to all others.

"He ripped off some stuff and took it to his mother's. Then he took off with some hood he met on the street helped him carry the goods."

"Go on," I said.

"His new buddy got into it with him, over money I think, tried to smack him with a stick, but before he could get a good windup, Billy broke his arm like it was a piece of kindling. I heard the sound from across the street in my car. Battle is some piece of work. You stay away from him. He's been drinking and doing drugs with a Seattle U student he met Friday night. Shacked up in some condo she's house-sitting in. He's only been out a couple of times since they shacked up. Broke into nearby apartments, stole CD players, televisions, cash, jewelry, and three pistols. I watched him sell two of the guns on the street. Then he went out yesterday afternoon and bought shells for a .357 Magnum. I lost him in traffic and ain't seen him since."

"You need a gun in this town, you just break into a house. Everybody's got one."

"That's right."

"Roxanne hired me to keep Philip and Billy away from each other, but since she hired me, they've both armed themselves. Now Billy has vanished. And you? You fall into a swimming pool and we'll never get you off the bottom. You're carrying enough steel to retrofit the *Missouri*."

"You would too, if you thought about it."

"He didn't go back to the condo?"

"No, nor to his mother's." Snake reached across to an ashtray, retrieved a matchbook, and wrote the address and the name of the young woman Billy had stayed with. "I know what you're thinking. I already talked to her. They fucked and did drugs. She didn't even know he had been in prison. He never said jack shit."

"You two are planning to kill him, aren't you?"

"What? Just because his girlfriend in high school disappeared a week after she broke up with him? Just because his best friend's house burns down when he's ten years old and of the whole family, only his friend survives? Just because the four-year-old kid who lives next door happens to drown in his wading pool? Just because every house in his neighborhood gets burgled? Just because he took a kitchen knife and tried to hack his foster brother to pieces? Just because he's planning to off an old man who had the balls to testify against him?"

"You're planning to kill him."

"A man commits a crime, Thomas, he commits a crime. He talks about it with somebody else, he's putting his own ass in a sling. Conspiracy. Most people get nabbed for something because somewhere along the line they opened their yaps and palavered where they shouldn't have. We might be planning something. We might not."

"You have any idea what you're getting yourself into?"

"You don't think I can do it?"

"I know you can do it. Just look in the paper. Anybody can do it. But it'll kill you."

"Phil's friend, Walter Clark, has been getting threats on his life."

"Walter didn't mention them to me."

"He's a proud man. And he wouldn't let us use the phone company to trace the calls. Or call the police neither. Philip only found out because he was over to the old man's place when he got one of the calls. A little later, the old man gets a call where somebody is laughing. Nothing else, just laughing."

"Philip didn't tell me all of this," I said angrily.

"Maybe you haven't noticed, but Philip doesn't much care for you."

I explained about the laughing calls I had been getting.

Snake said, "On the Larry King radio show years ago there used to be a nut would call up every once in a while. They'd put him through and he would laugh. Nothing else. Larry called him the Portland Laugher. It was weird."

"Did you realize my client had an affair with your client?"

"Phil and Roxanne? Gawd! She's old enough to be his mother."

"She was friends with his mother."

Snake buried the tips of three fingers in the scruffy beard growth on his throat, scratching and humming almost as if his throat were a kitten. "Well, well, well."

"Did you know Philip was a suspect in the murder of her fourth husband? Roxanne's."

I gave Slezak the details. When I finished, he said, "Thomas, I'm starting to get a real bad feeling about this."

"Like somebody's being had?"

"The trouble is, is it you or is it me?"

"I don't know. Look, we're both after the same thing. Why not pool our resources?"

"You know a gentleman named Dietrich?"

"Seattle Homicide."

"I took him out and had drinks with him the other night. He was in charge of the Alberg case seven years ago."

"Refresh my memory."

"Fifteen-year-old girl turns up missing in Madrona. Her ex-boyfriend, Billy, who she had jilted a week earlier, leads the neighborhood search party to a vacant house. It's been broken into and resealed. The girl's sweater is found inside. The cops, who are suspicious of Billy from the outset, think at first Billy has planted the sweater himself.

"Outside the house in the grass, a police dog discovers a severed finger that looks like it came off a woman. Six months later the FBI lab matches the nail polish to a bottle in the Alberg girl's bedroom.

"There were no fingerprints except for a few put there inadvertently by the adult males in the search party and the first cop. In the house they discover a spot on the hardwood floor where somebody has hammered about sixty nails into the flooring. In the shape of a human body. Yeah, that's right. Nailed her to the floor. By her clothing, they think.

"Dietrich found some surgeon's tools that had been stolen earlier that same year. They had been washed very carefully and laid out in a kitchen drawer, side by side. They ripped up that whole section of flooring and sent it to the state lab. They found blood, same type as the Alberg girl's.

"Dietrich took Billy Blodgett in for questioning. He didn't want a lawyer, but they had one there for him anyway, him being a minor and all. They weren't going to take any chances. Everybody involved knew Blodgett had done it. But they never got beans out of him. Not even with a polygraph. He's a full-blown sociopath, Thomas. Got no conscience whatsoever. He put something over on Dietrich, and when he was doing it he knew he was doing it, and they knew he knew they knew he was doing it."

"Could it have been somebody else killed her?"

"Yeah, and maybe his brother cut himself up in that alley. And maybe the bogeyman up at Echo Glen tied Billy's counselor to a chair and invited his friends in. Yeah, sure, maybe."

We had the waiter replenish our drinks while we surveyed the crowd in Mitchelli's. I said, "Philip used to hang out in that alley behind old man Clark's house and pine away for Roxanne. Her house was across the alley. I'm not sure, but I think the old man might know something he doesn't know he knows."

Snake stared at me with interest. "You sure about this?"

"Billy has been poking around in the murder of Roxanne's husband, a murder for which Philip was questioned. He's been to the old man's house. There are some snarls that need to be untangled here."

"Clients are always hiding shit."

I told Slezak where Billy had been Friday night, about his vigil in Madrona, the prowling, about getting lost in Bellevue, the long wait outside the pool house at Hunt's Point.

"Thomas? Why don't you and I go pay old Walter a visit? I'll betcha between the two of us we can convince him to let the phone company put a tap on his phone."

"It's a little late for a visit."

"Clark stays up for Arsenio."

"That's right. He does." On the way out of Mitchelli's I noticed Kathy and Philip were long gone, another couple ensconced at their table.

30

ONCE IN MY TRUCK, ELMER SLEZAK sat like a kid, with one leg and boot up on the bench seat and his spine squared up against the door so that should it pop open, he would shoot across the highway like a runaway corpse, a misadventure that had actually happened to Snake while taking a cab to his father's funeral, and, because it had happened to the kind of stubborn man that Snake was, he reacted in the nature of stubborn men by sitting that way pretty much exclusively from then on.

Dark thoughts about Philip and Kathy hounded me as I steered the Ford up the hill on Yesler. Snake courted his own hobgoblins. Neither of us spoke until we crested the hill and Bellevue's skyline peeked at us from the other side of Lake Washington like a comic book metropolis.

"We get Blodgett alone for a couple of hours, we could *make* him see the truth," Snake muttered, as if a ventriloquist were working him, his jaw clicking woodenly from some long forgotten horse-stomping or barroom imbroglio. His dim eyes looked as if they had been painted onto his head. "We might even get him to admit killing his girlfriend."

"None of it will help you in court."

"The court's got nothing to do with this, Thomas. The courts set that little maniac free. I know you're hoping the cops'll get him. You hope all you want, but hope is for when you're playing cards or flirting with some señorita. When you get down to blood and bone, hope isn't anything but a liar and a cheat. We gotta get him off the street. If we can get him in jail for the Alberg girl, so be it. If we can't, then we'll do something else. Maybe we get him where some bleeding-heart liberal lawyer isn't holding his hand and patting his fanny, maybe he just might begin to see the world through different lenses."

"I don't like it, Snake. You're playing this like some kung fu movie, and it doesn't work that way in real life."

When I reached to open my truck door, Snake touched my forearm and spoke in a soft voice I had not heard all evening. "Of course I realize we're buying front-row tickets for hell, Thomas. I ain't no moron. Hell is something you volunteer for. I know that. Philip is volunteering. I'm volunteering."

"It's an ugly world, Elmer, when you can convince yourself it's all right to kill somebody."

"Just quit psycho-annihilating the situation and try to use your head."

"That's what I'm doing. Using my head."

Snake squared up both feet on the floor mat in the truck and faced the windshield, arms limp at his side, head drooping as if he were about to nod off. "Let me tell you what I haven't been telling you, Thomas."

I looked across at him.

"I found myself with access to some detailed notes no-body else has seen. A gal named Sherry Finkelstein was his public defender. She's not practicing anymore. Got a face you could clean bricks on. Sherry claims Billy knew the girl was dead two days before they even mounted a search. He told her that later. Admitted it. Even knew how she had been kidnapped, a belt looped over her head from behind and tightened up until she lost consciousness. He went into some detail for Sherry, all without emotion, the way all these sociopaths are. Then the little molester had the nerve to claim he didn't have anything to do with it. He had a thousand theories about who did though."

"Did she believe him?"

"Hell, no. Billy's description was so vivid, Finkelstein still has nightmares over it. Claimed the girl had been held two days and two nights. It wasn't long after that Finkelstein quit the law. She's been clerking for five dollars an hour in a carpet place in South Park. She knew the cops already thought he did it. She could have said something to them. She wanted to. But she knew if she did and it ever came out in a subsequent trial, her actions could overturn a guilty verdict, and she sure as hell did not want to be responsible for freeing the little son of a bitch."

We thought about that for a while. Then we got out of the truck and approached the house. The streetlight outside Walter Clark's house spotlighted his dying vegetable garden so that the withered cornstalks and staked chrysanthemums looked like long-armed wraiths come to spook the neighbors. Several lights were on in Walter Clark's shack, the porch light, and inside in the back somewhere, another dim and steady glow.

I knocked lightly on Clark's door. No answer. I knocked

again. "Somebody's been here," said Snake. "I can smell
'em. It's like that scary, sweaty smell after bad sex."

"Scary, sweaty what?"

"You never had bad sex? It's that stuff you have with
your wife's divorce lawyer just before she takes you to the
cleaners. Later on she sends you a telegram telling you she
had VD."

I knocked again, louder. Crowding me away from the
door, Snake pressed his ear to the shabby wooden panel
and grew still. After some moments he removed the horse
pistol from under his jacket, cocked it, then stood back and
swung it up toward the door.

"Clark's not the kind of man to go to bed with the lights
on," he said.

"Put the gun away."

"We don't know what's in there."

"All the more reason to put the gun away." He shook
his head. I grabbed his forearm and held it. He tried to
move, failed, and used both arms trying to budge me. Toe
to toe, eye to eye, we struggled. My grip began leaching
the color from Snake's face. Finally, I grinned. After a moment he grinned too. Then he laughed and released the
tension on his arm and uncocked the pistol.

"Somebody's in there," he said. "Listen."

"Let's listen without the gun."

Pressing an ear up against the paint-peeled panels, I
heard the muffled sound of breathing through the thin
wood. It sounded as if somebody had his head up against
the other side of the door in basically the same posture I
was in.

"Walter. It's Thomas Black. I saw you Saturday. I'm
with a man named Elmer Slezak. I believe you've already
met Elmer. Walter? We would like to talk to you."

I pressed my ear up against the door once more and began to get a feeling that was difficult to describe, of im-
pending doom. Only once or twice in my life had I
experienced a sensation akin to this.

For a moment Snake and I exchanged looks and shared

one of those split-second, incredibly congruent moments you share with another human being maybe once every two or three years. Maybe never. We both knew. Neither one of us needed to put it into words, yet there was something in the air. Either Snake and I were turning into a couple of whacked-out paranoid conspiracy theorists with psychopaths on the brain, or there was something cock-eyed about this setup.

I gestured for him to guard the front door while I went around the face of the house. The tiny living room window behind the magnolia was obscured by old-fashioned yellowed shades pulled down snug with the warped wooden sill. Through a lighted chink along the edge I glimpsed part of the kitchen and a slice of the ancient refrigerator. I made my way through the flower beds and around the corner to the north kitchen window.

Adrenaline pooled in my stomach like old lies.

Edges curling, three crayoned pictures done by children were fondly affixed to the face of the refrigerator by magnets. On the yellow-topped, steel-legged table sat a small toaster alongside painted salt and pepper shakers. A piece of untouched cinnamon toast lay on a paper napkin on the edge of the kitchen table. In the living room, oversized crayons and a tablet were spread out on the low wooden tea table.

It wasn't until I took a step to the right of the window to get a better angle that I spotted him.

Walter Clark was up against the front door, a cork-screwed look of anguish on his face.

He was on his knees facing into the house, tilted backward at an awkward angle that was especially ungainly for a man of his age.

Mouth bound by several large pieces of gray duct tape wrapped completely around his head, Clark was clawing at his throat with his gnarled fingers.

It took me thirty seconds to figure out how it had been rigged. A section of piano wire six feet long ran through a steel eyebolt affixed to the wall beside his neck. From there it wrapped around his throat snugly and ran across his body into another steel eyebolt buried in the door lintel. The wire passed across the front door. Had we gone in the front, the edge of the door would have pushed on the wire and the wire would have ripped through Walter Clark's throat.

A gentle push would have killed him. Anything more and his head would have rolled onto the rug.

Before I could think about it, the front doorknob began to twist.

"Snake!" I screamed. I pushed off the house, hurdled a shrub, lost a shoe, skidded on the slippery grass rounding the corner, and bounced out of a three-point landing. "No! No! Don't do it! No!"

At the front of the house I gathered a fair amount of speed while Snake glanced casually over at me, one foot hoisted in the air to kick open the door.

The look of calm never left his face. He had undoubtedly heard me, but to his alcohol-dulled senses and paranoia-riddled mind, my pleas meant little. He had decided to do it. He was going to kick the door in.

I sailed through the air like a cornerback, taking both legs out from under him. The momentum of my flight knocked him off the porch and, for an instant, we were airborne in a tangle of legs, guns, grunts, silver-toed boots, and curses.

Somewhere from within the eye of our dervish, I heard a thud, but the fracas had begun and ended so quickly I could not be certain whether the noise was Snake's boot against the front door or our impact in the soft garden earth.

31

IN THE CONFUSION, I HAD TAKEN SOME-
thing hard and sharp against my right
cheek, could feel my flesh begin to numb up and pulse
with my accelerated heartbeat. We were twined together
like two wrestling drunks. I looked up. The door was still
closed, although it might have bounced open and then
slammed shut.

"You gone loco?" Snake asked, spitting out a mouthful
of earth. "Or was that a proposal of marriage?"

"The old man's wired to the door, Snake. You open it,
you kill him."

He embraced several moments of utter stillness while I
began untangling myself from the pileup, knees wet
against the damp ground, the fractured fence slats pricking
my ribs and chest. Snake's Ruger was beside my face, the
gun's barrel packed with moist dirt. The way his spindly
legs were wrapped around each other, I thought one of
them might be broken.

I pushed him off and tried to get up, felt a rusty nail stab
my left palm, then peered at the front door again.

Snake spat more dirt, wiped his face on his sleeve, and
said, "Damn! You hit me like some idiot schoolkid chasing
clown candy at a parade."

"What are you doing in Walter's garden?"

A pregnant woman stepped onto the porch, peering

down at Snake and then at me, a combination of amusement and suspicion in her dull green eyes. A dishwater
blonde, she was maybe twenty-three with a pitiless veneer
to her. She wore baggy, disheveled jeans and a green top
stretched over a bulging belly. She walked swaybacked,
the way some pregnant women do, as if to magnify their
achievement, or alleviate their discomfort. Her left arm
sported a tattoo of a motorcycle. Another tattoo on her
hand, homemade, spelled out the letters L-O-V-E, probably
stitched back in her teens on a rainy afternoon. Maybe in
jail.

Brushing her shoulders limply, her hair had been dyed
the wrong shade for her wan skin tone, so that it drained
the color from her face and made her look like a cartoon
woman somebody had taken an eraser to.

She had a hand on the front door and was ready to go
in. The only thing stopping her was our spectacle in the
flower bed.

"The door's screwed up," I yelled, leaping onto the
porch and pulling her hand off the knob. Snake was standing now, bending over to pick his hogleg up out of the dirt.
"Are you Nicole's mother?"

"I came to pick her up. What's going on here? Who are
you?"

"Listen carefully." I stepped between her and the door.
"I want you to walk back to your house and phone the police. Tell them—"

"I'm not walking anywhere! Who the hell are you to be
giving orders, asshole?"

"Look—"

"I'd be a fool to leave after seeing you two drunks in
the heather. My daughter's in there. And what the fuck is
the old geezer doing with that gun?"

"Elmer? I'm going around back to straighten things out.
I'll open it from the inside. Elmer?"

Cheeks smudged with garden residue, Snake clambered
onto the porch and clanked the .357 against his bony hip
to knock the dirt out of the barrel.

"Now you stand back off the porch, lady," he said. "We'll have you inside and reunited with the little pecker-wood in a jiffy."

"I will not stand back. I don't even know who you are. My daughter's . . ."

I jogged around the house. The sun porch at the back was empty, the screen door unlatched.

Through the back door, which had six small glass panes in the upper half, I spotted no people and no booby traps. The door was locked. Knocking out a pane with the edge of a flowerpot, I dressed the opening, dragging the pot around the square until the glass teeth were ground off, then reached inside and unlocked the door.

I walked through the kitchen, poked my head into the bedroom, the bathroom, and then the closet off the living room. I knelt beside Walter Clark. The wire had cut his neck under his chin, the skin of his face turning dark. His eyes were open, but unfocused, and too dark to tell if the pupils were reacting to light.

When I touched the wire, he gasped. "The little girl," I said. "Where is she?"

He could not talk, could barely breathe.

Outside the front door, Snake's dispute with the woman began escalating.

In the kitchen drawer there were no tools, just a set of mismatched silverware that Clark had probably picked up forty years ago at the Goodwill. On the screened-in back porch I located a battered mouse-gray toolbox, got out a pair of pliers and carried them back inside.

Even after I cut the wire near the eyebolt at the far right, even after I took all the slack out of the piano wire and un-loosed it from his neck, even after he pulled the duct tape off his face and took several deep breaths, even then he refused to relax. There was a trace of blood in the per-fectly straight line that ran around his throat.

I reached under his arms and helped him up off his knees, walked him across the room and assisted him onto the sofa. He was moving air even if he wasn't talking. The wind whistled in his nostrils and unspoken words gurgled in his throat. He smelled awful and bled onto me, bright red blood, from his nose.

"Where's the girl? Who did this? Did they take the girl?" Clark seemed almost embarrassed to have me in the room, as if he would rather die than have a witness to ignominy.

"Anybody here?" I said, approaching the closet door in the living room. The door handle was oblong and brass, darkened to a deep, greenish black, the sort of handle I recalled from my grandfather's home.

"Clark? Is she in here?"

He wagged his head sideways slowly. Somewhere deep in his dark eyes the life force was beginning to revive. Myriad possibilities lurked behind that door. A dead child. A muscular young man. Another surprise rigged up by Clark's intruder.

I cracked the closet door open half an inch, feeling no resistance, then scanned the length of the door for attachments, eyebolts, wires, little girls, maniacs. The closet held galoshes, two old coats hanging like poor ghosts on warped wire hangers, and a child's sweatshirt hooked on a wooden peg on the wall at the correct height for a child to hang it without help.

She wasn't in the living room or kitchen. She wasn't in the bathroom, not in the cabinet or the tub. Not behind the door. The bedroom was the barest and loneliest room in the house. If she wasn't here, he had taken her with him.

The bedroom had a dresser that had probably been secondhand when Clark got it. There were coins lined up in order of denomination and a shoehorn on the dresser top. Rabbit ears festooned with tinfoil topped a black and white portable television on a wooden stand, like some sort of exhibit from a museum of the shabby. Outrageously pretty women and bare-chested male models cavorted across a sunny beach on the mute television, selling beer or cars or maybe piano wire. Under the bed were two shoe trees and a bedraggled pair of slippers.

The bedroom closet was closed.

Standing to one side, I tapped the outside of the door. "Nicole?" I whispered. "Are you in there?"

"She run," said Clark from the other room in a raspy voice. "She run when he come."

Nicole wasn't in the closet, and neither was Billy Battle. A grouping of slope-shouldered shirts hanging off wire hangers greeted me, along with two dress hats on a shelf and a tatty robe hanging on the wall.

In the living room I could smell the funk of terror and the dour, stale smell of old age. I could smell the linoleum, the plaster and lath walls, shoe polish, the mild tang of an ammonia household cleaner. I could smell crayons. I could smell fear. But no matter how hard I tried, I could not smell a third man in the place.

Outside the front door, Slezak and the woman were conversing in normal tones now. I was not looking forward to telling her that her child was off somewhere in the night, maybe dead, maybe alive, maybe hauled off by a maniac.

I walked into the kitchen and, for some reason, opened the refrigerator door. He had one open can of beer and a shelf laden with juice containers like the one I had seen the little girl sipping from the other day. Cottage cheese. An open quart of milk.

"Who was it, Walter? Was it Billy Battle?"

"Dunno." I could see his reflection in the kitchen window. He was sitting like a cadaver propped up by pranksters.

"One? Two? How many of them?"

He held up one finger.

It was with a sick feeling in my stomach that I stood on a piece of linoleum that had bubbled slightly, rocked back and forth listening to the noise of it, like a piece of sticky tape being put on and torn off, put on and torn off. "Nicole," I whispered. "Nicole?" I might have stood there forever, since the alternative was confronting her mother. After a while I heard something somewhere deep in the bowels of the house.

"You got a root cellar, Walter?"

"Nope."

"Basement?"

"Nope."

It was a very tiny and very muffled noise. I stooped and began opening the kitchen cabinets. The third door had a flour sack, some spuds, and a little girl curled into a ball. Facedown, her blonde hair spilled across her shoulders. She did not move. She did not speak. She only looked at me sideways, thumb in her mouth, sucking. She watched to see what I would do.

I knelt lower and said, "Boy, am I glad to see you, Nicole. Your mommy's here. Right outside."

Springing out of the cubbyhole, she slapped her tiny hands together, then looked me over without recognition but with a great deal of trepidation. She was thirty-five pounds of blue eyes and plump cheeks and Osh-Kosh coveralls and shaky limbs and dimples and dread, and she was standing up against a man she had seen once and probably didn't remember at all.

"You're okay now," I said. "The bad person is gone. Your mommy's at the front door. Let's go see her."

Nicole's hand shot into mine and clutched tightly. The thumb on her other hand went into her mouth. I did not know how long Nicole had been hiding or what she had been thinking, but her own instincts had saved her life, and I had to applaud her for that. Now that it was time to trust somebody, I was glad to be the one.

She walked stiff-legged and refused to let go of my hand. In the living room she stared at Walter Clark, who in turn stared at a hooked throw rug under the battered coffee table. Tears of relief trickled down his face and across the white lines the tape had left.

When I opened the front door, Nicole looked up at her mother and spoke in a small, squeaky voice. "Bad boy gone."

32

"HE CAME TO THE DOOR. I THOUGHT it was Sumner, Nicole's mom. He had a gun. Talked in a whisper like I was a gal he was puttin' the make on. Put me against the front wall there. Looped the wire around my head, and before I knew it he was gone. I seen Nicole scamper into the kitchen behind his back while he had me at the door, so I threw a little conniption to keep him occupied. I guess it worked."

Clark didn't recall what his assailant was wearing or how tall he was, only that he was male, that he whispered, and that he wore a ski hood over his face and carried a revolver that he butted up against Clark's crotch. Clark could not swear to the caliber or make, only that it was large. Snake whispered to me, "Billy gets a piece; two days later this happens."

"Billy had a piece last Monday." I turned to Walter Clark. "Did you see his eyes?"

"I guess."

"Were they the same color?"

He thought about the question. "No way it was my friend Philip."

"What makes you so certain? Did you look at each eye?"

"No. But Philip wouldn't do such a thing."

"It was Blodgett," Snake said.

"I want to say it was, sir, but that is not something I can swear to," said Clark. "Not in court. This man was mean and he was about yea tall. That's all I really know."

Nicole's mother said, "It wasn't my old boyfriend, because he's in Walla Walla for stealing six motorcycles."

We all three stared at her.

An aid car from the Seattle Fire Department arrived just after the police. It was determined that Walter had suffered bruising and probably not too much else, though the recommendation was that he be seen by a doctor tonight, a recommendation he declined.

An evidence specialist collected fingerprints. It occurred to me that ten days earlier Battle had been there, a visit that would serve as a convenient explanation for any prints found tonight.

Patrol cars crawled through the neighborhood, wagging their spotlights through the shadows.

Walter admitted having received threatening phone calls during the past two weeks. The telephone voice, a whisperer too, had not been a voice he recognized.

Nicole's mother accused Walter Clark of endangering both her and her daughter by not telling her about the threats, then told him he would not see Nicole again, and marched out the door with her daughter in tow.

"Foul-mouthed, tattooed cow," Snake muttered.

After the police left, I got Walter a drink from the kitchen tap. Snake dropped to his knees and began unscrewing the eyebolts from the wall. "Seven years ago," I said to Clark. "How did you meet Philip Bacon?"

Snake shot me a look.

"He, uh, did a paper for his school. A dissertation on older blacks in society. I guess I was old even then." Clark attempted a laugh, then sipped water from a large plastic cup covered with depictions from a Walt Disney movie. He stared at the floor.

"How did he find you?"

"Why . . . you know I work out in that yard all day tending my plants. He used to go across the alley there and we'd say hello. Was seeing that Pitney woman behind her husband's back. A young man like that, getting his first nooky, he probably thought the sun rose and set out of her pussy." Snake looked up and grinned. Clark looked at me and I smiled. It took a few seconds for him to bring up his own smile and another few for us to boil over into a roomful of laughter. It happens sometimes like that when you need something to break the tension.

Inside the truck Snake said, "Now you know why Philip's got hisself a gun."

I had no answer to that and did not want to discuss it. My growing antipathy toward guns was one of the reasons I had mustered out of the Seattle Police Department. For years I had been a star on the department shooting team; then one night in downtown Seattle a youth in a stolen Volvo tried to run me down. I drew and fired and hit him in the face.

While we waited for the medic unit together, he wept bitterly and pleaded for me to apologize to his mother for him. It was a promise I never kept, was incapable of keeping. Later, when I looked up his record, I could see that until that night his biggest mistake was plugging up the toilets at Washington Middle School.

Everyone has pivot points in his or her life. An unexpected illness convinces you that you are not immortal, so you sell the antique Chevrolet you were restoring and begin spending more time with the family. A neighbor dies in a car accident, and you decide to propose to your girlfriend. The boss berates you once too often, and you resign to start a competing company that will eventually wipe him out.

Pivot points.

Me? I shot a kid in the face, quit the police department, and opened a one-man private investigation service. To Elmer, my not carrying a gun was akin to my not drinking, another habit he thought was sissy but which he couldn't quite square up with everything else he knew about me.

I said, "You realize when the settlers were crossing the

continent on the Oregon trail, more people were killed by accidental shootings than by Indians?"

"Sheeeiit. I don't believe that for a minute. That's bullshit! You make a mistake letting this cocksucker get away, and it's going to be the worst thing you've ever done. Whoever did this to Clark, this wasn't his first time out. A guy doesn't do something this smooth and it's his first time out."

"I know that."

33

IT WAS A FEW MINUTES AFTER SEVEN when Kathy knocked on the inside basement door that led up from her apartment. I was at the kitchen table waiting for the September sun to climb up over the spidery fingers of the crab apple tree and raise the vapor up off that end of the house.

"You knocked. Why not just come in the way you always do?"

"I always knock," Kathy said, voice subdued, hair frizzy from sleep. "Only you never hear me."

"Maybe I'll get my hearing checked."

"You do that, big boy."

Our friendship was foundering rapidly. You could hear a restlessness in the way she tried to kid me and failed, in the formidable dollops of both pity and kindness her voice lavished over me. Soon Kathy would be giving me that penciled-in smile she reserved for the freshly crippled, the newborn, the imbecilic. It was a heavenly smile, but not one I cared to be on the receiving end of.

"Care for some breakfast?"

"Thanks, but no. I came only to see how it went last night."

"How what went?"

"You and Philip."

"At Mitchelli's? He didn't try to slug me and I didn't throw him into the bay. Now that we get along so well, we're going to buy a boat and sail around the world together."

"That's the kind of answer I expected from you. Philip told me how hard he tried to be friendly. I was curious whether anything had changed between the two of you."

"Philip's a wonderful guy, Kathy."

"He really tried to be nice last night."

"He tried to be nice the way a broken front tooth in the wind is nice. You took off early. Snake and I missed you."

"We were talking. He guessed that I was vacillating, and I told him I needed more time to think it over—the marriage and everything. He's already sent for his mother's wedding dress. Gosh, he was crushed."

"Did he come clean about where he really was Monday night?"

"He was at the hospital. He's told me too much about it to have been lying."

"It's a good thing he's not lying. I know how you detest liars." We thought about that for a few moments. "Finally get to the opera, did you?"

"No. Philip said he thought Slezak was going to maybe interview somebody last night and there were some errands he wanted to run before that happened. I don't know what it was about." She stood over the table and peered at the grapefruit I had split open, glanced around the room the way she would if she had never visited before, or if this were her last tour. I could tell from her breathing that she was still upset from my comments. "Philip is taking me to lunch today. Then he'll shop for windshield wipers and antifreeze. Likes to be ready for the cold weather before it comes. I think he was going to write a letter to his mother. Want me to see if I can get you a copy?"

Had I thought of a reply before she turned on her heel and vanished downstairs, I would have issued it, but I couldn't and didn't.

Philip had left Mitchelli's minutes after I had spoken to him, mentioning an interview Snake might do. Snake, I knew, had been talking about Walter Clark. Moreover, Philip fit to a T the physical description Clark had given the police. Medium height; somewhere between five feet eight and six feet. Medium build. Caucasian. A neighbor saw someone in the alley fitting that description wearing a brown cotton jumpsuit of the type janitors and jail inmates donned. It was possible, it was just possible, that Philip had run over to Madrona and set us up to kill Clark with the front door. But what would his motive have been? I wanted to be suspicious of him, but I was more suspicious of my own bias. I was allowing my personal life to color my professional judgment and I knew it.

I telephoned the East Precinct and found out nobody had been arrested yet. If I wanted more information, I would have had to speak to the investigating officer, a man named Van Pelt, but he wouldn't be in until second shift.

At eight I phoned Sherry Finkelstein, the attorney who had represented William Blodgett seven years ago when he had been accused in the Susie Alberg disappearance. I told her who I was. "Ms. Finkelstein, I'm working with Elmer Slezak. I'd like to talk to you about a former client of yours."

"To tell you the truth, after I spoke to Slezak, I thought about it and realized I had overstepped my bounds. I'm sorry. I'm not going to be able to see you on this. Look, I have my family to think of. Also, I have a legal obligation to keep my former client's affairs confidential."

"Even if somebody dies because of your silence?"

"I don't see how my—"

"An old man nearly died last night. Along with the three-year-old girl he was babysitting. What do you think Billy might do to a three-year-old?"

She coughed or cried—I could not tell which—holding her hand over the receiver. After about a minute she said, "Still there?"

"I'm here."

"You do what you have to do, and I'll do what I have to, Mr. Black. Right now, I'm going to the doctor. I can't handle this. I am not going to talk about it or think about it again."

"If you change your mind, I'm in the yellow pages."

"I'll keep that in mind."

Ruben McGlover was a far easier nut to crack, although it took two hours and twenty minutes of phone calls to track down someone who had been working at Echo Glen while Billy had been there; yet once I had, McGlover was ready, willing, and eager to yak nonstop, night and day, on any topic I brought up, but certainly on crime, incarceration, and a young person he had once counseled at Echo Glen named William Blodgett. The nice thing about McGlover was that he didn't care who I was or what I was going to do with the information. Yackety-yak.

"I'm not saying we don't have problems up at Echo, Mr. Black, but the problems have gotten far worse in the last fifteen years. We used to have maybe one murderer on campus at a time. Now we've got so many kids who've killed that we lose track."

"About William Blodgett?"

"Even though he wasn't in for a sexual crime, he seemed to already have a twisted sexuality. Sometimes it is possible to treat that, but personally, I think with someone of Billy's age—and I think he was about sixteen when he arrived—that it's a waste of time to try. Billy was already hard-wired when we got him. It was because of what he did to Tanya that Billy was sent to Monroe."

"Tanya?"

"His counselor. Tanya Rivas. She lives in the boonies in

Montana or Wyoming or someplace now with her new
husband. No phone or TV. Trying to live off the land on
a little sheep ranch. She quit because of Billy, essentially.
She was treating him, this weird process I don't believe
in, where he's encouraged to . . . not encouraged, really,
forced to go into a room and masturbate to specific twisted
fantasies that he has, then, before he comes, he has a bottle
of ammonia he's supposed to hold under his nose to ruin
the fantasy. The theory is if a kid does this enough times,
the wrongful fantasy is no longer enticing.

"Now, nobody goes in there with him, so nobody knows
what he's doing, what he's thinking, or whether he's mas-
turbating or drinking Kool-Aid or what. And of course,
only a dope would follow the instructions. To make matters worse, he was supposed to write down all his fantasies
and share them with the staff, in particular with Tanya,
who was his counselor.

"Think about it. A teenage boy. Locked up. No normal
social contacts. Discussing his fantasies with a rather attractive woman three times a week. After a couple of
weeks she had a discussion with Billy in which she allegedly told him he was a misfit. He hit her and knocked her
unconscious, and when she woke up she was tied to a
chair and the room was full of young men. He went up for
assault. Indecent liberties. I forget what else. Billy claimed
that hitting her was an *isolated explosive disorder.* They
pick up the jargon right away."

"You think it is possible he's rehabilitated?"

"Billy will never be normal. The trouble with some of
these young sociopaths is they come up against the system,
and we teach them to mimic normalcy so well that we may
never again catch them doing anything unlawful. Which
doesn't mean they'll be law-abiding."

"Just one last question, Mr. McGlover. Why was Billy
being treated for sexual deviation? He was up there for assault, right?"

"The way I remember it—and you gotta remember, this
was years ago—the way I remember it, there were some

things in Billy's file that indicated he needed special treatment. I don't recall the specifics. We get so many kids
with similar problems."

I spent the remainder of the day searching for Billy Battle. Bridget canvassed the neighborhoods, while I talked to
some of the residents at the condo where he had been
shacked up over the weekend. The young woman he'd
been staying with knew nothing. I spoke to Millicent
Blodgett, who managed to smoke half a pack while we
visited. It was Wednesday and she hadn't seen Billy since
Friday night, when he brought her the stolen television.

34 To those of us huddled under the
umbrella of malfeasance, there is
the continual hope that we are hidden from the world. I
have lived with the misdirected belief that my coma was a
sort of armor, and since yesterday when Kathy visited, I
have lain snug and warm in that canister of false belief.

I am not breathing very well, having been flat on my
back for what seems like eons. Though I can now open my
eyes, move both arms, and can even talk, I have revealed
these abilities to no one. I cannot put a finger on why I am
hesitant, nay, unwilling, to alert my caretakers to the fact
that I am now sentient and reactive.

I have said nothing.

I have hidden the gift Snake left with me in the drawer

of the nightstand, where the nurses are not likely to look. When he comes back, I will return it.

Because I am toiling so hard to oxygenate myself, I pump her fragrance into my lungs quickly. I need only a whiff to know that it is her. I am listening to her walk. I know her by the cadence of her footsteps. By the way she breathes. By the precision and rhythm in which her shoes click on the hard tile floor.

She enters the room, sits on my bed, picks up my hand, and talks to me, even though she believes that I am still riding out the coma. Her entrance, her ministrations, and her beckoning voice arouse me. I can breathe now. I am alive.

Kathy Birchfield.

Though it will take an effort, I prepare to open my eyes and drink it in, but before I can do so, she speaks.

"Get well, you sonofabitch. If you weren't so jammed up, I wouldn't be here at all. In fact, it makes my stomach do flip-flops to come and see you. I don't want to be here. Get well so I can walk out of here with a clear conscience."

Kathy gets off the bed and walks to the window. I believe her back is toward me, and even though I would kill for a look at her, I do not open my eyes. She is cranky enough without knowing I have been playing possum. Besides, she has never spoken to me like this.

"I was stupid to get serious with Philip. Totally stupid. But then, once it began, I thought it was real. And I guess it would have been if you hadn't intruded. I wonder how many people marry the wrong person just because the right person doesn't show up? In fact, if you hadn't approached me that night with your stupid proposal, I would have gone ahead and married Philip. Eventually, I suppose, I would have figured out I was in love with you, and there we would have been for the rest of our lives, me married to another man.

"The mistake I made was sleeping with him. I don't care what they say. Making love with someone changes the whole universe. I began to think I was in love. I began to be in love. That is how it works with a woman. Funny, because that was the primary reason I never wanted to sleep with you. I didn't want to fall so thoroughly in love with you that there was no way out, especially since it looked to me as if you were not inclined to be romantically interested in me."

She returns to the bed and I feel her hot hand on my brow. She gets quiet for a few minutes, stroking my brow, and then she laughs. "Damn you, Thomas. You want to know something? I was only trying to find the right way to tell Philip goodbye when you followed us that night at the Egyptian. Damn you. Thomas, I miss you. And now I'll miss you forever." She laughs again, letting it go this time, working the trills until I worry about her sanity.

"You're always after me to tell you how Philip and I met. Well, this is as good a time as any. We were up at Ski Acres at the Pass. I was on the hill and the two women I had gone with kept skiing away from me. Anyway, I had to go to the bathroom, and when Shirley skied past for about the thirtieth time, I told her I had been stuck on that hill for an hour trying to get back to the lodge so I could pee. Shirley says—famous last words—'just head over in the trees here off this little trail.' There weren't many people around, so Shirley stands guard and I ski off into this little clump of Douglas fir and slip my pants down. What Shirley neglected to tell me was to take my skis off.

"I didn't have all that much control even with my pants up, but I had none with them around my knees, and before I knew it I was in this squat sliding down the slope screaming my fool head off.

"So I'm in the first-aid room and the ski patrol is giving me ointment for friction burns and who is sitting in there with his arm in a sling? Well, one thing leads to another and we get to talking and start asking each other about our injuries and Philip tells me he was okay until some madwoman came screaming down the hill without any pants on, which caused him to pile into a tree. I tell him I'm in there for a twisted ankle, which was partially true."

It grows quiet for a minute. Then I hear Kathy sniffling. When she leans close and kisses my cheek, I know she is preparing to leave. She says, "If you ever think about me, think about me as your friend, okay?"

Her weight shifts.

Before she can make good her escape, I grab her arm with all the strength I can marshal and pull her down onto me.

She has not been expecting this and flops across my chest. Pain shoots through my ribs and stomach and, when her hard hip brushes the catheter, I think I am going to scream.

She lets out a surprised squeal.

"Kathy."

"You were listening the whole time?"

"No, I just woke up. Stories about bare-assed women skiers would wake me out of the grave."

She is so pleased with my recovery, she has temporarily forgotten her anger. Faces pressed close, I reach behind her head with my good arm and pull her to me. Our lips meet. For a moment, maybe two moments, she does not seem to think this is such a bad idea, but then she wriggles out of my arms and sits up. "You bastard."

"Yeah. I can't remember why. But I think you're right." I am holding her forearm. She stares at me. "You've got to get Snake."

She attempts to pull away. I grip harder. "You're hurting me."

I loosen my hold but do not let go. "You've got to talk to Snake. He knows what this is about."

"Why don't you tell me?"

"Because my memory is like a sieve."

"You better let me go before I yell for a nurse."

"I let you go, I may never see you again."

"That's a given. Let me go."

"Kathy?" She is off the bed now and pain is shooting through me. "Kathy, you've got to see Snake. Promise."

She pauses, trying to decide whether I can handle what she has to say. "Yesterday Snake was hit by a truck. The police said he wasn't in a crosswalk and he had been drinking."

"Is he dead?"

"He'll pull through."

"Hit and run, was it?"

"How did you know?"

"It was a setup, Kathy. Just like what happened to me was a setup."

"What did happen to you?"

"I wish I knew. You're the first person I've talked to since I've been here. I don't remember a thing." For a moment I think she is going to sit back down, but then her eyes harden and she moves toward the door. "Do me a favor? Don't tell them I'm awake."

She is quiet for half a minute, giving me one of those long, studious looks she uses in court. "Thomas, you're not yourself."

"Promise me. And then see Snake."

"I told you he's in the hospital."

"Promise."

"Because you ask me to, I will visit Snake. I will take him some gumdrops and stand far enough back that he can't grope me the way you just did. And don't ask anything else of me. Ever."

**35** IT WAS 2:45 A.M. WHEN THE PHONE
rang. I picked it up on the twelfth
ring. "Yeah?"

"I need you to be with me tonight."

"Roxanne?"

"Thomas, I'm scared out of my wits. You're the only person I could think of."

Wedging the cool receiver between jaw and bare shoulder, I scooted to the edge of the bed and began tugging on a pair of pale blue jeans. "Tell me what's going on?"

"Didn't you hear me? I need you now!"

"I heard you and I'm getting dressed. Now tell me what this is about."

"Somebody sent me a thing."

"What thing?"

"I can't explain on the phone."

"Mrs. Lake. If you think you're in danger, my advice is to call the police."

"Not that I know of, I'm not. And no police. I don't need 'em." It was my first conversation with Lake where her voice had not been coy, or flirtatious, or calculating, or pretentious, or used as a weapon, or carrying any of the other carefully wrought effects she so patiently exercised. Stripped of affectation, she sounded very frank and completely frightened.

186

"Be there in a few minutes."

"Thank God. Let me give you directions."

"I know the way."

The Ford's bench seat was cold against my jeans, the blue steering wheel frigid in my hands as I drove to Hunt's Point. The sky was clear and the night had cooled the earth enough for my breath to be visible inside the truck. According to the cheap digital clock glued to the dashboard, it was five till three. Traffic pimpled the roads, mostly service trucks of one sort or another and people alone in cars. I liked to imagine the folks in cars were lovers returning to their own dwellings after incredibly romantic trysts, but most were probably sleepwalking their way home from the late shift or had just closed the neighborhood tavern.

Lake's driveway was dark as a dungeon.

Unassuming stars salted the sky overhead, but as I drove down through the tunnel of tall, dark trees, Seattle's glow blanked out the constellations on the horizon. I parked in the drive next to a pair of fairly dim antique ship's lanterns on posts.

Before I had taken five steps, the front door opened and a whiskered, bare-chested man in his early sixties wearing a grease-spotted sport coat, sagging pajama bottoms, and beat-up slippers, confronted me with an over-and-under engraved shotgun worth several thousand dollars. A handful of shells sagged his coat pocket. His breath smelled like a dead cat, and he had what looked like rat whiskers growing out of the tops of his ears.

As I began to identify myself, Roxanne Lake reached around from behind, grasped my arm in her steely fingers and towed me into the house so violently and quickly that I slammed into him.

She said, "It's all right, Max." Her bulging eyes told me she had been bouncing off the walls like popcorn in a pan.

The man in the doorway apologized for the collision while Roxanne trucked me through a foyer, down a level onto thick carpets, past a series of large, high-ceilinged rooms, one of which held a grand piano, and into a book-

lined den at the other end of the house. I caught just a
whiff of chlorine from the pool. Outside the window, part
of the pool house was visible, and from across the water,
Seattle's skyline.

Leather the color of cinnamon covered the chairs. An
enormous globe drawn from three-hundred-year-old navi-
gational charts stood next to the teak desk. Nautical instru-
ments, along with various shipboard items, hung from the
walls.

Roxanne leaned against the desk, crossed her legs and
folded her arms over her bosom. Her hair was a mess.
Over clashing green and periwinkle-blue flannel pajamas
she wore a peignoir that looked like the spray from a wa-
terfall. All of her makeup had been scrubbed off, giving
her the look of someone who had entered the first stages
of a lengthy terminal illness.

Fingers trembling, she held up a small, plastic
audiocassette tape. "This arrived forty minutes ago. I think
you should hear it."

Her lips were trembling at about the same cadence as
her fingers. It embarrassed her, but she clearly could not
put a halt to it. While she fumbled the tape into a deck in
the wall beside me, I said, "What do you mean *arrived*?
How?"

"Some kid, eighteen, nineteen, I never saw him, sat on
the doorbell until Maximilian, the groundsman, got up. He
told Max somebody at the Seattle Center paid him a hundred bucks to deliver this and make sure I listened to it tonight. Max took the tape with no intention of waking me,
and sent him on his way. I was having trouble sleeping, so
I came out to see what it was, then telephoned you. You'll
see why."

It was a sixty-minute tape, the final twenty minutes
filled with chatter and music from a radio station. The
other side of the tape, Roxanne informed me, was blank.

The recording started off with a man's voice. He tried to
be calm. He sounded old but not elderly, in his sixties, perhaps. He said, "What are you doing here? I don't keep any

cash in the house. The best you can do is my wall safe and the jewelry. I'll open it for you. It's in ... What? I'm not afraid of you. What?"

It had the ring of authenticity. A man in his home confronted by robbers. During extended periods when the tape had only the noise of people moving around, of chairs scraping hardwood floors, of objects being rearranged, Roxanne explained what I was listening to.

"As near as I can figure, Thomas, this is my late husband's voice. Randall. This had to have been taped the night of his death."

"Somebody got this from the police?"

"They never had a tape. Not that I heard about."

Whoever made the recording had been careful to either not speak, to switch off the recorder when speaking, or to edit the tape afterward, for the only voice was that of Randall Lake.

"Are you sure that's your late husband and not an actor?"

"It's Randall and that's our house in Portland. You can hear the regulator clock in his office. I can just see it all happening. Does he know this person? It doesn't sound like he does. God."

After they force him to walk to his office and sit him in a chair, the tape is relatively silent for a few minutes, until Lake says, "The wire hurts my bum ankle. Can you loosen it a little?" More silence and then Lake says, "Thanks." They have wired him to a chair. It is all very cordial. The recording played silently for a few moments, only the sound of the regulator clock's pendulum in the background, then someone comes back into the room and we hear the sound of liquid sloshing around in a can, liquid splashing out of the can.

"What are you doing? That's gas! What are you doing? Just take the jewelry and my wallet and leave me alone. You don't have to do that. What? Help! Help!" The last few words are the loudest on the recording, as Randall Lake begins to understand how it will end. Even seven years later it is making me ill. Even if it isn't real, it is making me ill.

A loud click sounds on the tape, as if the recorder has been switched off while some business is conducted. When it comes back on, the regulator clock is ticking but Randall Lake is quiet.

As if doping herself on oxygen, Roxanne Lake held her breath, then spoke slowly. "You want to know about this? Somebody broke into our house and confronted Randy. They bound him to a chair with coat hangers and then poured flammable liquid all around him and the chair. They jury-rigged a device so that when Dani opened the door to that room, it would knock over a lamp that would in turn set off the flammable liquid. It was simple and incredibly diabolical."

"Who's Dani?"

"Randall had a lover. He was named Dani, a body builder, and when he came into the house that night, he looked for Randall, and when he got close to Randall's office Randall told him that he was in trouble but not to come in, but Dani opened the door anyway, and it tipped a stack of books over, and on the stack of books was a lamp which broke and set a fire which spread rapidly across the room to Randall." The screams were on the tape. So was Randall's pleading for Dani not to open the door.

"They caught them, right?"

"Two runaways who'd been living on the street. They caught them. They both got life."

"The setup doesn't sound like something two runaways would come up with. Not unless they saw it in a movie or something."

"No, it doesn't."

"You attend the trial?"

"Never been back to Portland. Not even for the funeral. I hate that town."

"So where did the tape come from?"

Roxanne shrugged and let her arms fall limply to her

sides so that her palms slapped her thighs loudly. "I want you to get rid of it and make things right."

"I'll call the Portland P.D. first thing in the morning."

"You don't understand. I want you to destroy it. Get rid of it. Then I want you to find whoever sent it and get rid of them. At least make sure I never see them."

"There's a protocol here, Roxanne. The police, prosecutor's office, and the defense attorneys for those two in prison need to hear all this. This is new evidence."

"I'll pay you to hush this all up."

Before I could answer, the phone in the den rang. Glad for the distraction, Roxanne snatched it up, listened a moment, then said, "What?" and passed the receiver to me. By the time I got it, he was laughing. Insanely. He had to be responsible for the tape. I was fairly certain, no, I was positive that I had not been followed, for I had been watching my trail religiously the past couple of days. The laugher and the killer in Portland were one and the same. It had to be.

"Did you tell anyone I was going to be here?" I said.

"Not really."

"Who?"

"I might have said something to Phil. I phoned him right before I called you and asked him to come over and be with me. Only because he was the first person I thought of. He was with me the night Randall was killed. Except he refused to come over. What I needed was somebody to be with me. To calm me down." She wrapped her forearms under her breasts and stared dully at me.

"Did you tell him about the tape?"

"Not all of it. I couldn't."

A door opened and closed somewhere in the mammoth house. After a while footsteps on deep carpeting approached and Jerome Johnson poked his head through the doorway, saw me and said, "Oh."

Jerome wore his singing garb: baggy jeans, a white shirt and black tie, and black shoes with white socks. I filled him in, explaining to Roxanne for the first time what had happened to her ex-neighbor in Madrona, Walter Clark. Using a door as a trigger seemed to be a recurring theme, Jerome said, after we told him about the tape. "Walter Clark's door would have got him. And in Portland your husband was got by a door."

"You've got a point. Where's Billy?" I asked.

"I haven't seen him for a couple of days. Billy's got his problems, but he would never kill anybody."

"Honey," said Roxanne, "he almost killed you."

Jerome wanted to smile at times, but couldn't quite allow himself, almost as if he had been raised in a home where they charged a nickel a smile. "People thought he was a ghoul, but he just had this weird teenager's sense of humor, you know? He used to take this little white box and cut a hole in the bottom, stick his finger through, pack it with cotton, then put ketchup around the finger so it looked like he had a severed finger in a box. I think he pulled that trick on every teacher he ever had." Again, the almost smile.

"I'd like to ask you one question. I wasn't going to, but things seem to have taken a turn for the worse here, and we're pretty sure Billy's at the bottom of it." Billy or Philip. "What happened the night Billy cut you?"

The deer-in-the-headlights look behind Jerome's John Lennon glasses made me think he was going to bolt the room. Instead he ran a hand through his high, curly hair and spoke calmly. "Yeah. I guess you want to know everything, huh?"

"It would help."

"Somebody robbed the little grocery store up on Thirty-fourth that we used to go to, pistol-whipped the manager. It was the same store Susie Alberg was walking to the night she disappeared. Anyway, I found a sack of loose change, about twenty dollars worth, in Billy's sock drawer and asked him about it. Whoever robbed the store had cleaned out the till after beating up the manager, a Korean named Lee. And from some things Billy said, plus having seen the sack of coins, I figured he was the one robbed the

Korean grocer. I said I might have to turn him in, that I didn't want to, but I might have to, and one thing led to another and pretty soon he was after me. He was in enough trouble afterward, so I never said anything about the robbery."

"You recall who rescued you? Do you remember in what order they arrived?"

"It was like in slow motion, man. The old geezer. He was first. And on his heels, uh, came Phil. Then Roxy's husband. Ex-husband."

Jerome glanced from Roxanne to me and back again, as if he were trying to figure out whether we liked him. "Where have you been?" Roxanne asked.

"The group had an engagement at a place called the Pink Door down by the Market. And after, I had a date. I'm sorry. I guess I should have been here."

"You couldn't have known." She turned to me. "Would you stay over? This has really got me shaky."

"I'd feel better too," said Jerome, a tiny muscle in his cheek twitching. I had the feeling, for the first time, that Jerome's part in wanting me to investigate Philip and Billy had a lot more to do with Jerome's fear of Billy than he was willing to admit.

"I can bunk on a couch or someplace. Listen, Jerome, tell me about Billy's missing girlfriend."

"Susie?"

"Did Billy do it?"

"I don't think so. When she disappeared, he went completely goofy. Mr. Black?" Again he wanted to smile, but reined it in. "You don't think we're in some sort of danger here?"

"I saw a pretty fair security system on my way in. Maximilian's got a shotgun, and I can outscream a cheerleader on a whoopee cushion."

"And you've got a gun too, right?"

"Don't carry one."

Roxanne gave me a look of utter disappointment before showing me to a guest room down the hall that had its

own bath. I played the tape on the built-in stereo system in
the bedroom, searching for signs that the thing had been
faked. Using available blank tapes in the room, I copied it.
I marked the copy and put the original into an envelope
and sealed it.

It was hard to listen to the last bit, but I listened again
anyway. First, the heart-wrenching screams of a man
pleading for his life, his praying, then shouting in a state
of hysteria, shouting for his friend to keep out of the room.
The click of the door when his lover does not keep out. A
series of items falling to the floor. A sound that might
have been flames or maybe only the tension in the air as
the two men stare at each other, each realizing what has
been set into motion. Then, more shouts, these uncon-
trolled and panicky to the point that I was ashamed to be
hearing them, the death knell of a man who had not deserved to die, and certainly not in such a manner.

Even as I sat and listened, even as the sweat broke out
on the small of my back, I knew the tape was going to
stick in my head for years, and I cursed the individual
who'd made it.

36 EARLY THURSDAY I DROVE TO WEST
Seattle and listened to the original
with Foster Elwood, a free-lance evidence technician

whom I had considered one of my best friends from the day we'd met, maybe from the minute we'd met.

Foster was the kind of man who would bail you out of jail at three in the morning with no questions asked, loan you his car even when it meant he had to take a cab home, and give you his dog too, if you needed one. Once he had made up his mind about you, Foster became a lifelong friend, the kind of comrade few of us had or appreciated anymore. I accepted his friendship as some sort of merit badge, valuing it all the more because it had come so quickly and so wholeheartedly. Most ex-cops did not have that much good will left in them.

Though he had been a Los Angeles policeman back in the days of the original *Dragnet* TV series, had seen and heard his share of "spine ticklers," as he called them, the tape rattled him to a degree I found striking. He was shaking when he took it out of his machine. It wasn't until I had seen Foster's reaction that I realized how profoundly disturbed I was.

"People," was all he said.

He told me he supposed our original was a copy itself and that he would listen to it and run some tests, but our best bet in determining whether or not this was a recording of a murder was to secure a comparison recording of the late Randall Lake's voice. We both knew it was unlikely Randall Lake had dummied up a tape of his own death. If the voices matched, this was real.

Foster and I got to chatting about it, using logic to sand the specter of what we had just listened to out of our consciousness, the way you sanded a tabletop to get the nicks out, and we came up with some interesting conjectures. What if, for insurance, business, or perhaps personal reasons, Randall Lake had faked his own death? Sure, it was an elaborate and decidedly bizarre way to fake a death, but people had done stranger things. If the whole thing had been a rip-off, it would explain the unexplainable, why two street people would barge into a house, wire the owner to a chair, and attach him to a funeral pyre his male lover was bound to trigger.

But in order to carry off such a cruel crime, Lake would have needed some poor boob to take his place; and who was likely to volunteer for that? Then too, the victim would have to resemble Lake closely enough to string along the medical authorities and any relatives who might be called to identify the remains. The homosexual lover would have had to be in on it.

Perhaps that was why Roxanne was so adamant about my not going to the police. Perhaps she had been involved. Yet if a plot had been enacted seven years earlier, why would Lake have gone to such incredible and inordinate lengths to make it look like a crime instead of doing something simpler, such as faking a car wreck? And why would the tape show up at this late date? Was somebody trying to frighten Roxanne Lake? Blackmail her? Or had Randall Lake returned to play some sick game?

I drove to the office, parked, took the stairs up, and, once I was tipped back in my office chair, phoned the Portland Police Department. After two transfers I found myself speaking to a homicide detective named Doug Stutman. I had already spoken to Roxanne about finding a legitimate recording of her husband's voice, and learned that she had no idea how to go about such a task. "You're wasting your time, Thomas. It was Randy's voice," she said.

When I had given my pitch to Doug Stutman, he grew gruff and imperious and said he was "always extremely reluctant" to discuss a closed case. No, he said, there had been no tape and he was convinced anything I had in my possession was a hoax.

"I'd like you to hear the recording."

"I can't see why." His voice was flat, fixated, and patronizing in a way that was close to obnoxious.

"You mind if I drive it down today?"

"Look, we're busy around this place, and we already

nailed two little slimeballs for that torch job. Or didn't you know?"

"I was aware of it."

"I'd be willing to bet what you have is a hoax. In fact, I *know* it is. But I guess you better bring it on down. I'd be curious to see how much of it they got right."

After the call I malingered in my office with my feet propped on my desk, watching the sitting room and beyond, watching Beulah at her desk, watching the office traffic. One of the reasons I was taking this on was because I believed the exploits involving Philip Bacon, Billy Battle, Walter Clark, Roxanne Lake, and Snake were interrelated in some way that I wasn't privy to. The solution to the tape might be the solution to a lot of things.

As far as Roxanne could tell me, Billy had no ties to her old house in Portland, to the murder, to her, or to her late husband. As far as she knew, Billy had never met Randall Lake and probably hadn't even known she was married to him. Billy's current fascination with the house her husband died in, she believed, had come after the fact. I told her to call me if Billy showed up. I told her not to discuss this with him.

Logistically it was possible for Billy to have been involved in the Lake murder, since he hadn't assaulted his brother until two weeks later.

Outside my office, Philip Bacon entered through the main doors and went down the hallway toward Kathy's office, tossing a couple of flirtatious remarks over his shoulder at Beulah. Philip's day was never complete unless he had charmed every female within range of that wink.

Philip had hired Elmer Slezak, no doubt thinking anybody who swaggered and wore three guns and bragged about screwing virgins for a hobby and who claimed to have once actually caught a bullet, albeit a ricocheted bullet, in his teeth, and who had a name like Snake must be meaner than spit in a Minnesota winter. To the gullible and the naive, Snake portrayed himself as a soldier of fortune, a sworn foe of "thumb suckers, nose pickers, and bed wet-ters," yet Philip had no way of knowing what I knew, that Snake was no cold-blooded killer. Snake would get Billy in his sights, and Snake would choke.

I must have been daydreaming, because Philip had opened my office door and was standing in front of my desk. "Who let you in?"

"I knocked but you apparently were off in Never-Never Land. Your average adult needs seven to eight hours a night. You can't cheat it."

Closing the door, Bacon sat edgewise on my desk so that the soles of my shoes smudged his trousers. It was typical of him to make a maneuver that made it appear as if *I* were being rude. From the other room Kathy raised an eyebrow at me and walked back to her office.

"I know you feed peanut butter to dogs. You admitted it once."

"What? Listen. I visited Walter Clark yesterday. I didn't attack that old man. I was just now talking to Kathy about it, and we think perhaps you should see a counselor or something. Get your thoughts together."

"Get stuffed."

"Yeah, I thought you might say something along those lines. What are you doing with the tape?"

"The what?"

"The audiotape Roxanne got."

"You want to know about my dealings with a client, ask the client."

"She told me if I didn't come over she was going to call you next. I couldn't figure out how she knew you." I slid a paper clip off my desktop and began bending it with my thumbs until it was as straight as an ice pick. "Are you sending it to the police in Portland?"

"Driving it down this morning."

"I don't understand what that will gain. The jokers who killed her husband are in a cell watching a black and white TV. You should know that. Can I listen to it?"

"Not at this time."

"It would only take me a few minutes."

"I know how long it would take."

"Geez, I don't think it's a smart idea to give it to the Portland police."

"Geez, I don't recall asking you."

"How about if I go with you?"

"Sorry." I was smugger than a clerk in a pawnshop.

"You lost Billy. You bungled that. I knew you would. I could tell from watching you around here with your feet up on the desk all the time."

"Sweet talk will get you nowhere."

It was hard to argue with Philip because he never knew when you were taking coup, forever thinking he was the victor. It was like having a pillow fight with a blind man who always thought he was winning. The difference was you could feel sympathy for the blind man.

"Billy's got haunts in the Portland area, and I know where they are. I know where he eats and I know where he browses and I know where he picks up girls. You take me with you, or I go by myself and maybe find him without you. I know Portland like the back of my hand."

"How do you get your hair like that? You set it at night?"

"We can be friends, Thomas. After all, I'll be married to your best little buddy, so we'll have to work something out eventually, won't we? Otherwise you two won't be pals."

"Why did Mrs. Lake call you last night, Philip?"

His ears arched forward and his brow furrowed. "Roxy and I have been friends for quite a while."

"Since you cuckolded her husband?"

"I don't know where you're getting your information."

"Mostly from the local library."

"I'm an old and trusted friend. I told you."

In a deliberately poor Spanish accent, I said, "Bull sheeeeeit!"

"Huh?"

"She called you because you were with her the day her husband was murdered. You left her place at Hunt's Point in plenty of time to drive down, especially the way you drive. She got the tape, obviously made by the murderers, who are supposedly in prison, and realized maybe those weren't the culprits. I think she thought you might be."

"I don't know what you're talking about."

"I'm talking about a young man who has an affair with a married woman fifteen, twenty years older than him who promises she'll marry him after her divorce, then gets the divorce and turns around and marries some rich old fart. I'm talking about what people do when their dreams fall apart."

Slowly, he lapsed into what he pretended was a thoughtful reverie. Before he came out of it, he performed a series of mannerisms I had seen him fall back on before, stroking his chin and tugging his earlobe, the kind of attitudinizing a man might lock into after he's run over your dog and you're both deciding what to do about it.

"Look," Philip said. "The other night I followed Billy to a place up in the hills in Portland that used to be Roxy's house. You think Billy went there out of the blue? And now Roxy gets this tape. It's connected."

"The only glue I see in this pot is you. You're the connection."

More earlobe tugging. "That's patently ridiculous. Look, I didn't even want to get into this. I heard Billy was out and I looked him up and loaned him two hundred dollars, which I'm now pretty sure I'll never see again—even though we drew up a contract—and I figured if I maybe gave him a helping hand and got him started off right . . . you know."

"Then maybe he wouldn't be a psychopath?"

"No, it was just—"

"Get your galoshes. I'll drive."

37

PHILIP REFUSED TO BUCKLE THE SEAT belt in my Ford truck, a petty violation of the state traffic code I believed he committed because I refused to ride in his car after I found out he had been planning to charge me mileage. We passed the state capitol in Olympia before I broke the silence.

"So. Other than donating firecrackers with short fuses to orphanages, what have you been doing to amuse yourself?"

"For one thing, I don't play basketball with midgets."

"Kathy told you about that?"

"Kathy tells me *everything*." It was another ten miles before he said, "I take it you and Kathy had a serious relationship at one time?"

"We have a serious relationship now."

"You know what I mean."

"Kathy tells you everything. Why ask me?"

"You don't have to tell me about it if you don't like, but I keep wondering how it went off-line. I've never known ex-lovers as friendly as you two. I don't mind saying, it's a little disconcerting."

"You're actually very insecure, huh, Philip? That's why you try to submarine me."

"I don't try to submarine you."

"Even after she's agreed to marry you, you're still lying and trying to make me look bad."

"She's a beautiful woman. The most attractive I've ever gone out with."

"That's just the perfect reason to want to make her your wife."

"Yeah, well . . ."

"You told Kathy you were trying to be friends with me the other night in Mitchelli's."

"I told her I had made an overture and I thought we had come to an understanding. She may have interpreted it differently."

"Calling me scum is hardly an overture."

"Look, I'm risking my job over this. I've already called in sick on two weeks of school. Can't we just work together and find out what Billy is up to?"

"While you keep lying to Kathy?"

"Okay. I exaggerated a little. You're right. Where you and she are concerned, I am a bit insecure. Okay? It just fries me the way you kid around with each other. Look, I'll clear up any misunderstandings with her first thing when we get back. Deal?"

"Including where you were two Mondays ago? She still thinks I'm lying about Portland."

"I'll clear it up. All of it."

I thrust my right hand out and, after he flinched, for he thought at first that I was taking a swipe at him, we shook hands. "One-day truce," I said. "After that, you're a dickhead."

"There's no need for that kind of language."

"Sure there is."

After thinking about it for several long beats, he said, "And you'll be a dork."

"Dork is a little weak. No resonance. What would you think of numbnuts?"

"Uh, well, what about . . . butt?"

"Dildo might work." I gave him a goofy look, and something in the way I did it made Philip grin: a rare moment between us. I grinned too and said, "Dildo's not as heavy-duty as asswipe or as adorable as shitfurbrains, but it'll suffice." I laughed loudly and, after a bit, he laughed too, tentatively in the beginning, and then in a quick release of tension we laughed together, louder and louder. "Dickhead," I said.

"Dildo," he said.

"Motherless polecat," I said.

"Buttbrain," he said.

Philip talked about teaching, about the old neighborhood, about Walter Clark, about how many black friends he had, about the school where he taught, and about Snake, who had impressed him in ways that men do not often impress other men. Some of what he said touched me in a strange way that I hadn't been expecting. Whatever else he was, he was trying to be sincere, and letting me see that sincerity was an act of bravery that too many people would have dismissed too easily.

"Think you might teach me about guns?" he asked. "I'd like to have some skill with a pistol."

"Sure you would. You want to kill Billy."

"Snake said you were the best natural shooter he's ever seen. Said you could hit a Bible at fifty yards without even aiming hardly."

"Any good pistol shooter can do that. Here's two rules, free, if Elmer hasn't already given them to you. The first two rules of handgun ownership."

"Snake said the first rule was shoot first and shoot straight."

"Rule number one: all guns are loaded. There's no such thing as an unloaded gun. Rule number two: never point a gun at anything you don't want to kill."

"So I guess you won't teach me?"

"You weren't listening, were you?"

"It's just that I need to know about guns. In this day and age, a man without a gun is . . ."

Before we crossed the Columbia River and entered Portland, he mentioned Susie Alberg. He would have been in his early twenties when she disappeared, she fifteen. He grew wistful.

"I never even noticed her until one day she was walking home from school and got into a fistfight with some boy, slapped him around pretty good. And he wasn't a little guy either. Spunky? It made you sick to see her hanging around with Billy Blodgett."

"What do you remember about her disappearance?"

"I remember watching her mother in the street that afternoon. Looked like she was standing in front of a firing squad, her whole body quivering."

I was beginning to get a sick feeling because, as simpleminded and wooden as I found him, Philip really did seem like a nice guy, and because the closer we got to Portland, the more fidgety he grew, until sweat oozed out of his hairpiece, or hair, or whatever it was.

"I don't need to see the homicide boys with you," he said. "I just want to be there when you find Billy."

"You want to hear the tape, you're going to have to see Homicide."

"You can't play it now?"

"You afraid of the homicide guys?"

"I just never liked the way they treated people down here."

"It's the homicide guys or it's not hearing the tape. Take your choice. I'm afraid I can't stand to listen to it any extra times."

38

DOUG STUTMAN FROM PORTLAND Homicide met us in Cafe Coexistence, a pizza joint run by teenagers in T-shirts in a shabby little triangular building on Burnside. The walls were layered with flyers advertising avant-garde plays, poetry readings from last year, and banjo concerts in the park.

Stutman was a swaggering, no-nonsense man a head shorter than me with a Mexican bandit mustache and a football coach's belly that pulled the wrinkles out of his shirt. He wore a frayed sport coat and high-water slacks with white cotton socks. He was no fashion plate, and he looked at me and Philip the way a farm boy looked at a couple of sissies from a private school.

After we had introduced ourselves and ordered pizza, he led us to stools at a counter looking out on Burnside through a high window. He said, "You got something, pony it on up. I been pencil-whipping paper all morning and I'm in the mood for a laugh."

"You laugh at this," I said, "you're one sick cookie."

Stutman gave me a look that was colder than a mother-in-law's kiss. I explained where the tape had come from, then placed a small cassette recorder on the counter in front of him and switched it on, adjusting the volume so that Philip had to lean forward to hear.

When they called our orders, I carried them to the

counter in two trips. Before the tape ended, I finished off two huge slices of pizza and began eyeballing theirs. The recorder seemed to have vacuumed all the intelligence from their eyes. I noticed something in the drama I hadn't caught the first few times. At one point Randall Lake, or the man portraying Randall Lake, muttered something under his breath that sounded as if he were saying to his captor "You're a freak." I felt sure Philip caught it too.

When the tape ran out, Stutman rubbed a fat finger across his mustache east to west, then west to east. "What are you in this?"

"Me?" Philip asked, standing away from Stutman and dragging the paper plate with his pizza on it across the counter so that it made a greasy mark. He darkened it with pepper and then took a bite, as if being busy with food obviated an answer. He glanced over at me.

"Hell. I know you. You're the bum from Seattle. The Pig Man. What was it? Somebody . . . Bacon. What the hell are you doing here?" Finally, someone else who viewed Philip the same way I did. Of course, Stutman had seen him only from the wrong end of a murder investigation, but it was gratifying nonetheless.

Again Philip looked at me, but I only smiled, as interested in the reply as Stutman.

"I'm here at the request of Mrs. Lake."

"So who are you?" Stutman asked, turning to me.

I handed him one of my cards, the one without the machine gun on it. "Lake's my client. She asked me to take care of this."

"She asked both of you to come down here?"

"No," I said. "Just me. He made that up. There's no telling why he's here. He's engaged to a friend of mine is how I know him."

Stutman gave Philip a look, then took a bite of pizza and stretched the cooling cheese almost to the window before loudly sucking the strings into his mouth. He did not take his hard eyes off Philip. "You some sort of shithead who gets off on other people's tragedies?"

"Me? No. Of course not. Me? I knew the family. I was concerned. That's all. I'm trying to help out. Can't you see? Anything I can do. It was a terrible thing."

Stutman laughed. It came out as three barks and a woof. "Knew the family? You were banging the old lady the day he bought it! *Knew the family.* Jesus H. Christ."

For a few minutes Stutman ate in silence, and Philip shifted and scratched himself and looked around as if he were going to walk to the truck and wait for me there. You had to give him credit. He stuck it out. "It was in all the papers," Stutman said finally. "There was even a book written about it. A pretty good book, actually. So anybody could have made that tape."

"I don't think so."

Filling one cheek with pizza, Stutman looked at me. "Why not?"

"Because although we can't prove it yet, Roxanne Lake swears that was her husband's voice. And because of the look on your face when you listened to it just now."

After more thought and more chewing, Stutman said, "It does ring some bells. That clock in the background. I remember that clock. The fire gutted most of the room but never touched the clock. After you were in there awhile, it started getting on your nerves. I don't think it was ever mentioned in the papers or the book. And the muscle-boy. That high-pitched voice. We'll bring him back in, if we can find him. I don't know what it's going to prove. Besides, how did whoever taped this get the tape? It was obviously running until almost when we got there. And how did a recording device survive the fire?"

"You just said the clock did. Don't you think the existence of this tape indicates that the two men you got locked up might not have done it?"

"They did it all right. Couple of shitheads. It's more likely they had a third accomplice and he had the tape. Or somebody just plain found the tape. What's this about? Blackmail? She's loaded, right?"

"I wouldn't know," I said.

"She owns three hundred acres in Jamaica plus half of Kitsap County," said Philip. We both looked at him. "She's loaded all right." I could see how much having been dumped by Roxanne had hurt Philip. Before she broke up with him, he'd catalogued all her properties. Probably had the new Porsche picked out.

After our meeting I jaywalked across Burnside and went into Powell's Bookstore. "Where you going?" Philip asked when he caught up, having waited for the light. Here was a man who would lie to a homicide detective but would not jaywalk.

"Find that book. True crime."

"You didn't have to tell him I was fibbing."

"I didn't have to. Some things you do just for the sheer love of living."

"For all you know, Roxy did ask me to come down here."

"You some sort of congenital liar, Phil?"

"It's just . . . Billy makes me nervous and so do cops."

"So does Kathy, apparently. So do a lot of people. Which way to that house Billy was spying on?" Philip gave me a fishy stare. "You don't know where it is, do you? You don't know shit about Portland."

"I know parts."

"Geez."

We walked through the huge bookstore. "I know you think I'm a little strange. But I'm not. There's a Japanese saying that gets to the heart of it: *Deru kugi wa utareru.*"

"I didn't know you spoke Japanese."

"Read it in the newspaper. Loosely translated, it means, 'The protruding nail gets hammered down.' I've done everything in my life not to be the protruding nail. I guess you don't have much respect for that, but Kathy loves me, and I'm asking you to respect that.

"This is the most subversive and nonconformist thing I've ever done in my life. This thing with Mr. Slezak and you. Everything I've done in my life, I've done to conform. In fact, myself and Kathy. My parents have been after me for some grandchildren. The house is all fixed up the way I want it. The car is paid for. And then Kathy happened along at the right moment."

"Grandkids? Is that how you see Kathy? Some sort of breeding sow?"

"I can't win with you, can I?"

"Breeding sow. Geez Louise." I bought a copy of the book and we left. It was titled *A Kiss for the Devil, A Dime for Me*. "You see Stutman? He like to had a rag doll baby when he heard that tape. So did you, for that matter."

"It was . . . uh . . ."

"Of course it was. So where's Snake? Looking for Billy, or what?"

"Snake and I had a falling out."

"That so?"

"Yeah."

We drove up into the hills the same as we had two Mondays ago. After some searching, I found the house Billy had been watching and parked at a closed wrought-iron gate in front of a long driveway. I looked over at Philip. "You been here before last Monday?"

"No."

I was fairly certain he was lying.

It was an English countryside Tudor mansion, maybe twenty rooms, two stories, with a brick facade and leaded-glass windows, ivy growing up the walls. The grass was immaculate and the shrubbery had been sculpted.

We got out of the truck and walked through the delivery man's gate, up the drive to the front door. The mail slot was full. We hadn't rung the bell yet when she came bustling across the grass from the house next door in a flower print shift, waving her arms and saying, "Yoo-hoo. Yoo-hoo."

39 Trotting straight over to Philip, she said, "Is there something I can do for you? The Eastwoods aren't home. They're off vacationing in Bordeaux."

I had once seen a half-full rendering truck on an old farm road dripping whatever it was that rendering trucks filled with carcasses dripped. It was very reminiscent of the way Philip dripped charm as he explained that we were friends of the family that had lived here seven years ago. From the syrupy tone of his voice, you got the feeling he was going to ask her out on a date. She hadn't noticed me yet.

"Well, I'm Francie Zimmer. Phooey, they're not going to be back for weeks and weeks. I think the third of November. Would you like me to show you where it happened? I've got a key. Once in a while we get somebody driving by, but you're the first who's wanted inside. There's even a marvelous book been written, which I've been railroaded into autographing for all my friends. My picture's in it. You know how it is when you get to be a teensy-weensy bit famous."

Philip told her we had a copy of the book in the truck.

"Well, sure," said Francie Zimmer. "If you like. I think I have a pen right here."

"Would you, really?" I said. "Could you write *To my*

good friend, Thomas Black? No, could you write, *To a special guy, my very good friend, Thomas Black*? No, wait, could you—"

"Anything. Anything." She lit up like a Christmas bulb during a power surge.

In her early thirties, she had the blowzy, used-up figure of a woman who might have birthed a litter of kids, yet I doubted she had. She was braless under the print shift and quite conscious of the fact, holding her flattened breasts together by squeezing her pale forearms across herself. She had limp hair with pageboy bangs, dyed platinum. She wore sandals made of old tires and had shaved her legs, but not recently. Her exuberance seemed to partially annul her physical decline, so that spiritually and otherwise she seemed halfway between a little girl and on old woman. Exactly halfway.

We were beside the truck when my cellular phone hummed. I reached inside and picked it up. "Thomas? Snake. How's it hanging? Billy's back home with mama. I expect he was out riding a whore or two because he looked a little gamy when he wandered in."

I glanced at Philip and Francie Zimmer. "I'll be a minute. Go on ahead without me."

When they were out of earshot, I said, "I'm surprised you're still on this, Snake. Philip said the two of you had a falling out."

"Is that what he calls it, a falling out? I have yet to receive a dime from that deadbeat peckerwood. Not a single goddamned Jefferson dime."

"I think Roosevelt is on the dime. I heard he was cheap."

"Cheap? His retainer check bounced. We go out to dinner and he can't pick up his share of the tab because all his plastic is in his other wallet. One day he even had me pay for flowers and a new blouse for some floozy he was trying to dick, told me to add it to the bill."

"So why are you still working on this?"

"Billy got under my skin, I guess. Especially after what he done to the old man."

"So Billy's at his mother's? You talk to him?"

"Leaving that for you. The fingerprints the cops lifted from Walter Clark's house and pushed through the county's new ten-million-dollar computer failed to connect Billy to Clark, but that detective, Van Pelt, is on his way over to his mother's to interview him anyway."

By the time I reached them, Philip knew what high school Francie Zimmer had attended and why she had never been married, knew that her parents had left her a trust fund that paid for her house next door and expenses, also that she and Philip had mutual friends in Tacoma. At least, Philip claimed as much.

Guiding us to the room where a man had been burned to death perked her up like a lucky dog dragging a broken chain around town. As Francie led us through the sumptuous house to the high-ceilinged den overlooking a patio and, beyond that, a garden, you could catch just a whiff of magnolia in her perfume. The view outside the den was broken by several hanging wooden planters with purple and pink fuchsias, the last blooms of summer. A hummingbird, probably on his way to Mexico for the winter, whirred past the window.

Curiously, Francie took Philip by the hand and walked him over to the corner of the room. He had her hypnotized. I had seen women exercising the same sort of social voodoo, but rarely a male, and rarely had I seen anybody who did it as smoothly or who was as unerringly successful at it as Philip.

"This is where it happened," Francie said. "This is where he was wired to the chair, and this is where he sat and waited for his boyfriend to come in. You know, I used to watch all these young men coming over to the house, and I never thought anything about it.

"When they wrote the book, I spent simply hours with the author, Bette Hagan. Such a nice woman. Got killed herself about a year ago. Somebody she wrote a story about in Michigan got out of prison on appeal and ran her down in a golf cart. This whole incident has been absolutely bad luck for everyone. The neighbors on three sides got divorced."

"It didn't benefit Lake much either," I said.

"I didn't sleep for two years. I gained forty pounds eating chocolates. Of the ten closest neighbors down here, eight moved away. The police took fingerprints off some Pepsi cans they found in the kitchen garbage. At least that's how Bette Hagan wrote it. You see, they brought pizza with them. Bought it at a place all the students eat at down the hill, Cafe Coexistence. It's still there."

"On Burnside?" Philip asked. "We had lunch there today."

"Their fingerprints were also on a cigarette lighter they started the kerosene lamp with. A week later a couple of out-of-work cabinetmakers caught them trying to rough up some woman in Mount Tabor Park. What the police found in the shoe of one of the suspects was one of Lake's credit cards."

"You're certainly well informed," said Philip admiringly.

"Tell me how many times somebody gets murdered next door. The flames, you know, went all up to the ceiling here and scorched a painting that was worth over thirty thousand dollars."

"You see anything that night?" I asked.

"I was watching TV, and when I went into the kitchen to get another beer, I saw the flames. His boy pal ran clean out of the house, got in his car, and drove two hundred miles before the state police picked him up. Turned out he just panicked.

"Then later they thought it was some jerk from up in Seattle who had been having an affair with the wife. Can you believe it? Randall is having young men here while the wife is in Seattle getting it from some airline pilot? They hadn't been married a year. I'm telling you, civilization has come to an end right here in the U.S. of A."

"Amen," I said.

"Airline pilot?" Philip asked.

"I don't know. It wasn't in the trial. Bette Hagan told me about it."

"What kind of dork would have an affair with a married woman?" I asked.

"A jerk," Francie Zimmer said. "A regular jerk."

"Or a deadbeat peckerwood," I said. Philip gave me a look and then turned his back to us, standing at the window surveying the yard, the garden, and Francie Zimmer's house.

"You know, the funny thing was," Zimmer said, "they used to scrap like cats and dogs. Sometimes out here on the patio, so that if I sat in my yard behind the hedge, why, I could hear almost every word. I never could figure why they got married."

"It was a business cover," Philip said. "A lot of people fall into an arrangement like that. It's not as strange as it seems. She gets security and he gets respectability."

Francie moved beside Philip and gazed out the window dreamily. "I came over here one night in the summer. She was home alone, Roxy was. Crying. She was in one of those patio chairs in the most beautiful silk nightgown. To this day, I remember what she said: 'Just when you think life is finally fair, it dumps you back in the crapper.' "

"Was that close to when it happened?" I asked.

"Four days before."

"Francie, do you recognize this person?" Philip handed her a wallet-sized photo he had removed from his windbreaker, a snapshot of Billy Battle that Snake had probably taken on the street with a telephoto lens.

She held the photograph in her pudgy hands for a few moments and said, "That's one of the creeps who killed Randall Lake."

"Actually," said Philip, "I think it's a gentleman from Seattle. I was wondering whether you knew him."

"I know who he is. We bumped shopping carts and he

called me a bitch. He had this icy stare that was Idaho rude."

"Francie, he's somebody we're trying to get a line on," I said. "We think he's been watching this house."

"It was the day I bought fifty pounds of cat food and couldn't get it out of the trunk of my 9000. Know what else? I think I saw him at the gas station yesterday."

"You get a license number?"

"Didn't pay attention. But those two who broke in? I believe one of them was one of Mrs. Lake's castoff one-night stands. You realize when he was out of town, she entertained men?"

"I don't think so," Philip said.

"Oh, yes. Between the two of them, more strange men passed through this house the months they were married than an army induction center. One of those killers was an ex-lover. I just know it."

The visit to the murder scene seemed to have cheered Philip up after his run-in with Doug Stutman. Philip talked a mile a minute while we drove around Portland trying to locate some of Billy's alleged haunts. He didn't recognize anything.

On the drive back to Seattle, he tried every way he knew to connect Billy to Lake's murder while I was mentally trying to connect him to it. He said Billy might have known something—no idea of what—and was blackmailing Randall Lake. Billy might simply have heard that Roxanne had married rich, had traveled to Portland intending to burglarize the place, discovered the old man at home, and improvised thereafter. Randall Lake might have visited the old neighborhood with Roxanne and picked up Billy for sex, introducing Billy to the Portland house. This last was the only theory I thought plausible. Except for my own theory that Philip got jealous and drove down to kill the old man.

Philip's explanation for Harold Turner Weissman and Kenneth Toby Senters, the two men who had been convicted of the crime, was that Billy had recruited underlings to help. I told him I doubted it.

"But Francie knew him. She knew Billy right away."

"Francie has an act, Phil. At first she thought he was Senters or Weissman. Francie knows everything. You get her on a witness stand and any competent defense attorney will rip her to shreds."

"I don't think so."

"She said Weissman and Senters were arrested in Mount Tabor Park. They were arrested in downtown Portland, and not by two unemployed cabinetmakers. I saw that in the book. They were nabbed by an undercover cop trying to buy drugs. And the story about Lake's wife having an affair with an airline pilot. She was having an affair with you, or don't you remember?"

"Oh."

Thirty-five miles later Philip broke the silence, a queer tone in his voice. He was in his sincere mode now, and it worried me. "You know what I used to think was the worst thing in the world? Watching your parents get old. Because you realize eventually you are going to lose them. And it means you're next in line. But in the last few months I've discovered something even worse. Falling in love with a woman who might already be in love with another man. Especially when she doesn't know it. You know what I mean?"

It was the kind of thing he was good at, disarming you with a strange type of ingenuous statement that seemed to come, whether it did or not, directly from the heart. Along with his weird eyes, maybe that was part of his sway over women.

After a while I said, "I'm sorry about the F-person jokes, Phil. I'll try not to do any more of them at your expense."

"F person? What do you mean?"

"Nothing. I was kidding."

"Where are we going, anyway?"

"You'll see."

40

THREE HOURS LATER A MUTTERING Millicent Blodgett wheeled around the room in ellipses and semicircles, while belly up, Billy Blodgett Battle lay snoring across her bed, one foot marking the spread and one on the floor, his shaved head beside a TV speaker blasting out a black and white rerun of *The Fugitive.*

Billy wore shoes crusted with dried mud, jeans, and no shirt. His pale skin was hairless and satiny. One shoe had left smudges on her bedspread along with several small clods of reddish clay that had not yet disintegrated. You could see from the way his muscular chest rose and fell with his inhalations that he had gotten more than just a college education in the joint—he had pumped enough iron to put up a medium-size skyscraper.

"Maybe we should leave," Philip whispered.

"This is what you wanted, buddy. He's right here. Let's talk to him."

Wheeling her chair slowly around behind us, Millicent Blodgett said, "Oh dear. Now I'm in trouble. Oh dear."

"We won't let him be cross with you." I winked. Damn. I was doing them by accident. "We'll tell him I came to retrieve my pajamas and toothbrush." Laboriously she trundled down the hallway in the direction of the bathroom, but not before she had blushed ambitiously enough that I felt a stab of guilt over embarrassing her.

"That was the brown eye you winked, right?" Philip asked in a dull tone.

Except for Billy's mess, the small apartment was sparkling, bird cages scrubbed out and bedded with fresh newspaper, linen changed, carpet vacuumed, the knick-knacks every old lady kept dusted and washed and glistening.

"What if he comes up swinging?" Philip said.

I kicked the sole of Billy's shoe three times. "I'll let you handle that."

After he came fully awake, Billy Battle eased up into a sitting position, scratched an eyebrow with one blunt finger, coughed, looked at me slowly, then issued gas simultaneously from both north and south.

"An afternoon of surprises. Seattle's finest, Van Pelt, and now Seattle's worst, Phil, who gives me money and wants it back, and the private dick who's got nothing better to do than watch videos with my mum."

"Surprises make life interesting, Billy."

Philip said, "It was a loan and you know it. I need that money to pay a phone bill."

"Maybe I can't vote, but I got civil rights, buttwipe. You stay off my case."

"Buttwipe is a cuss word you should think about using yourself, Phil," I said. "It's mildly evocative and more colorful than dork."

"Yeah? You're a dork too. Both of you. Ma! Why the hell did you let these clowns in?" His mother was already closing the bathroom door behind her, switching on the fan to make her escape absolute.

"We just want to be sociable, Billy," I said.

"Like siccin' cops on my ass?"

"If I wanted cops on your ass, I'd tell them about this TV you stole." I stepped forward and knuckled the off button.

"Keeerist!" He swung his leg off the bed and dry-washed his face with his hands, working so hard at it I could hear the rippling of his palms against the stubble on his jaw.

Clearly intimidated by Billy's physical presence, Philip remained behind my right shoulder when he spoke. "My friend, Walter Clark, had a bad experience the other night. You have anything to do with that?"

"The nigger?"

"Please don't call him that."

"You're in my house uninvited, butthead. I'll call him anything I want."

"It's your mom's house," I said. "And very tidy. You clean it up for her?"

"Musta been Mr. Goody Two-Shoes. I'm in prison, he doesn't do stink. The minute I get out, Jerome's over here raking in the Brownie points."

"He cleaned this place up to make you look bad?"

"You got it."

"You are really something."

After a long, slow burn, Billy said, "Get fucked."

"Did you attack Clark?"

"I told the cops. They had anything on me, I'd be downtown right now."

"And how goes the search for work?"

Another long, slow look. "Yeah, like there's a lineup outside to hand jobs to ex-cons who can do twenty-five chin-ups, got zero work history, and spent a third of their life in state institutions."

"Actually, I might know a guy needs help unloading trucks. Of course, you're going to have to stop breaking into apartments and taking drugs."

"Yeah, and I know a lady'll hump the Vienna Boys Choir for two bucks. We should fix these two up on a blind date."

"I'm serious. I think I might be able to get you a job."

Battle came to his feet. "Don't bullshit me! You told the pigs all about me. Van Pelt said he was going to talk to the prosecutor's office. You made a bad enemy tellin' all that shit."

"Yeah, and if you're the one who visited Clark and attacked him, you made an enemy yourself. The hell, Billy. I followed you around in the dark, you're prowling Walter Clark's place. The next night somebody barges in on the old man and pretty near kills him. What am I going to do? Keep it to myself? On top of that, you come up missing."

"I was staying with a friend."

"Over on Seventeenth?"

"You know about Angela? Jesus. You're on me like stink on shit."

"You want it stopped, answer some questions. Convince us you're telling the truth." He reached across to the dresser, took a pack of cigarettes and lit one. I noticed three ugly, purple scars on his bare back when he turned, probably the result of mishaps in prison. "Let's start with what you were doing at Walter Clark's the other night. Friday."

"No problemo. I thought he might have had something I needed. I went to his house thinking he might not be home. When I saw he was, I got out of there."

"Something you needed?"

Battle hesitated, looked over our shoulders to see that his mother was still in the bathroom, and said, "Yeah. It was just something."

"You're not being straight with us."

"Look. This whole thing stems from Susie's disappearance. Right afterward this letter showed up in the mailbox with my name on it. No stamp or anything. It was maybe six months before I got arrested for the fight. The letter said she was close to home but in a spot nobody would think to look. So I went to the vacant house. Because I did, everybody thought I already knew where she was, and that's why the police dragged me downtown. It was a bitch."

"Wait a minute," said Philip. "You got a letter? What sort of letter? Who from?"

"It wasn't signed, for Christ's sake. It told all about her. Whoever wrote it was the one who did her."

"Where is the letter now?" Philip was getting very excited.

"I don't have it. It's gone."

"So if the letter said she was in a spot nobody would think to look, how did you know where to look?"

"I just did. I guessed."

"You guessed?"

"Yeah. It's not important. About six months later Jerome tells me some stuff about Susie's disappearance he shouldn't be knowing. That's when I lost it and went after him."

"What happened to the letter?" I asked.

"Like I know? I got back from visiting with the police, and a bunch of my stuff was missing. Including the letter. I never saw it again. I talked to Jerome about it, but he said he didn't know. Mom didn't know. At the time, I believed them. I thought the cops mighta had it."

"So what did he say?" I asked. "What did Jerome say that made you suspicious?"

"I just had the feeling he knew who did it. That they had talked to him."

"If he did, why would he cover it up?"

"That's what I was trying to find out when I got arrested."

"You have a funny way of finding out."

"Yeah? I'm smarter now."

"And you haven't asked him since?"

"We've talked some."

Philip said, "You weren't trying to kill him, you were trying to get him to talk?"

"I could have killed him in a second."

I said, "You two were talking and you went berserk? Is that what you're saying? He said something about this missing girl and you started cutting him up?"

"It wasn't that simple."

"How simple was it?"

"What makes you think, uh, he didn't provoke me? Like with a weapon? Maybe a gun. Maybe he had a gun on him, huh?"

"So why didn't you claim self-defense?" Philip asked.

"You don't remember, do you, bud? I told everyone he had a gun. Nobody believed me."

"Yeah, well, nobody ever found a gun, Billy," Philip said.

"How hard did they look?"

"That wasn't self-defense. You were murdering him."

"Somebody found it. Found it and hid it. If it had been self-defense, I might not have got sent up. They hide the gun. I go to jail. Big-time. Everybody in the neighborhood was out to get me. They all thought I was some bad-ass . . . I got news for them. Hard time makes a person worse. And we all get out. Sooner or later we all get out."

If what he was saying was true, or even partly true, Jerome might have spoken up for him at the trial and didn't. But what was Jerome going to say? I know things I'm not telling the police about the disappearance? It didn't wash. None of it washed. Billy was lying to us. "Are you trying to tell us Jerome had something to do with that girl's disappearance?" I asked. "Or knew who did?"

"He's trying to protect somebody. I want to know who, and I'll find out. Without going back to the joint. I'll find out." Behind him was a small library of true crime books, including several I had skimmed on my earlier visits, two of which contained graphic descriptions of torture sessions that had contributed to my recent sleeplessness. I found it hard to believe such books were in print, much less dog-eared and highlighted with blue grease pen.

"Listen," said Philip, irritation fogging his voice. "Let's bypass the ancient history here. Two weeks ago somebody tried to set fire to my car while it was parked under the Alaskan Way Viaduct. That was you, wasn't it?"

"I never set fire to nothing."

"You're lying." A bold statement, considering that it

was coming from a man hiding behind me. "You're telling us you had nothing to do with the old man the other night either?"

"I was rattling Angela Monday night."

"All night?"

"You want her phone number so you can look her up?"

"Billy," I said. "What's your interest in the house on Monte Vista?"

He seemed genuinely surprised that we knew about Portland. He stubbed the cigarette in his palm and shredded the remnants between his fingers. "What?"

"Monte Vista. You were outside the house where a man was murdered seven years ago. In fact, the murder happened maybe two weeks before you were originally jailed."

"I read about it, okay." He reached over to his small bookcase and pulled out *A Kiss for the Devil, A Dime for Me.* "I didn't like the way this thing stacked up, okay? Weissman and Senters still claim they're innocent. I got a feeling about it."

"Let's hear your feeling."

"Well . . . take Jon Pitney. He was a gambler. Serious debts. Roxy told the whole world about it before they got divorced. Maybe he was down there trying to get money out of that Lake dude. Maybe he was jealous of her new husband. He could have set that lamp and gasoline thing up to frighten him."

It occurred to me that Battle might have been describing a scenario he had played out himself. I said, "What about the evidence they got on those two, Weissman and Senters?"

"Could be the cops picked out two bums and hoked up the evidence. It wouldn't be a first."

I glanced at Philip. Aside from the fact that I doubted Jon Pitney had been jealous of Randall Lake, and aside from the fact that there had been no negotiations for money on the cassette tape we had listened to, this theory had possibilities. It might explain the nervousness and disquiet I had observed in Portland's homicide detective, Doug Stutman, after he'd listened to the tape. You didn't want to think cops framed people for murder, but sometimes when they thought they had the right suspects, the temptation to manufacture proof must become almost overwhelming.

I said, "Do you know anything about a package that was sent to Roxanne Lake's place at Hunt's Point last night?"

"The tape?"

"How do you know it was a tape?"

Billy sat back up and looked at me, then at Philip. "It was, wasn't it?"

"Maybe. Who told you?"

"I don't know. Jerome, I guess."

"You talked to Jerome since last night?"

"Mom must have. Jerome was over here cleaning—sure, he was over here cleaning and told her."

Philip and I looked at each other. Philip was edgy, and I could see he thought Billy was about to jump one or both of us, possibly with a screwdriver that was sitting on top of the television. I said, "Have you been spying on Roxanne?"

"Why should I?"

"You haven't scouted her house?"

Recognition sparked in his eyes right about the time I thought it would. If I had followed him to Clark's place Friday, odds were I had also followed him to Roxanne's. "Okay. Sure. I nosed around."

We pondered the situation for a while, the three of us, while the fan in the bathroom thrummed and broke into a rattle every so often. "Billy, I really do have a friend who needs help unloading trucks."

"From ex-cons?"

"From people with strong backs. He spent ten years in Leavenworth himself. He doesn't care where you've been."

Something jangled at the front door, and you could feel the air pressure in the apartment change as the door opened. Jerome walked into the room with a sack of groceries.

We all looked at each other for a moment, then Billy pulled a new shirt from a paper sack on the floor in the corner, chewed through the plastic loop that held the price tag on, and pulled it over his head. Jerome went into the kitchen and put the groceries away, then folded the sack and stuffed it into a drawer full of sacks. I noticed he put the goods in the lower cabinets where Millicent could reach them.

Jerome came into the room and took a chair behind Philip, near the bird cages, crossed his legs, and sat peaceably.

Roxanne Lake had portrayed Jerome as haunted by the assault. Billy had given us a different accounting. My decision was whether or not to bring it into the open by asking Jerome if he knew anything about Susie Alberg's disappearance.

"Well," Jerome said. "I guess Mom's not coming out. Tell her I bought soy sauce and macaroni. The raisin cookies she asked for are in the cupboard. And the Slims. How's everything going?" He was looking at Billy, but the question was meant for all of us. We were the last thing Jerome had expected in his mother's apartment. Surprise sat on his face like a meat packer's seal.

"We've been talking to Billy about the night of the attack, Jerome. He has some interesting assertions."

"I bet there isn't one of them I haven't already heard twice."

41 LIKE A LOT OF OTHER PEOPLE WHO'D spent time in the slammer, Billy blamed everything on someone else. Excuses, rationalizations, or straight-out fabrications helped him believe he was one of the good guys. Cutting his foster brother almost to death with a kitchen knife became merely another "isolated explosive disorder."

I said, "Billy claims the night of the altercation you had a gun. Also that you told him some things about his ex-girlfriend's disappearance you shouldn't have known."

Somehow looking younger and more inexperienced than he had before I spoke, Jerome did a slow take on the three of us, then addressed Philip, as if Philip were somehow his advocate. I felt badly for putting him in this position, since Billy was the one I was trying to goad, not him. And since I was certain from his body language and from other clues that Billy was lying. "You know none of that's true. There was no gun. There were a lot of people there. Ask them. Billy used to go nuts all the time. He still does for all I know. He just happened to have a knife in his hand that time."

"You been over here talking shit to Mom about me, haven't you?" Billy said angrily, fixing Jerome with his small, deadly eyes. Philip had been right. Billy had an in-

226

solent way of looking at you that made you want to hit him in the head with a length of pipe.

"What did I say to Mom?"

"Ah, forget it." The undercurrent of body chemistry and eye contact eddying through the room intrigued me, for although I was doing the probing and was covertly in the hire of Jerome, Jerome's eyes remained riveted to Philip, as if Philip were somehow his savior. I wondered what these two had in common that I didn't know about. Philip jammed his hands into his trousers pockets and shifted his feet uneasily.

"Billy," said Jerome. "You're out of the pokey. Let's forget ancient history and start fresh. Once you stop blaming everybody else for everything under the sun, you might have a chance."

"That's good advice," I added.

Battle tucked his shirt in, ignited another cigarette, then spit a piece of lint or a hair or something into the room in front of his face. "You could have come and testified for me," he said, to Jerome. "You could have told them you pulled a gun on me. Made them go easy."

"Easy?" said Philip. "When we got there he was covered in blood. And forget the gun talk. We know different, and you're not convincing Black here. Not a bit."

"You could have spoken up for me," said Billy, almost plaintively. "Nobody spoke up for me except Mom."

"Has this been bothering you all these years?" Jerome asked. "Why didn't you say something? If it's been bothering you."

"Fuck you. Get the hell out of here. I don't need you. I can solve my own problems."

"We'll talk, buddy." Jerome stood up and left.

When he had a hand on the front door, Billy said, matter-of-factly, "You made me mad that night. You knew better than to make me mad."

Jerome glanced back at us. It was the closest to a confession Billy would ever give. He had walked over so he could see Jerome up the corridor. "I'm sorry any of it happened, Billy. But nobody's blaming you anymore. For now, let's just have a little harmony in the family, okay?"

After the front door closed, Philip said, "I never saw a gun that night."

"That leaves Pitney and the old man," said Battle.

"Is that what you were doing at the old man's house?" I said.

"What?"

"Looking for the gun? The other night. Is that what you were doing there?"

"Uh, yeah. Didn't I tell you that already? Uh, one of them saw the gun and one of them kiped it. Yeah, that's what I was doing."

There had been no gun. Billy was focusing on a supposed piece of missing evidence the way a lot of flimflamming criminals did, as a way of exculpating himself. Even if there had been another weapon involved, it would not have excused the nature of his assault.

"Somebody hid it. One of you three."

"Give it up, Billy. The three of us jumped you," said Philip. "If you remember, you put up quite a struggle. There wasn't any chance for us to do anything except hold you."

"The only person there with any motive in hiding a gun, Billy, would have been Jerome. And the way I understand it, he was hurt pretty bad."

"He didn't move an inch, not until the medics moved him," said Philip.

"Okay," said Billy. "I don't care anyway. That knife I used. You know where I got it? Off Jerome. He had a gun and a knife. All I had was my fists. It was self-defense."

Philip and I both raised our eyebrows at each other. I said, "Why would somebody kill Susie Alberg and write you a letter about it?"

"I think it was so I would know things I wasn't supposed to know and maybe tip my hand to the police. That way I would end up taking the rap. Which I almost did."

Philip walked past me, halfway to the front door, turned and leaned against the wall, watching us.

"I want you to leave Roxanne alone," I said to Billy.

He knew I knew he had been watching Friday night through the pool house windows. "Sure."

"And Walter Clark? And Philip?"

"Are they going to leave me alone?"

"I think we can agree to that. You keep breaking into apartments, you're going back to the slammer anyway."

We were in the smelly outside corridor of the building, heading for the front door, when Philip said, "Are you crazy? We can't leave him alone. One of us has to follow him."

"You think he's going somewhere?"

"He always does."

"Philip, if we take it for granted that a missing fifteen-year-old girl is dead, we've got two old murders here, one of them unsolved. We've got Billy running around spying on people and thinking everyone else is spying on him. He's a dangerous man, but I'm going to keep my word for the time being and leave him alone. I think he's got mental problems, and the space might just help him relax."

"Are you blind? Billy is out for one thing, revenge. Can't you see that? Just the other night he came within inches of killing Walt. Doesn't that convince you?"

"The person who assaulted Walt was wearing a mask. It could have been almost anyone."

"It was Billy."

"Possibly. Maybe even probably. But I believe him when he says he's going to ease up. And besides that, I wonder what Billy would think if he knew the police had questioned you about the matter in Portland?"

Working his Adam's apple, Philip stood as tall as he could. "You wouldn't tell him?"

"On top of that, you were in a position to hide the gun Jerome allegedly was holding on Billy the night Billy attacked Jerome."

"You're looking at this from too many different angles,

Black. A reputable woman like Francie Zimmer tells you things and you think she's full of baloney, then Billy comes along, an ex-con and a primo pervert, and you swallow his story like a piece of chewing gum you lost control of."

"Gum builds up in your stomach into a big ball. You don't swallow it. Didn't you have a mother?"

"God. Can't you ever be serious? You know what I think? I think you're such an outsider that you automatically take the outsider's word. I think you actually believe half of this crud Billy's tossing around."

Depending upon your point of view, he had put his finger on one of my key traits. Sometimes it was a strength and sometimes a weakness. I *was* an outsider, and I usually sided with those of my ilk. The other problem was sincerity. I was a sucker for it. And everyone was sounding sincere today. First Philip and now, in bursts, Billy, at least when he wasn't lying. Or maybe he was a sincere liar. I had a feeling he really wanted to do good but was wallowing in some sort of mental trap of blame and denial he didn't know how to get out of. And Jerome. Jerome wanted this whole thing to dry up and blow away more than any of us. Maybe it was just the mood I was in. Yet my thoughts about Billy were tainted with suspicion, counterproposals, and forebodings. There was hurt and confusion and sincerity to what Billy was saying, and sometimes in the way he was saying it, but there was also anger and too many niggling questions. Too many outright lies. I had no doubt he was a criminal; my concern was in the scale of his criminality.

I found the Chevy Nova parked on the east side of the building, unlocked. I retrieved a key from the glove box and popped the trunk, which still had vacuum tracks on the carpet and was empty but for a spare tire and jack. The rest of the car was in disarray: food wrappers, empty beer bottles, gobs of matted Kleenex, a tattered map of Portland, another of Seattle, one of Washington State, a well-thumbed paperback book by a local fantasy writer, Terry

Brooks, an assortment of dirty rags I was afraid to touch, two stray women's shoes, the remains of several chicken dinners, a broken Polaroid camera, and some up-close photos of women's private parts, along with a half-empty box of prophylactics.

It wasn't until we had driven halfway across town to pick up his BMW that Philip broke the silence. "I've never seen pictures quite like that."

I didn't know how to answer that. In this day and age, Philip was unfortunately closer to the freak for not having seen them than a twenty-two-year-old ex-con probably was for having them in his possession. Francie Zimmer had been right about one thing: civilization was coming to an end right here in the U.S. of A. When we reached his car, he stretched his arm out to shake hands.

"Thanks, Thomas, for bringing me along. I've gotten to know you better, and I think maybe I understand you a little bit now."

"No problemo." Damn, he was sincere.

After I had dropped him off, I ran up to the office and let myself in. The building had been vacated for the day, though the odors of coffee, perfume, and human woe lingered. The mail had brought two bills, a check from a client, a personal letter from a woman friend I had dated for a time a year ago, along with some phone messages from Roxanne Lake and one from Doug Stutman.

"Black. Thanks for the tape. We found Dani Kirkdoffer, Lake's former playmate. My partner and I are going to see him this evening on our way home. Thought you'd want to know."

At home loud music rumbled the hardwood floors ever so slightly, like an offshore tremor, which meant Kathy was in the midst of a heavy session of aerobics. I noticed she played the music louder than ever these days.

After some phone calls and a snack, I donned shorts, a sweatshirt, a knee brace, my high-top Adidas, and dribbled a basketball with a little too much air in it three blocks to the school playground. I would have preferred a bicycle ride, but it was almost dark.

A full-court pickup game was in progress, but at their first break they realigned teams to include me and two other fresh players. We dribbled and waved our arms and passed and shot and catcalled into the night, until the occasional car lights turned us all into shadows and blinded us, until the bats that slept in the eaves of the school zigzagged over our heads. We played for almost three hours.

The only player who spoke English from birth was me, a giant on a court full of immigrants, the others shouting for passes and trick plays in Vietnamese and Chinese. There was nobody else on the court who came even as high as my chin. Playing basketball with short people was about the most fun you could have. Our team led by forty points before they traded me to the other team for two scrappy brothers.

On the way home I listened to the air pinging inside the basketball when it bounced up next to my face. Billy had a passel of theories to entertain himself with, but I wasn't so lucky. If Billy wasn't the primary mover in past murders and present assaults, who was? Roxanne's ex, Jon? Pitney had seemed blasé about Roxanne and their divorce, even more uncaring about her affair with Philip, about life in general in fact, about anything except a horse race and a roll of the dice. Jerome? Real doubtful. But then, there was always Mr. Sincerity, Phil.

Billy the local hoodlum, the boy with the temper, gets dumped by his first girlfriend, kidnaps and kills her, by accident or design or overzealousness, who knows; then, for whatever reason, becomes involved in the Lake murder. Two weeks after Lake's death, Jerome learns something he is not supposed to learn and gets sectioned up with a kitchen knife. It seemed very peculiar, too, that the very night after Walter Clark's attack, the cassette recording showed up at Roxanne's Hunt's Point home.

I had showered, eaten, paged through the evening paper where I read about a man who'd accidentally shot and killed his mother through a wall while playing with his hunting rifle, telephoned Roxanne Lake and found her out at some gala at the art museum, when the phone rang. "Thomas? I can't talk long. He's in the shower just this minute. Do you think he can hear me?"

"How are you, young lady?"

"I was feeling a little peaked until I had some wine. I couldn't help overhearing some of the things you talked about with Billy."

The only way Millicent could have heard us with the bathroom fan running would have been to press one ear to the hollow core door and screw her thumb into her other ear. "What did you hear?"

"Billy sometimes says certain specific things that might bear some correction by someone with a little better handle on reality. I love Billy. Don't mistake me. And it would kill me to see him behind bars again, Thomas. I do my best to talk sense to that boy."

"I know you do."

"But he tells a story about his girlfriend who disappeared, and he tells it as if he is completely blameless. I know there's nothing anybody can do about it at this late date, but since he was little, Billy always had a temper. I think he got it from his father, who more than once hung him out the window by his ankles when he refused to do something. But Billy, even at four, was too stubborn to say *uncle*, no matter. But that letter he talks about? That wasn't a letter. It was a confession. And I destroyed it. I read it and I destroyed it. I know Billy wrote it himself. I recognized certain things he said." Her voice was trembling. "It was the most frightening document I've ever read in my life. I don't want you to use this. I'll deny it. I only want you to know."

"Why do you want me to know?"

"You've treated me right. And somebody needs to know. Somebody more than his poor old mum. Oh, he's turned the shower off. I have to be quick. There's one more thing to tell you. When he was little, Billy liked to

dress up in my clothes. Does that seem like the Billy you
know? It doesn't, does it? It went on for some time, maybe
until Jerome came to live with us. I don't recall. But when
the police were asking around about Billy's girlfriend, they
brought scraps of a dress from the vacant house. They
asked if anybody recognized them."

"And?"

"They were from an old dress in the back of my closet
I didn't even know was missing until the police left and I
ran to check. I never told anyone."

"You're saying Billy took a dress out of your closet and
somehow used it in the kidnapping of Susie Alberg?"

"I'm not saying anything. I only want you to know that
everything Billy tells you cannot be taken at face value."

"And that letter? What did it say?"

"I've said too much already."

"But the letter?"

"I'll deny any of this."

Poor Millicent. She had discoveries that were too heavy
to carry, so she sat down and never got up again.

Just before I went to bed, Roxanne Lake phoned and
said she wanted to get together for a chat. I told her I
would be at the office most of the day tomorrow, and wondered if Jerome had reported our confrontation. It was the
first time in quite a while the laugher didn't ring me up.
Was it possible spending the day with Philip had something to do with that?

42 I AM WATCHING A FLY CAVORT ON the ceiling of my hospital room, no doubt in search of a corpse, when a bald man in a rumpled suit comes into the room. His dirty raincoat is spotted with droplets. When he moves just so, I can see the butt of a handgun in a holster on his hip.

Sober and businesslike, he acts just a little bit angry. "You know who I am?" he asks.

"I've seen you around."

"Know why I'm here?"

I sit on that for a while longer than he can stand. Time and I have become teammates, and this man is still out in the confusion where every action and thought is being broken in half with a stopwatch or a punch card or a commercial break.

"Look, don't play coy with me, Black. We know you know an individual named Philip Bacon."

"Sure. He's engaged to somebody at the office."

"What can you tell me about him?"

"Not a thing."

"You haven't seen him, say, in the last week?"

"I've been in this bed for some time. You try his house?"

"How about a kid named Jerome Johnson? He was injured a while back. Would you know anything about that?"

235

"You know, I'm not sure I know who you are." He hands me a white business card with blue writing and a little Indian head up in the right-hand corner. The Indian is supposed to be Chief Seattle. He is from Seattle's Homicide Unit.

I say, "I don't think I know anything about anything. I've been here a spell."

"Four days. You been here four days. They tell me you'll be all right. A little concussion. A few lacerations. You'll be all right."

"Will I be able to play the piano?"

"Sure."

"Wonderful. I've always wanted to play the piano."

The man in the raincoat takes a deep breath and tries to keep his anger from becoming visible. Anger, I can see, is one of his weaknesses, and it shimmers to the surface whether he wants it to or not. I have been waiting ten years to use that bedraggled George Burns gag.

"You happen to know where William Blodgett is?"

"Not really."

"Have you spoken to him in the last day or so?"

"I haven't spoken to anybody in the last day or so."

"Do you know where I might find Blodgett?"

"No."

"His mother says you were following him."

"If she's not mistaken, I guess I was."

"You're getting real cute here."

"Not as cute as a homicide detective asking questions to a man with a head injury."

"How about your friend Elmer Slezak? You think he might know where Blodgett is?"

"You'll have to ask him."

"You were a cop, weren't you. What'd you used to carry? A .45? That's a big weapon. Still carry it?"

"Not really."

"But you own a .45?"

"Last I knew, I did." I owned a couple of them.

"And you've got a permit to carry a concealed weapon, I notice."

"Been checking?"

"Where is it?"

"The permit?"

"The gun."

"I couldn't tell you."

"We went through your place with a search warrant. We didn't find any guns. We'd like to know where they are."

"I've got kind of an amnesia thing going here."

"Pretty convenient, don't you think?"

"From your point of view, maybe. From my side it's a little less than convenient." The phone rings. Three times. Four. I tell him not to answer. He picks it up. The look on his face when he hears the laughing insanity is priceless. He hangs up. "What'd I tell you?"

43

FRIDAY FIRST THING, I DROVE TO Walter Clark's, taking a sack of groceries that was heavy on the canned soups, which I had noticed he favored. Clark claimed not to have seen a pistol seven years ago on the night of the assault. "Billy wasn't as big in them days, and Phil knocked him to the ground from behind. Phil was having quite a tussle until Jon got there. Jon is a stocky man, you think about it. Strong as a bull. We all helped. I put my size thirteens on his hand, was all I did, kept that knife away from further work."

"And you never heard anything about a gun?"

"Oh, we all heard abut a gun. Didn't ever see nothin'.'"

I wasn't certain what the significance of a gun would have been. All I knew was that people were lying and I wasn't sure which people. When I listened to him, I tended to put some credence in what Billy was saying, though I had to remind myself that was the strength of a sociopath, that they could get you to believe things. On the other hand, Philip's lying had helped queer things between me and Kathy. Jerome was believable at first, but now I was beginning to have doubts. He seemed like a good kid, but there were things he was not telling.

I went across the alley to brace Jon Pitney on the question of the pistol that might or might not exist. A green-eyed housewife next door to the Pitneys told me Jon had jetted off to Florida to the dog races for three days, the aftermath, she thought, of a marital squabble. She had not been living there seven years earlier.

By the time I arrived at the office, Doug Stutman had phoned and left a message to call. Beulah told me about it just as Kathy came out of my cubicle and gave me the surprised look a friend might give if you accidentally met at the urologist, both carrying samples. "There you are."

"Morning, Sister."

"I wanted to talk to you."

"Sure. Has Philip spoken to you yet?"

"About what?"

"He was going to set you straight on a couple of matters."

"We spoke last night. Kind of a long phone call. You didn't threaten him, did you?"

"What?"

"Now don't get whiny. Threaten is not what he said, exactly, but I got the impression you had done *something*." Kathy looked across the waiting room at a client in a brown suit who had glanced up from his *Town and Coun-*

try several times, first to check her out, and then to check me out. Pumps clicking woodenly on the floor, she led the way into my office and closed the door behind us, resting her backside against the knob. She smiled perfunctorily. "Did you or did you not threaten Philip?"

"Phil's a big boy, Kathy. Even if I did, and I didn't, he can take care of himself."

"Even if you did and you didn't? What does that mean? Philip's an elementary schoolteacher, not an ex-cop who works out half his life and who used to be the top shooter on the department's pistol team. You leave him alone, understand?"

"The worst I did was call him a dickhead."

"You what? Thomas, he made me promise not to talk about this, but I think you threatened him. You've got that funny look on your face."

"He lied to you about me, and when I called him on it, he admitted it and promised to set you straight. Instead, he compounds the offense. The guy *is* a dickhead."

"Christ on a crutch." Kathy stalked out of the office.

A minute later Stutman answered his direct line. "Listen, Black. I owe you an apology. We got ahold of Dani and played that tape. It scared him shitless. The sonofabitch broke down completely, confirmed it was the actual murder scene, at least his part of it was. Obviously, he couldn't confirm what had gone on before he got there. You should have seen him shaking."

"So you think the tape is real?"

"Damn right. There must have been somebody else involved. We sort of suspected that at the time. Maybe even that putz you brought down with you. But why anybody would drag the tape out at this late date is beyond me. Tell me how you came by it again."

I explained in detail. Before hanging up, he said, "Say. What *was* the idea of bringing the putz down with you?"

"He wanted to come, and I thought, why not? I might learn something."

"Did you?"

"He's a dickhead."

"We knew that seven years ago. He was banging the old man's wife in Bellevue that afternoon. We figured he had time to drive down here, do the job, and get back to Seattle. I mean, he was living with his mother at the same time he was banging a woman old enough to be his mother. Weird."

"Then you got the fingerprints and found Weissman and Senters with the credit card?"

"And some other stuff. They claimed they had a meal early the evening of the murder at the Cafe Coexistence with some stranger they met. That later on the stranger saw Senters on the street and gave him some things, told him not to use them for a week."

"They give a description of the stranger?"

"They were both doing drugs heavily all during that time. They said only that he was young, male. From something he said, they thought he might have been from the Seattle area. We followed up to a point, but nothing came of it. There's always a stranger involved in these things. Only nobody can ever find him."

"Except this time there really is a stranger involved."

"Looks that way."

I phoned Roxanne Lake and left a message with her maid, who said she was still sleeping and had left instructions not to be disturbed. I phoned Bridget and asked her to come to the office, then dialed all the numbers I had for Elmer Slezak. No success there. After some deliberating, I called Philip and listened to his answer machine, remembering that he had once told Beulah the beauty of answer machines was that you could screen calls and "cull out the riffraff." After the beep, I said, "Philip, when you were a baby they should have knocked you in the head and sold the milk." It was something Snake's father had said to him almost daily, but I thought my application more apropos.

Even though we kicked the case around for two hours, Bridget and I came up with little. She had canvassed the Madrona neighborhood and found a couple of old biddies who had given her a rundown on the Blodgett family history.

William Blodgett Senior had been a wife-beater, a drunk, and generally the terror of the neighborhood. When Billy had been seven, his three-year-old brother had drowned. The next year William Senior served two jail sentences for domestic violence and then took the family car, their meager savings, and most of the pots and pans—he fancied himself a gourmet chef—and drove to the central interior of Canada, job-hunting. They never saw him again. Millicent managed to support the family on her salary as a grocery clerk and by babysitting. The house was a rental, the car a junker. With the youngest son buried, she had only Billy to feed and clothe and to worry about.

Then one night Jerome Johnson's family died in a house fire. Billy and Jerome had been ten at the time. The neighbors knew Billy had set other fires, and many of them conjectured that he had burned down Jerome's home, in spite of the official conclusion that Jerome's stepfather had placed discarded fireplace ashes too close to the house.

Working days for Boeing in the Everett plant where he hammered together 747s, Jerome's stepfather had been an avid coin collector. Jerome's mother, Bobby Jean Twerligger, had had two little girls with Mr. Twerligger, the riveter, the coin collector. Jerome was the product of an earlier marriage and thus had a different last name.

After the fire, Millicent, who had been a lost soul since the drowning of her toddler and the abandonment by her husband, volunteered to take Jerome in. He was the same age as her Billy, and they had been spending a lot of time together, and she thought she could do something for a foster son. The newfound responsibilities rejuvenated her to some extent.

Then, the month Susie Alberg vanished, something small but crucial inside Millicent Blodgett gave out. She quit reporting to work. Quit preparing meals. Quit taking care of the house. Within weeks she was unable to walk.

Nobody knew precisely what the physical diagnosis was, but one neighbor speculated, "Only so much grief a heart can absorb. The only thing that kept her alive, even, was that foster son."

A few minutes before noon Roxanne Lake, accompanied by a gust of cool air and a whiff of perfume, swept into my office and sat in the red chair. Underlined by the washed-out look of a recent crying jag, her eyes glowed with a false boldness. "You busy?"

"I was just thinking over your situation."

"Splendid. I have something to tell you. It's going to throw you for a loop, but I want you to promise you will keep this privileged. Can you promise?"

"I'm not a lawyer. In a court of law, I can be held in contempt just like anybody else. We get a lawyer in here and do it that way, I can work for the lawyer, and thus, what I hear would be confidential. Is it bad enough for that?"

"Let's do that, then."

We called in Allison, who was the only one left in the office, Allison in bangs and brown-blond hair that just brushed her shoulders. She was half pretty, with a round face and big calves, and, though she tended to brood, she took my vote for best future mother of the year. Roxanne wrote her a check, and she sat in the corner and did not ask questions. Allison was good that way.

"What you say now will be protected by the lawyer-client privilege."

Roxanne took a deep breath and lit a cigarette. I shoved a mug across the top of my desk with my fingertips, intending her to use it as an ashtray. She wore black high heels, black stockings, a skimpy leather skirt, and a leopard-print blouse with only three of the lower buttons fastened. Her hair was swept back casually and she wore large gold earrings. She seemed a woman who desperately needed to assert her ability to generate desire. But the eye shadow and the rest of her makeup did nothing to erase the circles under her eyes or the quivering flesh at the outer edges of her mouth.

"First off, Thomas. What have you found out about the cassette?" I told her. In detail. "That confirms what I had guessed. Let me say this clean and simple. Seven years ago, as you know, I had an affair with Philip Bacon. I don't like to say this, but it broke apart my marriage with Jon. It's easier to think the marriage was finished anyway, but it probably wasn't. Philip was very young and very inexperienced and clingy to the point that he sometimes talked of suicide if I wouldn't marry him. As you know, I met and married Randall Lake instead. Randall led me to believe that I would be allowed my own life and he would be allowed his own. What he meant was, he would be allowed his own.

"One night I met a man at Jake's in Portland and we went to his hotel room. Without my being able to see it coming or to do very much about it, things turned quite ugly. For some minutes I believed he was going to strangle me. I can't even tell you how ugly it was. Later, I put some things together that he had said with some things Randall had said and I realized Randall had hired him. I was furious. I confronted Randy and he admitted it. He said as long as I wanted to be a slut, I should be rewarded as a slut.

"There was something very wrong with him, Thomas. I never did figure out what, but there was something very wrong."

This confession changed things. Besides the money, we now had a second major reason why she might have been implicated in his murder. "Go on."

"I became unhappy with our marriage, but, for a number of reasons I would rather not go into, divorce did not seem a likely alternative." Several million reasons, I would guess. "I went a little crazy in my thinking and decided the most convenient thing for all involved would be if Randall were to have an accident. Shocked?"

"You're not going to shock us, Roxanne." She turned

and glanced at Allison, who hadn't moved or made a sound.

"I didn't know how to go about getting rid of somebody, so I went to someone I was fairly certain did know how to get rid of somebody."

"Billy Blodgett?"

"You're way ahead of me."

"Wild guess."

"I offered him five thousand dollars to make it look like an accident. He seemed to think of it as some sort of joke. He told me to get lost."

"What happened next?"

"Nothing. He told me to have Philip do it. I think he was kidding, but that was what he said."

"Did you speak to Philip about it?"

"Not at the time."

"Then what?"

"Then somebody broke into our Portland home and killed Randall. The police found the killers and they went to trial and, well, you know the rest. I thought it was the wildest coincidence until I heard that cassette recording."

"How long from the time you spoke to Billy until the night your husband was killed?"

"Eight days."

"And did you speak to Billy about it afterward?"

"No. It was too much of a coincidence. I didn't want to know if Billy was responsible. I was pretty shaken."

"Who else knew what you had proposed to Billy?"

"After it happened, I told two people. My ex and Philip. In fact, I told Philip just before it happened. That day. While he was out with me at Hunt's Point. If you want the time sequence, we were together for three hours before he left me at two in the afternoon. Randall was killed just before seven."

"Just thinking out loud. That was plenty of time to drive to Portland."

"That's what the police thought. Especially since he

didn't have an alibi. But then they caught the two guys. So I didn't worry about it after that."

I went over Billy's peregrinations to Portland with her, mentioning that Philip had followed him. The more Philip's name came into the conversation, the more Allison squirmed. She had been charmed too. This was a new view.

"Why tell me this, Roxanne?"

"I'm scared. I don't know what's happening, and I need somebody to watch out for my interests, somebody who knows what's going on. Somebody like you. Somebody who's dangerous."

I couldn't help laughing. "Who told you I was dangerous?"

"Snake."

"Snake is full of beans. This puts everything in a different perspective, Roxanne. I can't very well take what you've told me to Portland Homicide, now can I? It might mean nothing. Absolutely nothing. Or it might get you into a peck of trouble. Besides, the case is still officially closed. Billy never asked you for money afterward?"

"I never had any dealings with him afterward. Never saw him or heard from him, not until this month."

"Did he say anything about it this month?"

"Not a thing. He's been a perfect gentleman." I thought about Billy following her downtown, about Billy outside the pool house Friday night. Some gentleman.

"Does Jerome know this?"

"No. Of course not."

The three of us sat quietly for almost a minute. Finally, Roxanne said, "What are we going to do?"

"Whoever sent you that cassette had a reason. I assume they will contact you again. What I want you to do is keep Maximilian around and don't let yourself be alone with Billy. In fact, don't let him onto the property, if you can avoid it. I'd say the same goes for Philip and your ex."

"Jon?"

"A third party is implicated in your late husband's mur-

der, and my guess is it's somebody you know or knew.
Meanwhile, I'll keep poking into this and we'll see what
turns up. We'll get it straightened out, Roxanne. Don't
worry."

During the next two hours I drove out to Greenwood to
counsel a lady who last summer had asked me to tell her
whether her fiancé was solvent.

"He says he has a good job and owns his house, but he
borrows money from me like it's water." It turned out he
was a swindler who had left a trail of broken hearts, de-
pleted bank accounts, and disgusted fiancées across the
Northwest. She was a middle-aged woman who gave me
long, lingering looks when she thought I would not notice
and sometimes when she thought I would.

We spoke for over an hour on my nickel, me acting
more like a confessor than a private investigator. It seemed
her paramour had returned, pled guilty to his errors,
begged forgiveness, and, oh, by the way, could she loan
him eight hundred dollars to make the down payment on a
Toyota Celica?

They had made love, the details of which she seemed
anxious to share. She had been too hurt to tell any of her
friends or family the truth about the breakup, or about the
reconciliation, so I was the only one she felt she could turn
to with this new wrinkle.

I told her what she already knew, that tigers didn't
change their stripes.

When I got to my bungalow in the University District
that evening, I found several messages on my answer machine, the first from Philip.

"Thomas. I guess that was you this morning. I tried to
get to the phone to talk to you to clear things up, but you
hung up so quickly. Listen, Thomas. I spoke to Kathy at
great length on the phone today, and I believe there has
been some sort of mutual misunderstanding. I really do believe we got along rather famously yesterday, and I
thought you agreed. I'm a little puzzled at the tone of the
message you left, be that as it may. Anyway, I want us to

be friends. It's, uh, a little before noon. I'll try to get you at the office. Really. We need to work this out." Philip had not called the office.

The second message was from a woman who had contacted me several times. She told me she was "hanging in with her teeth" and needed my help because powerful state politicos were trying to discredit her because she was very attractive and had had affairs with most of them. There was "a lot of drama involved," she said, and by the way, would I help research her autobiography for ten percent of the royalties, of which there would likely be millions?

The last message was from Roxanne Lake. "Thomas, I need you over here so we can thrash out this situation. I'm in more trouble than . . . than I ever let you think about. If you have any suggestions, you might think about them on the way over. I called your office and they said you had just left."

I was starving, but I buzzed Lake's number and got her on the first ring.

"Are you coming?"

"Have you eaten? Maybe we want to do this over dinner."

"I haven't had a bite all day. But I'm not hungry. We have to be alone. Thomas? I hope you were being modest about not being dangerous."

"See you in a while, Roxanne."

I never knew what people were talking about when they talked about dangerous. To my mind, dangerous people were people who drove their cars onto crowded sidewalks, people who took infants on riding lawn mowers, people who spit into pay telephone coin returns.

It wasn't until I had already passed my last chance to exit that I realized there had been an accident in front of me on the floating bridge. According to the radio report, it would be a while. I dialed Roxanne on my cellular phone, but neither she nor the maid answered.

Almost onto the bridge proper, I watched the reflection of the sunset on a squadron of clouds over the Cascades to the east that were such a dark shade of gray they almost looked green, watched the glazed velvet surface of Lake Washington while the scullers from the university dipped their oars and stroked across it. In the distance a small sailboat searched for the breeze that wasn't there.

It was dark when I tunneled through the trees on Roxanne Lake's inherited estate at Hunt's Point.

As I approached the sprawling mansion, I glanced over at the spot in the shrubbery where I had concealed myself Friday night, and wondered if the man crouching there tonight really thought he was hidden.

 LAKE'S PLACE WAS DARK, THE ONLY vehicle in sight her white two-seater Mercedes sports car.

Swinging slowly around the circular drive, I headed back out to the street through the trees, taking a left on Hunt's Point Road. He had parked on the same gravel cut-out where I had left my pickup Friday night, seemed to be retracing my route step by step. I parked and jogged back down Roxanne Lake's long driveway.

Selecting a short stick, I threaded my way through the underbrush, only to discover he had abandoned his post and had traversed the crushed-rock driveway, was peeping into a window at the front of the house, this despite the fact that somebody had turned the porch lights on since my swing through.

From down on the lake on the other side of the house I could hear the sound of a small motorboat powering away from shore, a snoopy fisherman buzzing the shoreline to gawp at the upper crust, or maybe an old codger out for perch.

The trespasser must have been spooked by something inside the house, because he came like a springbok with a cat after it, making so much noise with his snarled breathing and hard-heeled boots he neither heard nor sensed me behind the bole of a Douglas fir not ten feet from him.

When he had turned his back on me and hunkered down, I crept close and moved the stick up against the center of his back, lowering my voice like a drunken man about to shoot a skunk. "You want to be around for breakfast tomorrow, you'll stand up real slow." He shivered with the surprise of it but followed instructions. "Now lower your trousers."

Ragged until now, his breathing ceased completely. "What?"

"You heard me."

He fumbled and muttered, but finally his oversized denim trousers dropped around his ankles and the heavy buckle and holster smacked the earth simultaneously. "Now take that hat and throw it on the ground in front of you. Stand on it."

"On the hat?" I prodded with the stick. "On my hat? I paid good money for that hat."

"I put a hole in your back, you'll fall on it anyway."

By the time he had it flattened, I was laughing so hard they could have heard me in Seattle.

Pants hobbling his ankles, Elmer Slezak turned and squinted at me in the dark. "What the hell you think this is, Thomas? A girl's seminary picnic? That's not even a gun, is it? You sumbitch. I could have shot your ass."

He reached low and hoisted the trousers, fastening the huge world championship bronc-riding buckle he had bought off a broken-down, hard-luck cowboy in an Albuquerque cathouse, or so he claimed, although there were times I suspected he might have won the thing himself.

"What are you doing here, Elmer?"

"I could ask you the same thing," he said, poking his hat back into some semblance of its former shape.

"Me? I'm rousting tramps."

"This ain't no time to fool around. I followed Billy here maybe thirty minutes ago. He's still inside."

"Where'd he park?"

"Drove that white Mercedes. I guess he stole it from her. I seen Jerome in it once or twice. He probably took it from Jerome. His mom's car don't seem to be runnin' 'cause he left it up there on Broadway this mornin' to get towed."

Nobody answered the front door. After waiting half a minute, I considered walking around the building, but instead I opened the front door, called out, went inside, then called out again. Snake was still in the shrubs. I gave him the high sign and then, just to aggravate him, I gave several other signals I knew he wouldn't be able to make any headway with.

Roxanne Lake's throaty voice was coming from a room off to my left. I called out, but she continued speaking to somebody else. I went down the wide main corridor on the Persian carpets laid over hardwood floors, past a suit of armor, of all things, past a vase on a pedestal, a painting of Ulysses S. Grant that looked to be an original, as if I could tell.

It was a large, ornately furnished room with sectioned windows overlooking the dark woods. The light in the room came from two table lamps off to the side and from a huge wall-screen TV. Roxanne's voice came from speakers hooked to the TV.

Six or eight times normal size, her face bobbed animatedly on the screen. Even though it was only a head-and-shoulders shot, I could see in the recording that she had on the same earrings and blouse, wore her hair the same as she had at lunchtime in my office.

"Roxanne!"

Nobody answered. Except for myself and the video, the house appeared empty. In this mansion, Billy and Roxanne and everybody else could easily be out of earshot.

On the video, Roxanne was talking about me, calling me Mr. Black, which she hadn't done in a while, familiarity being her goal, not distance. "He's going to keep everything I've said to him in confidentiality, don't you know that? Nothing is going to come out. Not a thing. He's going to fix it. Nothing will come of any of this if you just calm down and leave it alone."

It was possible that Roxanne didn't want to speak to me in person, that the videocassette was meant for me, but somehow I didn't think so.

The room had a second set of doors, sliding doors, which I went over to and cracked. They led to a larger room furnished almost identically to the first. It was dark.

Turning to the video again, I watched the camera pan to a wider shot. She was sitting in a straight-backed chair in a room I did not recognize but felt sure was somewhere in this house. Both arms were tucked behind her in a manner that made her breasts more prominent.

Slowly, the camera panned to wider and wider angles, until I could see that each of her legs in their black nylons was tied to a leg of the chair by strips of cloth, possibly towels. Now I felt certain her hands were tied behind her back as well.

I found the VCR and stopped the tape, muted the TV and walked to the front door, opened it, and, keeping my eyes on the interior of the house, made a sign. Snake was at my side in seconds.

"What the hell were all those signals?" he said.

"Something's happened."

"Billy?"

"Stick together, cover each other."

"Maybe I better stay out here in case he tries to get

away?" I began to suspect the fright I had thrown into
Snake earlier had stuck, because normally he wanted to be
in the thick of it. Asking to stand guard was not his style.

"Quiet."

We searched the main wing of the first floor, finding
nothing that looked the least bit peculiar. The rooms were
devoid of people, immaculately groomed, and dark. I
flipped on the light switches, leaving a trail of lighted
rooms and hallways. Snake had his hogleg out, following
me, his eyes bugged out.

"What's going on?"

I crossed my lips with a finger and shrugged.

We searched the main wing, the kitchens, then the wing
that contained the pool house. We went back and headed
up the staircase on the Lake Washington side of the house.
We made a cursory search of every room we came to,
Snake standing in the doorway with his .357 Ruger at his
side, me flitting through the rooms opening closets,
switching on lights, peering under beds.

She was upstairs in her own bedroom, still in the chair.
A clear plastic bag of the type supplied in most grocery
stores in the produce department had been pulled over her
head and knotted at her throat with a long piece of cord
probably cut from the Levelors in the room. The cord went
from her neck, across her lap, and across the floor to a tripod and video camera setup. She was dead.

"Keeriste!" Snake hissed through his teeth. "Did you
know we were going to find this?" Before I could reply, he
hightailed it across the hall into a room facing the driveway. I followed, gazing over his shoulder at the window in
time to see the white Mercedes kicking up dust as it exited
the premises. "That little bastard."

"Was it Billy?"

"Damn right."

"Positive?"

"As positive as I can be in the dark."

Neither of us felt like returning to Roxanne's bedroom.
We glanced at each other, then looked back out the win-

dow until the taillights in the trees were nothing but memories. There was no question she was dead. Her head was lolling, her eyes were still staring at her killer, and the inside of the plastic sack was full of condensation.

I looked at my watch. The police would want the time. I asked Snake what time Billy had arrived, and he consulted a small notebook he carried. Billy had been on the grounds forty-seven minutes.

For a while we stood in the doorway of Roxanne's bedroom, amazed at our discovery. "A bad way to go," said Snake.

"I was almost in sight of this place when it happened."

"Hell, I was outside the front door picking my nose."

The police weren't going to like two private detectives in a mansion with a dead woman. They weren't going to like all the hardware Snake carried, and they weren't going to like the fact that both of us had parked down the road. They weren't going to like us sneaking into the house, and they weren't going to like us finding a dead woman.

Hell, we didn't like it much ourselves.

45

SLEZAK HAD ALREADY REACHED FOR a phone in the hallway when I said, "Let's take a minute here and gather our wits."

"Wit gathering usually takes me longer than a minute, Thomas, me boy."

I tried to smile at him but it was one of those limp things you find yourself handing out just before heading into surgery.

"First off, there are at least three other people staying here. Jerome Johnson. I'm not sure if he's still around. Maximilian and a maid. They could be hurt somewhere, maybe even dying. We need to finish searching the house and we need to be quick."

The hired help lived in plush individual quarters on the first floor off the pool, suites actually, both empty. We found no signs of Maximilian or the maid, no signs of a break-in, and no more bodies. Now that we were certain nobody was bleeding to death under our noses, we back-tracked and went upstairs to Jerome's bedroom on the second floor.

My first trip through had left me curious. Jerome's was a messy room with an unmade queen-size bed, clothing strewn about, a pair of high-heeled shoes on the floor, a brassiere in the tangle of sheets, black lace panties to match the brassiere dangling from a chair back.

"Think the kid was rattling the old lady?" Snake asked.

"He mighta had a girlfriend up here."

"The old lady liked her sex."

Strangely, Jerome's personal library comprised four long shelves with many of the same titles Billy kept at his mother's. Volume after volume of true crime journals. *Whoever Fights Monsters* by Ressler and Shachtman. What appeared to be every tome ever penned concerning Theodore Bundy. Texts on serial killers, deviant psychology, and one called *Practical Homicide Investigation*, by Vernon Geberth, a book I had at home.

I explained the similarity between Jerome's library and Billy's. Snake said, "Jerome's studying the little pecker-wood. Gotta be. Wouldn't you if you had a brother like that?"

"Foster brother."

Snake used the telephone in Jerome's bedroom to call the police, while I stood in the hallway outside Roxanne's bedroom and contemplated Roxanne's slack body. There had been only the tiny window of time this evening for him to work, yet somehow he had done it. Where the hell was Maximilian?

He had tied her to the chair with nylons but had not gagged her, as if he were certain they would not be interrupted, certain Roxanne's shouts would not be heard. She was still fully clothed.

I had spoken to her at ten minutes after six. It was now five till nine. Roxanne had been unaccounted for and unreachable by telephone during a span of almost two and a half hours. Yet Billy had been on the premises only forty-seven minutes.

"Nobody is this good the first time out, eh, Thomas?" Snake was behind me in the doorway, his voice sputtering like an overheated radiator.

"You call 'em?"

"On their way. Don't touch anything. Just like Walter Clark's, eh?"

"Except this time we got here too late."

"The little shit."

"It's possible it wasn't Billy."

"We killed him when we should have, she'd be alive," Snake said.

"The thing I don't get is, why would he kill her like that?"

"Why would he kill her at all?"

"But why like that? Let's go review the tape. The police aren't likely to let us once they get here."

Watching the video was a blunder of monumental proportions. I hadn't been overly fond of Roxanne. I felt she used her womanhood as a weapon, and it offended me in more ways than I could say. But as a person, I had felt concern for both her plight and her station in life, a station I did not believe she had figured out yet. There were people around with too much money, and sometimes it became a growth on their souls.

In the TV room I switched on the VCR and rewound the

tape. The loop only had six or seven minutes on it, although it was clear from the beginning that Roxanne was
trying to stretch things out, believing, no doubt, that I
would show up any minute. She looked directly into the
camera, as if her captor had kept behind it or beside it,
sighting down the lens like an old-time movie director. After about a minute of trying to talk him out of whatever
was planned, the camera swung wildly to the ceiling for a
few moments.

During that span there were sounds of struggle, the rustle of a plastic bag, a couple of *you bastards*, then heavy
breathing and the filling and refilling of the plastic sack
with Roxanne's last breaths. When the lens had once again
been centered on her, the sack was over her head, a draw-
string running from her to the camera.

With her head in the sack and getting weaker, she continued talking to her torturer, though it was difficult to
make out the words. The only thing I knew for certain was
that she had not mentioned a name. The closest thing to a
clue was this line: "I've always been direct and honest toward you. I don't deserve this."

Snake was at the window when the loop turned to elec-
tronic fuzz. I shut both machines off and listened to the
whine of a siren in the distance.

"Hard to think it takes that long to smother," he said.

"I don't know, Snake. I feel responsible. I was out here
playing games with you when some of this was going on.
If I'd just gotten here sooner I might have stopped it."

"Our plan was to smoke the little fucker before he killed
again. Neither of us ever stated it in so many words, but
that was our plan."

"Just take him out in the woods and put a bullet in his
head?"

"Actually, Philip had a whole list of questions he
wanted to ask first. Wanted to know about that missing girl
years ago. Then too . . . what the hell is that?"

He unlatched and opened the window, stretched his
hand out and felt in the air for something, then brought it

into the room. It was a length of very fine wire hanging loose from somewhere above the window. Snake pulled the wire through his fingers until he got to the end of it, held it at arm's length until his eyes brought it into focus, then looked at me. "Ever see a Taser?"

"One of those electrical-shock guns? Shoots two wires at the target and puts them out of commission with a jolt of high voltage electricity?"

"Some people call them stun guns. This here is a wire from same." Snake leaned out the window and looked up. "Whose bedroom is directly above us here?"

"I'm not sure." But Snake already had one cowboy boot up on the windowsill and was launching himself into the bushes. I followed.

Jerome Johnson was on his back in the flower bed. At first I could not tell if he was semiconscious, unconscious, or dead. But he was breathing, albeit shallowly. From the looks of the trough he was lying in, like a shell hole, he appeared to have fallen from the second story, probably from his own bedroom window. The trough had been made in the freshly spaded earth by the impact.

A second Taser wire was fixed in his clothing.

He began to wake up just as a King County officer pointed his flashlight and pistol at us.

The rest of the night seemed endless, a wash of questions and answers and a sickening stickiness running through my veins like tar. From time to time when I glanced over at Snake on the other side of the living room, for they had separated us, I could see his emotions were running through the same gamut. After all, he had tailed Billy to this house and then sat calmly outside chewing a jawful of tobacco while Billy assassinated a woman Snake had been intimate with not three weeks ago.

Every thought that tracked through my brain that night centered around Roxanne. I did not often vow revenge. In fact, I did not believe in revenge, but I vowed that night to make an end to this matter if the police did not. I could see from the set of his jaw, Snake was having similar thoughts. When we got outside, our twin reflections in the window of a police cruiser were ugly and hate-filled.

46

BY THE TIME KATHY WANDERED into my bedroom in jeans, a sweatshirt, and thick wool socks, I had been lying on my back for quite some time. She hadn't been this cool and offhand since my unanswered proposal. Still fully clothed, I had been staring at a spot on the ceiling with the fixity of a client on a mortuary slab, and I felt about as lifelike. After glancing at her, I resumed my watch.

"I heard you come home," she said. "You all right?"

"Not exactly."

"I wanted to talk to you. I wanted to talk to you and Philip both. Separately, of course."

"It'll have to be some other time."

"You're really in a foul mood, aren't you?"

"You called it, Sister."

"Oddly enough, so was Philip. You two have some sort of dispute?" I bruised a pillow with my fist until it was swollen and puffy, wedged it under the back of my neck, and patted a spot on the bed. Kathy switched off the overhead light before padding over to sit beside me. Wasp-waisted and lean of limb, her slight weight didn't depress the bed much. Her hair was frizzed, probably from trying to sleep on it. The reflections from a small table lamp behind me made her eyes all the more violet.

"Philip was going to take me out to dinner at seven and then I was to see you later, talk things out. I haven't been fair to either of you. I've been playing the little princess, and relishing every minute of it, and I'm sorry. I'm sorry I was angry with you. You were and are in an untenable position, and I don't blame you for what you've said and done. Funny. Philip admitted lying. You'll appreciate that. He told me that last Monday night he wasn't watching a neighbor at the hospital, that he was following some ex-con who had threatened him."

"What time did Philip show up tonight?"

"I guess it was around quarter till ten."

"Where did he say he had been?"

"He was so visibly upset, I didn't ask. It's been a little ragged lately, between the two of us."

Kathy took a deep breath, yawned, and stretched. It took me a minute to figure out she wanted me to make a move, for, were I to sweep her into a sensual maelstrom, she could hardly be blamed for the decision to rid herself of the loyal but now no longer trustworthy Philip Bacon, could she? People weren't responsible for getting swept off their feet, even if they had planned it.

She looked away for a few more moments, then turned to me with a bewildered glint in her eyes that confirmed my theory. The look of expectation and acceptance she gave me was the most sensuous thing I had ever experienced. Now was the time to make my move, yet all I could think about was Roxanne Lake's face in that plastic sack, the condensation beading up on her eyelashes.

After a few moments Kathy leaned down, gave me a peck on the cheek, pushed herself off the bed, and walked to the doorway. A couple of our friends had infrequently accused Kathy of being a tease, but the reality was, we both flirted with each other constantly, all of it done with an understanding. It was to go no further than talk, and we both knew it. We had maintained a membrane of a platonic rapport until three weeks ago when I propositioned her.

After a minute or two I heard Kathy latch the basement door and go down to her apartment.

Philip had been missing until almost ten o'clock? Jilting females was not everyday deportment for the king of suave. Whatever had spurred this lapse in etiquette must have been compelling.

Jerome's story, after having regained his senses, had been understandably sketchy and disappointing, yet it left plenty of leeway for Philip.

Jerome told the police Roxanne had been on the phone all afternoon, that she had been upset, had been weeping, that she had raged at one caller shortly before Billy showed up. Billy had borrowed the car earlier in the day, claiming he had two job interviews lined up and that his mother's car had given out. So Roxanne had blithely loaned her car to an ex-convict I had warned her about only that noon. Was it that she didn't trust my judgment or, for some reason, couldn't say no?

Because Jerome's window had been open, he had heard Billy and Roxanne arguing in the TV room directly below. He had also heard Maximilian and Lupe, the maid, driving off.

A few minutes later he thought he heard something outside and went to his window to investigate. He saw nothing. At the time, the cool evening air had felt good in his stuffy room and he had kept the window open. He described what happened next as the most horrible shock he had felt in his life, along with "an incredibly weird sensation of falling in slow motion." Somebody hit him with the Taser and he fell out the window.

After Jerome regained his senses and partial use of his extremities, he found himself in the flower bed on his back. Before he could call for help or move, he lost consciousness again. Then we found him.

The Bellevue medics determined that he had incurred cracked ribs, a neck injury, probably not serious, and a broken left wrist. Had he not fallen into the freshly spaded flower bed, he would have been injured even more critically. In fact, because of the distance he had fallen, whoever zapped him with the Taser had probably written him off as dead.

When told about Roxanne, Jerome broke down and wept.

Maximilian and Lupe had been ushered out the front door by Roxanne with a hundred-dollar bill each and told not to come back before midnight. Despite instructions, they showed up in staggered succession around eleven o'clock to find a yard full of police vehicles and the King County Medical Examiner's blue station wagon.

Lupe had visited her sister in Medina, while Maximilian had visited a local bar where he had tanked up on margaritas.

Jerome was carted off to the hospital for X-rays.

The King County police issued bulletins for William Blodgett Battle, but by the time they released Elmer and me, nothing had come of it. They sent people to his mother's apartment to wait for him, and, upon our request, contacted the SPD and asked them to keep an eye on Walter Clark.

I mentioned that before entering the house I had heard a small motorboat on the lake. Twenty minutes later one of the uniformed cops told me they'd had a report of a stolen boat about a mile away at six o'clock that evening. The aluminum fourteen-footer had recently been recovered a hundred yards beyond the moorage from which it had been hijacked.

Combing the house with a police dog, one of the officers managed to locate the Taser, tucked away just inside a low crawl space that accessed pipes in one of the bathrooms on the second floor.

They took casts of footprints in the garden. Casts of footprints by the shore. They dusted for fingerprints in Roxanne's bedroom, on the camera, even on her glossy high-heeled shoes. When we left, evidence technicians were vacuuming the carpet around the chair she had died in with a machine that would collect hairs and fibers for later analysis.

Any way you looked at it, it was a freakish scenario, and I tried to fit it together in my mind. She had come to my office at noon and confessed, then had loaned the Mercedes to Billy. She had obviously been disturbed about approaching Billy seven years earlier, disturbed that Billy had been snooping in her husband's death, and disturbed over the audiocassette. I wondered whether she had mentioned any of this to Billy.

Still in my clothes, I woke up shortly after seven on Saturday morning, the bedside lamp burning. I had not slept in my clothes in years. There was a note on my kitchen table. *Sorry to bother you last night. If you need me, I'll be in the office. Love, Kathy.*

47

"ARE YOU HAPPY NOW?" PHILIP BELlowed from the waiting room.

Heads popped out of nearby doorways. It was Saturday but the office was full. He strode into my office and slammed the door. The veins on his neck danced, and a worm of a vein in his forehead bulged.

The nosy, the inquiring, and the morbid began massing in the anteroom outside my office, peering through the clear glass door with looks on their faces that rivaled a gang of children following a ruckus between a dog and a bird. Didn't these people have lawns to mow or ailing relatives to visit? Still wearing her headphone, a wide-eyed Beulah elbowed her way to the fore of the group. A year ago when a man had barged into the office waving a Luger at one of the attorneys, Beulah had taken the rest of the day off. Confrontations stressed her out.

"You stupid!" Philip shouted. "You stupid naive sonofabitch!" I smiled at Beulah through the window in the door and made a gun sign with my fingers, pointed it at my own head, and clicked down my thumb. She clearly did not find me amusing. Everybody knew my client had been murdered.

My feet were propped up on the desk, chair tilted back, none of it a reaction to Philip, as that was how I had been when he broke in. "At least *stupid sonofabitch* is heartfelt," I said. "Not like dork."

"Sure, try to cute the whole thing away."

"Philip, I'm as sorry as anybody."

"That would be your style. Cute it away. You don't face up to things, ever, do you? I ought to call you outside and beat the darn stuffing out of you. How would you like that? If you had listened, you sonofabitch, none of this would have happened."

"Tried and convicted," I said, keeping my voice level and low so the gawkers in the anteroom would not overhear. "Nobody's been arrested. Or tried. There is a suspect, sure, but that doesn't—"

"You stupid, stupid sonofabitch!"

"Calm down, Philip, before you make me mad."

"You're going to stand by all that American system of justice bullshit when the only woman I ever . . . when Roxy lies dead? Do you even have a heart, or are you just one big self-justification? You disgust me. You know that? You disgust me. You know what he did to her? It's bad enough he got to her, but now all the particulars are on the news."

"I know what he did."

"No, I don't think you do. Let me elucidate."

"I think I know, Phil. I found her. I know."

"You found her?"

"And if you think I'm not sick over it . . ." What I said dampened his rage, but how I said it silenced him long enough for Kathy to slip into the room.

It took a moment before Philip turned away from me and acknowledged her presence. "Hi, sweetheart," he said.

"What is going on?" Kathy asked.

"Me? I was just sitting here separating a sheet of stamps."

"I'm sorry, Kathy," Philip said. "I know you don't like scenes, but your lazy friend here has been butting into other people's business long enough. It's time somebody put him in his place."

"I don't understand," said Kathy.

The room was silent for twenty seconds. The onlookers outside began drifting away, all except Beulah, who I could see was pissed at me for letting this happen. For some reason, maybe it was some sort of unconscious vote of confidence, Beulah always thought I had complete control of everything in my life. It became irritating at times such as this, when she blamed everything solely on me.

"My client was killed last night, Kathy. Murdered. Philip knew her."

"Years ago," he said hastily. Philip and I had locked eyes, three brown and one blue. "I haven't seen or heard from her in almost ten years. But I know this. She died because of this man's negligence."

"What makes you say that?" Kathy asked.

"I'll explain it to you at lunch."

"Tell you what, Philip," I said. "You stop telling lies about me and I'll stop telling the truth about you."

"Wendell Corey did a better job of delivering that line to Walter Huston in *The Furies*. You always have somebody else write your lines?" He was halfway out the door when he added, "Kathy doesn't like scenes, and I don't like the way you've bungled this. We'll do things my way from now on."

"Why don't you explain the affair you had with her. The one that broke up her marriage. Explain her fourth husband's death and why the police questioned you about it."

"For Christ's sake. You let somebody kill her and film the whole thing, and you want me to stand here and explain myself. Screw you." He stalked out of the offices, walking like he had a stick down his trouser leg, or someplace.

Kathy closed the door, then came very slowly across the room and around my desk. "What was that all about?"

"Is he a film buff or something?"

"Don't be stalling."

"Roxanne Lake used to be his lover."

"Your ex-client? Lady Godiva in clothes? She must be fifteen or twenty years older."

"That's why he's so upset over her death. In a way, you can't blame him for this little scene. Geez, I didn't know he was a film buff, or I never would have used that line."

"First you hammer him, then you make excuses in his behalf. Somewhere under all those wisecracks you like Philip."

"Not enough to be the best man at your wedding."

Kathy sat on my desk so that her leg brushed softly up against my hip. She scooted back, crushing some letters with her rump, crossed her legs at the knees, and looked down at me. She had on a short navy skirt, a white blouse and white nylons. "Was your client's death related to what you were working on?"

Explaining everything from the beginning took forty minutes. Kathy asked the right questions in the right places, as she had been trained to do, then, when I had finished, she said, "You really were following us for a legitimate reason that night at the Egyptian."

"More or less."

"No, you were. I misjudged you."

"Philip's afraid Billy is going to get him."

"You think there's a chance?"

"I suppose there is."

Giving me a quick kiss on the forehead, she walked to the door. "You take care of yourself, buster. I need you."

It was easy enough to tell from the breaking tone in her voice and the slight stumbling hitch in her walk that she wanted to say something more but either did not know what it was or had decided for some reason that now was not the time to utter it.

Long after she left, I felt the imprint of her lips. There were all kinds of kisses: the kiss of a mother; the kiss of a lunatic; the kiss of someone falling in love, or out of love; but the craziest kiss of all was the kiss of a woman who didn't know what she was thinking. I had a hollow feeling I had just received one of those.

48

THREE DAYS PASSED DURING WHICH Roxanne Lake's empty Mercedes was found in a parking lot in downtown Seattle next to the Greyhound bus depot. Jerome came home from the hospital having suffered a mild concussion. Other than that the only visible marks were a bruised jaw and a cast on his left arm that extended from his palm to just above the elbow. He complained of not being able to sleep because of the cast and cracked ribs. He was consumed with the idea that Billy was coming back for him.

Snake and I were both interrogated twice more by the King County homicide detectives, who had taken a decided dislike to our protest of bad luck at being involved with Walter Clark last Friday night, and then the murder at Hunt's Point. There were drawbacks to working with Snake, and one of the drawbacks was that he managed to look as if he were implicated in any felony in his vicinity.

A group of society types in black skirts and tailored suits who I suspected had not known her well, if at all, mobbed Roxanne's funeral, wanting, I suspected, to be seen at the burial of a rich someone whose death had made a splash in the news. Interestingly enough, the plastic bag over her head and the rope had become common knowledge, featured at the beginning of every newscast on the murder. The police had withheld information on the video camera and the Taser, so that only insiders knew.

It was easy to imagine Billy wanting Jerome dead, for Jerome had been at the bottom of Billy's going to jail. And Billy had tried to implicate Jerome in Susie Alberg's disappearance as well. Billy also had grudges against Walter Clark, Philip Bacon, and Jon Pitney. But Roxanne? Why would Billy kill Roxanne? Even the knowledge that she had attempted to hire him to dispose of her fourth husband sparked few theories. Snake's idea was that she had hired someone else after attempting to hire Billy, that Billy had found out somehow and was blackmailing her, that she had balked at the blackmail and he had killed her. Yet, if blackmail had been attempted, surely Roxanne would have mentioned it when she told me she'd tried to hire Billy.

At the funeral, Lupe, Maximilian, and Jerome Johnson sat together in the front, managing to look almost like a grieving family. It was a pity when the family at your funeral consisted of a house guest, a handyman, and a maid. As had the servants, Jerome stayed on temporarily at the estate at Hunt's Point. He was jobless and glad for the room.

The executrix of Roxanne's will had earmarked a week's grace in which the three of them were expected to find other quarters. A twenty-four-hour security guard was stationed on the premises to ensure that nothing was removed from the estate. Had the guard been stationed sooner, Roxanne would be alive, an irony I couldn't help playing over and over in my head.

At the church, Elmer Slezak found me in the surging crowd of black-clad mourners. He followed me to a pew where he exhaled alcohol fumes strong enough to stun small invertebrates and said, "The detectives express doubts Jerome Johnson is actually telling everything."

"They don't think *we're* telling everything. How did you find that out?"

"Been drinkin' with one of them. He don't trust me, but he gives me tidbits hoping I'll give him same. They want Billy bad. Jerome didn't see Billy shoot him with that Taser. That's a little hard to swallow, isn't it? A man that size comes to your bedroom door and you don't see him? You think he's protecting somebody? Billy, for instance?"

"Why would he cover up for Billy on that? He admits he was in the house arguing with Roxanne."

"Only other person could have Tasered Jerome was Roxanne. But then who killed *her*? Max and the maid were both gone."

"I heard a boat leaving the estate."

"Billy did it."

"The police reported a small boat stolen from not far away. Returned the same night."

"It was just some criminal fisherman. The lake is crawling with 'em."

"Philip had a dinner date with Kathy that night. He didn't make it until almost ten. And he doesn't have an alibi."

"You look at how it was committed. She's tied to a chair. If you recall, it wasn't too many years ago up at Echo Glen that Billy tied a counselor to a chair. Got hisself a ticket to Monroe."

"I know. I've thought about that."

"Repetitions, Thomas. They run all through this. Somebody sends an audiotape cassette of her husband's death to Roxanne. Two nights later, somebody makes a videotape of her death. She dies tied to a chair. Her husband dies tied to a chair. Billy ties the counselor to a chair. There's no dancing around it, man. And you know as well as I do, he's going to get seven, eight years for it, be out in five. Then he'll do it again."

"This? He'll get the death penalty."

"Not if *we* don't give it to him."

As the service was about to begin, Philip paraded down the aisle, beside him a stunning Kathy Birchfield in a black dress, her hair loose and flowing and blacker than anything in the chapel. Roxanne would not be pleased to know she was being upstaged at her own funeral. Philip led her to the front of the church, where they sat near Roxanne's third husband, Jon Pitney, and his new wife, Hope.

At the service we learned things about Roxanne I never would have guessed, that she had been a track star in college, had been an alternate for the Olympic team, had high-jumped over six feet in high school, had taught fifth grade, and that she had lived two years in Borneo with her second husband, where they had lost a child to some exotic tropical disease.

Afterward, while the crowd mingled outside in the sunshine—there was to be no procession—Snake and I found Jerome commiserating with Roxanne's older sister and mother, both of whom wore dowdy brown suits and had all the homely aspects of Roxanne's features and none of the comely ones. The father, we had been told during the service, had abandoned the family when Roxanne was twelve, which might have accounted for, if you took a Freudian view of things, Roxanne's unbridled need to court men of any and all ilk.

When we got Jerome off to himself, Snake said, "Hey, kid. It's time to fess up."

"Huh?" Jerome butted his John Lennon glasses with the knuckle of a thumb and ran his palm across his high, wiry

hair. It was sunny and cool, a slight breeze that would
have taken the feeling out of our cheeks if we stood in it
long enough. Jerome wore dark, ill-fitting suit pants he
probably had borrowed, and a black jacket draped loosely
over the cast on his broken left arm.

"Yeah, sonny. Fess up. We know you saw more than
you're telling."

"I want to thank you both for scaring off whoever it
was."

Snake laughed wickedly. "My guess is Billy would have
taken you out into the lake and weighted you down with
rocks in your crotch. The lake is over two hundred feet
deep in places. Anyway, she's spending eternity just the
way she would have wished to. On her back. I'm drunk.
Forget I said that. She was a hell of a woman. One hell of
a woman . . . more woman than I am man."

"I never even saw Billy at the house that night," said
Jerome. "Only heard him."

Snake grumbled. "Well, I followed him there, so I know
it was him. What about the old lady? I heard you told the
cops you weren't banging her. Gimme a break."

"Yeah, well, I lied about that." Jerome turned pink.
"She was so nice to me. I didn't want to do it, but . . ."
Jerome was blushing.

When the festivities tapered off, Snake dragged me off
to the local pub, where he won a wager with one of the lo-
cals that he could swallow five raw eggs in less than ten
seconds. While we hashed over the case, I nursed a soda
and Snake downed whatever they put in front of him. Neither of us came up with anything particularly brilliant.

The next day two college-age daughters and a wife
came to my office to ask for help in finding their father
and husband who, it seemed, had walked out of the house
to go to the store and never returned. What made the case
titillating was that it had happened eleven months ago and,
although they claimed he had never disappeared in the
past, they had just recently begun to worry enough to seek

help. "For eleven months," I said, "where did you suppose he was?"

The daughters nodded and the wife gave me an answer I knew I would be taking to private eye conventions for the rest of my life. "Shopping," she said.

Saturday afternoon, eight days after Roxanne's murder, I took an eighty-mile bicycle ride with some friends who raced in category three, down Lakeside, through Renton and up into Bellevue, across Mercer Island, and then a couple of laps around the island and back home again across the new floating bridge. It was good to deplete myself on a long ride before taking on winter fat.

Wet and naked, I received a telephone call while stepping out of the shower. "Thomas?"

"Philip. You're not laughing."

"What does that mean?"

"Nothing. What do you want?"

"To tell you the truth, you're the one who's usually laughing at me. Honestly, I don't think this world is very funny. Never have. Listen, Jerome Johnson called me a few minutes ago."

"So?"

"So Billy's got him."

"What?"

"Billy's got him somewhere. Billy apparently conned Jerome into meeting him, then kidnapped him at gunpoint. He wants me to come and get him."

"Who wants you to come and get him?"

"Billy wants me to come and take Jerome home. Can you believe the luck?"

"Stop right where you are, and you call the police. Understand?"

"He's over by the First South Bridge somewhere. Jerome says Billy'll kill him if I bring the cops."

"So what's going on?"

"I don't know exactly. Jerome's scared. I can tell you that much. I think Billy may have done something to him."

"Like what?"

"Use your imagination."

"Why would Jerome meet Billy somewhere alone?"

"He said Billy wanted to turn himself in but needed Jerome to go with him. He was afraid somebody was going to shoot him."

"So why didn't you call Snake? Why me?"

"I did. And another friend of mine who I thought might be able to help. Neither one of them was home. Neither were you until just this minute."

"Where are you?"

"Down by Gas Works Park."

"And where are Jerome and Billy?"

"They're going to call again. You've got to hurry. Don't you understand? We don't see eye to eye on a lot of things, but we know how dangerous Billy can be, and we both want to see him where he can't do any more harm, right?"

"I'm not going on a hunting expedition."

"Of course not. But we've got to pick up Jerome. Will you help?"

"I'll be there in ten minutes."

"Thanks, Thomas."

"Sure."

After toweling off, I stepped into some old jeans and a sweatshirt, a pair of broken-down Pumas that I had played several hundred hours of basketball in, then went to the back of my bedroom closet and knelt, fumbling with a panel that didn't look as if it was removable. After I got it open, I disabled the alarm and pulled out the kind of pistol a lot of ex-cops probably wouldn't have chosen: a .45 Colt Government model. I had done a lot of combat-style shooting with this and with similar pistols, and I trusted the weapon and liked the load. I filled three clips, popped one into the handle of the gun, and dropped the other two into the left pocket of my windbreaker. I took half a box of Remingtons and dropped them into my right pocket. Then I clipped a holster onto my belt and put the .45 in, snapped the buckle. Though I hadn't carried a gun in years, I still had a concealed weapons permit.

As I drove toward Gas Works Park, I tried not to visualize the possibilities. It was go with Philip or not go with Philip. I hadn't had much choice. All I knew was that I had already lost one client and wasn't about to lose the other.

49 MY HAIR WAS STILL WET FROM THE shower and I had been in too much of a hurry to put socks on, so I could feel the truck's heater on my bare ankles and the cold air sucking on my skull. Because of the long bicycle ride, I was pretty near starving. I managed to grab two bananas and an orange on the way out the door but had consumed them before I cleared the University District.

When I got to Gas Works Park, I spotted Philip alongside his BMW on Northlake Way. The park was full of people flying exotic kites. It took him a while to notice me.

Braking to a stop in the street, I said, "Get in."

"No way. Sucker. You get in." Angrily, he opened his car door, sank into the driver's seat.

I parked, locked the truck, and walked to the passenger side of the BMW, feeling the mild burning sensation in my muscles that meant my body and bloodstream were overloaded with lactic acid from the bicycle trip. I was hungry and worn-out, and the fleeting thought occurred to me that Philip might be running some sort of dipsy doodle to get me out into the woods and put a bullet through my brain.

"They call?"

"On my cellular. Thank God for these things." He touched a small, black leather case at his side, fired up the engine, and pulled out into the street before I even had my door closed.

"Where are they?"

"You ever hear of Detroit Avenue?"

"Over near West Seattle by the First South Bridge?"

"We're supposed to drive there and walk up the hill into the woods. I hope we can find it. It's clouding up and starting to get dark."

I showed him a five-cell flashlight from my days as a patrolman. He told me there was a flashlight in his glove box, but when I got it out and turned it on, the bulb shone weakly. He put his flashlight next to the gear shift and pulled out his gun as we cruised onto the freeway at Forty-fifth, absentmindedly pointing the big Smith & Wesson at my stomach.

"I brought this too," he said.

Reaching across, I grabbed the barrel and twisted the gun up and backward, almost breaking his fingers, and took it away from him.

"Darn you," he said. I directed the muzzle at the floor-boards between my knees. As guns went, it was a beaut, blued, with an eight-and-three-quarter-inch barrel. The problem with a .44 Magnum was that every bullet you fired had the potential to go through car doors, skulls, houses, you name it, to kill two, maybe three people and a couple of cats to boot. Most city police departments didn't allow them for that reason. "I told you not to aim this at anybody."

"Don't be so touchy. It's empty."

"You didn't listen when I spelled out the rules, did you?

All guns are loaded, and you never point one at anything you don't want to kill."

He thought about that for a while. "What makes you the expert?"

"Four years on a combat pistol team. Three state championships."

He thought about it again. "What makes you think I don't want to kill you?"

He may have been smiling, but he looked as if he could chew through a log with those teeth. I broke the cylinder open and found it empty, then laid it on the floor at my feet, cylinder open.

"Give it back."

"Like I'd give car keys to a drunk." He began slowing the car to pull onto the shoulder of the freeway.

"Give my gun back or we don't move another inch. Jerome gets whacked by Billy, it'll be your fault."

"I'm not the one driving. It'll be your fault."

"I can be as stubborn as anybody. So we'll watch Jerome die. That'll be two deaths you've caused in one week." We were going thirty-five now, pulling off the freeway onto the shoulder. A foreign car full of young men in baseball caps honked at us.

"I thought Billy wanted you to take Jerome home, not kill him."

"You want to take a chance?"

It was not likely I was going to win a stubborn contest with Philip. I picked up his Smith & Wesson and handed it to him, whereupon he accelerated back onto the freeway without downshifting, lugging the engine.

He took the Michigan Street exit, but I had to help him get to the other side of the river. Years ago when I had been on patrol, I lost half a night on the hillside above Detroit Avenue chasing a couple of teenage boys who had raped an elderly woman who had been living in her car. I lost them, then returned in the daylight with my partner, trying to figure out where they had gone. There had been some construction activity in that part of town, and I won-

dered if it had encroached on the wild acreage I remembered.

Philip said, "You only took my gun because I'm going
to marry Kathy next Tuesday."

"Say again?"

"Oh, cripes, I guess I put my foot in it. Darn. Maybe
she was going to explain tonight. She turned me down on
a Vivaldi concert at the Seattle Center for some reason. I
should have guessed she was breaking old ties."

If I had swallowed a half gallon of diesel fuel, I couldn't
have felt much sicker. "What were the directions again?"

"That we'd see his truck. Walk up the road to the south.
Supposed to be an old house up there somewhere. That's
where they are. In the house. Listen, Thomas. About me
and Kathy? She told me a few days ago you had asked her
to leave me. There's no hard feelings, I trust. We can be
gentlemen about this, don't you suppose? Because I think
some day we'll be close friends, you and I. All three of us.
That's what Kathy wants, and—"

"Listen, Philip. I don't want you taking a gun up there."

"You've got one."

"That's different."

"How is it different?"

"I'm not going to shoot anyone."

"Then why bring it?"

I had no answer for that, at least none that I could give.
Mine had come along because I didn't need to get executed or to watch anybody else get executed by a punk just
out of prison. I had no intention of carrying out any death
sentences. In my heart, I believed in the legal system. I
knew there were inherent oversights in the arrangement,
but for my own peace of mind I needed to support it. I
didn't know how to square these thoughts with what I had
decided at the funeral, because at the funeral I had decided
to kill him if I ran into him again.

Until Philip blurted out that he and Kathy were getting
married Tuesday, I harbored a wee suspicion that this trip
might be some sort of con. But his announcement of the

wedding had been so smug I knew he wasn't planning anything. Shooting me would be anticlimactic.

Inside the city limits of Seattle lay a multitude of green belts, of wooded gullies and hillsides, and in some cases, acres of vacant and overgrown, largely forgotten land. Full of potholes, Detroit Avenue was an obscure little road most people didn't know existed. It ran parallel to West Marginal Way, only a few blocks southwest of the First South Bridge, which was one of the most heavily traveled bridges in the state.

The broad hillside to the west of Detroit Avenue was wooded and shrouded in brush and blackberry vines. Several businesses, their parking lots booby-trapped with mud puddles, lined the north end of Detroit, but the farther south we drove on the short road, the wilder it got.

A primer-gray pickup truck, one of those small foreign numbers without a rear bumper, was parked nearly at the end of the road. I had seen the same truck sitting outside Roxanne Lake's garage at Hunt's Point with a bumper sticker on the front that said, ANOTHER MAN AGAINST VIOLENCE AGAINST WOMEN, and had assumed then, as I did now, that it belonged to Jerome Johnson.

A rutted, gravel lane with a hump of weeds between the wheel tracks led south from there, up through a knot of blackberry bushes and overhanging apple and cherry trees.

Years ago, when my partner and I scouted this hillside, we discovered a huge old abandoned house halfway up the hill. Higher on the slopes, beyond the ramshackle house, we discovered old barns, stables, outbuildings, and above that, wild and overgrown pastureland. The property looked out over the smokestacks and industry of the Duwamish Valley and probably had belonged to wealthy folk who had come on bad times.

Philip parked the BMW, reached across me to the glove box, and fetched his flashlight and a small case that held opera glasses. He sat with his door open and began pushing the fat .44 Magnum bullets into the Smith & Wesson's open cylinder. When he moved, his jacket pocket clinked with spare cartridges.

It was hard to know what to do.

I did not wish to confront Billy Battle with a gun-happy Philip alongside.

It would be dangerous for Billy and for anybody else within range of that Magnum.

The thought of racing him up the hill occurred to me, for I knew where we were headed better than he did and might be able to lose him, but it was getting dark, there was no telling what Billy was thinking, and the last thing I wanted was to stumble blindly into an ambush. Besides, after an afternoon of battling to keep pace with my bike-racing friends, I wasn't sure I could beat Philip in a foot-race.

There was the option of jumping him then and there, but I didn't want a wrestling match with a loaded pistol be-tween us either. I could hit him in the head with a rock, but that might kill him.

"You don't happen to have a Snickers bar, do you?"

Philip got out, locked the car and said, "Why, no. Are you hungry?"

"Not really."

"It must be up that way," he said, pointing at the rutted tracks heading up the side of the hill.

"Must be."

"Listen, Thomas. I really don't want you to feel bad about this marriage thing. I really don't. We'll still be friends. All of us. I really want us to be friends."

"Don't forget your light."

"I know this is sudden. But would you honor us by be-ing our best man?"

"Let's you and me have a reality check, Phil. Okay?"

"What do you mean?"

"First of all, we're not going to be friends, you and me. Probably not me and Kathy. Secondly, I don't like you, Phil. I never have and I probably never will. When Kathy marries you, it'll make me like you less. Not more. So cut the crap about my being the best man. And you're not six feet tall. I could eat soup off the top of your head."

"Did anybody ever tell you you were uncouth?"

"And juvenile and a lot of other things. Right now I don't give a rat's ass."

The road climbed at a steady rate, and Philip and I began breathing hard. The tall, brown grass at our feet was still damp from rain. From time to time the long prickly branch of a runaway blackberry bush reached out for us, then clawed the air wildly as we pried it out of our clothing and moved on. Spiderwebs glittered with gems of moisture. It was dark enough that in another half hour we would need the flashlights to get back down. Below us to the east on Highway 99 most of the cars had their headlights on.

Surreptitiously, I unsnapped the hammer loop on my holster. "Phil, just one little thing."

"Sure, Thomas." He was huffing hard, pushing on his knees with his hands on the steeper sections.

"The other day when you busted into my office—"

"Thomas, I really want to apologize to you for that. I was out of line. Kathy was upset. I know you were upset, and I just want to tell you I was out of line that day. I was."

"Naw," I said. "You were upset about Roxanne's death. But you mentioned something about somebody killing Roxanne and filming the whole thing."

"Did I?" He readjusted the sagging weight of his Smith & Wesson in his waistband and changed his wallet from one back pocket to the other.

"How did you know about a film?"

"I suppose I heard it on some news report or other."

"No, you didn't. The police are keeping it hushed up."

He huffed some more, stopped walking, and propped one leg on a dirt outcropping at the side of the road. The air was warm with the smell of wet earth and moist vegetation. "Well, then I guess somebody told me."

"Who?"

"Maximilian, I suppose. I spoke to him at the funeral."

Keeping my eye on him, I took a few more steps and stole a quick glimpse up the road. It continued to wind and climb, the portions ahead even more overgrown than the narrow track we had been through. I could see long strands of spiderweb spanning the trail at the height of my head. "Maximilian doesn't know about the video. Besides, you spoke to him at the funeral after you told me about the filming."

"Gosh, I don't know who told me. Somebody. Are you sure we're going the right way?"

"They said go south up the dirt road. That was Jerome's truck back there. We're going south."

"I thought this was east."

"East is that way. How did you know about the film?"

He huffed some more and chewed his lower lip while he looked me over. "Somebody made a film of her death, didn't they? Maybe Jerome told me."

"I'm pretty sure Jerome doesn't know about it."

"I think he did tell me." Unconcerned, he began walking again, leaning into the hill. I walked beside and slightly behind. "No. Wait. Snake told me. Yeah, he did. This whole past week has been an ordeal, Thomas. In the last seven years I don't think a day has gone by that my thoughts haven't reached out to Roxy at some point, and then, to have something like what happened to her . . . and to know it was my fault."

"Your fault? How do you figure?"

"Billy killed her. I had a chance to make certain Billy didn't, but I let you talk me out of it."

"We're not going up here to kill this guy."

He took ten more steps before he said, "I know that."

There was an ever-so-slight possibility that Snake had told him. I hadn't been in touch with Snake in almost twenty-four hours, and whether or not he had spoken to Philip was not something we had discussed. Whatever else Philip was concerned about, he did not seem concerned over my catching him in an apparent slip-up.

Before arriving at the house, one had to cross a deep ditch, natural or man-made we could not tell. It was a sheer thirty-foot drop in some places, shallower in others. The floor of the ditch was a forest of spiny thistles. The only way across the gully was to take a long path in the grass that led around to the right near the woods.

Seventy-five yards away stood a fine old house that hadn't been lived in for maybe thirty years. Three stories, it was sinking on one side. The front porch had caved in. There were two windows near the porch. A light shone in the one farthest to the right. The light was intense and white, and after I stared at it long enough, I thought I saw a shadow waver in front of it.

Philip opened his opera glasses. "There's a light in the window."

He handed me the glasses. One of his eyes was so much weaker than the other that the left lens looked like somebody had smeared a gob of margarine across it. I futzed with the focusing knob. "We're going to get Jerome," I said. "If Billy wants to turn himself in, we'll take him back too. We're not going to fight it out with Billy. Not here. Not with Jerome in the way."

Philip did not answer, only stared up the hillside with a look in his eyes that told me nothing.

"You've been giving me orders for over a week now, and all you've done is get a very special lady killed. You don't give any more orders."

It was time to cold-cock the sonofabitch, kick him in the nuts, remove and unload his weapon, and I would have done those things had his gun not been pointing at my sternum.

"Listen, dickhead," I said. "You put that thing down or I'll make you eat it." We were standing four feet apart when he cocked the hammer back.

Without earplugs, the concussion alone might do permanent damage to my hearing. I wanted to tell him I could draw and fire my weapon in about the time it took him to blink, wanted to tell him how foolish and damned danger-

ous he was being. I was about a tenth of a second from
dead and so was he and I didn't like the feeling. Nor did
I want him to even have a glimmer of my expertise, rusty
as it was. I didn't need to spook him. He was nervous
enough. He was sweating and the pistol was shaking.

50

"JUST YOU AND ME MOSEY ON UP
this little trail, and we'll see what
they're up to," said Philip, gesturing with the barrel of his
Smith & Wesson.

I jammed the fingers of each hand into my jeans pockets
and stiffened my arms against my rib cage. "I don't like it
when people point guns. I told you that already."

"Don't get all tight. This is just two friends talking, one
of whom doesn't know gun etiquette because his fiancée's
buddy wouldn't teach him."

"Philip, this is why most people shouldn't be carrying
guns. Exactly this."

"What's over there is the purpose for carrying a gun. I
may not be the expert you are, but Snake showed me
enough."

"That include showing you how he accidentally shot
most of his butt cheek off two years ago?"

"You're making that up."

"He was practicing his quick draw, and now his wallet
doesn't show. We're going over some rough ground here

and it's almost dark. You step in a hole and that thing goes off, half of Seattle's going to get up from the dinner table and look out the window. Billy might even hear it."

He motioned for me to step back, and when I did, he let the hammer down while the gun was still pointing at me, which didn't piss me off at all. I was already so angry there was nothing he could do that would make it worse.

Dropping the opera glasses into my pocket, I walked away from him.

The trail in the damp, brown grass led slightly uphill to the right and around the end of the gully, zigzagging through some knee-high prickly brush, around the shallow snout of the ditch, then back toward the falling-down mansion. Philip kept ten feet behind.

We walked along the side of the house, past a rusted washing machine cattywampus in the weeds, past eight or ten scattered wine bottles with the labels weathered off, past doors lying flat and blanketed with moss, past a rhododendron that must have been forty or fifty years old that extended to the second story of the house. I had seen larger rhodies growing wild on the Olympic peninsula, but not many and not often.

The night was quiet except for a large bird squawking higher on the hillside and the distant rushing noise of traffic on the highway.

I kept a watch on the windows that weren't blotted out by the rhododendron and saw movement in one. My hope was that if anybody saw us and felt the need to fire a gun in our vicinity, they would see that Philip had a revolver in his hand and target him first, which would give me a second or two to react. Dramatic imaginings. Even as I laughed at myself for the melodrama playing itself out in my head, I began to get a bad feeling in my bowels, as if this were the second day of a Mexican vacation. It came on with incredible swiftness. I had had the feeling before, and things had always gone badly.

Philip remained a few paces behind while I crept past the glassless windows without incident. I stepped onto the front porch. It was soggy and soft. I went through the cockeyed front door. Somebody had pried the knocker off the middle of the door, leaving a maw now black with rot.

It was night inside the house. A very white light splashed from a room thirty feet beyond the front door, dim at first, then almost blinding as we entered the structure and caught it at the proper angle. Philip was close enough that had we been alone, I would have jumped him and broken all the fingers he had wrapped around that damn gun.

The corner of the entranceway was littered with damp *National Geographic* magazines, hundreds of them, flattened, covers tattered and slippery under our feet. The furniture in the living room was gone except for a broken-down sofa that reeked of mildew. A legless chair sat on the floor near a window that, remarkably, still had some glass that hadn't been shot out by boys with slingshots.

Walking across the floor with my right hand on the butt of my holstered pistol harvested a certain amount of small noises from the house, creaking floorboards, a tiny knob of glass crackling under my shoe.

At the doorway, I poked my head around the corner and peered into the lighted room.

Jerome gazed up at me from the corner, silent, scared, and somewhat bewildered. His confusion was alleviated when he saw Philip over my shoulder. Jerome seemed to be nursing the broken arm, as if the cast had taken some unwarranted strain. His other wrist was handcuffed to a pipe inside a wall. He was kneeling next to a kerosene lantern. Any slight movement projected shadows onto the walls, the shadows we had seen from outside.

Sprawled on a sleeping bag on top of a mattress on the other side of the room under the high, glassless window, and oblivious to our entrance, Billy Blodgett Battle snored methodically. The butt of a pistol protruded from the waistband of his jeans. Philip, now that we had reached the objective, looked as if somebody had turned on an egg-beater inside his brain.

I walked across the room, reached down, and took the gun from Billy. The jostling did not wake him. I removed a folding knife from his windbreaker pocket and another sheathed knife from his belt. I patted him down. He had no other weapons.

Jerome said, "God, am I ever glad to see you two. You oughta hear him."

Philip remained in the doorway staring dully at Billy. He had a look that reminded me of a hyena about to poke at a downed rhino to see if he was really dead.

"You know where the key is?" I said.

Jerome pointed at the windowsill. I reached over Billy, then moved across the room and unlocked Jerome, took the cuffs and snapped them onto Billy's wrists, cuffing him in front, which was a no-no to any experienced cop, but I figured it was less hassle, since I could do it without waking him. I was thinking only a real psycho could get into a situation like this and sleep this hard. Jerome said, "There might be another key somewhere, but I don't know where."

"We'll worry about that in a minute."

Now was the time to disarm Philip, except that he had lined his back up against the wall and raised the Smith & Wesson slightly. His eyes looked like a pair of porch lights that some old man left on day and night. It was easy enough to see that he had no plan other than taking the next breath and letting it go.

Billy Battle continued to snore, adding the percussion of a gentle fart to the symphony. Under different circumstances, the three of us might have laughed, but the tension was electric. Jerome got up slowly and rubbed his wrist where the handcuffs had chafed, tried to get circulation into his shoulders and legs, then retreated to the wall next to Philip in what was basically a defensive posture. From the look of him, he had been chained to that wall for a good long while. It was the second time I had seen him

turn to Philip for succor. It was almost as if these two had
some sort of alliance I didn't know about.

"How long have you been here?"

"Seems like forever, but it was a few hours." Using both
hands, he seated his broken glasses delicately on the
bridge of his nose, one earpiece awry.

"You all right?"

"I am now. He said he was going to kill me and Phil
here and bury us out on the grounds somewhere. I didn't
know what to do. He made me call Phil. Said if I didn't,
he'd kill me then and get Phil later. I didn't know what to
do."

"How did he get in touch with you?"

"Called Mom and left a cellular number. He told me he
wanted to give himself up. Said he was afraid to try it
alone because he thought he'd get shot. I was supposed to
come and pick him up and help him. God, I was stupid.
After everything—Roxanne, Susie, him cutting me—I believed him."

"He say anything about Roxanne?" Philip asked.

"No. I asked, but he won't talk. He's been telling me
other stuff. Susie Alberg. He knows everything about her
disappearance. Claims she's at the bottom of Lake Washington."

It was hard to believe Billy could sleep. Yet, if you had
five suspects and you knew one of them had committed a
crime, a murder, say, the thing to do was put them in a
room and let them stew. The first one to go to sleep was
your killer. The others would be keyed up trying to figure
out all the different ways they might get shanghaied or
tricked or fooled. To the guilty man who had been on edge
for days or weeks already, it was the second shoe dropping
and he could relax somewhat and stop waiting. To the innocent man, it was only the first shoe dropping.

Stepping across the mattress, I kicked Billy hard on the
bottom of his foot, twice, three times. It was an old patrolman's trick, although it was usually done with a nightstick,
standing beyond somebody's feet where it was next to im-

possible for them to spring up and surprise you. It took half a minute to wake him.

"He drunk?"

"He's always slept like that. Since he was a kid."

When Billy finally awoke, he fought the cuffs, then saw us, saw Philip's gun, and realized his was missing. After a moment he slithered backward across his sleeping bag like a lizard with a broken spine and leaned against the wall. As he sank his weight against it, part of the wallboard caved in.

"We're going to take you in, Billy," I said. "They want to question you for the murder of Roxanne Lake."

"Question him?" Philip was shouting. "They want to hang him, they got any sense!"

Billy looked from Jerome to me and then to Philip. A smile you could classify only as demented crossed his face. From the look of cool competence he tried to fake, he had been in jams like this before.

"How're you doing, Billy?"

"You wouldn't believe me if I told you."

Striding across the room, Philip whipped his pistol around in a circular rotation and struck Battle across the brow with the barrel. "You're going to answer, you little weasel. You're going to answer every question we ask."

Before he could hit Billy again, I kicked Philip in the back of the knees and hammered my automatic down and across his right wrist as he fell. The Magnum dropped softly onto the mattress. I scooped it up before anybody else in the room thought to.

I spoke softly. "You're turning into a bully, Philip."

"I think you broke my wrist." He rubbed it and crawled away from Battle. Being strong and being deliberately cruel so that you would look strong were two different animals. Philip had evidently transposed them.

"*Mucho hombre*, Phil," Billy said sarcastically. "With a gun in your hand. *Muy malo hombre*. Why don't we try that same routine man to man, huh? I'll make you eat your nuts."

Billy's scalp had erupted with a bright scarlet torrent. I tossed him a T-shirt that had been on his bedding and told him to compress it over the wound.

Using one hand, I popped the cylinder on Philip's revolver and tilted the assembly until the bullets slid onto the floor. I holstered my automatic and held his gun through the open frame. Billy mopped the trickles of blood zigzagging down his face and onto his forearms.

"We've got kind of an interesting situation here, Billy," I said.

"Don't we, though?"

"For once in your life, why not tell the truth?"

For a moment I thought I saw a spark of amusement in Billy's pale blue eyes. "The truth? Sure. First thing you should know is I wasn't holding Jerome prisoner. He was holding me."

"It's going to kill Mom," Jerome said, near tears. "This is going to finish her off."

"You should have thought of that before you framed me," Billy said. "Before you came up here with a gun."

"You don't have to impress anyone with your crazy theories anymore," said Jerome. "You're going back to jail. You can't talk your way out of it. You never could. But you never quit trying."

Billy dabbed at his head with the balled-up shirt, then pulled it away and stared at the blood, pressed it back on the wound. He said, "You came up here and started talking shit, Jerome, phoned Philip pretending I had you prisoner instead of the other way about. After you hung up, I jumped you, got the gun and cuffed you to the wall. Took a little siesta. If I was planning something, why would I take a siesta?"

"Say your piece!" Philip barked.

"About the murder? I didn't kill her. I got there, nobody's around, so I go upstairs to put the keys to the Mercedes in Roxy's bedroom and I find her tied to a chair, that plastic sack over her head, and Jerome was I don't know where. She was already dead. I take the video from the camera downstairs to where I know they got a TV room, but before I get settled in, somebody shows up and I hide."

"Why the heck would you hide?" Philip asked.

"I'm scared by what's upstairs."

"Then what?" I asked.

"Then whoever came in goes upstairs and I'm outta there."

"It was me came in," I said. "With another investigator named Elmer Slezak. We found the tape running. We found Roxanne upstairs and a little later we found Jerome unconscious outside."

Billy looked at his foster brother and said, "You weren't lying?"

"How do you think I broke my arm?"

Battle pondered this new wrinkle for a few moments. So did I. He seemed genuinely surprised to learn Jerome had been hit with the Taser and had gone out his window. "I don't know what to believe anymore. People are lying faster than I can straighten it out in my own head. All I know is, I'm twenty-two and just out of the joint. I blow off Roxanne, I would have humped her first."

"Shut your mouth," Philip said.

"Geez, Billy," I said. "You trying to dig yourself in or dig yourself out?"

Jerome spoke softly. "Billy? I heard you downstairs arguing with her. The next thing I remember, I'm waking up in the garden and my ribs feel like a sack of broken glass."

"She was dead when I got there," Billy said. "If you heard an argument downstairs, it was someone else. And I don't know who shot you with that Taser."

We mulled that over for a few moments, all of us, liars and nonliars alike, then Philip said, "Like you don't know what happened to Susie Alberg?"

"Like you weren't all over Susie yourself, Phil. She told me about you. How you were always trying to give her a lift in your car, but only when she was alone, never when she had a friend with her. How you asked her to go to a

motel with you. How she caught you peeping at her out of
your house with a pair of binoculars one day. You gave her
the creeps, Phil."

"That's not true. We talked often, Susie and me."

"You want the real scoop?" Billy asked, looking at me.

"Sure. I guess." What was the point? Billy had never
told the truth in his life.

51

"LET ME EXPLAIN HOW SOME RUMOR
from your past can make people be-
lieve almost any kind of lie. It's all about Susie's disappearance. That's what convinces everybody I'm so bad."

"And cutting up Jerome," I said.

"And beating up a counselor while you were in Echo
Glen," Philip added. "Tying her to a chair. Does that remind us of any recent events?"

"You're not going to fluster me," said Billy. "All this
poison people are throwing around is based on Susie's disappearance. Bear with me, Black. I don't expect these
other two to listen, but I'm hoping you'll give me a hearing."

"Let's take him back now," said Philip. "This is a waste
of time."

"The only one bleeding here is Billy. If he's got the
time, I guess we have too."

"About a week after my ex-girlfriend disappeared, I got

an unsigned letter that said Susie had been on her way to the store when she was dragged into a vacant house. It went on to explain what happened to her in there. I thought I was tough, but I didn't know anything about tough until I read that letter. The hell of it was that I didn't have a clue what to do with the letter. To tell you the truth, I was afraid to give it to the cops. Plus, her father and older brother had already threatened to kill me. I was hoping it was some sort of hoax until I found her sweater in that house."

"This is a good example of how you defend yourself with half-truths," Philip said. "The girl's sweater you claim to have seen from the window of that vacant house was not visible from any of the windows. So how did you know it was in the house? That's the little item that got the police on to you."

"Hell, you dope. I popped the lock. I went in. I saw where it looked like somebody had been in there, and I found the sweater. So I went back out and called everybody over. You think I'm going to announce to what is essentially a lynch mob waiting to form up that I can pop a lock? After all those burglaries?"

"Who else saw the letter?" I asked.

"It disappeared with most of my other stuff when they had me down at the jail."

"Mom threw it out," Jerome said sheepishly.

"What?" Billy was wide-eyed.

"She read it. I read it too. How could you do that?"

Billy said, "You read the letter?"

"It's been the family secret for years. Mom was screaming up in your room. I went up to see what it was about. She wouldn't let me have it at first, but then she gave up and I read it. You're sick, Billy. They should have kept you in forever."

Billy looked pleadingly at me. Oddly, he seemed to be near tears. "Jerome and I were driving somewhere—he never said where—but we don't even get to the end of the alley when the fucking car breaks down. So we're working on it and talking about Susie, and Jerome knows too many things about Susie's disappearance. I figured he knew who did it and was protecting them for some reason. And now you tell me you read the letter?"

"I told you stuff you wrote yourself, Billy."

"I didn't write it."

"Whatever. Somebody did. Anyway, I got it from the letter."

"Why didn't you tell me you read the letter?"

"Mom made me promise not to. She wanted to pretend everything was normal."

"Oh, Christ. I thought you were involved. I thought you knew the person who did Susie. That's one of the things I've been trying to prove."

Jerome looked at Philip and Philip looked at me. Billy continued, "I figured you got your information from Philip here. Or Mr. Pitney. Or somebody." The room got very quiet and stayed that way for a few moments.

"You were having one of your fits," said Jerome. "One of your blind rages."

"And we scuffled and the next thing I know there's a bunch of men with bad breath pinning me down."

Philip began rocking his weight from one leg to another like a blind man holding onto a jukebox. "You cut him to pieces. And you were trying to pants him. What were you going to do when you got his pants off?"

Billy glared at Philip. Jerome, who had looked frightened and bewildered all evening, looked even more frightened now. "I don't remember any of that part."

"There's only one question left," said Billy. "Why lie about the gun that you had?"

"I don't remember any gun," said Jerome. "In fact, I hardly remember any of it."

Billy began staring at Jerome and Philip in a manner I was certain he had perfected in prison. He was an odd combination, with his surprising ability to marshal arguments and speak clearly. The education he'd gotten in prison had helped him and contrasted starkly with his tough-guy act. "Ask Jerome why he pulled the gun on me."

"There was no gun, Billy. We were working on your car. And I never knew anything about Susie that I didn't read in your own confession."

Billy began to turn pale. He scratched the top of his head with both cuffed hands. "You know what I think, Black? Maybe one of these two here killed Susie. Maybe both. I think they probably killed Roxanne's husband down in Portland that same year. If I had more time, I might be able to prove this. I also think Jerome set fire to his own house when he was a kid and killed his whole family."

"Now wait a doggone minute," said Jerome. "Don't let's get ridiculous. That was *my* mother and *my* father and *my* sisters, and we know the fire department said it was accidental. And if it wasn't, I'm not the one who had all the trouble about lighting fires. I'm not the one who got kicked out of the fifth grade because his desk caught fire under suspicious circumstances.

"I'm getting tired of covering for you and then having you come back on me. With you, everything is always somebody else's fault. Who's fault was this?" Jerome pushed up the sleeve on his right arm and disclosed a set of scars running from his palm to beyond his elbow.

Billy looked at me and then at Philip, trying to think of more ways to muddy the water. "I always wondered how *this* fucker got there so fast that night. The other two lived right on the alley."

"Yeah, how did you get here, Philip?" I asked.

"Luck of the draw. But you took Susie Alberg to that vacant house. Nobody else. You, Billy." Philip was still rocking, had begun to speed up the cadence.

"She was afraid of you, not me, Bacon."

"And that was her mistake," Philip said. "She was a sweet young girl." We all looked at each other for a few moments, the stark lamplight turning our eyes bright and watery, shrinking our pupils to pinpoints.

"Recognize this?" I asked, pulling an object out of my pocket.

Passing both cuffed hands over his freshly shaved pate and then leaving his arms in the air in a James Dean pose, Billy looked up at us and shook his head. "Cigarette lighter?"

"I took it out of your pocket a few minutes ago. The initials are R.L."

"Somebody put it there."

Philip said, "Enough of this surprised junk, Billy. You're not fooling us. Or do you expect us to believe other people are hiding things in your pockets? Maybe Jerome put it there while he was handcuffed to the wall. Maybe Black brought it with him."

"Did she have it the day she was killed?" I asked Jerome, who shrugged and began edging toward the door. Clearly terrified of Billy's explosive potential, he had the uncomfortable look of mild panic you would see on a reverend caught in a nudist colony.

"You're a killer, Billy," Philip said. "You're a sadistic psychopath, and if somebody doesn't stop you, you're going to repeat."

Battle put his head down on his chest and for a minute I thought he was laughing. But he wasn't. "Everything gets blamed on me anyway. Why shouldn't I confess? I'm responsible. I won't deny it. I'm responsible for the failed space program too. And the drop in the yen. I'm the reason kids watch too much TV."

"Be serious. Did you kill Roxanne?" I asked.

"You care?"

"In fact, I do, Billy. I particularly care about the way you did it."

"Eat shit."

"Get up. Get moving. Let's get out of here before it gets too dark."

Battle rolled slowly to his hands and knees as if he couldn't find his balance, and then, instead of standing upright, sprang at me with a growl. If he hadn't been so deceptively quick, he never could have made it work.

Philip's broken open revolver was in my left hand, but Billy ignored that, clawing for the automatic in my holster, bulling me backward with his head and shoulders, pushing me up against the opposite wall, pinning Philip against the wall behind our bodies. I clamped my right hand over the butt of the automatic.

He was stronger than I expected, and I had expected him to be strong. We wrestled. I dropped the empty gun in my left hand and punched at his stomach with my fist, punched three, four, five times, got maybe two decent shots in. Things got crowded when Philip stooped and snatched at the revolver on the floor, stabbing his hand in and out between our feet. We struggled, the three of us, and finally I elbowed Battle across the side of the head, squarely on the temple, and then kicked at him. My foot caught Philip instead, amidships, hard.

Woofing like a bear in a garbage dump, Philip collapsed at my feet.

Billy, stunned by my elbow, stood in front of me with only a small amount of spark remaining in his eyes. I dimmed it by slugging him in the solar plexus. He flew back across the room, spraddled onto his back beside the kerosene lantern and was still. His skull was bleeding again.

Philip looked up at me, then rolled painfully onto two knees and one hand, his other hand clutching his belly. He tried to catch his breath. His voice was hoarse and had almost no wind behind it. "Kathy's not going to be happy about this."

"Screw you."

When I turned to see how he'd weathered our tussle, Jerome Johnson was missing.

We heard heavy footfalls outside the windows, migrating away from the house. Then a sharp yelp that sounded like an animal getting hit by a car.

I went to the window to scan the hillside, keeping Billy, who still had not moved, well inside my peripheral vision.

Philip had spit up what little fight he had left and was hovering over the puddle as if looking for a contact lens. It was dark enough outside that I could barely see the other side of the gully. The trees in the woods had melded into an amorphous blob.

"He fall in the gulch?" Philip asked, coughing wetly.

"Looks that way."

"Why'd he take off like that?"

"Scared." I hollered his name through the empty window. His yelp had seemed a combination of surprise and pain. Animals sometimes bounced back from impacts like that, but people with arms in casts and cracked ribs weren't always so resilient.

It took some moments to decide how to handle things. Billy was dazed now, but if I took him outside, he was going to stumble and balk every inch of the way. He might even make me carry him. Philip wasn't going anywhere; not now and not in five minutes. Kneeling on Billy's neck, I removed the handcuffs from one of his hands, rolled him over, and forced the other arm around in back, then cuffed him in back. His body remained lax, eyes shut.

"Watch him," I said to Philip, picking up my five-cell flashlight.

"Give me the gun, darn it," said Philip. "He's strong as six football players. Who knows what tricks he learned in the pen?" Philip was still on his hands and knees staring up at me. "On my honor, Thomas, I'm not going to do a thing. You go find out how Jerome is and I'll watch this lunatic until you get back. Word of honor."

It was with some misgiving that I handed him back his gun.

52

NIGHT-BLIND FROM THE BRIGHT LAN-
tern, I was compelled to use the
flashlight, flicking it around the landscape like an old man
chasing a mouse with a stick. Jerome, besides being night-
blind after having been chained to the wall for hours, had
probably forgotten how close the gully was.

I danced the beam through the thistles below and past
the chunks of fallen dirt, past an old car hulk. There was
no sign of a man or beast, no fresh marks on the red dirt
walls and no trace of Jerome's blue jeans or dark navy
sweatshirt.

Walking slowly along the rim, I continued to sweep the
floor of the ravine with the light. From somewhere I heard
a sound that might have been a tree branch rubbing against
another branch. It might have been a moan too.

From this side the only way to get in was to fall in, yet
the other side had ridges one could scramble down.

It occurred to me while I retraced our route around the
gully, while the dampness from the long grasses wetted
and cooled my bare ankles, that behind me in the house
Philip was planning to shoot Billy. The thought hit me at
the same time as the chill autumn wind whipped across my
face.

Somewhere in my gut I must have known he would, yet
I had left them together anyway. Had given him the gun

anyway. Although part of me must have thought it was the right thing to do, another part of me realized it was probably the greatest sin I had ever committed. Snake had been right. You did something like this, you were buying a front-seat ticket to hell. Then again, maybe Philip was planning no such thing. Weak from hunger and shaky from our scuffle, it was hard to think.

I had not gone far when I heard a noise that made me stop and cock my head this way and that. A rhythmic thumping noise like somebody slapping a rug with a broom handle. Then another sound that might have been a man sobbing.

It was not coming from the gully. I peered into the dark woods but saw nothing, no light, no movement. Cool and moist, the wind whistled across the brush on the hillside, numbed my cheeks and injected teardrops into my eyes. Below, traffic pulsed along Highway 99. An airplane unzipped the night along the horizon.

I remembered Philip's binoculars in my pocket, brought them out and focused. Shadows flickered in the room. Two loud popping noises came from the house. Philip's .44 Magnum. The sounds had been very close together and did not have the authenticity of a staged execution. It was more the sound of panic. It was only then I remembered that Jerome had said Billy might have another key to the handcuffs.

I ran. Recklessly.

I sprinted, but even then it was going to take a minute to reach the house, another twenty seconds to reach the room. I stepped in holes and realized the chance of breaking my leg was almost as great as the chance of getting shot entering the building.

It didn't seem possible that Philip had gathered up his courage and done what he considered the moral thing, which would probably be to shoot Billy as he lay handcuffed on the floor. The sounds of a struggle in the room continued. Maybe he had fired and missed and Billy had gotten the jump on him.

In the space of a few seconds a dozen thoughts assailed me. Philip had been accused by Billy of having some part in the high school girl's disappearance seven years ago. Philip had denied it, but Philip was a liar. If Philip was implicated in the disappearance, he would have a very personal reason to kill Billy. And a personal reason was what had been lacking all along. Supposedly, Philip had been following Billy out of sheer public spirit. I had never swallowed that. In fact, his antipathy toward Billy might have been over the missing girl from the get-go. Billy had been investigating. Philip had wanted to quash it.

Another shot rang out. The third.

I rocketed past the window and reached the back porch, skidding once on a slick patch of turf. Though three shots had been fired, the thumping inside continued.

Skating on the magazines in the entranceway, I slammed into a wall, bruised my shoulder and felt nails tearing at my clothing. An earsplitting explosion cracked the center of the house. Simultaneously, something whizzed over my head, either a sonic boom from a bullet or the bullet itself. Without pausing, I rebounded off the wall and continued my gallop toward the room.

Momentarily silhouetted by the brilliant lantern, a figure dodged out of the room and scurried off to my left, down a long, dark hallway.

Crossing the hallway into the room where I'd left the two of them was foolish, but I got away with it. The gunman had not fired again, was still darting about somewhere in the back of the house. I could hear his pounding footsteps.

He was propped against the wall on his knees, his head a mass of knots. His face and head were so swollen he wasn't even recognizable. The fingers on one hand were crumpled and broken, and he held them away from himself like a huge spider someone had smacked with a shovel. Although most of the damage had been done to the top of his head and face, a single tooth lay with its bloody root on the fold of his shirt.

"Goddamned sadist," I said. His chest rose and fell regularly, but I knelt anyway to make certain air was entering and exiting his lungs.

I activated the slide on the .45, letting it go forward to slot a bullet into the chamber. The thumb safety on the side was off.

Two loud noises came from the room beyond the wall. At the same time the wall above our heads shuddered. Scabs of plaster and dust particles shot into our hair and onto the floor. Chips peppered my windbreaker. I pushed him over onto his side. He fell like a wooden dummy. So far it was only plaster, but it was only a matter of time until one of the bullets the gunman was firing through the walls hit us.

Stepping hastily to one side, I pumped four shots in a random pattern into the wall. The house grew quiet.

Dropping into a squat, I listened, waiting for a cue as to where the gunman was now. I dropped the half-empty clip into my palm and slammed a full one in. I took four bullets from my windbreaker pocket and refilled the first clip.

The bloodied man in front of me wobbled his head and opened one eye. It was the blue one.

"Are you all right? Did you lose consciousness?"

"I must have. I was dreaming."

"How'd he get your gun?"

Philip's words came in bloody burbles. "Who would have guessed he was so quick? Or so mean? After all of this, it still came as a surprise. We were sitting here one minute. Wrestling with the gun the next. When he hit me it felt like a chimney fell on me."

"Why did he fire?"

"I don't know. He fired? I guess he did. Did we have Billy? I thought somebody shot me. I could feel the heat."

"Look, Phil. Go down to the car and wait. He's somewhere in the back of the house. I'll keep him pinned. And watch out for that gully."

"Can you come with me?"

"If I did, he'd shoot us both. That's what he's waiting for. This way I can keep him occupied."

With my help, Philip struggled to his feet and stood dizzily, leaned against my shoulder. "Gimme the other gun."

Handing him the revolver I had confiscated from Battle earlier, I patted his jacket pockets and found them flat. Billy had all the ammunition. Thirty rounds or more.

I walked him to the back door and watched the night gulp him down.

Heading back into the dark house, I bypassed the lighted room the beating had taken place in and moved swiftly across the first large room until I saw part of a kitchen through a large entranceway at the far side.

The first enormous room in the house contained only a few sticks of broken furniture, a fireplace, and to my right the passage that led to the lighted room. To my left was the kitchen, a handful of wires dangling from the ceiling. I could see some of this by the refracted light from the lantern. In front of me on the other side of the room a cracked mirror was nailed crookedly to the wall.

After my breathing calmed, I listened, but heard nothing but the rustle of my clothing when I moved.

By now Philip was probably on the other side of the gully working his way toward his car. With only one good eye and a headache the size of Tacoma, it would be a rough trip. Jerome was probably at the bottom of the gully. Billy was crawling around somewhere with a .44 Magnum and, thanks to Philip, more ammunition than a pickpocket at a turkey shoot. Moving to the far side of the fireplace, I stood against the wall and pressed the back of my head to the plasterboard.

"Billy?"

When he returned the salutation, his voice was soft and close. He didn't sound as if he were more than five feet from the entrance to the kitchen.

"I guess you're taking this all pretty seriously, huh, Mr. Black?"

"I guess you could say that. Throw the gun down and let me take you in. I'm not going to hurt you."

"Listen, Mr. Black. Roxanne asked me to ice her old man. Seven years ago? The old fart in Portland. Okay? She thought I was some sort of stone killer and offered me money to off him. Okay? I turned her down. She was still fooling around with Philip, and I think they wanted the old fart out of the way so they could be together. Okay? The only thing that could have happened was Philip went down to Portland his own self and killed that old bastard. 'Cause I sure didn't do it."

"They've got two people locked up in Salem for it, Billy."

"Two people who claim they're innocent."

"What about Roxanne? Who killed her?"

"I don't know." We chewed that over for some moments. "Hey, Mr. Black. You're getting awful quiet."

I had been moving a few inches each time he spoke, knowing the sound of his voice would help cover the rustle of my motion. The house was close to pitch-black now, and the farther I got toward this end of it, the blacker things became. The only light I could see was a dim reflection now and then against the boarded-up windows in a bay twenty feet away, and the lantern light reflecting off the mirror from the wall. Just a glimmer.

Turning my head so my voice was directed back in the direction from which I had come, I said, "Billy, why beat the hell out of Philip?"

I turned my head back in time to see a movement in the large mirror across the room. He was in the center of the kitchen doorway pointing a pistol at me. "Look out, Mr. Black," he said calmly.

I lunged across the room, landing on knees and belly and one shoulder as a flurry of shots boomed through the house. Each time he pulled the trigger, a spurt of flame brightened the interior of the house enough that I could see chunks of the wall and splinters from the floor flying off in all directions. He was still shooting and I was still rolling when I directed the automatic at the doorway.

After I began pulling the trigger, the room brightened considerably. He had ducked behind the wall and was shooting through it. I was shooting through it too.

Each shot had vibrated the structure like a tuning fork, except that it lasted only a fraction of a second. The longer I held him here, the better the odds were for Philip. And for Jerome. I put a new clip in the handle of my .45. After some moments, my ears still ringing from the gunshots, I heard brass shell casings clinking onto the floor in the other room as he reloaded.

"Mr. Black? Mr. Black? I don't want you to get hurt. Okay? Why don't you just leave."

"You act awful funny for a guy who doesn't want me to get hurt."

"Just leave."

"Ummm. Not just yet."

For a while neither one of us breathed. I hadn't been this close to my own death in quite a while, and I found, to my great annoyance, that it inoculated me with a fair high.

During the next few minutes he quietly inched his way back toward the door. He moved with infinitesimal slowness, something I wouldn't have judged Billy capable of. In fact, if I hadn't been utterly still, I wouldn't have heard him at all.

It took almost two minutes before I judged he was a step away from the doorway again, one of those triple-width doorways that might have had a pair of sliding doors in it at one time. The floor had creaked twice, but other than that he had disturbed nothing. An incredible feat in a house so dark I couldn't see the white on my sneakers.

For six or seven minutes we remained like that, I on the floor pointing the .45 at the door frame, he sneaking toward me. It gave me time for my neck to begin cramping, but more important, it provided time to think. It also allowed my hearing to return.

Something seemed to have changed at the edge of the door frame. For a few moments I couldn't figure out what it was. Then, he reached around the doorway with one arm and began firing blindly.

Again the room filled with muzzle flash.

Strangely, it looked like the flash cartoonists painted at the tips of guns in comic books.

I fired three times into the wall, then three more, spacing the bullets out and firing at what would have been just below his waist level. Even as the heavy .45 was bucking against my palm, I heard him running in the other room, through the kitchen and somewhere into the back of the house. The building shuddered a little and some floorboards creaked. The only thing I could figure was that he was going up a set of stairs.

I shoved another fresh clip into the handle of the Colt, got up and walked to the doorway. I flicked on the flashlight and surveyed the room. Gun smoke hung in silky strands. Shiny brass empties littered the floor. I saw no blood.

The kitchen had been gutted years ago and the floor was spotless, which accounted for his ability to move so quietly. A sink lay upside down near the counter. Cool air wafted through the house here. I could smell the kerosene lantern, too.

I swept the light around the room and stepped forward.

 **W**HEN **I** HEARD THE FIRST STRAINS, I was standing in the center of the kitchen.

It was the same misbegotten, run-on insanity I had been hearing on the phone for the past two weeks, except that tonight he was laughing intermittently instead of in one long, steady campaign; five or ten seconds at a crack and then a silence that somehow seemed itself bizarre and unnatural after the din, the calm lasting half a minute or more.

Then more laughter.

Listening to the laughter, I knew it had been Billy's voice all along. How could I have not known?

The laughter was louder than I thought a man could laugh—maniacal, explosive, almost mechanical in its rhythms. It appeared to be coming from a room I had not been in yet, a room from which Billy had fired through the wall at Philip and me. I had been fairly certain he had gone upstairs, but I must have been mistaken.

Cupping the flashlight in my left hand so that only a pinkish sliver of light slipped out, I hoisted the automatic in my right hand and proceeded through the extensive kitchen, down the hall toward the laughter.

I stopped during the silences, moved on while he heehawed.

It was easy to visualize Battle huddled in a corner of some small room pointing the cannon at the doorway while he laughed his fool head off. None of these old walls would stop or even unduly slow down a .44 Magnum slug. All he had to do was hear me somewhere close and let loose at the noise the way we had both already been doing.

For more than a minute I perched near the lip of the doorway, listening to the mindless laughter as it cut in and out. Then it occurred to me that there was something wrong with this picture.

Suckered in like a goat to a salt lick, I stepped into the room and found myself ankle-deep in garbage. Billy Battle was not here. He might be behind me, down the corridor, or in the next room. He might have been laughing through a hole in the wall, but he wasn't in the room. He might have found a spot upstairs from which to pop me through a loose floorboard or an old plumbing cutout.

I turned my flashlight on and flicked the beam around the room. Some hobo had holed up here seven or eight years ago, to judge by the vintage of the brand names on the discarded food containers—probably for a couple of weeks—until the trash was knee-deep. I did not spy any voids in the walls or ceiling large enough to stick a gun barrel through.

When the laughter ruptured the silence again, I almost jumped out of my shoes. I waded over to the corner and booted garbage aside until a large, black two-speaker portable radio and tape deck was showing. Obviously, he had selected this house and location with care, had staffed the building with a shrewd inventory.

It was hard to believe I had gotten into the room alive.

The trick would be getting out in a similar condition.

I switched off the machine, pocketed the tape, waded through the trash to the other side of the room, and turned off the flashlight.

I listened to the house for a time, allowing my eyes to adjust to the darkness. The lantern was casting just the tiniest wash of refracted light into the hallway outside the room.

Tucking the flashlight into my belt, I stepped back and eased my spine against the wall. Slowly, I lowered myself. I dropped my arm and the heavy pistol and let the circulation in my shoulders restore itself. I breathed through my mouth to suppress the faint whistling that occurred when air passed through my nose. I waited and listened until I fancied I could hear blood pounding in the veins in my skull. From this quiet outlook I would be able to hear any sound in the house.

You had to give him credit. It took him nearly two hours to crack.

It started as a squeak twenty feet down the hallway. Then nothing for two or three minutes. Then a tiny popping sound, as if a large, shelled insect had fallen off the wall and hit the floor. I don't know what it was other than some part of his movement. I glanced at my watch. Ten minutes after nine. It had been over three hours since Philip had called me.

Moving like a caterpillar, he forged his way toward me. When I thought he was getting close, I raised the gun in both hands and wedged my arms between my knees. The house was so still I could hear my fingers clasping and unclasping the wooden grips of the .45. I was shaking from the cold, from the hunger, but most of all, from the hunt.

After a while I heard his breathing at the doorway. He must have been going crazy trying to figure out what had become of me. He knew I had gotten this far because I had turned off the boom box, but what then? In the darkness it took me a while to figure out what I was seeing. A gun barrel. Once again he was reaching around the wall to fire blindly.

I fired first. Eight shots.

I squeezed them off one after the other until the slide remained cocked back, then ejected the empty clip into the garbage and heeled another one into the butt of the gun, let

the slide ram a fresh bullet into the chamber. The whole
thing had taken less than five seconds.

Footsteps banged somewhere in the house, far away,
thundering along the floor, or maybe down a set of stairs.
They pounded through the front rooms and evaporated
outside. I could hear or maybe sense the vague vibrations
through the earth in the yard from a running man. What
the hell was going on? Had I missed him so completely
that he was able to drop his gun and run out of the house?
For I had seen the gun drop.

I kicked away the pistol in the doorway and switched on
the flashlight. He was sprawled on his face, blood showing
between his shoulder blades.

I ran through the house and out the front door.

When I got into the long grass, I spotted a figure up the
hill jogging toward the far outbuildings. I sent the light
beam after the runner, but it didn't quite do him justice.
While I debated whether or not to chase, the figure
stopped near a weathered outbuilding and two rude popping sounds broke the silence. Dropping the flashlight into
the grass, I stepped away and sent a dollar's worth of lead
and powder up the hill. An instant later I heard him crash-
ing through the brush, blackberries mostly. If nothing else,
he was going to cut himself.

I went back to the room with the lantern and retrieved
the cellular phone Jerome had used, then poked through
Billy's belongings. I dropped the clip out of my gun and
into my palm and then slowly fed in two bullets to replace
the shots I had fired outside. There was nothing important
here, just the sleeping bag and some provisions and the
holes in the wall where we'd shot at each other.

Swinging the lantern near my waist, I went down the
back hall to the body.

Five of my eight shots had penetrated his back on either
side of his spine, and as I drew closer I could see that another had hit him in the buttock. He was deader than Elvis.
Deader than dead. Deader than my love life.

"Stupid," I said. It was wrong to curse a dead man, but

I couldn't help myself. I rolled him over and stared at the astonished look on his face. "What the hell did you think you were doing? What on earth did you think you were accomplishing? You idiot."

I stooped and fingered the carotid artery at his neck, just in case. My hand came away dripping a warm and somewhat sticky concoction. His lungs were quiet. His heart motionless. For a split second so was mine. Then, as I began to think about things, it started to gallop like that of a small animal in a medical school lab.

I stared at the blood, the limp body, the pale skin, at the wide open eye.

As one might have expected, the brown one remained swollen shut.

54

I WAS WELL DOWN THE HILL AND out of sight of the house when I noticed the blue lights of a police cruiser on the frontage road just west of the highway, its spotlight licking up the hillside like a Komodo dragon tongue. Using their rack lights in the hopes of scaring away whoever was up here, these cops weren't overly enthusiastic. They rolled along for a couple of minutes, then drove away.

A fat raindrop hit me in the face when I looked back up the hill.

Billy was hiding up there somewhere with a gun, but I

had forgotten Jerome. I went back up the hill and looked around at the woods, at the house, then wagged the flashlight beam into the gully and dissected the dark tangle of timbers where a trestle and plank road had once been. Unless he had fallen into some crevice and been swallowed up by thistles, he was not in the gully. But then, why should he be? It had been hours. I stood alone while raindrops kissed the grass and spanked the dirt. I would have to go back into the house. I had forgotten to retrieve Philip's car keys. While I thought about that, the rain petered out.

Killing Philip had been accidental; but whether or not I would be charged with a crime, whether or not I would be convicted if I were charged—those were entirely different matters.

Plenty of people were in prison behind accidents.

I could put up a reasonable argument. I felt I could convince most people it had been unavoidable. After all, the house was riddled with bullet holes from two different handguns. There was empty brass all across the floors. Evidence of Philip's beating, blood spatters on the wall and so forth, abounded. The tape recorder was still in the room, no doubt with Battle's fingerprints on it, and I had the laughing tape in my pocket. All of it supported my story.

I was ready to dial 911 on Billy's stolen cellular phone when I saw the first ragged arms of flame waving about the interior of the house.

When I turned it toward the building, the flashlight's beam punctuated a river of gray-black smoke squeezing through cracks and knotholes and windows, puffing out the front door.

Twenty seconds after I spotted the flames, a fluttering sheet of orange began tonguing out the back of the house. Fire washed out the window of the room where we had found Billy and Jerome. I watched the enormous rhododendron plant alongside the house catch and flare up, and for half a minute flames shot seventy feet into the night sky, lighting up the countryside. Steam whispered off my clothing. There went the bloodstains. There went the bullet holes. The body, most of it. There went my evidence.

The first SFD pumper tried to grind up the steep, narrow path but got bogged down a hundred feet after it left the pavement, its rear duals sinking axle-deep into the damp earth. The three firemen gave up and began unloading hose where it sat. You could tell by their heavy movements the house was a grounder. By now the fire on the hillside was crackling like an NRA Youth Group with .22 rifles.

Forty minutes into the operation, Elmer Slezak showed up at the intersection down the road. Ten or fifteen cars had parked along the block, occupants gawking up the hill through their windshields like ferrets waiting to be let out of a box.

I got into the Mustang and we drove away. About a mile later Snake said, "You been a sorry sight these past couple of weeks, Thomas, but tonight you look like somebody stole your testicles and buried 'em."

I said nothing.

We drove in silence and I directed him to my parked truck at Gas Works Park. Once we were alongside my truck, I said, "Snake? Philip ever say anything about Portland?"

"Every damn time I seen him. Something about me talking to Homicide about an old case. Never did get a straight answer when I tried to link it to this business. Say? That fire back up yonder didn't have nothin' to do with Philip, did it?"

"You talked to him in the last day or two?"

"Can't find him. He knows he owes me money."

"You tell him about the video at Hunt's Point? About the setup?"

"Are you shittin' me? I ain't told nobody. The cops find Billy and he knows about that, they got their murderer, don't you guess?"

"I thought so too. Somebody knows about that video, they're either a cop or they did it." I opened the car door, thanked him for the ride and got into my truck and drove away. At least I hadn't killed an innocent man.

55

IT IS FUNNY HOW ADRENALINE CAN sometimes take the place of food. I had been starving for hours and now I couldn't eat.

Aside from my mood, the strangest aftereffect was a thin swathe through my hair, a line that might have been cut by a barber. I was sure a bullet had done it. I also found scratches on one arm, bruises on one shin, and a funny feeling in my sternum where Billy had butted me with his head.

In the morning I would call Bridget Simes and ask her to see if she could locate Jerome in the event that the fire department had not picked him up.

Whether to turn myself in or to go out to the garage and hacksaw the .45 into chunks, blowtorch the chunks into a heap, and heave it all into the bay in the morning, that was the choice. If I decided to cover things up, I would have to take any casings that had run through the .45 and destroy them too, since casings could be traced to the gun that had ejected them.

At a quarter after two the neighborhood was quiet and I still hadn't slept, was trying to think up more ways in which Philip had helped precipitate his own demise. Or maybe I was waiting for the cops to knock on the front door. Philip had done a stupid thing. If I hadn't killed him, Billy would have. No one but a fool would put a mongoose in a box with a cobra and then reach back inside to see how things were going.

Then too, there was the nearly unthinkable prospect that Philip had been planning to murder both Billy *and* me—he had certainly pointed his gun at me enough times to singe my tail feathers—that he had waited only because he thought he needed my help in subduing Billy. I knew why he wanted Billy dead, at least I thought I did, but I couldn't be sure there was a reason he would want me dead other than eliminating the competition from his love life. Certainly I was a thorn in his side, but people like Philip Bacon did not kill you because you were a thorn in their side.

It all boiled down to one crucial and inexplicable fact: Philip knew Roxanne's death had been videotaped.

There was only one way for him to have that knowledge.

He had done the videotaping.

Maybe Billy had been telling the truth. Maybe Philip had been involved in Randall Lake's death. Maybe he had hired those two in the Salem prison. Or tricked them? Philip's motive was obvious and as old as the world. Even during the past two weeks, he had several times mentioned Roxanne with a longing and fondness I had hoped Kathy would not fail to see.

The audiotape of the killing had given Doug Stutman pause, for most likely it meant someone connected to the crime was running around loose. Maybe when Billy told me he was investigating the crime in Portland, he had been telling the truth, and that was why Philip had wanted him stopped. Then too, if Philip had been involved in the Randall Lake murder, the odds were that Roxanne had been also. Had he killed her to keep her from implicating him? Yet, why do it in such a bizarre manner? Perhaps to implicate Billy, who was known for his bizarre crimes?

When the hinges on the basement door squeaked, I

bolted upright, heart pounding, gun in hand, then leaned over and placed the .45 back in the drawer in the nightstand beside the bed.

"Thomas?"

Silhouetted against the impossibly bright yard light Horace kept burning next door and which shone through my kitchen window, she moved across my bedroom doorway.

Smelling of mint and lavender. She padded across the floor and climbed into my bed, where she melted against me. She knew and I knew that she couldn't keep crawling into my bed like this without something happening. She placed her lips up against my face so that when she spoke I could feel them moving, could feel her hot breath. "Thomas? You awake?"

"We have to talk, Kathy."

"We were going to talk, but you never came home."

"We have to talk, but this is not a good time."

She propped herself up on one elbow and began to nuzzle my neck. I placed my hand on her shoulder and gently pushed her away, then removed my hand. I was tempted to take her in my arms and forestall telling her until morning, but that would have been a rotten trick.

"Listen to me, Kathy."

"No, you listen to me, Thomas, you galoot. You court me, you tell me to break off my engagement with whatshisname—"

"Whatshisname?"

"I'm amazed at how easy it is to say that now. We had lunch together today. We—"

"Don't tell me, please. I have to say something first."

"Mine is more important."

"I have something to say that's going to change the way you think about me. Forever. You're only making it harder."

"What?" She sat up and looked at me. Her mood sobered.

"Kathy, you're my favorite person in the whole world.

No matter what you do, Kathy, you always will be my favorite person. I hope you remember that."

"Are you crying?" When I could not gather up my nerve to say what I had to tell her, she blurted out, "I broke off my engagement this afternoon. It was the hardest thing I've ever done, but I went to lunch with him at Stella's and we talked and I told him I thought he was a sweet guy and I had at one time thought I was in love with him but I had made a mistake, that I was in love with you. That I had been for a long time. Maybe since the day we met. That I just hadn't been ready. And neither had you."

"You *dumped* Philip?"

"I'll remember the look on his face for a very long time. It was terrible."

"Philip told me the two of you were getting married next week."

"We told everybody we were getting married."

"He told me next Tuesday."

"Tuesday? When did he say that?"

"Tonight."

Kathy stiffened, fingered a strand of her hair and began nibbling it. "Why would he tell you something you would find out was untrue by tomorrow?"

I could think of a number of reasons, including that Philip thought I had no more tomorrows. I took her into my arms and pulled her close. She said, "I love you, Thomas. I've always loved you. I think you knew that. You know why? You're loyal and brave and trustworthy and a little goofy and you make me laugh and you see right through me. You may be the only guy I've ever met I can't fool."

"You don't try to fool anyone, Kathy. That's what's nice about you. Listen. I have to tell you this. Philip called this afternoon. He said Billy was holding Jerome hostage and he wanted us to go up there and take him home."

"Are you making this up?"

"Jerome was handcuffed to a pipe in this old—"

"So you called the police, right? The two of you called the police."

"Billy claimed he was afraid the police would do something to him before he got booked."

"But you called the police anyway, because you're loyal and brave and trustworthy and you make me laugh, right?"

I took a deep breath and let it out slowly. Kathy sat up on one elbow. I remained flat on my back, the way I had been since she'd come in. Certain parts of our bodies were touching. She was hot. Me? I was as cold as a gravestone.

"We were up in an old house on some vacant property in West Seattle. Billy had Philip's Magnum. Somehow when I was outside, Billy got out of his cuffs and got hold of Philip's gun. I'm not sure what happened. He fired off a couple of shots—"

"Philip did?"

"Billy did."

"He didn't hit Philip?"

"No. He didn't hit Philip."

"Because I don't know if I could forgive you, Thomas, if you took Philip out in the woods somewhere and let Billy shoot him."

"No, I don't suppose you could."

"So then what happened?"

"Billy pistol-whipped him. Philip. Pretty good. I got back inside to stop it, and Billy took a potshot at me and hid somewhere in the house. By that time it was dark inside. I sent Philip back down the hill to his car while I tried to keep Billy occupied. He had Philip's gun and a ton of ammunition. Philip thought we were going to a dance at the Alamo."

"Philip doesn't have a gun. He told me just the other day he would never own a gun."

"Philip has been known to lie."

"I guess so."

"We were in there shooting at each other through the walls mostly, when somebody came creeping up the hall.

As far as I knew, it was me and Billy alone in the house. I emptied my .45 into the wall."

Slowly, Kathy disentangled herself from me and sat on her knees on the edge of the bed. Her glossy black hair covered her shoulders. In the dim light I could see the slope of her chin and the bulge of a breast. We listened to a clock in the living room. A dripping faucet in the bathroom. We listened as the rain spattered off a clogged gutter into a puddle outside my window.

"You killed Billy Battle?"

"I don't think so. Philip had come back into the house. What happened was an accident."

"What are you saying, exactly?"

"I killed Philip."

"My Philip?"

I nodded in the darkness.

"No. No." Kathy held her hands up, palms out. "No, no, no, no, no, no, no. You're not going to sit here and tell me you've been needling my fiancé for six months, telling dumb jokes about him, and that this afternoon you took him out on one of your stupid expeditions and shot him? I dumped him at lunch and you killed him at dinner? I'm not going to let you tell me that. No, no. Because if you say it, we're through, and I was years getting your stupid little dinosaur brain to this point and I thought things were straightened out and we were going to share the rent and eat off the same plates, and now you've thought of the one thing that would muck it up and you've gone out and you've done it!"

There was nothing to say to that.

I wanted to tell her I thought Philip was a killer, except where was the proof? I wanted to tell her there was a chance Philip, who had been beaten so severely he could hardly see or walk, might have been trying to murder me. I wanted to tell her that somebody had set the house on fire afterward so that I had no verification of any of this. Except where was the proof?

"Thomas, you are a *son*ofabitch!"

There was nothing to say to that.

"What did the police say?"

"I haven't had the nerve to tell the police." Briefly, I explained why, including my belief that Billy Battle had framed me in some way that I probably wouldn't be privy to until it was too late.

"Wonderful. Now I have to decide whether or not to rat on the man I love for killing the man I was going to marry, or whether to let the man I love get away with killing the man I was going to marry. How dare you put me in this kind of situation. *Bastard*."

There was nothing to say to that.

She continued to curse me for a few moments, and when she was finished, she sat beside me breathing hard and cried for a short time, then got up and walked out of my bedroom and out of my life.

There was nothing to say.

 I BELIEVE I AM DOING BETTER.

My breathing no longer involves so much pain, and the lines have been removed from my arm. The worst part is that people know I am recovering so they visit and want to gab.

I have been thinking.

Beulah swooshes in and immediately makes the room smaller. Tonight she is boisterous and loud and tells me

Kathy has gone through some sort of metamorphosis that she cannot comprehend. She has been on a crying jag for days, has canceled all her appointments, and, as far as Beulah can tell, has not eaten all week. Beulah gauges the psychological health of those in her vicinity by their eating patterns. I lay still and let the chitchat wash over me.

When she wants answers, I wince and blurt one-word replies. Yup. Nope. Maybe. She gets the idea, gives me a kiss on the forehead and vanishes in a swirl of Giorgio. At the door she says, "If you blow this with Kathy, there are a number of us who will never forgive you. Everybody thinks you two are perfect for each other."

"Right," I say. Our almost-union, the death of Philip, and our separation have become the office soap opera.

Richard, from the office, visits, and speaks in a whisper. He must think I have AIDS. Allison comes in and is too polite also. A couple of cops I know drop by. One of them, Smithers, immediately inquires about Beulah Hancock. They once had a rather torrid affair. One of my bike-riding buddies shows up and wonders how long until I can ride, seemingly a cold-blooded question, but it is the first thing anybody says to me that actually cheers me up.

Visiting hours are nearly over. It is a Monday. They tell me that six days ago I got into my truck, turned the ignition key and blinked as a piece of the fire wall and some fragments from inside the engine compartment hit me in the head and sent me into a coma. The blast broke three of my ribs and blessed me with a litany of smaller complaints. It also gave me time to work things out.

I have spent the last three days trying to concoct a foolproof scheme to prove Philip did something wrong and to prove also that his fate was his own doing and not mine. When I am not concocting, I am musing about my extraordinary predicament. Killing your best friend's fiancé is usually a bad move.

It is going to be difficult to claim shooting Philip was an accident. If I talk or if Kathy talks, my chances of not being indicted are almost nil. If I keep my mouth shut, I doubt they will come up with enough to get me. Which option favors justice? Which is the right decision? Which do I want to happen? As it stands, only three people know I killed Philip. Kathy, because I told her. Billy, because he was there. And Snake, who, if he hadn't already figured it out from the way I had been acting Saturday night when he picked me up, would have figured it out by now.

It has been in the papers, the discovery of Philip's charred body.

Bridget Simes saunters into my room and sits beside the bed without comment.

She is looking prettier than usual in a soft silk blouse, her auburn hair pulled back into a French braid. She folds her hands on top of a purse that I know contains a device capable of inflicting 150,000 volts to a would-be attacker, a device I have seen her use once—on a three-hundred-pound skip tracer who called her sweetie while palming her butt. The jolt knocked him to the ground, where he wet his pants.

"I remember asking you to find Jerome Johnson."

"You know your truck blew up?"

"The doctors told me."

"Remember who did it?"

"I knew who?"

"You told the paramedics you got into your truck and saw his face at the end of your driveway. You don't recall that?"

"No."

"Well, nobody knows who it was but you."

"Have they arrested anyone in Roxanne Lake's death?"

"Nope."

"Any word from the police on Billy Battle?"

"Not yet."

"What about Jerome?"

"The police talked to him when he came to reclaim his vehicle a few days ago. He said Billy had kidnapped him and that you and Philip Bacon had gone up to some house off Detroit Avenue in West Seattle to rescue him. He said he ran outside and fell into a hole and didn't wake up for several hours, and when he did, the house was on fire. The Medical Examiner discovered a bunch of bullets in what was left of a charred corpse.

"You know who it was, don't you? They found a car parked nearby that belonged to Philip Bacon. It was him. They interviewed Jerome about the body. They seemed to think he might have done it."

"He didn't do it."

"Poor Jerome. His foster mother had a stroke. He found her yesterday tipped over in her wheelchair. She's upstairs. I saw him in the elevator. Recognized him from Roxanne Lake's funeral, but he didn't know who I was so I didn't say anything."

"Tonight?"

"Just a few minutes ago. Yesterday I visited Snake in St. Joseph's in Tacoma. He was asking about you. Somebody hit him with their car and left the scene. A bystander got the license. Turned out to be stolen. Snake says he's been hurt worse bulldogging, but I can't see how. I smuggled him a bottle of whiskey because he smuggled one to me when I had my surgery, even though I don't drink."

"He does that."

"And now he says he wants to marry me. When I told him I was with Tamara, he said that was perfect. He'd marry her too, give us both babies."

We are silent for a minute. The clock on the wall says we have five more minutes of visiting time. They are officious about that here and will kick her out. "What did you find out?"

"How much do you want?"

"Every little scrap."

"Lupe, the maid, is Mexican, been in this country thirteen years. She doesn't do much besides work, go to church, and send money home to her kids. No boyfriends. No lovers. I don't see anything there. She tapes daytime TV and watches it late into the night.

"Maximilian has been arrested for drunk driving but not

in the past five years. He's worked at every type of job you can think of. Boat builder. Gardener. Auto-parts-store flunky. He was a nude model back in the Fifties. Used to pump iron at Gold's Gym on the beach. He's had two wives. Both died. One of pneumonia and one of MS. No kids. He sees a frumpy little housewife hooker in Federal Way every other Thursday night and pays her eighty dollars. I could get the details if you wanted. He likes to fish. He reads sci-fi and visits a bar in Kirkland called Percy's a couple times a week.

"The stolen boat? I looked at it. It was just a boat. Nobody left anything in it. Nobody saw anything."

"Philip?"

"Straight-A student in high school. A little withdrawn. No girlfriends. Not even a picture in the yearbook. He tried out for most of the teams, but he never made varsity at anything. Kind of sad, when you think about it. His parents live near Palm Springs now. Dad was an engineer for Boeing. With that and some investments, they did rather well. From talking to the mother, I gathered they were a little overly protective of him. He had an older sister, but she was out of the house by the time he was five, so he was raised pretty much as an only child. After high school he went to Harvey Mudd on a scholarship, but moved back home and finished school at the U of Dub. Lived at home that whole time.

"He seemed to lead a pretty boring life except for two things. One, he had a love affair with a neighbor lady that lasted a couple of years. It started when he was in his early twenties, and I'm not sure how long it lasted. Two, sometime after he came back home, a nephew he was babysitting drowned out in the backyard in a wading pool. Philip's mother swears that the little boy was murdered by the local psychopath."

"Was his name William Blodgett?"

"You'd be good on *Jeopardy*. Anyway, nobody ever proved anything. It seemed to be a turning point in Philip's life. He felt very guilty about it, decided to live for others

from thereon out. He changed his major and decided to
become a teacher. Then, a couple of years ago, his grandfather died and left him and his sister a tidy little sum.
Couple hundred grand each. He put most of his into a
house. I talked to three of his old girlfriends, and all three
said basically the same thing. He dated them until it had to
either get serious or fizzle, and at that point it fizzled."

"You talk to Doug Stutman in Portland?"

"The homicide dick? He's a hard case if I ever met one.
I drove down there and took him out to dinner. He thought
we were going to end up in some motel, so I think he told
me a little more than he might have. I tried to get him to
admit they had played footloose and fancy free with some
of the evidence on the Lake case, but everything seemed
legit. I asked around. Stutman's thought highly of."

"What about Bacon's possible involvement down
there?"

"Doug still thinks he was involved but can't pin it
down."

"That's okay. I think I know how it went."

"Thomas? He's tagged you, he's tagged Philip, and he's
tagged Snake. It seems like everybody who's been involved, even your client, has been either hurt or killed.
This guy is real good."

"Watch yourself, but don't worry too much. It's about
over."

"You sure?"

"Just about positive."

We sit in silence awhile longer, then Bridget kisses my
forehead in the exact spot Beulah kissed it. I wonder if
there is a mark on my head that says KISS HERE. When she
goes, she deposits a small sack on my nightstand. I don't
have the flexibility to want to reach for it, but I know there
is a chocolate chip cookie inside.

57

I AM ALONE IN MY ROOM WHEN Jerome Johnson knocks softly and pokes his head around the edge of the door.

As usual, he is timid. He mumbles something. When he mumbles again, I realize he's asking if it's all right to come in, despite visiting hours being officially over. I do not nod. Nodding makes my neck feel as if I am hanging by a rope. I say, "Come in, Jerome."

He cups his hand over one ear to hear better, and then, closing the door, steps into the room. He pussyfoots the way people visiting hospital rooms pussyfoot. He remains on the far side of the room.

His hair is wiry and standing high. He still has the cast on one arm. His John Lennon glasses have been repaired. He is a small, inoffensive person with the build of a bookworm.

"How are things going, young man?"

He smiles. "Fair. I found a place to stay. We've got a bunch of singing jobs lined up for November and December. Some Christmas office parties. And we got some guy maybe wants to finance us on a demo. Can you believe that, man?"

"Terrific."

He grins and shrugs. Life is good to him, but he tries to let it roll off his back. "I was upstairs visiting Millicent."

"How's she doing?"

"She'll recover," he says matter-of-factly. "Everytime Billy does something like this, she has some sort of relapse. They tell me you can't move." I say nothing. It is close enough to the question I have been waiting for. I stare at Jerome until he becomes uncomfortable. "Can you move, Mr. Black? Because if you can't, I'd just as soon get these into some water for you. The nurses are having some sort of problem up the hall."

In his uncasted hand he carries a paper sack that has three scraggly carnations jutting from it. He is gripping the sack at the neck, closing his fist tightly on it. It is a pathetic gift, but gifts in this room are few and far between.

Jerome starts across the room. I say, "Stay where you are."

Being the obedient young man that he is, Jerome stops and looks at me curiously. "Sir?"

My right hand is under the covers. I raise it slightly, putting a small hump in the bedspread. He watches with interest.

"What?"

"Before you step over here, why don't you tell me why you would nail a fifteen-year-old girl to the floor?" He is incredulous to the extent that I want to laugh. But then, sociopaths are experts at replicating emotions, innocence being an emotion they must fake more often than most.

"Look, Mr. Black. I'm not sure you're really feeling well. I'll just put these in water and—" He takes a step forward, closing in on the foot of my bed.

"Like hell you will."

He stops. He gives me the almost-smile. "What?"

"One of the books in Billy's collection at his mother's was about a hit man. I thumbed through it. Somebody found a passage about using an ice pick inside a paper sack and highlighted it. The book had been given to Billy by you, an inscription on the first page. I'm willing to bet the book is still there for the prosecutors to find. I'm also willing to bet the inscribed page is missing. Kill me.

Frame Billy. Everything's a two-for-one deal with you, isn't it?"

"Kill you? What are you talking about? I was visiting my mother. Billy is the bad guy, Mr. Black."

"Don't patronize me, Jerome. I saw you flip that 'Do not disturb' sign on the door when you came in." My body is beginning to stick to the sheets. I am sweating like the pig at a barbecue. A bead of sweat rolls down the side of my skull and plops onto my pillow. "Billy's a trouble-maker, but you're a psychopath."

Jerome's face becomes like live rubber, deviating from grimace to smile and then back to grimace. It is the first time I've seen his features so mobile. Usually he has a stone face or that half smile. "What's under the sheet?"

"An innocent person doesn't ask what's under the sheet."

"You've got a gun under there? Really? In your condition, how could you have a gun?" He says it in such a way that he may only be humoring a sick man. "A gun?"

"Mail-ordered it from the back of a *Boy's Life* when I sent for my replacement pair of X-ray glasses."

Jerome smiles, almost. "I'd say you're on a lot of meds, Mr. Black. If you have a gun, maybe you'd better give it to me. I don't even think you have a gun."

"You buffalo pretty easily for someone who thinks he's so smart."

"You are on meds."

"A few."

"Okay, let's analyze this, Mr. Black." He butts his glasses onto the bridge of his nose with a pale knuckle. "I happen to know you killed a teenager when you were a policeman, and it bothered you so much you quit the po-lice. Also, if you had a gun, the nurses would have taken it away. You are known to prefer automatics. A .45 in par-ticular. I don't think you have the strength to work the slide on a .45. The other thing is that that's a book. I can tell by the shape."

"On that videotape, Roxanne said she had been direct

and honest with you. She hadn't been direct and honest with Billy particularly. But she wasn't talking to Billy. Roxanne was talking to you."

"She had been good to Philip, don't forget."

"I have other reasons for thinking it wasn't him. Now you, you jumped out a window to make yourself look innocent. You happened to hit the only freshly spaded spot on the whole estate. I wondered how that happened until I called Maximilian and asked him. He said you spaded it up that afternoon yourself. The laughing phone calls. That was you, mimicking Billy. You're trained in voice, so it probably wasn't too hard. Trying to give me clues. Trying to make the contest more even."

"You're brighter than I would have guessed, Black."

"Sure. I'm bright and you're a killer."

"This is all very slim."

"It's not slim if you have a weapon in that sack."

He grips the sack and then loosens his grip. His uncasted hand is scabbed with small scratches. So is his face in three or four places. "The blackberries nailed you pretty good, huh? When I chased you up the hill."

"These? I got these falling into the gulch."

"When Billy jumped us, you went outside and yelled as if you were in trouble, then went around to the back of the house. When I went outside to look for you, you crept in the back way and surprised Philip. You grabbed his gun and beat him with it. Maybe he gave a little fight, so you fired the weapon to make him keep still. More likely, Billy objected to the beating and you fired to keep him from interfering. When I got in there, Philip was so disoriented he couldn't remember how it happened.

"I got back in there, you shot at me, then had Billy talk to me in the dark. You had the gun. He did the talking. He knew if he told me you were there, you would kill him. When you ran down the hall, he probably ran out the back way. Maybe afterward, if I'd bothered to search the area, I would have found Billy. After I chased you outside and up into the blackberries. Or did you burn him up too?"

Jerome gave me the almost-smile.

"You played around too much, Jerome. The laughing phone calls. You like to toy with your victims too much. You're planning to kill me in a minute. Why not tell me about it?"

"You call that toying? I ruined your love life and almost got you into prison, and you call that toying? If you'd called the cops last Saturday night, you'd be in jail instead of in a hospital. If Billy hadn't made me fire off those shots inside, the shots that warned you, I could have beat Philip's brains in and stuck you with that. And then later, I screwed up that bomb in your truck. That was my fault. Hey man, it was my first bomb. Give me a break."

"No breaks for tough guys."

"Hah. You going to shoot me with a book? I was tempted to pillow you when you were out, but that old man with the belt buckle kept hanging around. I finally got rid of him down in Tacoma. But this way is better because I get to talk to you. Tell you about it. The trouble with being a genius at this stuff is only dead people know about it. Even a genius needs applause."

"What did you have against Billy?"

"Used to kick me around when we were kids. What put you off Billy, anyway?"

"Billy broke one of the cardinal rules. Sociopaths are almost always model prisoners. Their one aim in life is to get out. They are good at convincing most people of most things and, in particular, at convincing prison personnel they have changed. Billy did not get along in Echo Glen."

"That was it?"

"Also, the crimes Billy had proven against him were all crimes of a disorganized offender. Attacking you. He did that wildly. Same with hitting his counselor up at Echo Glen. But most of these other crimes seemed well planned. It got me thinking. A different type of criminal personality seemed to be involved. The capper was when I called Jon Pitney this morning and made him admit he'd found a revolver in the alley the night Billy attacked you.

He sold it for fifty bucks to help pay gambling debts. The way he figured it, Billy deserved the slammer anyway, and he was going with or without the gun as evidence. And the pistol was worth money. He wouldn't testify publicly, but he would hide evidence and sell it privately. What I've been having trouble with is Randall Lake."

Jerome chews on something in his mouth with his front teeth, then breaks into that almost-smile. "I did a few kids, but I always wanted to kill an adult. Lake was my showpiece. That was the reason I was worried about Philip chasing down Billy. Philip wanted to torture Billy to find out about his nephew who drowned. I had a bad feeling Billy would spill the beans about Roxanne's offer to pay him to kill Lake. Billy told me about it when it happened. Nobody knew except me. I had never talked about it to Roxanne, so she didn't even know I knew. But I didn't need Philip finding out. He was such a conspiracy theorist, it would have led to all kinds of things."

"Why didn't you just do something to Philip the way you'd done it to whoever else got in your way over the years? Why hire me?"

"Why play checkers when there's somebody willing to play chess? Roxy wanted to hire you because she was worried about the same thing, that Billy would tell Philip, or somebody, about her offer. I thought I could have some fun with it. Shit, it was her money. Admit it. We had a good time."

"So seven years ago when Billy told you about Roxanne's offer, you went down and killed Randall Lake?"

"Had a little fun and set up a lifetime of blackmail at the same time."

"You were afraid under torture Billy might convince Philip of his innocence? Or you were afraid he would tell Philip about Roxanne's offer and Philip might guess that you went down and did it?"

"Both. See, I really did tell Billy enough about Susie so he knew I did her. That was another thing. But under normal circumstances, Billy was never going to convince anybody else."

"You were blackmailing Roxanne for hiring a hit man, when all the while you killed her husband?"

"I never got around to blackmail. She started giving me things before I could steal them. Blackmailing her was only one of many complicated strings I was waiting to play out. My life is blessed with infinite complications, Black. Have you ever met a god before?"

"A god?" I laugh. The back of my head is so sweaty it slides on the pillow.

"Somebody's going along in a perfectly good life and they do something shitty to somebody. Me, for instance. If there were a God and He were just, He would get them. But there is no God. So I become a god. In the beginning it was little things. I get kicked out of Mrs. Drysdale's backyard, and two days later Mrs. Drysdale's cat gets hung up to dry.

"Billy's been pushing me around, so I do the cat maybe an hour after Mr. Drysdale chews Billy out for sitting on his car. See how it works out for everybody?"

"You manipulate."

"You'd be surprised how much control a god can exert. A snobby girl won't give a kid the time of day. Somebody steals her homework. Somebody makes a few dirty phone calls. Somebody puts her dog on a stick by her window. Pretty soon she's not quite so snobby. Pretty soon, she's having a nervous breakdown and the family is moving out of town. You may call it a god complex. You may call me a god. But remember that old saying, just because you're paranoid doesn't mean people aren't after you? Just because you have a god complex doesn't mean you aren't divine."

He laughs. It is loud and raucous and I recognize it immediately from the telephone calls and from the recorder Saturday night, this mania emitting from the young man I cannot get to smile.

"You realize your girlfriend has to go too. What I've

got in mind will be perfect." He grins the toothless, all-lip grin of a man controlling destiny for those around him. "Film at eleven."

"Why Kathy?"

" 'Cause after you die, she'll want to investigate."

"Thanks for telling me. It gives me all the more reason to shoot you with this book."

"Book, hah. It's your fault. If you hadn't been so squirmy up at that vacant house, you'd either be dead or in jail, and she'd be safe. But I know the type. You die in bed here, she'll be sniffing my tracks. Or Billy's tracks. For weeks, months."

"Billy never did a thing, did he?"

"Oh, he used to set fires and wet his bed. But only when he was little. He burgled a few houses. Took Susie away from me. But I got her back."

"Why kill Roxanne when she had all that money waiting? Blackmail is more profitable than murder."

"I heard her on the phone talking to her shrink. She was going to ask you to investigate the possibility that Philip had killed her husband. I knew once you got going, you would figure out the truth. You ever talked to those two in Salem, they'd give a fair description of me. It didn't mean anything to the cops, but it would to you."

"And Walter Clark?"

"An easy way to get Billy out of the picture. He goes back to prison, Philip Bacon doesn't get to question him."

"Philip knew about the video because you told him."

"That's right. When people find out things they're not supposed to find out, they look criminal. You should know that."

Jerome takes a step toward me with the flowers.

"Don't do it."

Jerome grins. "Look at you. You look scared, Black. You've already killed at least two people in your life. If you weren't such a pussy, that would make you a god too. Even if you have a gun, you're not going to do me.

You're all bluff, Black. You always have been. Don't forget. I'm a god. I know."

Jerome takes another step. I sweat. Jerome grins. Under the blankets my hand shakes. Jerome laughs. And then laughs some more. He laughs until I can see the back of his throat and hear the bottom of his lungs.

He proffers the sack with the flowers, holding it rather high and stepping toward me. He is near my legs. I want to have the nurse's button in my hand, but nobody is going to get here in time to stop the pain. I am on my own and I know this will hurt. It will hurt as much as anything has ever hurt because Jerome is not one to make things easy on a victim. Funny. I am the victim. I, who have always been the rescuer, now pray for salvation.

"Please, Jerome."

"I love it when they beg." Before I can pull away, he slams the paper sack with the flowers in it against my lower leg. The sack crunches up under his fist. I shudder and want to scream but I cannot. The steel shaft of the ice pick is protruding from the bottom side of my leg. I can feel the pick catching in the threads of the mattress. So can he. Our eyes are locked.

When my sudden screeching intake of breath stops, he slowly wiggles the sack right, then left, maintaining eye contact while inflicting as much agony as he can. I am waiting for the jolts to stop so my brain will engage, but they do not stop. He is enjoying this immensely. He knows I do not have a gun.

My arms are shaking. My whole body trembles.

He pulls the sack upward, out of my leg, and I can clearly see, below the broken carnation stems, the shaft of an ice pick. The pick is not even bloody, although part of the ruptured brown paper sack is. He is gritting his teeth and preparing to slam it downward again. He will move higher this time. It may even be fatal. He is grinning.

"Scream all you want. The nurses are all busy up the hall. I made sure of that." Ice pick in midair, he stops and looks at me curiously. I let out a curious little crazy laugh myself. And then I scream.

The bedding at my right erupts and leaps two inches. It does this four times. Flame spurts up at an angle from the spot on my bed.

The reports are loud and sharp.

Jerome leaps backward, staggers and slumps against the wall. One eye is open. The other has been replaced by two of my slugs. He is on the floor. The flower sack remains in his right hand.

After some moments a nurse bangs the door open and spots my guest on the floor in a pool of his own making. I try on a smile, but the weak attempt does not reassure the stricken nurse.

"Good God," she screams.

Smoke curls toward the ceiling. "I believe my bedding has caught fire. Do you think you might tell somebody?"

By the time the extinguisher arrives, the bed is going pretty good.

58

SNAKE CAME BY ON A COLD AND sunny Saturday afternoon, parked his Mustang in front of my house, and got out with the aid of a cane.

In a sweater, jeans, and high-top basketball shoes, I hunkered on my front stoop watching jubilant stragglers from the Husky game trickle toward various rooming houses and parking places. L.C. sat beside me, his head on his front paws.

"Found yerself a dog, eh?"

"Last Chance, this is Elmer Slezak. Watch your woman, L.C."

"Is that the ugliest dog you could find?" Snake asked, sitting hard on the wooden porch beside me.

"Yeah, but to make up for it, I trained him to limp."

"Eh, we're all limping these days. I'd of held out for one painted blue."

"Hell, I could paint him myself."

"Don't use latex. He'll lick that right off."

We sat for a while. "Thanks for watching over me while I was in the hospital, Snake."

"Nah. Forget it. That dog is uglier than a plowed-up graveyard."

"He was hanging around the Dumpster down at Safeway. Followed me home one day."

We stopped talking long enough to watch a herd of football fans carrying thermos bottles, blankets, and Husky pennants. "We beat UCLA?"

"Thirty-one, twenty."

"I saw Kathy the other day down at the courthouse. She actually stopped and talked to me."

"What'd you talk about?"

"The weather, mostly."

"And?"

"The elections."

"That it?"

"She wanted to know if you were recovering. Started to get a little quiver in her voice when she asked. You get details like that because I'm a trained investigator."

"What'd you tell her?"

"I told her if she wanted to know, she should mosey on over here and ask you her ownself."

"What'd she say?"

"Nothing. I'm guessing you let that damned fool up in

the hospital stick ya so you'd have proof of self-defense, if nothing else."

"It was a mistake. I'm limping worse than you."

"Couple of gimps. What if he'd brought a machete?"

"He didn't."

"What if he had?"

"I'd be less of a man."

We laughed. "He tell you much?"

"Enough to fill in the cracks." I explained almost as much as I knew, all of what I had guessed, and some of my mistakes. Snake listened and nodded, observing the street, occasionally tapping his new silver-toed boots. His old ones had been cut off by the medics the day he got hit by Jerome in a truck with stolen plates.

"You know, old Phil wasn't a bad sort," Snake said, placing a chunk of Bubblicious bubble gum into his mouth and offering me a hunk. When I declined, he fed the hunk to the dog before I could stop him.

"You shouldn't have done that."

"Ah, he'll be okay. You know, Phil wasn't a bad sort. He sure didn't deserve to go all shot and burnt up."

"I think Phil was kind of useless, like a book you bought in hardcover and then never read. He lived a scrawny, sucked-in stomach of a life, and when he thought he'd found a woman he never thought he could have, he held on for dear life. But you're right. He didn't deserve to die for any of it."

"No. What about Billy?"

"Billy was never a prize citizen, but he never kidnapped Susie Alberg either. He never drowned the four-year-old neighbor boy. Jerome did all that. And Jerome set fire to his own house too. Can you imagine what it must have been like to be taking the blame for all that? Billy must have thought he was going crazy. Everybody on earth, including his mother, thought he was a fiend."

"Is he unloading trucks?"

"He's unloading trucks."

"They took a bunch of .45 caliber slugs out of that body in the burnt-up house. Seems like you used a .45 mostly."

"Seems to me I don't use a gun mostly."

"You had one that night."

"What night?"

"Right. What night. Right. I just wish I knew half of what was going on."

"Jerome murdered Roxanne because she was getting ready to blow open her husband's murder by having me launch an investigation. Jerome killed her husband as a way of toying with her and so he might eventually get most of the money. He waited seven years partially because he had other things going on in his life. He was about ready to start blackmailing her when Billy got let out. He found out Philip was going to mess with Billy, and they hired me to stop it. Jerome killed the high school girl—probably jealous—then made it appear as if Billy had done it."

"I never did figure out how he buggered those two in Portland. Or why."

"I'm guessing. He went down there, met a couple of runaways on the street, treated them to pizza and a couple of cans of pop, then took the half-empty cans and remaining pizza to Randall Lake's house and went in and killed him. He put the cans with their fingerprints in the kitchen. Then tracked them down again and gave them Lake's credit cards. They were runaways. They never read the papers. They didn't know anybody had been murdered until they were arrested for it themselves."

"I heard the governor's going to commute their sentences."

"Probably. The night of the fire, Jerome was planning to kill Philip and me both. He had a gun on Billy, but before he could get everything ready, Billy jumped him and cuffed him to the wall. We set Jerome free and made it even easier on him by refusing to believe Billy when he told us what had actually happened."

We watched another group of Husky fans trooping up

the sidewalk. Snake laughed as L.C. worked over the gum, chewing and then spitting it onto the porch to examine it, then picking it up and chewing again. "You and Kathy have a falling out?"

"You could say that."

"I'd be in the gutter with a bottle of Night Train."

"Hell, I got a dog."

Snake laughed and scratched L.C. behind the ears. L.C. did not move. L.C. had swallowed the gum and did not think he liked Snake. "You got anybody living downstairs yet?"

"Haven't been down since she moved out."

"Can't keep it vacant, Thomas. I'll go down with you. Hold your hand and all that shit."

"Maybe some other time."

"It's *been* two months. Let's go see what's down there. Don't worry. I'll scare the boogerman."

By the looks of the daylight basement, she had cleared out in a couple of hours, hauling clothes and personal items upstairs to a waiting vehicle, probably by the armload, probably with a bunch of women friends, because under those circumstances women rarely tolerated men in the company.

Snake lingered near the foot of the stairs while I poked around the small apartment. Dust balls and a slab of the *New York Times* from that Sunday greeted me. In the bedroom closet I found a stray shoe. On the narrow kitchen counter that served as a table I found a tape of *In Dreams*, Roy Orbison's greatest hits, the cellophane wrapper intact. Kathy did not favor Roy Orbison, but knew I did.

"You okay?" Snake asked.

"Sure."

"It's not like it's the worst thing that ever happened to you."

"All in all, Snake, it is the worst thing that ever happened to me."

"Well, hell. You might get her back. Men have gotten women back. You might."

"I will get her back."

"Yeah, well, I was saying you might."

"If it kills me, I'll get her back. The question is when."

"Now don't get your hopes up, boy. People get their hopes up and things happen and then they get hurt."

"I've *been* hurt."

After Snake left, I lay on the couch and played the Orbison tape straight through. "Crying" was probably my favorite song of all time, always had been, but it held special meaning now.

I was off work for almost two months, and by the time I got back to the office, I found that I had been moved out by a combination of default and common consent, since Kathy had threatened to leave the office if I didn't. For a few weeks I worked out of the house, then found another place in Pioneer Square. I sold my guns and shooting equipment to a couple of policemen I knew, but even as I did so, I realized selling off my weapons was not going to absolve me of anything. I was a changed man, certain the change was for the worse.

In the weeks that followed, I looked for her everywhere but ran into her only once, just after the first of the year on the street outside the Alexis Hotel. It was well after dark. I was on my way to meet clients at the Painted Table in the Alexis. She was alone, cradling a bundle of work in her arms. She wore a long black wool coat and her hair fell across the shoulders of the coat. Her cheeks were flushed with the cold. Snowflakes starred her coat, jeweled her hair, and melted against her face.

I had a thousand comments rat-holed and waiting, but, sensing that this was too soon for anything more than the trivial, I spoke like a country boy with dirt in his ears. "Kathy."

"So. How have you been?"

"Fair to middling. You look busy."

"I've been keeping myself that way. I'm doing some pro bono work for a group that puts homeless families into houses. And you?"

"Some employee theft problems for one of the department stores in town."

She nodded and shrugged. As we spoke, our breath formed cartoon balloons. I said, "Have you been well?"

"Well enough."

"Yeah, me too." It was cold, and under normal circumstances if a man like me met a woman like Kathy, he would have asked her inside for something warm to drink while they caught up on things, while he got lost in eyes so violet they should have been up on the silver screen. But we both knew I wasn't going to ask and she wasn't going to say yes if I did ask.

We stood awkwardly for a moment, then she stepped close, stared up at me, touched my hand and said, "I feel really bad about what's happened between us."

"Then why don't you do something about it?"

"My brain tells me to but my gut won't let me. I need some time, is all."

"So we're going to be friends again?"

"It's just going to take some time."

"I love you, Kathy."

"I know."

I watched as she walked to the corner of First Avenue and disappeared around the corner. Snowflakes fluttered down past the street lamps, falling slowly at first, and then with greater and greater swiftness. I had been thinking about her for months, yet I had forgotten the swing in her walk, the serenity in her eyes. I had forgotten the calm sense of presence she carried with her. I had forgotten that cool voice.

Standing alone in front of the Alexis, I watched a million snowflakes drift to the ground and begin to obliterate the trail of tidy little footprints she had left, watched until they were barely visible. Seeing the marks of her passing disappear altogether would have been too much to bear. I went inside to a warm place and let a cool whiteness bandage the city.